Lethal Dose of Love

Cindy Davis

L & L Dreamspell
London, Texas

Cover and Interior Design by L & L Dreamspell

ISBN: 978-1-60318-360-4

Library of Congress Control Number: 2011923439

Visit us on the web at www.lldreamspell.com

Published by L & L Dreamspell
Printed in the United States of America

Most times my dedications read: for Bob, he knows why. I always thought it was sort of self-explanatory, but people wondered. So here goes:

It's rare in life to meet your soul mate, the one person who understands and loves everything about you, which in my case is—well, let's not go there.

In 1990 I met my soul mate. Rather than a long-winded story about soul mates, I'll relate a short story that happened in 2005. We were chugging along in our motorhome in upstate New York when we approached a sign saying Welcome to Historic Sackets Harbor, established 1801. Nothing unusual about this sign. Nicely done, fresh paint. Strategically placed. An author never knows when inspiration will strike. But strike it did. I shouted, "Stop!"

Bob stopped. Dogs flew off couches. Toaster tumbled to the carpet. Most husbands would've said, "What the...is wrong with you, woman!?" Not Bob. He said, "Here's a pen."

We spent three days in lovely Sackets Harbor, a village of 1,400 nestled on the shores of Lake Ontario and the fantastic Black River Bay. We interviewed helpful historians, friendly chamber of commerce members, and gracious shop owners—and came away with the plot outline for this book. The mystery is finally a reality.

So...now Bob isn't the only one who knows why.

Part One

One

What on earth were Sean and Payton doing in the middle of Main Street? Claire stopped the little hatchback two feet from Sean Adams' left elbow. He never flinched, never looked her way. He stabbed an index finger in the air just above Payton Winters' left breast. Payton held her ground.

Good girl. Time someone stood up to him. Claire turned down the CD playing Neil Sedaka's "Bad Blood." She lowered the window and was assaulted by a chilly May wind off the harbor.

Sean's index finger moved up, now poking the space just under Payton's nose. "We had a deal."

Payton didn't back an inch. "There was no deal." She said each word with definition, no backing down there, either.

He took a step and a half forward and leaned in her face. "We had a deal."

"You're crazy, you know that?" She made two sideways steps left, but he grabbed her arm and jerked her back. She shook him off, shooting him a glare rivaling Scarlett's to Rhett.

He was going to hurt her. Claire got out of the car and dashed toward them. Why couldn't he just leave people alone?

Sean spotted Claire. "What do you want, you interfering old biddy?"

Claire positioned herself arm-to-arm with Payton. The united front—or possibly the crowd of onlookers who'd gathered on the sidewalk—forced Sean to slap his mouth shut and stalk across the street and inside his café.

Two taps on a horn spun Claire around. She threw the driver

a shrug and went to move her car out of the way. What were Sean and Payton fighting about? Yesterday at the yacht club meeting everything was fine. Wasn't it?

Come to think of it, maybe everything hadn't been fine. Sean had asked Payton to be his sailing partner, and she said she was buying a boat and partnering with someone else. Still and all, that shouldn't lead to something like this. He'd been spouting something about a deal. Deals meant money. Claire got out of the car and pocketed her keys. Maybe Payton wanted to talk; when Claire was upset it helped talking to Mamie.

But Payton had disappeared.

On the sidewalk, two men on tall ladders were fastening a covered sign above the long-vacant hardware store. Claire watched the workmen, hoping they'd drop the covering and reveal the newest shop addition to their small-town Main Street. Maybe she could sneak under the ladders and peer through the plate glass window. No, the window was covered with newspaper; sheet upon overlapping sheet of the *Watertown Daily Times* taped to the glass. Claire wouldn't like the job of scraping off all that stickum. Besides, it was bad luck to walk under a ladder, probably twice as bad to walk under two of them. She resumed her original plan, a trip to the post office. Overhead, bare branches on the row of young crabapple trees rattled in the wind.

Not that the opening of a new store was a big event in Sackets Harbor, New York. Flatlanders did it all the time thinking they'd make a killing with the tourist trade. What they invariably forgot was that tourists only came from Memorial Day to Labor Day. That left seven months to pay rent and utilities with no income, because chances of the locals buying cheap ceramic dragons or chintzy imported vases were slim. Most of the shops folded in two seasons. Through all the openings and closings, the hardware building remained vacant: too large for a gift shop, too unwieldy to be divided into smaller shops, and too expensive to be bought and torn down. Till now. Apparently someone thought they could make it work.

Who? And how could this information have slipped past the

Sackets Harbor gossip committee? There were permits to be applied for, leases to be signed, utilities to be connected and advertising to be bought. Surely someone would've heard something.

Claire finished her business at the post office and went outside where the workmen still fought with the heavy-looking sign. Maybe they should have picked a less blustery day. No good. There were few days without some sort of bluster off the harbor. One of the men climbed down two rungs and knocked on the window. Claire didn't try to squelch the gasp of surprise when Payton came out carrying a clipboard and pencil. She stepped off the sidewalk and returned to the middle of the road. Claire glanced at Sean's café to see if he was watching out the big, wide window, waiting to race out and rekindle the argument. He wasn't.

Payton tilted her head, giving the sign a critical gaze. After a moment, she nodded approval. The men gripped identical white ties at either end of the sign. Payton nodded. In unison the workmen tugged on the strings and the covering dropped away. With a crack like thunder, the giant nylon sheet snapped into the air. An enormous moth now, it lifted, dipped, lifted again and then landed, taking down a whirlwind of dry oak and maple leaves under it.

The sign was exposed: white background, green vines twining the edges, green and gold lettering. *Payton's Place ~ Exotic and Domestic Plants.* The gossip pipeline had really missed this one. As a matter of fact, they'd missed the whole boat on Payton Winters' arrival in town. She'd been here four months and so far all anyone knew was that she had once been married and apparently had a bottomless gully of money.

"What's so funny?"

Claire roused herself and blinked the owner of the voice into focus. Payton's face was beautiful and smooth. High cheekbones, almond-shaped eyes. Auburn had to be her natural hair color—it matched her brows. Payton repeated the question. Claire pointed to the workmen and quirked a sheepish grin. "When the cover dropped, I sort of expected them to wave magic wands and say ta-da."

Payton smiled. White, square teeth. Was anything *not* perfect about this woman? Claire bet she didn't even wake up with bedhead. Payton wore a bewildered expression; had she read Claire's thoughts? People always said her face was an open book. To cover the awkward seconds, Claire said the first thing that came to her mouth, "You're opening a flower shop."

"Exotic plants. Come see."

Payton's hair, pulled through the strap of a Twins baseball cap, swung like a pendulum on her shoulders. She wore blue Levis and a pink hooded sweatshirt topped by a fleece LL Bean vest.

The shop door stood open. Brown leaves lifted in a mini-tornado in the doorway. Payton and Claire pushed through and climbed the pair of cement steps. "I warn you, the place is a mess." The room was a rectangle stretching toward the back. The walls wore a fresh coat of white paint. Beneath the paint smell was a mustiness that would probably take months to erase. Tools and wood everywhere, shelves of every shape and size piled at one side, cardboard boxes stacked against the far wall. Sawdust floated in the air, brilliant twinklers in the afternoon sunshine.

Payton waved at the wall on the side of the building that faced an empty lot. "I'm having a door and a large bay window put in there. Outside will be a patio area with a lattice enclosure and flagstone paths." She took a breath. "Patio furniture and chimneas, lots of hanging plants."

Claire turned in a circle, imagining. "It sounds lovely."

A squeak and whoosh of cold air made them whirl around. Someone stood silhouetted in the doorway. From the shape, which included an apron, it had to be Sean. The twister that spun leaves outside the door became one in Claire's stomach. Damn him.

"What the hell do you think you're doing?" He lashed out an arm that encompassed the room and repeated his question.

So, he'd just learned about the shop, too. That meant their discussion in the street was about something else. Claire thought back to what they'd said: "We had a deal." "There was no deal."

Payton's voice was calm. "I'm showing Claire my shop."

"Your shop?"

"As if you didn't see the sign," Claire couldn't help saying.

"You stay out of this."

"Leave Claire alone. What do you want?"

"You aren't taking up all the street parking with a-a flower shop."

"What's wrong with a flower shop?" Claire was unable to keep from mimicking his tone of voice. When she corrected herself, saying, "exotic plant shop," Payton flashed her a grin.

"There's not enough parking on the street as it is," he continued.

"Calm down, Sean," Payton said. "I have it covered."

Claire stepped forward. "Since when are you complaining about parking? I've never seen you grumbling about the bookstore, or about Mamie's gallery taking up spaces." He didn't reply. As a matter of fact, he didn't even acknowledge her. She forged on, "You can't be worried Payton's *plants* will take business from your *café*."

"Don't be ridiculous."

"You're the one being ridiculous," Payton said. "What I do is no concern of yours."

"It is so long as you owe me money..."

She owed him money? His words echoed in Claire's head: "We had a deal."

"Get out." Payton marched toward him holding the clipboard like a shield. Claire readied herself in case he balked.

Sean laughed but backed outside anyway. The women watched him cross to the café and disappear inside.

"Does he act like that all the time?" Payton asked.

"You mean obnoxious and domineering?"

"Exactly."

Claire looked down at her hands, clenched like gnarly wrestlers. She forced the fingers apart, making one hand grip the purse strap and the other drop to her side, feigning nonchalance. "In grade school he conned other kids out of their lunch money and toys. In high school he cheated on tests and fooled around with married women. He—" Claire squeezed her eyes shut. She'd never spoken these images out loud. It left her feeling empty, sick. She opened her eyes at Payton's touch on her arm and changed the subject. "What did he mean about you owing him money?"

Payton's groan resonated in the empty room. "I showed interest in one of the paintings for sale in his restaurant. We dickered on a price but couldn't come to an agreement. Next thing I know, he's calling to ask when I'm picking it up. I reminded him we hadn't agreed on a price. He insisted we had and I'd better come through."

Typical Sean.

"The price wasn't the real reason I backed out."

Claire recalled yesterday's yacht club meeting. At the time certain comments hadn't seemed odd, but in light of today's developments… "Amanda March, right?"

"Yes. I was late getting to the meeting and didn't catch the whole discussion, but Amanda was clearly upset. I thought it had something to do with that painting of the Commodore she bought from him. After the meeting I cornered her and asked about it, but she wouldn't talk." Payton shook her head, twitching her ponytail forward over her shoulder. "I'm glad I decided to stay away from him."

"I'm not sure you'll be able to."

"Because I'm opening across from his café?"

"That yes. But he won't stay away from you."

Payton blew out a sigh. "I thought moving to Sackets Harbor was such a good idea." She dragged two wooden crates and dropped on one. She leaned the clipboard against the side, then gestured for Claire to sit too.

"Why *did* you choose Sackets Harbor, if you don't mind my asking?"

"It's a long story. I won't bore you with it now."

"It wouldn't bore me." Claire definitely wouldn't be bored. Everyone in town was dying to know why someone as rich and beautiful as Payton moved to an out of the way place like Sackets Harbor, New York. Rumor had it she was hiding from something, or someone. Till a few minutes ago, Claire sort of believed it. But if she *were* hiding out, why would she open a retail business where anyone might recognize her?

"God, I hate confrontations." Payton tipped her head left and then right, as though working kinks out of her neck. She glanced around the shop. "I'm trying to open a week or so before Memorial Day. Just in time for the tourists' arrival." Payton took off her cap, shook the shoulder-length tresses, then combed absentminded fingers through them.

"Are you really having second thoughts?"

Payton didn't reply.

"Because of Sean?"

More silence. If only Claire knew Payton better, she'd tell her about a plan that, for months—no, years—had been brewing in the back of her mind. Some days the stress of keeping it inside was more than she could stand. "What did you mean when you said you had parking covered?" she asked instead.

"Besides this building, I bought the vacant lot next door. Part of it will be turned into the patio I mentioned, but the rest will be off-street parking—for everyone to use."

"Somehow I don't think that would have made any difference to Sean."

Payton stood, ran a hand through her hair again and put the hat back on, easing the hair through the strap. "I'm not letting him ruin my plans. People who act like bullies are just covering up their own weaknesses. He probably had a bad childhood."

Claire's stomach flip-flopped. "Yes. Yes, that must be it." She pulled up a sleeve and checked her watch. "I, er, just remembered an appointment. Very nice shop. I wish you much good fortune." By the time the last word was out of her mouth, Claire had burst outdoors.

It was all her fault. This whole bloody mess was her fault.

Two

Claire hurried away, scrubbing tears with tense knuckles. To get to her car she had to go near the café. For now that strength just wouldn't come. She turned right, walked twenty feet up the sidewalk, then crossed the street. Payton's new sign stood proud and shiny for everyone to see.

Claire took a breath of the cold air and went into Mamie's Artpost, two doors from Sean's place, yet in the same building. Between their businesses was a vacant shop, empty since fall when the woman selling goodies for dogs closed up and went back to Connecticut. The ever-present scent of oil paint and damp cardboard pushed out of Mamie's gallery as the door squeaked open. How could she stand that smell day in and day out?

"I'll be right with you," Mamie hollered from the back room.

"It's just me."

Round, plain Mamie Coutermarsh appeared, wiping her hands on a wad of paper towel. Her eyeglasses were perched atop a beehive of grey corkscrew curls. "How does the place look?" This was asked without Mamie making eye contact. She almost never made eye contact with anyone. She'd look up, down and around, and would, if the subject was serious enough, focus on a person's chin or top button. It was the one thing about her friend that drove Claire nuts. Still, they were best friends, had been for more than ten years, since the death of Mamie's husband.

Claire turned in a circle, squinting, searching for the slightest bit of dust, the smallest thing out of place. "Perfect."

"Oh, Claire, I'm so nervous. Mr. Arenheim will be here in the morning."

"Stop worrying. He'll love the place. You'll be Sackets Harbor's first internationally-known gallery owner."

"Do you really think so?"

"He's going to love you. Just make sure you look him in the eye while you're talking. Now stop worrying. Everything will be fine."

"I wish there'd been time to get next door cleaned up a little. It'd be easier for him to envision."

"Didn't you sign a lease with Helen?" Helen Mortenson, besides being figurative head of the gossip committee, was a real estate agent and owner of the building.

"She said she'd have one ready. If Mr. Arenheim agrees to the deal to expand the gallery, all we have to do is add our signatures. Oh, Claire, I'm so nervous."

Just then, a thump came from the very space under discussion. Mamie frowned. "Someone's next door."

"Probably Helen cleaning up." Claire put up a finger for Mamie to wait. She stepped outdoors, cupped her hands and peered in the window of the empty shop. Sean was hefting a cardboard box atop two others. Midway along the left wall, the connecting door to his restaurant stood open. Claire felt a momentary dizziness that sagged her against the cold glass.

"Is it Helen?"

Claire jumped at Mamie's voice. Her shoulder jolted Claire as she too looked through the glass. "Oh gosh."

"You'd better phone Helen."

Mamie dashed into the gallery.

Talking with Sean wasn't something Claire wanted to do again so soon, but Mamie's future was at stake. He spun around as she hammered on the window. The glare on the glass prevented reading his expression, but the way he strode to the door didn't say, I'm happy to see you again. Claire jammed her hands in her pockets and dried sweaty palms on the lining.

Sean opened the door three inches. "What?"

"What are you doing in there?"

Sean's nose wrinkled and his eyebrows dipped into a vee. "It's really none of your business but I'm expanding my restaurant."

"You can't. Mamie's renting this space for her gallery. The guy's coming from the city in the morning."

"I don't think so." Sean shut the door, giving a definitive twist to the latch.

Claire put a palm on the doorframe to steady herself. Helen wouldn't have rented to him without checking with Mamie.

The news would hit Mamie like a truck. Ever since Donald's death, her emotions had been on a rollercoaster. God knew she deserved something good to happen. Life with Donald hadn't been great; he was some kind of inventor at the Technical Institute in Watertown and worked long hours. Like many people he hadn't planned for his death and left Mamie penniless. With Claire's encouragement and every cent she could scrape together, Mamie had opened her dream gallery. When Miles Arenheim called from the City a month ago, Claire thought this would be it—a world class gallery—Mamie's big chance.

Claire pulled open the Artpost door and went in. Mamie said, "Helen's line was busy."

"If I were you I'd go right over there."

"You really think so? I hate when people just drop in on me."

Another thump sounded next door.

"You should go. Now."

Mamie's head tipped and her nose wrinkled as she listened. "Will you watch the place while I'm gone?"

"In case you didn't notice, it's after five o'clock."

"Heavens, I didn't realize."

"Call me later and let me know what happens."

By seven thirty Mamie still hadn't called. Claire had phoned both her house and the gallery at least a dozen times. She was about to go out searching when Mamie's car crunched into the driveway. Claire listened for the familiar slam of the door, the hollow footsteps across the porch, the opening and shutting screen door, but none came.

She went to the bedroom window and looked down on the roof of the green Ford Escort. No movement at all. Claire shut off the computer and went downstairs to look out the kitchen window. Mamie sat like a statue in the front seat. Claire knocked on the glass. Mamie didn't react.

Claire hurried outside and rapped on the car window. Still Mamie didn't move. Claire jerked open the door, a tear rolled down Mamie's cheek. Claire eased her friend out of the vehicle, into the house and down the long hallway to the living room sofa. Then she went to the dining room and poured them each a shot of bourbon. As an afterthought, she splashed more in both glasses.

Claire sat on the coffee table facing Mamie who didn't reach up for the glass so she pried the fingers open and folded them around the glass. After a hearty sip, Claire spoke. "The deal fell through with Helen."

There was the slightest nod of Mamie's head. Claire wanted to scream that there'd been a verbal agreement, that Helen all but promised the place to Mamie.

"Tell me what happened."

She erupted into spasms of heart wrenching sobs. Claire got a box of tissues and set it in Mamie's lap. It was a full fifteen minutes before she could speak. "God, Claire, I wish I was dead."

"Tell me what happened."

"When I got to H-helen's nobody was th-there. I went home and c-called. There was still no answer. "

"Did you leave a message?"

"No. I just figured I'd keep ph-phoning till she came home. I called every ten minutes for two hours. Then I wanted a cup of tea and realized I was out of milk. I went to the corner market." Mamie sucked in a breath and new trails of tears squeezed from her eyes. She blew her nose. "Helen was at the market. Sh-she'd been downtown m-meeting Sean."

The dread that started on seeing Mamie sitting statue-like in the driveway, detonated like Fourth of July fireworks. Acid churned into Claire's esophagus. She didn't have to hear the rest.

"Sean told Helen that my deal with Mr. Arenheim fell through. And then he told her how he'd been thinking what a good idea it would be to enlarge his café. Helen believed him and, since she had the contracts all ready, th-they just substituted his name for mine on the lease. God, Claire, I wish I was dead."

Claire slid off the coffee table and onto the couch beside Mamie. She put an awkward arm around her friend's shoulders and pulled her close. For a fleeting moment Claire considered divulging the plan that had been taking shape over the past year or so. Little by little the way she'd murder Sean Adams had achieved reality. She would poison him—that she knew for certain—what she hadn't determined was which poison she'd use.

After hearing the plan, Mamie would realize her coveted store would be available. Two stores even, because without Sean, the café would close down. What a gallery that would make, to expand the length of all three shops!

But, no, Claire couldn't speak up. Even though she was positive Mamie would be all for the idea now, Mamie was too weak. At some point years down the road, the guilt would eat away at her and she'd either tell or go mad keeping the secret inside. No, Mamie most definitely could not be trusted with a secret like this.

Claire urged her friend to lie down. She put two ruffled throw pillows under her head and tucked in the handmade afghan. Mamie sobbed for a while and eventually fell into a fitful sleep.

Claire went upstairs and turned on the computer. When the Google home page loaded, she typed in the little white rectangle: poisonous plants. The computer was old and slow, but the search eventually yielded more than two million hits.

"Claire? Where are you?"

Claire glanced at the bedside table and was startled to see more than two hours had passed. "I'll be right down."

Footsteps on the stairs. Panic. Mamie couldn't see this. Enormous blood red letters screamed across the screen: YOUR GUIDE TO POISONOUS PLANTS. Claire clicked on the *sleep* mode and the monitor went black just as Mamie waddled into the room. Her eyes were rimmed in red, her flowered housedress crumpled.

"I said I'd be right down."

"I know, but I have to go to the bathroom. What are you doing?"

"Checking on new books to buy for the library." Claire hopped to her feet, grimacing when the chair scraped on the varnished floor. She moved away from the computer, forcing Mamie to step back. Mamie frowned but went into the hall. After she disappeared into the bathroom, Claire raced in and shut down the computer.

How to get Mamie to go home? No, that wasn't nice, Mamie was suffering. She'd been dealt a cruel blow by Sean Adams and shouldn't be alone right now. But Claire wanted nothing more than to be alone with her research. Just before Mamie came upstairs Claire thought she'd found exactly the right poison—monkshood. It was fast working and was lethal via absorption, injection *and* ingestion. The only drawback was Sean would suffer terribly. Claire didn't want that, but it was unavoidable.

"Want to watch a movie?" Mamie suggested once they'd gone downstairs.

Claire settled at her usual end of the sofa. Mamie fluffed the pillows, tucked the afghan around herself and started clicking the remote.

"Did you know Payton was opening a plant shop?" Claire asked.

Mamie nodded.

"You knew and didn't tell me?"

"What?" Mamie turned a scrunched up nose at her.

"Why didn't you tell me Payton was opening a shop?"

"Payton's opening a shop?"

Claire stifled a groan of exasperation. "Across from Sean's place, she's opening…" She recited the words from the sign, "Payton's Place, exotic and domestic plants."

"That's nice. You love plants."

"I thought you did too."

"I like them—outdoors." She set the remote on the table. "Let's watch this."

Claire gave a mere glance at the old black and white movie. One of the actors looked familiar, but she didn't care for television. She preferred more cerebral activities that tonight included research on monkshood plants.

THREE

Claire sat on her stool behind the check-in desk, the perfect vantage point to watch over her library. She'd come to think of it as hers. She'd been head librarian for nearly nineteen years, ever since Edna Adams died and left Claire the job through osmosis. Every book, every shelf, every event was Claire's doing. The pride was felt as a tingling all the way to her toes every time she stepped in the building. It was like her child.

Children. She just hadn't been blessed that way. Well, not in the traditional sense. The memory burst into her brain. Twenty-seven years, four months and seventeen days, so long ago. She swallowed a scalding mouthful of tea that burned her throat. But, she didn't flinch. It was part of her due, her punishment.

To bury her misdeeds, Claire had thrown herself into her career. Not much of a career, but she had a measure of respectability around town. Dedication to her career couldn't negate her shortcomings or erase the past, but for the most part it kept the memories hovering only in the back of her mind, at least during the day. Daytime she kept busy with her job, but also with gardening and a few clubs around town. She rarely left Sackets Harbor. As a matter of fact, since moving here, she'd never been far from this little town at the northern tip of Lake Ontario where winter winds wailed like lost children and summers teemed with tourists and sunshine. Where was there to go that she couldn't go in books? There were thousands here at her disposal.

Nighttime was another story.

The heavy door whooshed open. Payton Winters entered wearing a teal colored spring jacket and matching beret.

"Good morning," they said at the same time.

"I'm looking for some books on small business management."

Claire slid off the stool. "They're down this way."

Payton didn't follow. She spoke quietly. "I heard about Mamie losing out on the shop. Did Helen really just substitute Sean's name?"

Claire nodded. "It's not Helen's fault. Sean told her Mamie's deal fell through. Helen didn't have any reason to disbelieve Sean."

"Mamie must be a basket case."

"Helen is too." Claire stepped into the appropriate aisle. "The books are down here. Are you going to Wanderlust this afternoon?"

"Just what is Wanderlust anyway?"

Claire gave an elaborate eye roll. "A bunch of travel wannabes who share ideas and experiences. We talk about art and things like that. Whenever one of us takes a vacation, if we don't return with a slew of photographs…" Now she gave a dramatic sigh. "Helen's probably thinking the influx of new blood—yours, that is—might stimulate the group. We're quite sick of each other's stories."

"I've never been much of a joiner."

"They're a nice group of people."

"Does Sean go?"

Claire laughed. "No. Very few men." She slipped a book off the shelf—*Small Business for Dummies*—and handed it to Payton. "I saw you talking to Aden Green at the yacht club meeting."

Payton groaned. "Don't you start too! Everyone's trying to set us up. What country is he ambassador to? I can never remember."

"Uzbekistan. Don't you like him?"

"He seems very nice. Good looking."

"Understatement! So why are you avoiding him?"

A shadow crossed Payton's face. She busied herself thumbing the book's pages.

"I wouldn't have thought you were shy."

Payton closed the book with a snap. "My husband only died two years ago."

"It takes time." Claire patted her arm in a motherly fashion. The front door opened and closed. "Well, I've got to get out there, someone just came in."

Claire hurried to her desk. No reason to hurry really. People mostly wanted to browse, but she felt funny not greeting each person. It was like welcoming them into her home. Brighton James stood in the foyer. He was tall and distinguished, a businessman who spent much of his time in the City as a stockbroker. He had a book in one hand and dropped it through the slot under the front edge of the desk.

"Looking forward to the first meet?"

"It's been a long winter. We took the boat out of storage yesterday." He lowered his voice and glanced about. "Er, is there somewhere we can talk?"

Claire led him behind the desk and into her miniscule office, overcrowded with boxes of books. "Sorry for the mess. They're for the upcoming book fair." Claire waved him to a chair then leaned against the desk.

There was a long moment of silence where Brighton stared out the tiny window behind her, twisting the narrow silver band on his ring finger. "This is very awkward."

Four

It was just before two when Mamie picked up Claire for the Wanderlust meeting. She rolled her window all the way down to inhale the delicate aroma of lilacs, her favorites. Their season was far too short to waste a moment's appreciation. They passed Payton's house where a crew slapped on a coat of stucco. Another crew was busy removing trees from both the front and side yards.

"Arrogant to flaunt money like that," Mamie said.

"How can you say that? She doesn't drive a fancy car. She doesn't—"

"She wears cashmere and a huge diamond ring."

"Her husband gave them to her. Is she supposed to throw them away just because he's dead?"

"She's a widow?"

"Yes. Two years." Claire reverted to the original discussion gesturing at the narrow band embedded in Mamie's left hand. "You still wear Donald's ring." Mamie didn't reply. Claire continued, "Payton doesn't brag about what she spends. It's Helen who… Besides, the house wasn't livable the way it was."

Mamie turned left into the community of Madison Barracks, the military post named after President Madison. Much of it had been renovated into homes and apartments, but some remained as an historic site for visitors. Daffodils and tulips marched up walkways the way the soldiers had marched there in the 1800's. Claire liked that analogy.

How could she get Mamie out of her funk? Help find a suitable place for a new gallery; that was about the only thing. But where could she find that Mamie hadn't already thought of?

The plan to get rid of Sean needed to be sped up. With him out of the way, a number of situations would be served. First, the original gallery plan could be adhered to. Second, the tension between he and Mamie would be removed. Ha! Lots of people's tension would be eliminated. Thirdly, Claire's own guilt would be gone. Twenty-seven years, four months and seventeen days of it—ever since she'd given birth to him. Yes, Sean's passing would erase a lot of problems.

"What's so funny?"

"Oh nothing."

Mamie turned the car into the short driveway that led to Felicia's impeccable brick town-home. Not a ripple in the white trim paint. Not a weed in the flowerbed. Weeds probably didn't dare grow in Felicia's yard. The driveway was cobbled. Talk about flaunting.

"I didn't expect Helen to be here," Claire said.

"Why shouldn't she? None of this is her fault. It's entirely mine. My stupid do-nothing personality." Mamie was near tears again.

Claire changed the subject. "Brighton came to the library this morning. He wanted to talk about Felicia."

"What about her?"

"Last night he woke up and she wasn't there. He found her standing at the living room window, just staring out. He asked what was wrong and she said nothing, that she just couldn't sleep. He's sure there's more to it. That wasn't the first night's sleep she's lost. He wanted to know if she'd said anything to me."

"He should be talking to Amanda. They're tight as thieves."

"He said he did and she pretended not to know anything."

"Did you tell him we saw them at the diner the other day? That they had their heads together and clammed up when we said hello?"

"I only said I'd talk to her."

They ambled along the curved walkway. Mamie was curiously

silent. Did she know something more about this? Mamie was sort of scatterbrained and it often turned out she knew more than she realized. Now wasn't the time for interrogations. The big front door with the shiny brass knocker opened.

Helen Mortenson smiled down at them. The round woman wearing a denim skirt and white sweater stepped out. She pulled Mamie into a hug. "I was afraid you wouldn't come," she said in her gravelly voice. Mamie's shoulders tensed, she was holding in tears. In her condition she wouldn't be able to hold them very long. Helen urged Mamie inside and down the short, brightly lit hallway. Claire followed, breathing in cinnamon-scented air. Nice.

As soon as the three women entered the dining room, Amanda leaped toward them, dark eyes bright with excitement. She engulfed Mamie in another hug. "I heard about your gallery! Congratulations."

"Yes, wonderful for you. Wonderful for the town too," said Felicia from the far end of the long table where she poured coffee into tiny china cups. "What a coup for your gallery, to have such a famous man as Miles Arenheim want to—"

Mamie burst into tears. She dropped into the nearest chair and buried her face in her hands. Everyone gathered around.

Helen faced the group, her hand on Mamie's back. "I screwed up royally. Last night, Sean came to me. He was very upset, saying how Mamie's deal with Mr. Arenheim had fallen through."

Amanda put her hand on Mamie's shoulder. "I'm so sorry."

"The problem is," Claire said, "the deal hadn't fallen through."

"I don't understand."

"Sean *told* her the deal fell through. But it hadn't."

"That scumbag. That low-down piece of—"

It was unusual for Amanda to curse. Helen sank into a damask covered chair. "When Sean told me about Mamie's deal not working out, I felt terrible, of course. We commiserated: how nice it would have been for Mamie, how nice for the town, and all that. Then he acted like he'd had this brilliant idea. 'Gee, Helen, I know how you were counting on renting that place. Maybe you'd consider letting me have it. I could enlarge my restaurant.'"

"I allowed…no, I helped him replace Mamie's name with his on the contract. God Mamie, I'm so sorry."

"He's a filthy rat."

They all turned toward the new voice. Sylvie French, in her traditional polyester slacks and knitted vest, removed her coat and laid it across the back of the chair beside Mamie. "I thought he was bad when he screwed me out of the commission on that house he bought in Chaumont. But this beats it all."

"I went to my lawyer this morning. I can break the contract. Since Sean duped me—"

By now Mamie had wiped away her tears and stood stoic and brave. "Thank you, but it'll cost too much money."

"Why?" Amanda asked.

"Because Sean will fight just for the principle of it."

"I can't believe he's capable of something so despicable," Amanda said.

"What!" Felicia turned a hollow-cheeked face to her friend. "After what—"

"No!" Amanda's eyes flashed with anger.

No one but Claire seemed to notice the exchange between the women. Claire knew right then that what kept Felicia up nights had something to do with Sean.

"I went to his house last night," Helen said, "to appeal to his human nature."

An unladylike snort came from Felicia. She covered her mouth with an expensively manicured hand.

"I'm sorry, Mamie," Helen said. "As Felicia so eloquently expressed, I wasted my time. He said he regretted the way things went down, but ultimately his business had to be at the forefront of his thoughts."

"Let's see how good his business is when we all boycott it!"

"It won't matter. Our boycott won't keep the summer people away."

"It would if we picket or something," offered Amanda.

Sylvie rapped her knuckles on the table. “We should call the meeting to order. I have an appointment in an hour.”

“How can you be so insensitive?” Helen asked.

“I’m not insensitive. It’s just obvious there’s nothing we can do, so why waste time beating a dead horse? You’re just encouraging poor Mamie’s depression.”

“I guess Sylvie’s right. We can’t accomplish anything right now. But I promise you, Mamie, I’ll find a way to fix this.”

Mamie patted Helen’s arm and went to sit. Felicia passed tea and coffee cups and a plate of Amanda’s homemade sugar cookies. She took a seat at the head of the table, framed by light from the tall windows. “One more thing I want to say before we get started. Let’s get together in the next day or so to decide what we can do about Sean. Legally.”

Mamie’s eyes fixed on the coffeepot in the center of the table. “No, don’t. I don’t want to be the reason for any more trouble.”

“Sean’s making the trouble, Mamie, not you,” Amanda said. “There’s got to be a way to handle it.”

There is, Claire wanted to shout. Don’t anybody do anything yet.

Claire realized Amanda was watching her. As their gazes met Amanda’s flicked away and became interested in how much sugar Payton added to her coffee.

She knows my plan!

“We were talking about Payton’s shop,” Felicia said. “We’re all very excited about it. It’s just what this town needs.”

“Gosh yes,” added Amanda. “I’m so tired of all the gift shops and junk stores.”

“I’m having a Grand Opening party the Saturday after next. You’re all invited. 9 a.m.,” Payton said.

“Can’t we get down to business?” Sylvie complained.

Helen gave her a squint-eyed glare behind wire-rimmed glasses. “First on the agenda is to welcome Payton.”

There was a chorus that made Payton blush. “Don’t you take a vote whether to let me in or not?”

Claire shook her head. "You don't get off that easy."

"Heavens no," Helen said. "I told you we're free and easy here. You want to be in, you're in."

Amanda pushed the cookie plate toward Mamie, who shook her head. Helen broke off a piece of cinnamon-sprinkled sugar cookie and aimed it at them as she spoke. "Payton, tell us about yourself."

"We heard about her at the yacht club meeting already," Sylvie whined.

"What I meant was, maybe she'd like to tell us about her travels."

"I'm interested in hearing where you all have been," Payton said.

Felicia set down her cup. "We already know everything about each other. That's why we want to hear about you."

"She's been to Washington," Helen prompted when Payton threw her a *help me* look. "She was there when Mount St. Helens erupted."

"Really? What was it like?" Claire heard herself ask, even though she'd read countless articles about it.

"Awful. We were sure the world had come to an end. Ash was several inches deep on everything, and as soon as you cleared it away, it was back. We got out of there as soon as the planes were airborne again."

"Ever been abroad?" Sylvie asked.

"I've been to Greenland."

"Really? What's it like? And don't tell us it's green," Amanda said.

"It is green, though. It's very pretty with wide open spaces and brilliant blue skies."

Mamie spoke softly, "I've been to New Zealand...to visit my uncle. I painted a landscape of his hometown." Her nose wrinkled as if trying to think of its name.

Felicia broke off the corner of a cookie. "I've been there, too. I went for—"

"Can we get back on the subject?" Sylvie asked.

"I thought travel *was* the subject."

"We've heard your damned New Zealand story a dozen times."

Payton frowned and picked at something on her sleeve. Claire wanted to tell her that was how these meetings went, someone opened a subject and they worked around the table, finishing, adding and embellishing—a conversational free-for-all. Sylvie and Felicia's sparring was part of it, as commonplace as the breeze off the harbor. They both seemed to enjoy the relationship and carried no enmity when it was over. Well, none except for the usual class barrier. Felicia's only real friend was Amanda March. Claire had never measured up and didn't care to. She didn't want to spend her days sipping Bacardi and finding fault with people.

"Did you, er, have a career?" Felicia asked.

"That's not about travel."

This time everyone ignored Sylvie. Payton took a fork-flattened peanut butter cookie and set it on a napkin. Then she picked up her spoon and stirred the coffee. Round and round Claire watched the liquid swirl. Finally Payton said, "I'm a retired school teacher."

"You look too young to be retired," Amanda said.

"That's not about travel," Sylvie said.

"What's the matter with you today?" Helen asked.

Helen was right. Sylvie was frequently argumentative but never this bad.

"I told you I have an appointment."

"So, go to it. Why keep disrupting the meeting?"

Sylvie stood, tight-lipped. "You— Oh, never mind." She jerked her coat from the back of the chair and left.

"Sheesh," said Helen.

Amanda laughed.

For all their faults, Claire really liked these people. Every time they complained of Sean's exploits, she felt ill. For all her forty-three years, she wondered why she'd been put on this earth. God must have had some Great Plan, but so far she'd been unable to fathom what it was. The one thing she thought she'd done right—giving her son up for adoption—had blown up in Sackets Harbor's face.

Well, she'd rectify all that. Soon. Very soon.

"You do look too young to be retired," Mamie said, shyly.

A flush spread from Payton's cheeks down her neck, looking harsh against her purple blouse. She cleared her throat. "Retired just means that I don't do it any more. I taught seventh grade math. I gave it up because students are too unappreciative."

"Isn't that the truth!"

"Felicia Ann Marie Dawson Featherstone, you're so naughty!" chastised Amanda.

Everyone laughed. "In my day the teacher put a ruler to your knuckles if you didn't shut up and pay attention. But, you actually learned something."

"Were you born in Minneapolis?" Amanda asked Payton.

"Virginia. Richmond."

They compared stories about Virginia for a while; Helen and Felicia had both been there. Then Amanda stood and tapped her knuckles on the table. The meeting was at an end. "I want to welcome Payton Winters to our group and say—I think for everyone—that I hope you'll return." She moved toward the door. Everyone piled their dirty cups on the tray.

"I almost forgot," said Felicia, "I want to show you my painting, it's called *Sunset.*" She disappeared into the living room.

Claire followed. It was a beautiful room, bright and airy, with a tall ceiling and lots of open space. A long sofa with flowered upholstery in coral and brown graced the longest wall. The matching chair sat beneath the artwork and Claire instantly knew the furniture had been upholstered to complement it. The painting was small, about six by nine inches.

"Who's the artist?" Claire asked.

Both Mamie and Felicia answered, "Frederic Edwin Church."

Claire braced herself with a palm on the back of the chair and leaning in for a better look at the painting Felicia had bought in Sean's restaurant—he had several hanging on the walls there.

Claire wasn't much on art, couldn't see the big deal about possessing an original over a print—until now.

"Stunning," she said, meaning it.

"Yes," Amanda agreed. "Church really captured the evening's serenity."

"And the value is ever increasing," Felicia said.

"Only if the economy increases." This from Helen.

"Art will always sell."

"You sound like Sean," Claire said.

As though mesmerized, Mamie moved closer. Claire backed to make room, but Mamie stopped six feet away.

"How does Brighton like it?" Helen asked.

"Loves it," Felicia replied. Then she laughed. "That's because he has no idea what I paid for it."

"Will he be upset?"

"Upset! He'll have chickens if he finds out."

"Your secret's safe with us," Helen said.

There were tears in Mamie's eyes. Claire smiled. She could see how something that beautiful could move a fellow artist to tears.

The group filed into the hallway. "I'll see you all at the meet next week," Helen called, rubbing her hands together in anticipation. "Can't wait to get the cobwebs out of my brain. I hate winter."

"I'll be there," Claire said.

"You'd better be!" Helen laughed and left.

"I didn't know you raced," Payton said.

"I've been the team's official timekeeper for twelve years. I love the water, and racing, but the motion makes me sick," Claire said.

"Do you race?" Payton asked Mamie.

She shook her head. "I hate the water. Besides, Mr. Arenheim is coming."

They said their good-byes to Felicia and Amanda, who retraced their steps to the living room.

Payton caught up to Mamie and Claire in the driveway. "Wait."

Mamie faced Payton, her eyes settling on the little cleft in

Payton's chin. Claire wondered if Payton felt at all discombobulated by Mamie's inability to look people in the eye. She didn't appear to notice.

"I was wondering how you left the gallery situation with Mr. Arenheim."

"I-I haven't told him yet."

"She picks up the phone, dials his number, and hangs up before the call goes through," Claire said.

"Except once," Mamie said softly. "His secretary answered, and *then* I hung up. I j-just don't know what to say. I'm so embarrassed. I led him to believe things would be fine."

Claire opened the passenger door. "He'll realize it wasn't your fault."

"People like Miles Arenheim expect things to go smoothly."

"I might have a solution," Payton said softly.

Mamie almost looked into Payton's eyes. Almost.

"What if, for the summer, we use my house for the exhibit? It'd give you time to find another situation."

Mamie's face turned white, except for her cheeks, which grew a bright tulip red. Then she shook her head. "No, I couldn't. It's too much of an imposition."

Payton put her hand on Mamie's arm. "If you think it's something that might work, then we'll do it." She turned to Claire. "Convince her, will you?"

"Give her a few minutes to digest your offer, and she'll be bouncing all the way home." She gave Payton a *you're a lifesaver* smile. She plucked at Mamie's sleeve. "Come on."

This roused Mamie. She looked Payton in the eye—actually looked her in the eye—and whispered, "You are an angel."

"Let me know what Mr. Arenheim says."

"That was so generous," Mamie cooed after strapping herself into the car.

"Seems like we should celebrate. Want to go to the Boathouse for supper? Felicia's painting was really something, wasn't it?"

"I thought you didn't care about art."

"I noticed it brought tears to your eyes."

Mamie didn't reply. When she stopped in Claire's driveway, she didn't shut off the car.

"Aren't you coming in?"

"No, I have a lot of planning to do."

"Glad to hear it. If you need any help, gimme a call."

Claire waved good-bye to Mamie and walked around her house, checking the perennials sprouting in the small gardens around the property. Tulips in a dozen colors on the driveway side. Daffodils, even pink ones, along the back. Everything needed raking again. But even so, it looked beautiful. This was her artwork, her specialty. People who couldn't, or wouldn't develop their talents—people like Felicia—bought art from people like Mamie and, she guessed, like Sean. Where had he purchased *Sunset*? Maybe Claire could find out.

She went inside and phoned Felicia. "I was just curious. Did Sean tell you where he bought that painting?"

"He said he got it from a gallery in the City." Felicia told Claire the name, but she didn't recognize it. After hanging up, she typed the gallery name in the computer search square. Why wasn't she surprised to find it had come from one of the places owned by Miles Arenheim?

Five

When the postmistress pushed the rectangular package across the counter, Claire felt a surge of elation so strong it was like being hit with a blast of January wind off the harbor. She glanced at the vacant table in the corner but swallowed the urge to open the package right there.

A wall of rain hit her head-on as she stepped outside. She held the door for old Mrs. Campe, already soaked just running from her car. Claire opened her umbrella, ducked her face into her jacket collar and started down the steps, the words "it's here" repeating in her head.

On the bottom step, Claire's left foot slipped. She turned her ankle and went down hard. The umbrella and package flew out of her hands. Razor-like pain shot up her leg and into her spine. Cold rainwater saturated her pants. Her vision clouded. She squeezed her eyes shut and forced her brain to override the messages of pain.

A firm hand gripped her shoulder and someone knelt beside her. "Are you all right?"

Even through the viscous haze, Claire recognized the owner of the voice. Her eyes shot open. Blood rushed to her cheeks. "My package. Where is it?"

"Right here. It's only a little damp," Sean said, shaking it near his left ear. "Don't worry. Doesn't sound like anything's broken. Are you hurt?"

Claire shook his hand off her arm. A vein throbbed in her

temple and a migraine materialized as if yanked from a magician's hat. She grasped the iron railing and tried to get to her feet but the feet just wouldn't cooperate.

Faces bent to hers, asked if she was hurt. Features blurred together. Suddenly they all had Sean's bright blue eyes and high cheekbones. She blinked several times to displace the vision and tried again to pull herself up. This time her right foot worked.

Sean held her down. "Don't move, an ambulance is on the way." He peeled her hand from the rail and warmed it in his.

She wrenched it from him and tried once again to rise. "No ambulance. I'm not hurt. Someone just help me up." She seized the railing and planted her boots firmly in the puddle. "Please."

Strong hands grasped her upper arms from behind and she was set carefully on her feet. Another wave of pain seared up her back. She tried not to grimace. Swallow the pain. Her eyes darted toward the package in Sean's long lean fingers.

"Ms. Bastian, are you sure you're all right?" Officer Vaughn Spencer's face evolved from the mass of images before her.

"I'm fine. Will someone just help me to my car?"

"Why don't you go to the hospital—" Vaughn tried to say.

"No! Home."

"Okay, okay, take it easy. I'll send the ambulance away when it gets here and take you home myself."

She recognized the panic in her voice and warned herself to remain calm. She took a breath, then another, put a little weight on the injured ankle, then let the foot take all the pressure. The pain was bad but not unbearable. "I'll go home now," she said firmly.

"I'll drive you. Sean will follow in your car."

"No, not..." Claire started to say, but she was suddenly overcome with fatigue. "Oh, all right. Where's my package?"

"Right here." Sean wiggled it before her.

She wanted to demand he hand it over but instead allowed them each to take an arm and help her to the police cruiser. With them at her sides, she didn't have to put much weight on the ankle and it hardly hurt at all.

The sound of a siren loomed in the distance. "No hospital."

"It's okay. You can just sign a paper that says you don't want treatment. But I still think you should go." Vaughn's voice was soothing, his grip calm and steady. He threw open the front door of the SUV and helped her inside. He'd left the motor running and it was toasty warm. He patted Claire's arm. "I'll go talk to the ambulance guys. Be right back."

Claire leaned back on the headrest, the throbbing pulse of her ankle repeating all the way into her ears. She closed her eyes and willed her brain to ignore it. How easy it would be to fall asleep in this warm, safe haven. Away from her problems.

Her eyes shot open as Vaughn opened the door. She blinked guiltily, aware she had indeed fallen asleep. He didn't seem to notice, just shoved a clipboard in front of her and placed a pen in her right hand. Claire switched it to her left and skimmed down the page looking for the signature line, not bothering to read any of the typewritten words. She scrawled her name and the date and handed the things back to him.

Rain pounded down, echoing inside the SUV like a tunnel. The windshield wipers were on full speed and still she couldn't see the road ahead. Vaughn drove so slowly she thought she could have walked faster. If she *could* walk, that is. Then it dawned on her that she wouldn't be walking much at all for the next few days, possibly weeks. Claire said a quick prayer the ankle wasn't broken. She hadn't heard anything snap. She'd read that when women reached a certain age, their bones tended to be a little more brittle and wondered if she'd reached that age yet. She was only forty-three and had taken good care of herself: mammograms, vitamins, the works.

Vaughn pulled the police SUV to a stop and cast a concerned glance at her. He opened his mouth to speak but clapped it shut when she shot him an icy glare. Sean swung her little car through the river of rain at the side of the road and into her driveway. She tried not to let her emotions reach her face as he raced toward them.

Vaughn ran around to open her door. "Give me your house keys."

"He's got them," she said.

"Okay, swivel on the seat and put your feet on the sidewalk."

A stab of pain went up Claire's leg when she banged the foot on the door but she didn't even flinch. Both feet were on the ground. She reached out for something solid and felt herself grasped on each side by strong hands. They practically carried her across the sidewalk, up her recently swept walkway and onto her nice dry front porch. Home. On her right side, Sean's hands burned through the jacket, cotton blouse, and into her upper arm. Each finger etched into her like torches.

The key rattled in the old lock. Sean wiggled it, then rattled it again. She was just about to jerk the keys from his hands when the door sailed open. A blast of warm chocolate scented air rushed outside.

"Mmm." Sean put his nose in the air and sniffed, like a wolf scenting out a rabbit. "Do I smell one of your famous chocolate cakes?"

"It's got to be. Ms. Bastian, you make the best chocolate cake in town." Vaughn kicked the door shut as they guided her into the living room.

"MaryAnn made it once and it didn't taste anything like yours," Sean said.

"Your wife is a wonderful cook," Claire said, unzipping her coat. "You're smelling chocolate chip cookies. There's some in the cookie jar on top of the refrigerator."

She held her breath while Sean helped her off with her jacket. Once again his fingers burned her flesh wherever they touched. The two men eased her into her flower patterned chair, placed so she had the best view up and down Broad Street. Then they stood, arms crossed, dripping on her highly waxed floor. Claire could almost see the silence hanging in the air. "My package. Where is it? And my umbrella."

"In the car. I'll get them," Sean said.

"You can go now," she told Vaughn. "I'll be all right, really."

She knew he was reluctant to leave her alone in that big empty house, but he also knew she would insist on it. Vaughn shifted restlessly, putting his hands into, then out of, his pockets. "Are you sure? I can come back..."

"I'm sure. Really. Thank you."

Sean returned. Instead of bringing the package to her, he traipsed down the hall to the kitchen. She stifled a groan thinking about the footprints on her floor. Claire heard the rattle of the cookie jar lid and footsteps return down the hallway. Sean stopped in the living room doorway, three cookies in his left hand.

"Well, I guess we'll be on our way," Vaughn said, spotting a newspaper rack beside the chair. He picked up the topmost one, took a pen from his pocket and wrote two phone numbers in the margin. "You know to dial 911 if you have an emergency, but here's my home and cell numbers. Please call if you need anything; a cup of tea—" His cheeks reddened. "—help to the bathroom, anything. I'll stop during my rounds and check on you in a couple of hours anyway." He laid the newspaper on the small table beside her comfortable chair.

"Sean." It was hard for Claire to say his name. He flashed those brilliant blue eyes her way, eyes that had captured several Sackets Harbor's citizens. "Felicia's painting is beautiful."

He put a finger to the cleft in his chin. "She bought *Sunset*, right? Yes. It is very nice."

"I was wondering where you got it."

"At an auction in Boston."

She nodded, hoping her face didn't show the consternation she suddenly felt.

They left. Finally.

The cruiser pulled away, sadness clutched her insides. Was Mamie in for another downfall? Was Sean somehow at the background of this new gallery? For now, she shook off worries about Mamie. There was nothing she could do without further proof.

Claire gazed at the wet spots on her imported Persian rug.

Of course, she hadn't imported it—had bought it used—but preferred to think of it the other way around. She struggled to her feet, taking plenty of time. After all, no one was there to see her pain now. The ankle wasn't broken. To prove it, she leaned heavily on the arm of her chair and flexed the foot gently in a circle. It hurt but moved freely. She hobbled into the hallway and threw a disdainful look at Sean's trail of footprints. She blew out a breath and, using the wall for support—usually a no-no—made her way to the kitchen.

The mail and package were on the table. The brown paper was a little spotted but didn't look soaked through. She shuffled to the sink, ran water into her favorite mug, dropped in an herbal teabag and popped it in the microwave. Her eyes kept roving from the digital blue numbers on the microwave to the package on the table. What a blessing credit cards were. You could call or e-mail to order absolutely anything and they sent things out the same day.

Her plans were finally coming to fruition. The temptation to tear the wrapping off right in the post office had been almost unbearable. She'd hurried to get home to open it and fell in her impatience. How many times did mothers warn their children to slow down and pay attention?

Claire dunked the teabag up and down in the cup. On the table, the package emitted a heady magnetism. She squeezed a wedge of lemon into the cup, dropped the fruit in a zipper bag and returned it to the refrigerator. She dribbled a little milk in the cup and stirred, looking out the kitchen window. It was still raining so hard the house next door was invisible. She wiped up the drops of lemon juice and milk from the counter and once more gazed down the hallway at the water spots but knew if she got down to clean them up, that's where Vaughn would find her later.

Claire cradled the cup in both hands, savoring the warmth oozing through the heavy ceramic, and went to the table. She pulled out the chair, sat and took another sip before allowing her full attention to settle on the plain brown package on the corner of the vinyl tablecloth. The sound of the telephone brought a muttered curse. She tottered to the wall phone. "Oh, hi, Mamie."

"How are you? I heard you took a tumble at the post office."

"I'm just fine, really."

"You should go for x-rays."

"Really, I'm all right, a little stiff perhaps. Did you decide if you're using Payton's house for the exhibit?"

"Yes. What a wonderful thing for her to do. She doesn't even know me."

"It *was* nice. When are you going to check it out?"

"She's invited me over tomorrow. Will you come with me?"

What a perfect opportunity. Claire had wanted to see the inside of Payton's house. "Sure, I'd love to."

"I'll call you and let you know what time. Go to bed, rest your ankle."

"Thanks for calling."

Claire hobbled back to her chair. She picked up the parcel and tore off the paper. The cover shone in the lamplight, beckoning. Claire ran a hand over the glossy green paper, then brought the book to her nose and sniffed. There was nothing better than the scent of fresh ink. Claire could almost hear the thing say "Open me." So she did.

Six

An hour later, Claire hung up the phone with an ache in the pit of her stomach. Mamie was on her way over to take Claire out for lunch. Her eyes roved to the table, to the brightly colored book beside the damp pile of mail. Speaking of damp. Claire ran a hand over her narrow backside. She'd been so wrapped up in the book she hadn't even noticed the cotton fabric clinging to her bottom. She pulled the cloth away, but it rippled back in place as if drawn by a magnet. Claire glanced at the ceiling and then at the plastic rooster-shaped clock on the kitchen wall. She sucked in a breath then let it out in an exasperated hiss. All she wanted was a few hours of peace and quiet.

She searched for a place to hide her treasure. Behind the bread maker? Seemed like she never found time for it any more. On top of the refrigerator? No, it'd be just her luck Mamie would show up wanting cookies. Claire finally settled on a spot behind a stack of flowerpots under the kitchen sink, chuckling a little thinking of all the trouble it was to hide something in a house where she lived all alone.

Claire had a sudden wish that she could move away and restart her life like Payton had. Not to hide from something, as Mamie seemed to believe about Payton, but just to begin as another person. She could establish herself as a recluse. People would leave her alone. She wouldn't have to deal with old memories, wouldn't have to face her misdeed every single day.

Who was she kidding? The memory would still be there,

lurking in the back of her mind, choking her dreams. She sighed again and poked the paper wrapper deeper into the trash. She wouldn't always want to be alone. Sooner or later, she'd seek out company and the cycle would begin again. Claire pushed the wad of paper and the invoice deeper, burying it under the morning's coffee grounds.

She took a fortifying sip of the now-cold tea and limped down the hallway. The old banister creaked with Claire's weight against it. It took four minutes to climb the thirteen steps to her bedroom and another two minutes to peel off the sodden clothes. The skin of her upper arms still tingled where Sean had touched it. She massaged the limp flesh.

A wave of grief hit like a punch in the gut. How ironic was it that he'd carried his own murder weapon? Tears came, but she brushed them angrily away. No time for regrets. Claire lowered herself on the edge of the bed and removed her socks, wondering why the wet things hadn't bothered her; usually a tiny splash on her blouse during dishwashing was enough to send her scurrying upstairs to change.

Finally she was ready. The bedside clock said there were still twelve minutes before Mamie was due. Maybe time for just another short glance at the book. Claire's heart thumped with excitement, but by the time she'd struggled downstairs most of the time had evaporated.

Three minutes left. Not enough time. Mamie was never late.

It was eight p.m. before Claire returned home. Mamie had insisted they watch television. After the movie, Claire urged Mamie to drive her home, but she'd risen and prepared leftover meatloaf for dinner. "You always say it's so much better the second time around."

Even though she'd barely touched her lunch, Claire wasn't hungry. But Mamie wouldn't listen to protests. When dishes were done, Mamie tried to enlist Claire's interest in a video, but she'd finally put her foot down. "I'm tired. I want to go home."

Mamie had looked at Claire's top button. "I've been doing my best to keep you here. I know the mood you're in. You're going to go home and brood, though God knows what you've got to brood about."

"I'm not going to brood. I'm going to bed, to sleep."

Finally they stood on the sidewalk, Mamie talking about the dismal weather, Claire trying to figure out how to dissuade Mamie from escorting her inside and tucking her in bed.

"A bit like being in a cave, isn't it?" Mamie was looking up at the branches of the maples, heavy with rain.

"Hmm? Oh yes. As though none of the outside world can get in and ruin things."

"Ruin things?"

"Nothing. Never mind." Claire had turned away from the frown on Mamie's round face and hobbled up the steps. Taped to the front door was a piece of paper. *Stopped by to see if you were ok. Hope this means you decided to go to the hospital. You should've called. Will stop again in morning. Vaughn.*

Claire left her boots in the tray beside the door, hung her coat on the hall rack, tossed a rueful glance at Sean's long dried footprints and limped to the kitchen. The cabinet doors looked undisturbed. The tiny smudge of flour she'd left on the handle was still there. Claire wiped it off with the tip of her thumb. She poured a double shot of peach schnapps, gathered up the book and hobbled upstairs. No more delays.

Finally in nightclothes and under the fluffy down comforter, she clutched the book to her chest. She'd actually bought three books: one on poisonous plants and two on gardening and landscaping. The one on poisonous plants was destined for the trash. No need for it again. After all, how often does a person go around poisoning someone?

In the light from the pink-shaded bedside lamp, Claire smoothed her palm over the glossy cover with its mass of bright green leaves splashed across it like a jungle. *Poisonous Plants and You.* A twinge of excitement, almost carnal in nature—that is, if she remembered correctly—coursed through her. And another when the spine crackled as she opened the cover. Claire savored the aroma of the fresh-off-the-press pages. It was well after midnight before Claire shut off the light. Her eyes were on fire and refused to read another word.

But sleep was as elusive as was the way to carry out the plan. Her ankle throbbed. The pulses were like sheep on a sleepless night. At 3 a.m. she began to think something might be more seriously wrong than a simple sprained talus, but she channeled thoughts of pain into thoughts of Sean and his demise. She hadn't felt this hopeful, nor this depressed, in a very long time.

Claire woke to sun streaming in the windows. She loved the east facing room for that reason. She stretched her arms over her head and arched her back to work out the stiffness. As she flexed her legs the memory of yesterday's tumble came roaring back. Pain bolted up her leg. She grimaced and lay back on the pillows, realizing today would be the first time in seventeen years she'd call in sick to the library. She'd been very proud of that record, but while tossing and turning last night, Claire had done some thinking about her life. A wasted life, really. Who the heck would care if she never missed a day of work? Would they put it on her tombstone? Big deal.

The one thing she'd done, that should have turned out good, was all crap. She would rectify it. She'd make it right for Sackets Harbor—and *that* could go on her tombstone.

Here lies Claire Bastian ~ She Saved Sackets Harbor

Just as General Jacob Brown did in 1813

That would be Claire's legacy. It was all she had left.

The book lay on the bedside table, a Hay Memorial Library bookmark stuck in about a third of the way. She glanced at it, then at the clock, 8:10! A knot formed in her stomach, then dissipated as she remembered her decision to take the day off. She hadn't slept this late in years. Today would be a day for blazing new trails. Maybe she'd just call the library director and say she was retiring—at age forty-three. Wouldn't that just shake things up?

Claire slid her legs over the edge of the bed, the braided rug rough on the soles of her feet. She stood, letting the right ankle absorb the weight. Not that her weight had ever been a problem. She'd always been able to eat anything and it didn't show up on her hips or thighs the way it did with other women. Particularly Mamie. She was always complaining about her weight. Never did anything about it though.

The ankle was painful but not unbearable. Still, she wouldn't be tripping the light fantastic for at least a couple of weeks. When was the last time she'd gone dancing—God, had it been twenty years? She took one step away from the bed. The air was chilly and her nipples stiffened. The nightgown rubbed across them, and she fluffed the fabric away.

After a shower, Claire sat on the bed and wrapped her ankle in an Ace bandage, slipped on a pair of heavy socks and finished dressing. The journey down the stairs was easier than yesterday afternoon.

She called the library director. Once the phone was back in its cradle, Claire hid the book under a pile of mail and set about making coffee and breakfast. She had no sooner popped two slices of wheat bread in the toaster when she heard tires swooshing on water. Down the long hallway and through the window on the front door, the roof of a car was visible—Vaughn's SUV. A long, deep sigh issued from her throat and she hurried to hide the book in the cabinet.

A second later, his smiling face appeared in the glass.

"Coming!"

Vaughn stepped onto the mat and wiped his shoes. "I came to see how you were."

"Come in. Do you have time for a cup of cocoa? I might just have some homemade muffins in the freezer too."

"I'd love it." He unbuttoned his police issue jacket and hung it on the peg beside hers on the wall. "How is your ankle this morning?"

"It's sore, but it'll be all right." Claire pulled up the leg of her polyester slacks and displayed the bulky wool sock.

"I stopped in last night to check on you."

"I was at Mamie's."

"I figured as much. You didn't go to the hospital?"

"No. I'm fine, really."

He took her elbow and helped her to the kitchen where he set the kettle to boil. When her toast popped up, Vaughn buttered it. He dropped it on the waiting plate while she defrosted a blueberry muffin. The phone rang. She considered not answering. Vaughn was enough company for now. Claire gave him an apologetic look and went to the living room to answer the phone on the small table.

"Good morning." She forced a brightness she didn't feel. "Hi, Mamie."

"How are you this morning?"

"Wonderful, Thanks."

"Why are you home?"

"I decided to take the day off."

"Then you are hurt. I'll be right over to take you to the hospital."

"No! I'm fine. I just didn't feel like working."

There was much hesitation in Mamie's voice when she said, "Okay, if you need something, call. I'm on my way to the shop. I'll call later and let you know what time we're going to Payton's. If you're still going."

"Of course I'm going. I'll talk to you later."

The smell of warm muffins was in the air. Vaughn had settled himself at the table and was munching on a butter-smeared muffin. "I didn't know where you kept the cocoa mix. Otherwise I would have made it."

Claire opened the middle drawer near the sink and took out a packet of mix. "Sorry, I'm all out of whipped cream."

"A little milk to cool it off. Here, sit down, I'll get it. Your toast is getting cold." He poured her another cup of coffee and sloshed milk into his cup. "Do you take milk?"

"Only a dribble, thanks. So, what's on tap for the local constabulary today?"

"Just patrol."

"Must get boring after a while. The same old scenery."

"I love the job." He chewed and swallowed. "I've been thinking about yesterday...about Felicia Feathersone's painting. I didn't know Sean sold art."

"He sells it in his restaurant."

Vaughn swallowed some coffee. "I don't go in for that stuff much."

"Neither do I."

He put the last of the muffin in his mouth, took the plate and empty cocoa cup to the sink, rinsed them and put them in the dishwasher. "You don't like Sean much, do you?"

"It's not that. I just have no use for him."

"I grew up with him. We never hung out together though. He was always the jock. I was the bookworm."

"I haven't seen you in the library in years."

"I buy my books. Probably could start my own library." Vaughn went down the hall to get his coat. Claire started to get up to see him out, but he waved her off. "Don't get up. I'll stop by later to check on you."

"Thank you for everything."

She listened for his car to drive away. Then she got up and made the trip down the long hallway to lock the front door. She hobbled back to the kitchen and did the same with the back door, then pulled all the shades in the downstairs. Claire retrieved the book, grabbed her cup and headed for the living room. She folded herself into her chair in the living room to reread the paragraphs on monkshood for at least the hundredth time.

Every time, though, she prayed the words would change and become items that were easy to obtain, like at the supermarket or pharmacy. She'd racked her brain but couldn't figure how to get monkshood without it being traced back. Granted, she had no police record. She probably wouldn't even be a suspect when

Sean was found dead. Everyone liked and respected her. Well, almost everyone.

Trouble was, as soon as Vaughn or the State Police, or whoever handled murders, began checking, they'd find a number of people, perhaps dozens, with reason to want Sean Adams dead. Claire didn't worry about them pinning the crime on someone else. Sure there were plenty with motives, but who would have means and opportunity too? Besides, she planned for Sean to die at home. The only one there was his soon-to-be ex-wife, MaryAnn. And she didn't have a motive to want him dead. They'd done what few divorcing couples could, remained friends.

As for herself being accused of Sean's murder, Claire didn't think they'd be able to turn up a motive. Except for yacht club meetings and a rare trip to his restaurant, their lives rarely intersected. If they did, well, she'd suffer the consequences. Hadn't she been doing that for almost twenty-eight years?

No matter how hard she thought about it, the main ingredient presented a continued difficulty. If she knew members of the criminal element down in the City, she could just hop on the bus and be there in a matter of hours. Someone there surely could point her in the direction of...heck, in the City they probably had stores that specialized in such things.

Claire envisioned herself walking from the bus station—couldn't risk a cabbie who might recall her face—to the seedy neighborhood where her *contact* hung out. Maybe he had a place in an abandoned building, replete with litter-strewn rooms and holes in the graffiti-painted plaster.

She put down the book and shivered. Without the monkshood plant, she might as well be reading a romance novel. Where on earth was she supposed to get it? Claire thumped a finger on the printed word *monkshood* and decided to try the Internet. She hobbled upstairs. Her ankle was already feeling better. Maybe she'd go back to work tomorrow. Or maybe not.

Claire booted up the ancient computer, wishing she could use the one at the library. It was much newer and connected to some fancy high-speed cable network. At the library they couldn't be certain it was she who'd been looking up the information, but couple that with her purchase of the main ingredient and she'd be off to the penitentiary before you could say "John Kerry would have been a great president." Then again maybe she'd be better off doing the research at the library because *if* they focused on her as a suspect, they would definitely know to look on her own computer. She'd just have to figure out a way to delete it from the innards of the thing. There had to be a way.

While the home page loaded, Claire undressed and donned a comfortable flannel nightgown and slippers. She took a large gulp of brandy, coughed twice, then realized she hadn't eaten a thing since the toast with Vaughn that morning. No matter. She wasn't hungry.

This had to be a perfect murder—unsolvable. Was that a word? A librarian should know such things. She frowned. It was the second time today she'd failed herself.

All was black outdoors except Sylvie French's porch light diagonally across the street. The only sound was the rustle of branches against the house siding. Claire typed the appropriate words in the search square and waited. She opened the book and read the bold captions:

Ingredients
Consistency
Dosage
Storage

The plan had been brewing in the back of her mind for a long time; almost three years. But over the past weeks, Sean had gotten more and more out of hand. So far no one had done anything about it.

SEVEN

"It'll be bigger than Funny Cide," Helen remarked, standing beside the refreshment table in Payton's shop, sipping tea from a steaming paper cup.

"Funnyside?" A little wrinkle formed across the bridge of Payton's nose.

"C-I-D-E," Helen spelled. "He's a race horse owned by some businessmen from town. The news people dubbed them the Sacket Six. It put us on the map and in the news when they entered him in the Kentucky Derby."

Claire took a cookie from the plate on the table. "Did you make these?"

Payton gave an unhesitating giggle. "God no. I can't cook. I bought them at the *Galley*."

"It was nice of you to offer your place for Mamie's showing. She's really excited."

"Please stop saying how nice it was. I hated to see Mamie get the short end of things."

The door creaked open, then shut. Amanda March stood in the doorway. "Ooh. I love what you've done here."

"Isn't it lovely?" Claire agreed.

"I can only stay a few minutes. Edward's up to his ears at the store." Amanda and Edward March owned the marina at the bottom of the hill.

"Come on, I'll give you the grand tour," Payton offered.

"I love how you've made it like a regular home," Claire said.

"Thanks. I thought it would give the customers ideas of how to decorate with plants without having it rammed down their throats."

"I wonder if we could do that at the marina," Amanda said.

"Yes, Amanda, I can see it now, framed boat parts on the walls," said Claire.

"And as knickknacks on the piano," Payton added.

"We don't have a piano," Amanda said, and they all erupted in laughter.

"What's so funny?" Felicia stepped in from the patio.

"We were just being silly," Payton said. "I was giving the nickel tour. Leave the money on the counter on your way out."

"Where did you get this furniture?" Claire asked.

Payton fingered a discretely placed price tag. "I struck a deal with a used furniture shop in Watertown. They'll rotate the pieces on a regular basis. I found a woodworker here in town who makes these wonderful shelves and arbors."

"What's the vine wound through this one?" Helen asked.

"Virgin's bower."

"Beautiful," Amanda said, twining a length of it around a finger. "What's that wonderful aroma?" She bent and sniffed the virgin's bower.

Payton picked up a small plant beside it. "It's a *luculia gratissima.* Isn't it nice?"

"I bet you put it near the door on purpose."

"A marketing technique." Payton gave a modest grin.

"Well, it worked on me. Can I have two?" Felicia said.

"I'll box them before you leave." Payton straightened a plant on one end table, pinched a dead leaf from a peperomia and blew a whisper of dust from a lampshade.

"I'll have one also," said Helen.

"Me too," said Claire. And while you're at it, give me a monkshood plant.

The door whooshed open. "Good morn… Oh, what is that wonderful smell?" cried Mamie.

"It's working!" Helen announced, then explained it to Mamie who asked if it was difficult to grow.

"No, though it will eventually need quite a large pot. Just so you know, I have a repotting service. And free pickup and delivery." Payton showed Mamie the special tag attached along with the price. "The yellow tags indicate the easiest to grow. Green tags are moderately easy and the red ones require a special touch. And, see this shelf?" She pointed to an antique hotel mail holder on the wall near the front counter. "There's a care sheet for every plant in the shop. If I don't put one in your bag, make sure to ask for it."

Mamie ran a finger along a satiny leaf. "Can I have two? I'll put them in the gallery. Maybe they'll cover the smell of paint and canvas."

"A gallery isn't a gallery without those smells," Felicia said.

"You're probably right. I'll still take two, but I'll take them home. I have to run, some people just went into the gallery. I wanted to come and say congratulations on your opening."

"Thank you. I'll box up the plants and send them over before the end of the day. So, have you been in touch with Mr. Arenheim?"

Mamie's pale blue eyes lit up. In the artificial lighting she was almost pretty. "That's another reason I stopped by. Can he come on Monday to look things over? I hope it's convenient for you. He's such a busy man, and that was the only time he—"

"Monday will be fine. I'll probably be here, but you can go in."

"Oh, I couldn't…wouldn't want to be there unless you were."

"It's all right, really. Workers are everywhere right now anyway. You'll probably be tripping all over each other."

"Oh, you're such a life saver."

"Question: someone mentioned you were once going to give painting lessons."

Mamie's smile faded. "I offered classes, but only two people signed up, so it wasn't worth doing it."

"I'd like to take a class or two."

"Maybe…well, I'll see if I can… I'll talk to you later." Mamie closed the door and hurried across the street, a new bounce in her step.

"That was nice of you," Claire said.

"What?"

"Do you really want painting lessons?"

Payton smiled. "Of course. Do you want the rest of the tour?"

"Everything is so beautiful."

"Thanks. I wanted people to see that they can use their plants as decorations rather than just something to set on a windowsill. Like this *ficus radicans*, for example." Payton pointed to a plant on a wall shelf beside a photo of a little blonde girl. The plant's tiny tendrils twisted through the shelf's openwork back. "This plant looks best winding around something. Obviously this one has to be sold with the shelf, but I sell them separately also. Then I have these hand painted Mexican planters. They were made to hold herbs and sit on a windowsill."

Two steps led down to the outdoor patio. A five-foot latticework fence had been erected on three sides, shielding the area from the road. Tall umbrella palms made subtle privacy curtains at the street. Different shapes and colors of stones had been laid in a meandering pattern on the gravel.

"Absolutely beautiful." Helen sat in a white wicker chair and put her feet up on the matching ottoman. Sunshine filtered through the overhead lattice casting Helen's face in warped squares of light. Hanging plants swayed in the warm breeze; the gentle aroma of peppermint wafted through.

Amanda took a chair beside Helen. "Payton, this is lovely."

"Thank you."

Claire sat in the third chair. Felicia took the fourth. Payton remained standing. Helen sipped her tea and pointed to a potted plant on the next table. "Tell me about this. We're almost finished with our breakfast room and—"

"A breakfast room?" Claire asked.

"Yes. One day Payton pointed out how nice a sunroom cum breakfast nook would be, so I talked Carter into demolishing that old attached shed and replacing it with a glass room. You should see what a difference it makes. Anyway, I'll be looking for plants to put out there. How would this be?"

"You don't want that. It needs beaucoup sunlight, and your room will have filtered sun because of the surrounding chestnut trees," Payton said.

"It's so refreshing to have someone to tell me what's going to work or not. Usually, I just hope a plant will live long enough for me to get it home from the supermarket. You know what you should do, dear? Start a home service where you go to people's homes and tell them what sorts of plants they should have."

It was hard keeping her ears tuned to Helen's words because Claire's eyes had spotted something that sent a thrill of excitement literally from her head to her toes. Nirvana. It had to be. She was experiencing total and all-encompassing bliss because, in the center of the glass topped table, not three feet away, sat *the plant*! In an unassuming plastic pot, eight inches of shining green leaves and a young cluster of blue/purple flowers, was her monkshood plant. Claire leaned back and closed her eyes. The others could think she was enjoying the pleasant weather and relaxing furniture if they wanted. In reality Claire was experiencing an emotion something like childbirth: the overwhelming emotion that hits when the pressure's released from your vagina and everyone yells congratulations.

Congratulations, Miss Bastian. Your baby has arrived.

Claire's fingers twitched. She forced her hands to fold in her lap, presenting the vision of leisure and cheer. Two tags were affixed to the pot. She couldn't read the price, but the cost didn't matter, she'd mortgage her home if she had to.

"What are you smiling at?" Felicia asked.

Would any of them suspect she was the one who'd murdered Sean Adams? Would they care? She'd seen movies where people in town banded together to protect a murderer. She'd better not count on something like that. Face up to it, that's all she could do if the time came.

Felicia's eyebrows lifted and Claire realized the woman was waiting for a response. "I was just enjoying the day." Her eyes roved casually to the plant. A yellow tag meant it was easy to grow. That didn't matter. It would only have to live a couple of hours. No, she'd probably keep the plant, minus the necessary number of leaves. If authorities came asking questions, would those missing leaves be incriminating? Could they tell leaves had been snipped off rather than simply dropped on their own?

How many others had Payton sold? It was pretty. The flowers smelled nice. It rebloomed without much effort from the owner, so the tag said. People would buy it by the score. No they wouldn't. People with children or pets would be advised to stay away. The entire plant was poisonous, including the roots. "The drug toxins are absorbed not only through the skin, but also can be ingested or injected. There is no specific antidote," the book said. Monkshood had a toxicity rating of six out of a possible six stars, which meant it was quickly fatal.

She leaned a little deeper in the wonderful chair and crossed her arms, her mind racing with fervor.

"Look who's here."

Even though Helen whispered, the trepidation in her voice snaked into Claire's thoughts. Panic bubbled up inside her seeing Sean standing on the top step to the patio. His blond hair, flecked by the overhead lattice, was tousled as though he'd just gotten out of bed. He ran a casual hand through it, and the locks remained in place for a second before tumbling back onto his forehead.

Helen was looking at him with unveiled anger. Amanda gave a quick, unemotional glance, then turned away. Felicia's fingers were tight around the padded wicker arms. Claire mentally checked her own fingers—loose, at rest. Nobody would guess what she'd been thinking. None of that mattered, Sean only had eyes for Payton.

She threw him a benign smile. "Help yourself to some tea and cookies on your way out."

Claire managed not to grin.

Sean opened his mouth and shut it several times, looking like a goldfish who'd fallen out of the bowl. He shut his mouth for the last time, turned on his heel and left.

"He's such an ass," Amanda said softly.

"You mean he *has* such an ass," Felicia said. "Wonder what he wanted."

"I don't." Amanda laughed and stood up. "I've got to get going. Edward's got things to do down in the boatyard so I need to man the store." Out front, between the lattice criss-crosses, traffic flowed in a steady line and people were already filling the sidewalks. "Looks like it's going to be a busy weekend."

"I've got to be going too," Felicia said and hurried after Amanda.

"Rumor has it Felicia and Sean had an affair," Helen whispered.

"What?" Payton and Claire exclaimed at the same time.

"It's just a rumor. And the source gives me reason to question the whole thing. I wouldn't have mentioned it if I didn't see her reaction for myself. She was struck just about speechless when Sean got here."

"What's the source of the rumor?" Claire asked.

"Sylvie said she saw them together in Chaumont a couple of weeks ago."

"Sylvie's not reliable?" Payton asked.

Helen gave an elaborate shrug. "She likes to embellish, if you know what I mean. I didn't believe it till just now, though."

Claire rose. "I've got to get to work." She shot a long parting glance at the monkshood and followed Payton and Helen into the shop where several tourists were browsing.

Claire crumpled her cup and tossed it into the trash as Payton helped Helen decide which plants would be best suited to life in her new breakfast-nook-cum-sunroom. "On the driveway side—that's where you'll have the most sunshine—I think a tall *cussonia spicata*—"

"A what?"

"A cabbage tree. From South Africa. The natives eat the roots during times of famine."

"What a relief to know everyone else in town could perish and we'd still have our—what did you call it?"

"*Cussonia spicata.*"

"I love the sound of the name." Helen repeated it twice. She removed her glasses then resettled them on her nose.

"I'm sorry, but the image of cabbages hanging on the ends of the branches leaves a little to be desired," Claire said. "I've got to get to the library."

"I forgot to ask about your ankle."

"It's much better, thanks."

"Are you coming with Mamie tomorrow night? She's taking a tour of the house so she'll be familiar with it because Monday Mr. Arenheim's coming. I just had a thought, why not stay for dinner?"

"I'd love to. What can I bring?"

"Nothing. Just yourselves."

"We'll bring dessert."

Claire climbed into her little car and headed to work, little monkshood plants dancing in her head. It was here. It was accessible. Now, she just had to summon the courage to buy it.

EIGHT

Claire couldn't sleep. A tiny voice she could only attribute to the monkshood plant kept calling her name in a high-pitched squeak. Even when she pulled the pillows over her head and pushed her hands on both ears, the sound still penetrated. The digital clock had just clicked over to 4:22 a.m. when Claire flew to a sitting position and yelled, "Just be patient a little longer, I'm coming." Right after, she laughed out loud. If any neighbors heard, they might think she had a visitor.

How long had it been since she'd had a man? A date? She wouldn't let that thought remain in her head. She replaced it with thoughts of how she'd introduce the poison to Sean. Chocolate cake. Everyone loved her cake, especially Sean. Hadn't he said so the other day? Yes, hopefully the chocolate would cover any flavor added by the monkshood—the book didn't say how strong it would be.

By morning, she was bleary-eyed and dopey. She staggered upright and went to look out the window, the bright sun making her blink fiercely. After two cups of coffee and the last blueberry muffin from the freezer, Claire felt ready to face the world. This might just be the biggest day of her life. She needed to be prepared. And to screw up the courage to purchase the plant.

The ankle felt better. No twinge of pain going up the steps to Payton's shop. She stopped in the doorway letting the heady aroma of the *luculia gratissima* work its magic on her senses, just as it did in her living room on the little table beside her favorite chair. Claire sucked in another scented breath and looked for Payton. The main store was empty, but voices came from the patio area: Payton, Amanda and Felicia. Claire remained inside, ears perked in their direction.

She wandered around noticing how Payton constantly changed plants and furniture arrangements, keeping things new and interesting. Claire's fingertips examined the crinkled leaves of a tiny peperomia. Those same fingertips carried it to the front counter. It would look nice on the table between her bedroom windows. Another trip around the shop added another *luculia gratissima* for the dining room table.

Amanda's muffled voice said she had to be running along. Claire's fingers examined the raised design of the Mexican windowsill planter as the three women moved toward the doorway. The planter would look wonderful over the sink. Basil, oregano, sage—the aromas would fill the kitchen.

Payton was first to enter. Claire ducked out of sight. "I want a visit to Payton's Place to be one of the best and most sensual experiences a woman's ever had."

"What about the men?" Felicia asked.

"Men aren't sensual creatures by nature."

"Tell me about it!"

Payton laughed. She had a great voice, not the least bit abrasive, even when laughing. "Men are very basic. They'll come here in a hurry because they've forgotten a holiday or birthday and buy something just to avoid sleeping in the dog house."

"And they'll tell their wives where they got it," Amanda suggested.

"Right. But if they don't, these little ditties will." Payton indicated the care sheets that went with each plant.

The women passed by. Claire slipped out to the patio, stopping at the bottom step. How nice it would be to have a patio just like this, with greenery and flowers and privacy everywhere. She had the money and the space. Why hadn't she done anything like this? Because except for her living room chair, Claire's creature comforts weren't something she generally put at the forefront. For years her concentration had been on the library. During the days she catalogued and filed and tried to devise more efficient ways of running the place. Nights she was consumed with thoughts of what new books the meager budget could purchase, what new events or classes to offer.

The smell of damp soil brought back memories of childhood summers when she and her brother chased grasshoppers in the empty field across from the school.

Six hanging fuschias graced the lattice barrier, bright tri-color flowers sprinkling drops of water every time the breeze rippled through. Claire tiptoed across the gravel and halted at the wicker patio set where the monkshood sat regally on the glass-topped table.

Her finger muscles twitched. She closed her eyes and let the plant's aura flow into her, become part of her. After all, they were about to embark on a relationship that would change two lives. Perhaps even end them both. That notion had been wiggling around in her head like a mass of earthworms ever since she'd made the decision. She might be caught and sent to prison. Did New York State have the death penalty? She didn't know, didn't want to know right now. Nothing could get in the way of the plan, whatever the final outcome.

No, that was stupid. There was no reason for anyone to be caught, no reason this couldn't be the perfect crime. Her hands clenched open and then shut. Claire opened her eyes and walked toward the plant. She sank into the poofy flowered cushion and pulled the plant close. From her research, Claire knew it should eventually reach more than three feet in height and would need to be put outdoors; being only eight inches tall meant it was a baby. What did they call baby plants? Seedlings? Didn't matter right now. Being a baby, would it still have the poisonous properties of its adult counterpart? None of the books or the Internet had divulged that information. Unfortunately there was only one way to find out.

Out on the sidewalk, Felicia and Amanda stopped a half dozen feet from where Claire sat. The wind pushed Amanda's words into the patio. "I feel like sinking Sean's boat…with him in it."

"I know what you mean," Felicia replied.

"Trouble is, I'd be the first suspect."

"I doubt that."

"I can't believe I let him talk me into paying fifteen thousand for that painting."

Claire recalled the yacht club meeting at the marina two days ago. As they'd been ushered into the marina store, Amanda introduced them to a painting of Commodore Melancthon Brooks Woolsey hanging behind the cash register. She'd bought it for Edward's birthday; he was a history buff. "When Edward finds out what I paid, he'll kill me."

"No he won't because when Brighton finds out what I paid for *Sunset* he'll kill me, and Edward will be busy comforting my husband." Felicia gave a harsh chuckle. "We should make a bet as to who gets it first."

"Don't joke like that."

Felicia sighed. "I wasn't joking." She switched the red plastic shopping bag from one hand to the other. "What if Sean finds out you haven't told Edward what you paid?"

"I don't even want to think about that. God, I hate that man."

Claire sighed and let her eyes rove to the monkshood plant. Who would believe such a beauty could be so lethal? Behind the innocent façade beat the heart of a monster. Two-faced, that's what it was. Just like people. You never knew what was behind their smiling faces. There was a song about smiling faces. Who sang it? Some group from back in the 80's. Claire couldn't think who it was. She slapped her thigh. She should be able to recall such things.

What if, instead of buying the plant, she plucked off the necessary number of leaves? Surely no one would notice missing leaves. Even the sap was poisonous. If she got any on her skin…

She picked up the pot and went inside.

"Claire!" Payton said. "I didn't know you were here."

"I've been sitting on your comfy patio furniture. Almost took myself a nap."

"Ready for the yacht race?"

"My stopwatch is all polished. I hope the weather holds."

"I've been watching the forecast very closely. They said it might rain tomorrow morning for a while."

"It wouldn't dare. Are you sailing with Helen and Carter?"

"Just for a couple of practice races. The extra weight will slow them down, so I don't want to be a hindrance. Carter said it didn't matter, but still..."

"Are you buying Aden's boat?"

"I am thinking of buying *Zephyr*. If I can find a partner, that is. Are these yours?" She gestured at the plants on the counter.

"Yes. And this, too." Claire set down the monkshood.

"Did you read the tag? *Aconitum napella* is quite poisonous."

Claire perched a frown between her eyes and backed a step away from the counter, feigning fear. "Really?"

Payton laughed. "If you don't have children, cats or dogs, it won't be any trouble."

"I don't like pets. They make too much mess."

"I like dogs. One of these days I'll get one." She pointed at the monkshood. "I've sold quite a number of these little fellows. As a matter of fact, Felicia and Amanda each just bought one."

"Really?" Was the delight in her voice noticeable? She quickly hid the elation behind a giggle. "Sorry, I'm having a hard time picturing Felicia with a plant. I can't imagine her putting her hands in dirt."

Payton giggled. "She's got a gardener. What are you bringing to the potluck before the race?"

"I haven't decided yet."

"I'm making a tossed salad. I can't mess that up too badly."

This was the second time Payton lamented her cooking skills. Claire began feeling a little dread about tomorrow's dinner invitation.

"Felicia's bringing ham salad sandwiches," Payton said. "Amanda's decided not to make her famous macaroons, she's doing chocolate cake instead. She's using the recipe from The Galley's cookbook."

This was a terrible turn of events. When Sean died from chocolate cake poisoning Amanda would be the first suspect.

The door opened and Sylvie stepped inside, turning in two circles before stopping in front of the counter. "Nice shop," she announced. She looked past Claire to Payton. "It's my sister's birthday. I thought a plant might be a perfect gift."

"Does she have plants now?"

"Her husband calls their house a botanical garden."

"Good, that gives us a place to start. Come with me."

Not knowing exactly why, Claire followed them to the patio. Payton picked up a beautiful bird of paradise. "What about this?"

"Is it easy to grow?"

Payton wiggled her hand in the air to indicate a medium range. "If she's a plant person, it will be easy for her."

"What's this?" Sylvie pointed to an overhead shelf where bright flowers wiggled in the breeze. There was another monkshood, bigger than the one Claire was buying, with larger, more fully developed flowers.

"Does your sister have children or pets?" Payton asked.

"Yes."

"Then she wouldn't want this, it's poisonous," was all Payton could say before Sylvie's fingers released it. The plant thunked to the walkway, leaves, soil and beautiful purple flowers shooting in all directions.

Sylvie pushed past Claire, holding her hands out as though she'd been sprayed with acid. "How dare you—" She ran to the hose and began washing herself.

Payton followed, trying to explain, but Sylvie cast a venomous glare at both Payton and Claire and sped dripping from the store. Both women watched open-mouthed as Sylvie raced down the hill to her real estate office.

"I didn't mean to shock her like that." Payton swept up the plant and deposited it in the trash.

The front door opened and in walked the largest bunch of roses Claire had ever seen. The roses lowered onto the counter. Behind them stood Aden Green. Payton was smiling from one side of her face to the other.

Not ready to date? Humbug. Payton was as ready as she could be. Claire would bet her next paycheck that Payton and Aden would be an item before the month was out.

Claire paid for her plants, said bye to Aden and left. If any onlooker had concerns about her injured ankle, they would have been quickly erased. Her pace was as light as a five year old's. She not only had her plant, but many other people had purchased them too. Could life get any better than this?

Claire was actually giggling out loud as she made the trip from car to house with the box of plants. She set the monkshood in the middle of the kitchen table atop the handmade doily in place of the basket of wax fruit. She folded her arms and closed her eyes and drank in the aroma of the silky blue-purple flowers.

After putting the other plants in their respective places, she took a paper cup from the package in the cabinet over the stove and filled it with water. Was the water supposed to be hot or cold? Or room temperature? Claire knelt on the immaculate floor and retrieved the book from under the sink. Settling back on her heels, she turned to the page describing the *aconitum napellus.* It didn't specify water temperature. Claire put the book back in its hiding place, and stood up, ignoring the twinge in her ankle. Maybe too-hot water destroyed the poisonous properties. And maybe too-cold water would do the same thing. To be on the safe side, she'd use water just out of the tap.

Claire filled the cup to a half-inch of the top. Then, with shears from the utensil drawer, snipped off two leaves like the book instructed. But, this was a baby plant, the leaves smaller than the ones in the picture. The directions hadn't specified mature leaves. Were two of this size enough? Why couldn't this be like the cookbooks and be specific? A tablespoon of this, a half cup of that; amounts that left a person knowing where she stood.

Claire lopped off two more leaves, taking them from different spots on the stalk so the stubs would be less noticeable. The snipped areas stood out like acne on a teenager. She dropped the leaves onto a paper towel, folded the edges of the towel together and shook the leaves into the cup of water. She placed the cup on the windowsill to "brew" beside the new Mexican planter. As an afterthought, Claire put the book on poisonous plants into her satchel. Perhaps she'd have time to look at it again, to learn something more about the plant.

She stashed the paper towel in the trash, careful not to touch any of the sticky white sap. Claire washed the scissors with the hottest water, using an old toothbrush to scrub the joints, dried the shears with another sheet of paper towel and put them away. She crossed her arms and eyed the paper cup, sitting like a toddler that was soon to erupt into the vilest of tantrums.

She decided to walk the quarter mile to the library. It was a beautiful day, the air was fresh and clean and she felt great. Claire buttoned her jacket and inhaled deeply. Someone had just mown their lawn.

Claire heaved her satchel on the counter and made a beeline for the phone. Edward answered on the second ring, "Good afternoon, Sackets Harbor Marina, Edward March speaking."

"Hi, Edward, it's Claire."

"Well, hello there, what's cookin' good lookin'?"

"Nothing much. I hope the weather holds for the race."

"How's your ankle?"

"It's okay, thanks."

"But you didn't call to talk to me, did you? Amanda's not here. She's down below with a customer. Want to leave a message?"

"Will you remember to give it to her?"

"Probably not."

Claire laughed. "I heard she's making her chocolate cake for the potluck." Claire twisted the phone cord around her finger. The library door opened, a pair of elderly women entered and waved hello.

"I think she mentioned cake," Edward said.

Claire lowered her voice. "Well…I just love her macaroons and she's the only one who can make them right. I wondered if—"

"Say no more." Edward laughed. "I'll tell her everyone's calling to vote for cookies."

Claire hung up feeling sick to her stomach. She hated lying. She rubbed her palm in a circle on her abdomen feeling the gurgle of acid beneath her hand. After opening the library mail, she settled on her tall stool and took out *Poisonous Plants and You*. The title glowed like neon. Each and every customer was sure to spot it. She reached under the counter, removed the jacket of a Grisham novel and wrapped it around her book. She tapped the cover with a forefinger. Much better, now it could sit right on top of the desk. The day passed without incident. Customers came and went, chatted and gossiped. Claire responded but by late afternoon could recall nothing of what anyone said. The only thing in her head was the cup of leaves in her kitchen window.

The door opened and Felicia entered. Claire slapped the book shut and pushed it aside with an elbow. Felicia ducked down the fiction aisle saying, "I know you're getting ready to close, don't forget and lock me in."

The big wall clock said ten minutes past five, ten minutes past closing time. She shifted in the chair working out the kinks, then glanced at the cart full of books to the left. She hadn't even put them back on the shelves. The top book was Stephen King's *Carrie*. Claire started pushing the cart toward the K fiction aisle when Felicia returned.

Claire followed her to the counter where she dropped a Lisa Scottoline novel on the counter. "Beautiful day."

"Mamie told me you and Mamie have been invited to Payton's for dinner. I took a painting in to be cleaned and she was bubbling all over about it."

"Wasn't it nice of Payton to offer her place for the gallery?"

"A big sacrifice."

Felicia would never put herself in such a position. Even though she'd love to show off her belongings, she wouldn't chance one of her precious things getting damaged or stolen.

Claire rotated the chair forward, putting her elbow on the faux Grisham book. The movement caused Felicia to notice the book and reach for it. "What are you reading?"

Claire pressed her elbow tight against the cover. In spite of that, Felicia kept pulling. The only option besides jerking it back and crying "Mine!" was to let her have it. Every muscle in Claire's body knotted as she watched it slide into Felicia's hands. Felicia studied the cover blurb. "I've never read Grisham before. This looks good. I'll take this too."

"Um, ah." Claire couldn't think of a single lucid word to say.

"Oh, you probably haven't had time to check it back in yet. I'll wait."

"Um, it's just that, er, this has a long waiting list."

Felicia opened the front cover and read the inside flap. Claire tightened her butt muscles against the threatening diarrhea. She took a breath and focused on the computer screen. "It looks like you owe a fine. Two dollars."

Felicia slammed the book shut, dumped it on the counter and leaned across to gape at the monitor. "What!"

Claire set the book atop the farthest pile.

"I *always* return my books on time."

Claire squinted at the screen, scrunching her rear end tighter. "Oh dear, I'm sorry, that's not you at all. So sorry for the confusion. Would you like to be added to the Grisham list?"

"Yes, please." Felicia sounded distant, confused.

Claire scanned the bar code on the Scottoline cover. The computer made a pinging sound, and printed out a receipt that Claire tucked inside the book cover. "You're all set, it's due back the fifteenth. Sorry for the confusion."

"Well, I'll be on my way," Felicia said, her eyes flickering toward the faux Grisham book. Claire resisted the urge to push it out of sight. She didn't breathe until Felicia's convertible whooshed past the window. Claire hurried to lock the door.

Nine

Claire hefted the satchel and purse on her shoulder and began the walk home. The book was a comfortable thump against her spine with each step. Excitement about dinner at Payton's built. What should she wear? She wasn't one to buy new things, styles came and went too fast for her to keep up. Claire did a mental examination of her closet: blue A-line, too baggy; green wrap-around, too informal; brown print, hideous. Nothing came close to rivaling Payton's wardrobe. Perhaps something that had been relegated to the back of the closet. Hadn't she read that sooner or later everything comes back in style?

Before going to Payton's, Claire also wanted to check the ingredients for what she'd begun to think of as Sean's Deathday Cake. He'd said often enough that *Tin Pan Galley's* chocolate layer cake was one of life's best things. Maybe it was one of death's best things too.

Claire stepped over a root that had grown through the sidewalk. Not a twinge from her ankle. The gods were certainly shining down with goodness today. That meant her decision was the right one. Surely if what she planned was evil, if Sean wasn't meant to leave this green earth, things wouldn't go so smoothly. Tonight promised to be very busy, but rather than disturb her sense of order, Claire felt an almost giddy excitement.

As she crossed the intersection of Main and Broad streets, someone headed the other direction jostled her arm. "Oh my." Claire's satchel thumped to the ground.

"I'm so sorry," said Payton. "My mind was spinning in a hundred directions."

"Mine too. Must be the weather."

"It is a beautiful day, isn't it?" Payton handed Claire her bag.

"Thank you. I'll see you in a while." Claire flung the strap over her shoulder and went across the street. Her foot had barely touched the opposite curb when Sean's Grand Am pulled up. He leaned forward, looking at Payton, but Payton already headed home.

He got out of the car. "Wait. Payton."

From where Claire stood, she could see the pique on Payton's face as she turned around.

"I need to talk to you."

"How many times do I have to ask you to leave me alone?"

He stepped onto the sidewalk, a shark looking for his next meal. "I wanted to apologize, that's all."

"Okay, apology accepted. Now, I'd appreciate it if you leave me alone."

"I want us to be friends."

"Sean, we're never going to be friends. I am willing to accept your apology because we are fellow business owners and take part in some of the same group activities, but that's as far as it will ever go." She turned away.

He grasped her left arm just above the elbow and yanked her toward him. Her hip banged his. She shook off his hand. She took another step away and he took one toward her in a jerky two-step dance.

Claire had seen enough. She recrossed the street.

"Fine, bitch. I told you the other day you were going to be sorry. You—"

"You don't intimidate me, Sean Adams. Now get away from me or I'm calling the police." Payton produced a cell phone. She flipped open the lid and dramatically punched a number. "Are you leaving?" He didn't move. She hit another number.

Claire stepped onto the sidewalk, just four feet behind Sean.

"I know why you left teaching."

Payton poked another number. Claire hefted her purse, prepared to knock him silly.

"It wasn't voluntary."

Claire's fingers tightened around the handbag. Neither of them had noticed her standing there. When Sean said, "Conduct unbecoming a teacher," Claire lowered the purse.

Payton closed the phone. But instead of pleading for him to keep her secret, her fist flashed out, her knuckles making contact with his nose. The blow staggered him backwards. He tripped over the curb and landed with his rear end on Broad Street, his heels propped on the sidewalk.

He was up fast, like one of those punching bag clowns Claire's brother used to have. Sean braced his feet, one fist clenched in front of him. Blood and anger swelled as he glared at Payton. Then he spotted Claire.

"Did you see what she did?"

"I certainly did."

"Go call the cops, will you?"

Claire shook the handbag at him. "What's wrong with you? Do you sit up nights thinking of ways to piss people off? Ways to screw them?"

Confusion trickled between his fingers along with blood from his nose.

Claire narrowed her eyes, took a few steps forward, and aimed a finger inches from his face. "How dare you? Your poor dead mother would be ashamed. Now young man, tuck your sorry tail between your legs and get the hell out of here."

Another dribble of red oozed between Sean's fingers and onto his leather bomber jacket. He glanced down at it, then back to the pair of women. "You haven't heard the end of this."

"Git!"

Sean slithered into his car, performed a u-turn and sped away. Payton rubbed her upper arm. There was a small, appreciative smile on her face. Vaughn's cruiser slid to a stop in the same spot Sean's car had just stood. He raced from the vehicle and to Claire's side. "Are you all right? Did you injure your ankle again?"

"Yes, so stupid of me. I was crossing the street and twisted it as I stepped off the curb. So dumb."

"You shouldn't be out walking with a sprained ankle."

"Goodness, Vaughn. That happened ages ago. Besides, I wasn't out for a joy walk, my car broke down."

"Why didn't you call for a ride?"

Claire gave him a motherly smile. "Because my ankle didn't hurt. And you aren't the Auto Club."

"Get in. I'll drive you home."

"Thank you. That would be very nice."

Payton waved as Vaughn helped Claire into the passenger side of the SUV.

At home, she booted up the computer while the muffled roar of water coursed through her old pipes and into the tub. She clicked on the homepage and typed Payton's name in the white search rectangle. She waited while Yahoo searched its databases. Nothing. Claire gave an audible sigh, selected a dress from the closet and went to the bathroom. Just what was Payton's secret?

Just as she'd lowered herself into the tub, the word "widow" flashed before her eyes. Of course, Payton was a widow. What was her husband's name?

Her brain churned, but try as she might, she could not recall Payton's dead husband's name.

Mamie and Claire arrived at Payton's at one minute past six. It was the first time either of them had been inside. What a far cry from what the neighbors used to call it: Brice's Eyesore. Harry Brice had been a crusty old codger, as Mamie referred to him. Grouchy, arrogant and slovenly. An insurance salesman, intense in his career, able to talk people into twice the coverage they originally wanted. His wife had died twenty years before him. In those ensuing years, the house had fallen into disrepair. The grass hadn't been mowed, except for once when the son came to visit. Inside, boxes and junk were piled shoulder high, with only narrow pathways for a person to crabwalk from one place to the other. That was the rumor anyway. Sylvie French's agency had handled the sale. She complained that she'd spent weeks hauling stuff to the dump. The place sat for seven or eight years before Payton came along. Apparently no one wanted a fixer-upper that needed everything fixed.

Mamie and Claire stood on the sidewalk. Mamie held a foil-wrapped plate that she said contained a banana cream pie, her specialty. Seemed like most every cook in town had a special recipe. For Claire, it was chocolate cake. Amanda made coconut macaroons. Sean's was chocolate caramel cheesecake. Count Felicia out. She didn't bake, as apparently, neither did Payton.

The grass was freshly cut. Payton's Intrepid sat in the driveway. It was shiny and freshly waxed. Before Claire could ring the bell, Payton opened the door wearing a shimmering blue-green caftan. Claire instantly felt underdressed even though she wore her best cotton shift. Payton also wore a genuine, welcoming smile. She stepped back so they could enter. Plucky Mexican guitar music greeted them.

"This is for you." Mamie handed Payton the plate. "It's a banana cream pie."

"Thank you so much. It'll go perfectly with the cordial I got. Come in." She shut the door and moved around them. "Let me put this in the kitchen, then I'll show you around."

Payton disappeared in a flowing cloud of aqua. Mamie gazed open-mouthed around her. Claire had to admit, the place deserved open-mouthed inspection. It was an absolute delight to the senses. From the energetic guitar chords that seemed to ooze from everywhere, to the aroma of something herbal and pungent, to the open living area that assaulted the eyes with color and texture. Wood furniture in straight solid lines, upholstery in large flowery prints, floors of highly polished hardwood. All from the pages of *House & Garden*.

"Beautiful," Mamie murmured.

Payton returned and gestured to Claire's right. "This is my den slash library slash office. I don't know what to call it yet." She laughed. "Frankly, I haven't been in it long enough to give it a name. Seems like I spend all my time at the shop."

"I feel that way about the library. Like it's monopolized all my time."

"Claire, you love that job," Mamie scolded.

"I know, but recently I realized I haven't changed anything about myself in a very long time."

"Are you contemplating anything in particular?" Payton sounded genuinely interested.

"Yes. I'm just not sure what it's going to be yet," Claire lied.

"What kind of rug is this?" Mamie asked.

"It's called Spanish Revival."

Mamie toed the red zigzag border, then almost immediately her attention went to the wall of bookshelves. "I guess you meant it when you said you liked to read."

"You have quite eclectic tastes." Claire ran her hand over the spines at eye-height. "Christie, Francis, Cummings, Thoreau."

"I read any chance I get. Lately though, it seems like all I have time for are sales brochures and invoices."

They passed through the foyer and into a small area, separated from the main living and dining space by the discreet placement of furniture. Payton pointed at the far wall, at the painting she'd bought in Mamie's gallery. *Ocaso*'s bold sunset colors blended perfectly with the furnishings. The yellow wall paint seemed to have been selected just for it.

Mamie nodded in appreciation. "Wonderful, just wonderful. You have an impeccable sense of color."

Payton led them to the main living area. Up till now, Claire wondered if Payton's motive in inviting her to supper along with Mamie was to show off this masterpiece of a home. But during Mamie's unabashed compliments, a red flush crept up the back of Payton's neck. Claire realized she'd totally misread things. This woman wasn't stuck-up and ostentatious. She was shy and reserved, cautious. Claire's regard for her soared.

"I thought we could just remove all my art to make room for whatever you're going to exhibit," Payton said.

"Except for *Ocaso*," Mamie said.

"Except for *Ocaso*. Thank you for selling it to me. I love it. Tell me if I'm wrong, but I think there's enough lighting and space here to make a really nice showing for you."

Mamie didn't speak. She wandered around, running her hands across the backs of sofas, the surfaces of shelves, the rims of vases. Suddenly she spun on a heel and said, "This will be absolutely perfect."

"Do you think Mr. Arenheim will agree?" Claire asked.

Mamie looked Claire directly in the eye and took a hefty breath. "I'm not going to wait for his opinion. I'm going to call him the moment I get home and tell him this is what we're doing."

"I think he'll value your opinion," Payton said. "After all, he trusted you to sponsor the whole shindig."

"That's right."

The dining table was set with thick ceramic plates on woven straw mats. A centerpiece of canna lilies completed the setting. Payton turned right past a set of glass doors leading to a patio civered in deep shadows by the approaching sunset. The kitchen was just as brightly colored as the rest of the house. The floor was some sort of tiles the color of red clay, the walls a shade or two lighter. Copper pots dangled from a wrought iron rack on the ceiling. Seeing Claire looking at them, Payton laughed. "Funny isn't it?"

Claire knew she was referring to her professed inability to cook, but if the scents emanating from the stainless steel-fronted oven were any indication, Payton was a liar of considerable caliber.

"So, that's the downstairs, except for the pantry." Payton jabbed a corkscrew into a bottle of wine. She gave it several no-nonsense twists and popped the cork from the neck. "I'll show you the upstairs later. There's a wide hallway where I think we can expand the gallery also. We'll probably need to install more lighting, though."

"I will pay whatever it costs," Mamie said.

Payton moved the bottle to the center of the counter that was the same color as the floor. "While that breathes, I'll show you the patio." She pushed aside wispy gauze drapes and shoved open the glass door. The breeze off the harbor smelled like spring—earthy and damp. The backyard was lined with mature trees that lent privacy and insulated it from neighborhood noises.

"That chestnut tree is coming down tomorrow," Payton explained.

"My goodness, why? It's beautiful," Mamie said.

"It is pretty, but it's responsible for mildew on both my house and Helen's. It's so big that no sunlight gets through. I had a couple of others removed a few weeks ago. This was an afterthought. I held off because it's so pretty, but it's just got to go. I'll replace it with something, maybe a Japanese maple or a Russian olive; something that doesn't get so big. Later, I'll do up this spot with brugmansia and summersweet and some foamflowers and lilyturf. Over here, I'll put in an arbor and grow moonflowers on it. I love their scent. Don't you?"

Mamie gave a nervous chuckle. "After you said Russian olive, I didn't understand a single word you said."

Payton laughed too, but hers was heartfelt, not poking fun in any way. Mamie seemed to realize this and joined anew, apologizing for being such a horticultural dunce.

"That's ridiculous. Not everyone is interested in or knows about plants. Just like I know next to nothing about art."

"You knew about *Ocaso*," Mamie said.

"All I knew was that it had a southern feel and the colors matched the room. So I'm an artistic dunce. Anyway, I should have the plantings done in time for the gallery opening. Did I hear you say it's slated for the Fourth of July weekend?"

"Yes."

"Things are falling right into place. Shall we eat now?"

Claire followed the other two inside. "Claire, would you pour the wine? I'll put the food on the table."

"What are we having?" Claire asked.

"I thought we could start with Tuscan onion soup. Then lamb noisettes with braised asparagus."

"You shouldn't have gone to so much trouble for me," Mamie said.

Claire heard the trepidation in Mamie's voice. Not one to be very adventurous in her culinary attempts, Mamie had probably spent the afternoon stewing over the menu. It didn't matter to Claire. She wasn't a picky eater. And though she'd never heard of lamb noisettes, the aroma was simply wonderful. Claire was a good cook when she wanted to be, but her fare tended more toward the traditional.

Claire sipped the soup. "Payton, why do you say you can't cook? This is like silk."

Payton lowered her voice, as though she was about to tell the secret of the century. "I didn't cook any of this. I ordered it from the Barracks Inn. They do a wonderful job, don't you think?"

Mamie eyed Payton sadly. Just as Payton's embarrassment over Mamie's compliments had raised her in Claire's esteem, the confession seemed to lower her in Mamie's. Mamie believed everyone should work at something until they succeeded. She would rather have eaten a poorly cooked meal stirred by Payton's own hand than this gourmand's delight. Not Claire, she liked quality and perfection wherever possible. If this was Payton's way of achieving it, so be it. Payton was smart enough to know her limitations.

The upstairs of the house looked as beautiful as the ground level. The hallway was wide with long walls between the doorways, perfect for hanging art. There were a couple of pieces already there, and from Mamie's reaction, they were originals. Payton and Mamie talked about one in particular, making Claire feel left out.

"We'll have to install some track lighting, I think," Payton said.

"I agree. I will pay for it," Mamie offered for the second time. And for the second time, Payton said nothing.

The long narrow guest bedroom was bright and fresh and

looked out over the street. The twin beds and windows were covered in colorful Mexican and Spanish fabrics. The furniture was all square edges of some light colored wood.

"I might have put my office in this room," Claire said.

"I thought about it, but the downstairs room just seemed so perfect for a library. Problem is, I have more rooms than I need."

"Maybe someday you'll get married again and raise a family," Mamie said. "Then you'll need more space."

"I don't have the patience for children."

"I don't believe that for a minute." Claire noticed Payton hadn't ruled out another marriage, only children. Did this have something to do with "retiring early" from teaching?

Mamie's face had turned serious. Another strike against Payton. Mamie had wanted nothing more than to have a houseful of children. She'd blamed her and Donald's childless state on herself, but Claire always believed it had been Donald's choice. He was just too cold, too self-centered.

"I think I would have liked the master bedroom here. You can see all up and down Broad Street," Mamie said shyly.

"Come, I'll show you why I didn't."

Payton led them across the hall and flicked on a light switch. Claire's eyes were accosted with a vision of white. The master bedroom took up most of the back of the house. The tall four-poster bed of some rough finished wood was covered in layers of pouffy white fabrics: cotton, seersucker, eyelet lace. A multitude of ruffled pillows graced the headboard. There was a white braided rug on the gleaming hardwood floor, an armchair in white brocade in the far corner, white drapes framed the French doors.

Claire suddenly broke into harsh laughter, collecting a pair of disbelieving stares. "I was just picturing old man Brice in here."

"This is definitely not a man's room," Payton said.

"Especially not Mr. Brice," Mamie added. "He was very old country."

Payton slid open the French door and stepped out onto a brand new deck. Across Sackets Harbor, a mere strip of amber-colored light separated the dark layers of sky and bay. The sky was a deep navy blue, cloudless and dotted with gold twinkling stars. The bay was mirrored charcoal, the town's lights reflecting like cloned images.

"Wow," Mamie said. It was an uncharacteristic word from her, but it truly described the view.

Claire wished she had such a haven.

"I love to sit out here with a glass of wine, watching the lights and the stars compete for twinkling space," Payton said.

"How poetic," Mamie said.

"Does anyone smell peppermint?" Claire asked.

Payton went to the rail of the deck and peered below. "There's a porcupine walking through the herbs."

Ten

Claire didn't arrive home from Payton's until after eleven. She was exhausted but there was much to do. She had managed to talk Mamie out of driving her home saying a walk was just what she needed. And it was. The air was cool and fresh, the streets quiet. It seemed like she had the whole world to herself.

Dinner had been fantastic. Payton's house pristine. Claire thought about making some serious changes to her old Victorian. Not Spanish/Mexican like Payton's, that wouldn't suit this house, or her personality, but basic things like opening up the small rooms into larger, airier spaces. That was the style these days. Besides, the rooms would be easier to heat and keep cool. She walked around her downstairs, picturing which walls might be knocked out, what furniture could be replaced. Certainly not her old recliner. Not that antique sideboard in the dining room that Sean's adoptive mother Edna had given her. And not that beautiful dining set.

What about a glass room like the one Helen was getting? Or a deck off the bedroom? By the time she'd made the circuit, Claire had decided that some new wallpaper and curtains would be just fine—but later. Now, she would concentrate on the Sean situation and worry about redoing the house afterward.

Looking at the *Tin Pan Galley* cookbook, she thought back almost thirty years into the past. Should she have done things differently, made the only other decision available and kept Sean to raise herself? No, things would have turned out the same, of that she was certain. The only difference would be that his actions would have hit much closer to home. She'd still be faced with baking this Deathday cake. Killing someone she'd once loved dearly.

Claire shook off the memories, drew two mixing bowls from the bottom cabinet and clunked them beside the canisters. She took matching layer pans from the drawer under the stove. Claire rubbed a generous dollop of shortening around inside both pans, doused them with flour, set them aside and turned the oven to preheat.

A tear poked from each eye. She was about to kill her son. Her only child.

As Claire measured dry ingredients into the larger bowl, not for a moment did she consider whether this was the right thing to do. She'd been over that in her mind dozens of times through the years. Sean never should have been born. Since she'd brought him into this world, it was her duty to remove him, pure and simple.

She sniffled and removed the paper cup from the windowsill, careful not to slosh the liquid on herself. She mashed the leaves against the side of the cup with a Popsicle stick she'd found in the junk drawer. Where it came from, she had no idea. Next she poured the concoction into the two-cup measurer, holding the leaves in the cup with the rounded tip of the stick. Were the fumes toxic? No time to check the book. Claire flung open opposite windows, then for good measure, the back door also.

She added milk to the liquid in the cup to make the total measure required for the recipe. This she poured in the other bowl and followed it with the remaining liquid ingredients. She whisked them together, just enough to blend in the eggs and hopefully not enough to ruin the poison properties of the monkshood because, though she knew it was the only answer to the problem, she didn't think she could do this a second time if it failed.

Through it all, Claire held her breath, just in case the fumes weren't entirely pushed away by the frigid breeze. She poured the liquid from one bowl into the dry ingredients every now and again stopping to run into the hallway to take a breath of clean air. It took a while, but at last the batter was in the oven. She had been unable to find information regarding the mixing and baking properties of monkshood. Would noxious baking fumes asphyxiate her? Just in case, she found a blanket and hung it in the kitchen door leading to the hallway. She set the oven timer, put on a jacket and went for a walk.

A few lights shone in people's houses, mostly the ambient blue of televisions. Damned television. Nobody read books any more, just planted themselves on their asses watching that stupid box. Even Mamie. Movies movies movies. Claire put up with it because she was lonely, just as she expected that was the reason Mamie put up with her. Claire knew she wasn't perfect. Her fastidious housecleaning grated on Mamie more than once. But that wasn't as bad as ruining your brain in front of an inane brown box. Was it?

12:22 p.m. The cake should be half done. She turned and retraced her steps, her heart fluttering and a cold clamminess breaking out on her palms. She jammed her hands in her jacket pockets and wiped them on the lining. All the way up the driveway, she pictured herself handing Sean the plate, the slice of cake resplendent under its thick layer of dark chocolate frosting and symmetrical row of chocolate chips around the top edge. He'd thank her profusely, might even kiss her cheek. That thought gave her a funny feeling inside. Her son had never kissed her. How could he? He'd grown up thinking Edna was his mother.

Edna had done a marvelous job with him, Claire had to admit. It wasn't her fault he'd taken his father's genes. Claire pushed the thought of Sean's father from her head. He wasn't worthy of anything more than a fleeting memory. The slime had run for the hills as soon as the "p" word had come from Claire's lips.

The air was filled with the delicious chocolate aroma. She wondered how potent the poison was all the way outdoors. Should she hold her breath or would the air disperse it? Claire walked slowly up the driveway. As she got about halfway, the timer went off. Her heart did a flip-flop. She took an extra deep breath and stepped indoors.

She took one pan from the oven, hurried to set it on the back porch to cool, raced away and took a breath, then did the same thing for the second layer. Sitting on the windowsill, they looked perfectly normal.

Claire left the blanket hanging in the doorway and the ingredients on the counter. Her meticulous nature pecked at her to clean things up, but she wasn't certain the air was fit to breathe yet. She'd wait till morning to wash up and whip the buttercream frosting. One single slice of cake for Sean. Not the whole thing because he might give a piece to someone else.

Claire poured some brandy. Yes, morning was soon enough to dispose of the remaining cake; break it into chunks and wash the pieces down the garbage disposal. Just some bleach afterwards and it would all be gone. The authorities would determine that the cake killed Sean, but who'd baked it would remain a mystery.

Claire couldn't sleep. Just after 3 a.m., she got up and went downstairs. She pulled back an edge of the blanket and poked her head into the room. A blast of cold air hit her. She sniffed. Was that a chocolate smell, or her imagination? The air should certainly be all right to breathe by now, shouldn't it?

Everything seemed all right. At the stove she put the kettle on for chamomile tea. While the water heated, she went out to the porch and peeked at the cake layers. They were beautiful—tall and fluffy. The potion hadn't destroyed the rising properties of the baking powder. Well, the tasting would be the most telling factor. And only one person was slated to taste this cake. Too bad. Such a lovely specimen.

Usually while making frosting, Claire couldn't keep herself from sampling thick fingerfuls of it, but today she couldn't get the image of the monkshood mixture from her brain. She hadn't put poison in the frosting, but the vision was too strong to take the chance. By 4:14 a.m., the cake was iced in wide sweeping swirls of creamy goodness.

She slipped on a new pair of gardening gloves and took a china plate from the dish drainer. It was a pretty plate, with tiny roses etched along the outer edge, and a gold rim. Claire didn't know where that had come from. Maybe the same place as the Popsicle stick. For some reason, the notion was humorous, and she spent some time envisioning the people who'd visited her home, bringing food. Would one of them have also brought Popsicles? She couldn't recall the last time she'd eaten a Popsicle.

Still smiling, she wiped around the plate's surface, making sure all the fingerprints were removed. It had crossed her mind to use a paper or foam plate, but one—she didn't have any in the house, and two—the cops were good at tracing such things. Surely some store clerk would recall her buying a package just a day before the murder.

Claire took the gloves off long enough to cut a wedge of cake. If her townspeople thought she'd been famous for her cake before, what would they think in a week? She laid the slice on the plate, careful not to smudge frosting or drop crumbs. She rinsed the cake cutter under scalding hot tap water, then put the gloves back on. They were too unwieldy and she had to try more than once to pull plastic wrap from the box, tear it along the little metal cutter and shape a double layer around the plate. Finally it was done. She stood back and viewed her work. It looked good. Nothing to trace back to her. The plastic wrap was a common variety.

The rest of the cake had to be disposed of, but right now it was most important to get the kitchen cleaned up. She had a dishwasher but didn't trust it to remove all the trace evidence. She'd learned about trace evidence on CSI. So maybe television wasn't so bad. Claire boiled water in her largest pot—a lobster cooker—and drank tea while everything soaked for at least ten minutes. Next she hand washed each item, scrubbing the nooks and crannies with an old toothbrush. This had to be the perfect crime. No one could be blamed. It took more than an hour, but

Claire finally had the kitchen cleaned to her satisfaction.

She wanted Sean to have the cake first thing tomorrow morning. She could bring it to the café, but there was always the chance one of his employees would get hold of it or see her delivering it. No, it would be better if she waited till late at night and brought it to his home, a small ranch twenty minutes away in Chaumont.

What if MaryAnn was there? Claire hadn't seen Sean's soon-to-be ex-wife around lately, hadn't heard any new rumors. At least there was no danger of MaryAnn eating any cake. She was deathly allergic to chocolate. Everyone knew that, still talked about the time she'd eaten—what was it now—the item escaped Claire, but it was at the Church Bazaar last year. MaryAnn had been raced to the hospital gasping for every breath.

Claire climbed on a chair. A slight tingle in her ankle reminded her to be careful. It wouldn't pay to fall. A vision of ambulance attendants rescuing her but taking along her cake and gorging themselves on the way to the hospital erupted goosebumps along her arms. She removed a few items from the topmost shelf over the sink, pushed the cake in back, then replaced the things she'd taken out. She made another cup of tea and took the cup upstairs. She removed her robe and climbed into bed. One sip of the brew was all she had before falling asleep.

Daytime had spread across the sky in a gray and gloomy mess of clouds. Rain pattered against the window. It was a sound she'd always found comforting. Claire sat up, stretched her arms over her head and emitted a deep satisfied sound. The heady aroma of chocolate drifted into her senses.

She sniffed, once, twice, and then flew to a sitting position. What if she really *was* smelling it? The kitchen had seemed all right last night. She'd done the dishes and not suffered any ill effects. What if the poison was floating through the house? Sticking in the tiny hairs of her sinuses. Was the poison in her nose, too? Of course not. The book said the effects worked very quickly. The poisonee—was that the right word?—was affected within minutes. She must've received only a glancing blow, from the aftermath of the aroma. Would that mean she'd just die slower?

Claire forced herself to take several breaths and calm down. It had to be all right. She'd made it through the night. Felt all right. She took another breath. There was no pain, no tightness.

Late. She'd overslept. Mamie would be there in less than an hour. It was Claire's day off; Mamie closed the gallery at noon. They traditionally breakfasted together. Then later on, cooked a big lunch, did some gardening or puttered around one of their houses. They sometimes went for a drive and ate lunch leftovers while watching that damned television. Mamie would work on her latest painting project and Claire would get out her crocheting. Same old same old.

Were they friends or just two lonely souls with nothing better to do? She shrugged. She guessed it didn't matter in the long run.

Claire raced through her toilette. She still had to dispose of the rest of the cake. And hide Sean's slice. She donned the gardening gloves and took Sean's slice of cake out to her car to lock in the trunk. If they went out later, she'd insist they take Mamie's car. What excuse she'd use Claire didn't know yet, but she couldn't chance Mamie wanting to put something in there.

As she put her sneaker on the bottom step, Mamie's Escort pulled into the driveway. *No!* For one horrible second, she couldn't recall if she'd left the cake on the counter in plain sight or had put it safely into a cabinet. That's where she'd *thought* about putting it. She flew inside.

As Claire raced through the back porch, the scent of chocolate wafted into her senses. Her imagination was working overtime. It had to be. It better be. Mamie was absolutely addicted to chocolate. If she found the cake, she wouldn't stop till she'd eaten two, maybe three slices. Claire stumbled on the doorstep. In a slow-motion chain reaction, Claire's feet went out from under her. She pitched into the table. The table skidded into the opposite chair. The chair slammed into the cabinet. The monkshood plant and handmade doily slid across the tabletop. Mid-fall, Claire groped for it. Missed.

"No!"

Somehow things worked in Claire's favor. The plant and doily stopped halfway off the far edge. One movement might jar it from its perch, one tiny breath. Claire reached for the plant. Pushed the pot back onto the table.

The cake!

Not on the counter. The counter shone bright and spotless in the dim morning light. So did the sink and faucets. Claire's memory returned. The cake was safely in the cabinet above the sink. The doors were shut tight.

Mamie waddled inside. Claire let out the breath she'd been holding and turned, rubbed her shoulder and slipped on a welcoming smile.

"What happened here?" Mamie asked.

"I tripped," Claire said, pushing the table and chair back in place.

"You shouldn't have been running."

"I thought I'd left the burner on."

Mamie peered at the stovetop. "It isn't even red."

"I said I *thought* I'd left it on. What do you want me to pick up at the grocery store later?" Did her voice sound normal?

"I was thinking soup would taste good today."

"It's supposed to be beautiful and warm, I won't feel like eating soup. And you won't either. What if I put together a picnic and we eat down at the battlefield?"

"That's right, today is dress rehearsal, isn't it?"

Claire had forgotten about that. Dress rehearsal was Edward's term for the practice meet the day before the yacht club race. "Yes. What about finger foods: carrots, cucumbers and fried chicken?"

"Sounds good. Will you make some of that horseradish dip for the chicken?"

"I can. And I'll make extra chicken so we can have it for supper. What about potato salad?"

"Good. Should I pick you up at lunchtime, or will you drive?"

"I'll walk."

"You've been doing a lot of walking lately. Do you think it's good for your ankle? Besides, you'll be carrying that heavy basket of food."

"My ankle is fine. I'll be fine." Claire slid the plant to the exact center of the table and made sure the doily lay flat underneath.

"What a pretty plant." Mamie put out a finger to touch one of the shiny leaves.

"Don't!"

Mamie yanked her hand back as if the plant were a hive of angry hornets. "What?"

"It's…I just…" Claire stammered. What to tell her? The truth? Sure, Payton was telling everyone anyway. "It's poisonous. Well, I don't think it is if you touch it, but Payton said it's got poisonous sap. And I just didn't…"

"Why on earth would you want a poisonous plant?"

"Well, it's only poisonous if you're messing with it. A lot of houseplants are that way, poinsettias, lily of the valley, cyclamen, amaryllis. Payton said they're only dangerous if you have children or pets who might be putting leaves in their mouths."

"So why did you jump down my throat?"

"I'm sorry. It was a knee-jerk reaction." Claire handed Mamie a small notepad. "Here, help me make a shopping list."

Mamie peered at her suspiciously. Claire had never needed help with a list before. She began dictating; chicken, cucumbers…

"I bought some nice plants at Payton's shop." Mamie was still eyeing the monkshood. "Didn't see this one there. Maybe you could give me a cutting."

"I don't think it propagates that way. After a while it'll be too big to keep as a houseplant. Eventually I'll have to put it outdoors. How did you like Payton's house? Do you think it'll work as a gallery?"

"That reminds me. I called Miles this morning and told him we were having the exhibit there. He was excited I'd found something so quickly."

Finally Mamie left to open the gallery. Claire did the grocery shopping, but her mind wasn't on fried chicken, potato salad or carrot sticks, it was on the Deathday cake delivery. Sean would suffer. The fastest working poisons generally had the most horrific symptoms. It had to work fast. She couldn't take the chance some magical antidote would be available. This had to be done right the first time. There wouldn't be a second chance.

Driving from the supermarket, all she could smell was chocolate. Could that single slice in the trunk emit that much aroma? Suddenly Claire felt ill. The chocolate smell was so powerful her stomach rumbled. Acid churned. She sped home.

Eleven

With her stomach in turmoil, Claire decided to drive to the marina instead of walk. The sky was still overcast, but now there were breaks in the clouds with blue sky visible between. She left the picnic hamper in the car and joined the others already gathered for the dress rehearsal under the big white canopy in the parking lot. Tomorrow long tables would be set along two sides to hold the potluck lunch they served before each race. Chaumont, the team they'd race against, would be invited, too.

She spotted Sean talking to Brighton and Aden. Brighton pointed at something down the dock and Sean nodded. He said something to which Aden disagreed, tweaking his mustache between thumb and forefinger.

Payton's words popped into Claire's head. "Helen's been trying to fix me up with him ever since I moved here." For once Claire had to agree with Helen. They would make a handsome couple. Both tall and slim, both educated and well off, both calm and collected. Yes, definitely a nice match.

A flicker of jealousy whacked the back of her head. Payton had been in town for just a few months and already had men fawning over her. Claire had been there almost thirty years and hadn't had one. Nobody tried to fix her up. The envy was replaced by a wave of loneliness. Since Sean's father, there hadn't been a real relationship with a man. Not a sexual one anyway. Not that the relationship with Sean's father was anything to write home about. A two-night stand. Claire's loins twitched in response.

Helen, Amanda and Payton stood to one side of the canopy, chatting. Claire stepped around a puddle and joined them. "Who's watching the store?" she asked Payton.

"I put a note on the door inviting people down to watch."

"Good idea. Will you be hiring anyone to help during times like this?"

"I've thought about it. My housework is suffering."

"Your house is pristine," Claire said.

At that moment Sylvie arrived somewhat out of breath. "I've had the worst day so far. First I overslept. Then the percolator overflowed all over the counter. And then I dropped the ironing board down the cellar stairs." Her eyes narrowed as she spotted Payton.

"Morning, Sylvie."

Sylvie gave a snobbish turn to her head.

Claire puffed in irritation. "Sylvie, you're being childish. Payton wouldn't sell plants that would emit poison right through the pot. They're not dangerous if you—"

"Who're you to tell me what someone else would do, Claire Bastian?" Sylvie slammed her purse strap onto her shoulder and stalked away.

"What was that all about?" Amanda asked.

Claire told of Sylvie's escapade with the monkshood. "I can just picture her barreling back to her office and taking a bath in disinfectant!" Amanda said.

"Anyone heard who Sean's teaming with during the race?" Helen asked.

"I heard it's someone named Frank Simpson. He's from Watertown but can't be here today. He's got some family get together."

Edward's shout of, "All right everyone! Gather round," halted further discussion.

Claire followed the racers into the circle where Edward would give a pep talk and prayer for safety. Everyone stood in rapt attention except Amanda. Her head partly turned toward Sean, her expression one of careful indifference, but Claire knew the anxiety she felt. The same thing Claire experienced every time she saw Sean, every time his name was mentioned. Except Claire had the added burden of guilt of his birth in her soul.

The racers did high fives, signaling the end of Edward's benediction. They clomped down the dock toward the sailboats. Claire used her sleeve to polish the face of the stopwatch. She punched the buttons a few times to make sure everything worked smoothly.

One by one the yachts moved under motor power from the marina to the starting point in the harbor. Aden and Brighton on their bright new *Diplomat* followed Helen and Carter's *Paves the Way,* Amanda and Edward lined up third on *SHARE,* Sylvie and her partner from Henderson were next, and last was Sean on *MaryAnn.* Claire wondered if he planned to change the name once his divorce was final. Claire had heard it was bad luck to change a boat's name. Wouldn't matter, she guessed. Sean was soon to be overflowing with bad luck.

Felicia joined Claire and they walked the path along the top of the stone barrier wall on the south side of the bay. On the left were the now-famous one hundred maple trees planted in 1912 to commemorate the War Centennial. This was where, in the year 1812, soldiers had fired at ships attempting to make their way into the United States via the St. Lawrence Seaway. A north wind, that strongly favored sailing, pushed small whitecaps on the harbor to the right.

Felicia and Claire stood on the point where the land curved southward. Claire inhaled, savoring the aroma of freshly mown grass. This point was the best spot from which to watch, and time, the race. The sun poked its happy yellow face through the clouds as the starting buzzer sounded. It was just over seventy degrees. Overhead, the clouds sped past as though shoved by the same tailwind the boats received.

As far as she could tell, the practice was going smoothly. She and Felicia, silent for the most part, sat with their legs dangling over the stone wall. The sailboats were nearly out of sight as they proceeded to the first and second pins. From the second pin to home they would be back in view.

As usual, Brighton and Aden were way out in front. Their first boat always had the wings of an angel and this new one seemed to be the same. She clicked the stopwatch as they passed the finish line. Second to them were Edward and Amanda on *SHARE*. Following a close third was a Chaumont boat *Bank Account*. Fourth was *Paves the Way*, Carter hauling firmly on the jib line, his feet planted beneath him braced against the choppy water. Helen wound the stern line with a vengeance, changing the height of the jib sail as the wind switched direction. Claire couldn't see Payton at all because the mainsail was in the way. Far back was Sean on *MaryAnn*. Although slower than the others, it sailed straight and smooth into the bay.

Once all the boats were battened down and the participants gathered in the tent area, Amanda broke out the champagne that Edward poured into long stemmed plastic glasses. They all toasted the successful run.

"Whew, that felt good!" Amanda ran a hand through her short-cropped hair. Edward watched her, the love obvious on his face. Claire felt her second twinge of jealousy.

"It sure did," Helen agreed. "Makes you realize what a long winter it was."

"No longer than any other," Sylvie groused.

"Children, children," Amanda called. "Let's not spoil this wonderful afternoon." She held up her glass. "To tailwinds and angels, full sails and untangled lines."

"Here here," Aden called, holding his glass high.

"Congratulations on your record fast time," Claire announced, holding up the stopwatch for everyone to see. "Let's hope you can do it again tomorrow when it'll be official."

Aden checked the timer and whistled. Helen and Carter groaned in unison.

"Sorry, folks," Aden said.

Claire put her empty glass on the table. "Well, it's time for me to shove off."

"Me also," Payton said. "Got to get back to work." They walked up the long marina driveway together.

"See you later," Helen called.

"What did she mean by that?" Claire asked.

"I have no idea," Payton replied.

"I've been so absentminded all week. I'm sure there's something I'm forgetting. Mamie and I are having a picnic lunch at the battlefield in a while. I'm getting her at the gallery."

Payton brushed windblown auburn hair from her face. "Have fun."

Claire thought how pretty it looked. When her own hair got all windblown, even though it was short, she thought it made her look like a mad woman.

They separated, saying they'd see each other later. Payton crossed Main Street. Claire continued on to the art gallery, but Mamie wasn't at her easel. Voices from the back room echoed. She found Mamie and a handsome looking Italian, whom she assumed was Miles Arenheim, standing on the back stoop. He had a cigarette in his hand, which explained why they were outdoors. As hesitant as Mamie usually was around people, she would never allow anyone, even someone as suave and famous as this man, to sully the gallery air with cigarette smoke.

"Claire, hello." Mamie turned to Miles. "This is my friend Claire Bastian."

Miles blew smoke out his mouth, self-confident, well educated and obviously rich. Other than the round eyeglasses that lent a mousy expression, he could give Aden Green a run for his money in the looks department. "Nice to meet you," Claire said.

"Same here. Mamie speaks often of you." The moment he spoke, Claire felt a surge of dislike for the man. The soft-spoken sentiment never reached his eyes. She always believed her grandmother's tenet, that eyes were the "mirror to the soul." People could disguise their emotions with words, Grandma said, but couldn't keep the truth from their eyes. This man didn't mean a word he said.

"I'm sorry, I won't be able to have lunch with you today," Mamie said. "Miles and I are going to Payton's to make a list of things we need to ready it for the exhibit."

"Don't worry about it. Have fun. I'll see you at my place for dinner."

Outside, the sky had turned a sodden gray. Funny how fast the weather could change. Drizzle blew off the harbor and slammed her in the face. She hadn't gone twenty feet down Main Street when the sky erupted. Claire dodged a pickup and raced across the street. She was sopping wet by the time she flew inside *Payton's Place*. Payton looked up, startled, from the front counter. Claire realized the vision she must have presented to the always impeccable Payton, and before Payton could laugh at her, she said the most inane thing she could think of, "It's raining."

"Would you like a bar of soap?"

Twelve

Wouldn't Mamie ever finish eating? Bone after bone got piled on the woman's plate. A second and third helping of potato salad. Endless one-sided conversation about Miles Arenheim's delight with Payton's house. Finally, she pushed back from the table and patted her round tummy. "I could really go for a cup of herb tea."

Claire leaped up. "I'll get it. Why don't you go watch television and I'll bring it."

Mamie patted her stomach again and waddled out of the room. The television came on.

Minutes later Claire placed the steaming cups of tea on the coffee table.

"There, finished." Mamie turned the easel so Claire could see. "What do you think?"

Mamie was undoubtedly the worst painter in the world. Everything was one-dimensional, unimaginative. Which made being her friend very hard at times like this. Claire wanted to be honest, but Mamie loved to paint more than anything else. Once, Claire had lied and said how great the thing was, then received the damned thing as a Christmas present. She stole a glance at the painting on the far living room wall, a wild landscape of the arctic tundra with a polar bear chasing a frantic seal. It wasn't as though it had been given to her by a far-away relative and could be relegated to a spot in the spare bedroom. Mamie came here often, and Claire was faced with looking at it day in and day out.

Claire went for a closer inspection of Mamie's work in

progress. “You’ve really captured the mother’s love for her pups. Do you have a buyer yet?”

Mamie sighed. “Claire, you know no one ever buys my paintings. I’m a terrible artist and everyone knows it.” She gave a wistful smile. “It’s just that I love it so.”

“That’s what’s important.”

Mamie stood and arched her back. “I’ve got the munchies. Got anything sweet to eat?”

Claire nearly lost her balance and toppled into the wet painting. “How can you be hungry after what you just ate?”

“It’s probably the excitement of the gallery opening.” By now, she was halfway down the hallway.

“I don’t have anything in the house. You told me you were cutting back on sweets, so I didn’t make anything.”

Claire heard cabinets opening and shutting and launched herself from the room as total silence descended upon the house. She ran, choking down a mouthful of panic similar to the feeling of waking to the sound of a wailing smoke detector. She stopped dead in the doorway; Mamie stood on a chair clutching Sean’s cake in her chubby hands. She narrowed her eyes. “What do you mean you don’t have anything in the house?”

Was it too late to pray? “That’s…ah, for the potluck tomorrow.”

Mamie stepped down from the chair holding the cake at eye level turning it this way and that as if it were a pair of shoes in a store. She brought the plate to her nose and sniffed. “Yum. Come on, let’s have a slice.”

“Mamie, I just told you…”

“If you made it for the group, why is there a slice missing?”

“I-I couldn’t help myself. That’s why I hid it in the cabinet.”

“In that case, it shouldn’t matter if I have just a skinny little piece.” She set the cake on the counter and plundered in the silverware drawer.

Claire vaulted into the room. The unexpected movement shot pain up her leg. Her ankle went out from under her and she crashed to the floor.

Mamie slammed the drawer. "Goodness, are you all right?"

"Twisted my ankle again."

"Did you hurt anything else? Can you get up?"

Claire allowed Mamie to help her up. She braced herself with one hand on the doorframe. Oh god, there was chocolate frosting in the corner of Mamie's mouth!

Claire stood for a moment, testing the ankle. Finally she'd delayed long enough and shook off Mamie's hand. She limped to a chair and dropped into it. One corner of the cake wrapping gaped open. A three-inch scrape marred the frosting on one side. "Mamie! I told you that cake was for the sailing club."

"Sorry. I couldn't help myself. Your cakes are to die for."

Mamie reached out a pair of fingers to take another swipe at the frosting. Claire's hand thrust out and slapped her arm. Mamie reeled back.

"Oh God, I'm sorry, Mamie."

"It's not like this is the first time we've had to make another dessert."

"I know. I just..."

"Okay, okay. It's your damned cake. Do what you want with it."

"Mamie, don't be mad. It's just a cake."

"Exactly my point."

Their eyes met in a silent challenge/apology. Mamie was the first to break the gaze. She took two plates from the dish drainer and fumbled in the drawer for several seconds. "Where's your cake knife?"

She opened the dishwasher and uttered a gratified grunt. Claire's blood went sour. She bounded out of the chair. Her ankle turned and she fell forward clawing the air. Her fingers found only the edge of the cake plate. They closed around it. She went down, banging her chin on the counter and taking the cake with her.

Mamie knelt on the floor beside her friend, now painted psychedelically in brown and red. Claire's face was a mask of pain. Blood trickled from a gash on her chin. A wad of chocolate cake clung to her left ear. Mamie removed it with an index finger and started to put it in her mouth.

Claire's hand flashed up and batted it away.

"What the hell's gotten into you!"

"Help me up." Claire struggled to rise, deliberately slipping and sliding and mashing the cake into brown goo on her once-spotless tile floor.

Thirteen

Wordlessly she and Mamie cleaned up the chocolate mess, somehow without Mamie attempting to eat any more. Through the dessert-less evening, Claire watched her friend for signs of poisoning even though she'd been reasonably sure Mamie hadn't eaten more than a few fingerfuls of frosting. What if she *had* eaten cake and the poison hadn't worked? Not that Claire would want it to work on Mamie, but it raised uncertainty in her mind.

She'd fended off another apology for ruining the cake, several offers to help make another and finally closed the door against her friend's round backside at 11:30.

Claire brewed herself a cup of tea and went to the living room to sip and let the troubles of the past few hours ebb away. Mamie's newest painting gaped at her: a nondescript mother dog standing over a basket of yellow pups depicted as a swirling mass of yellow fur, hard to tell where one ended and another began. Claire tried to count the tiny black noses, no easy feat since the blanket in the basket was black and white polka dots. The expression on the mother dog's face was the only redeeming quality. She gazed adoringly at her pups like Madonna over her brood. Claire rotated the easel to face the wall.

She sat again and leaned her head back on the handmade doily. Her lids felt so heavy. She'd just close them for a second.

Claire bolted upright, adrenaline pumping so hard she could barely see that she'd slept three hours. Time to go. She limped upstairs to don dark colored clothes. Her ankle throbbed with each step. Where had all that good luck gone?

Sean's car sat in his driveway. Claire drove to the end of the block, made a U-turn and went past again. All quiet. She turned and drove partway back, parking under the overhanging branches of a lilac two houses away. The luminous dial on her watch said 3 a.m. She hadn't been outdoors at this hour in many years. The sky was inky black. No stars or clouds. The moon a mere slit. She touched the flashlight on the seat, comforted by its presence. It had fresh batteries and a new bulb.

Claire's heart slammed against her ribs as though it were trying to escape. Her hands sweated so badly she feared not being able to hold the plate. She took in enough breath to fill her lungs. She held it, then let it out slowly. Calm. Be calm. Everything will be fine.

Sean's house was a long ranch with a breezeway and an attached two car garage. Both doors were closed. Sean's Grand Am sat in front of the right-hand side. The front porch was a small cement stoop, wide enough for one person. The light to the right of the screen door was on, bright, probably 60 watts. Too bright.

A screened breezeway, picture window in the living room, two windows to the right. She didn't know which one was Sean's room, or which was MaryAnn's. Considering their situation, he and MaryAnn were hardly likely to be sharing a room—if she still lived here. Regardless, except for the porch light, all was dark. Not even a television flickered.

Claire rolled down her window. Most of the houses along this street were bordered by lilac bushes. The air was laden with their heady aroma. The hedge-like shrubs would make good cover.

She opened the door and stood beside the vehicle. The lone streetlight illuminated Sean's entire front yard. Hopefully the breezeway door wasn't locked. Claire had read all the Lawrence Block's *Burglar* series, but none of Bernie Rhodenbarr's lock picking talent had rubbed off on her. She should have sought out MaryAnn and asked discreet questions that wouldn't raise eyebrows, like whether they had a dog or were insomniacs. Too late now.

Claire wiped her palms on her slacks, put on gardening gloves, dropped the flashlight in her pocket and picked up the plate. She pushed the car door closed, till the dome light shut off but keeping the latch from clicking shut. She stepped out of the arc cast by the streetlight and into a black corridor between the house and the lilacs bordering the property. Unfortunately the corridor ran below what had to be bedroom windows. But Claire had surprise on her side and knew how to be quiet. The dewy grass soaked her canvas sneakers as she tiptoed across the shaggy lawn. She stopped till her eyes adjusted to the darkness.

Darkness had never been one of her favorite things. Her father always laughed and forced her into dark forbidding places, a beefy hand securely set against her backside should she balk, saying she would "get her over it," but he'd been wrong.

Only the tiniest bit of light penetrated the shadows. Enough to give shape to objects she hoped were just bushes. Her father's invisible hand pressured the base of her spine. Claire groped for obstacles with her left foot, then slid the right to meet it, wishing she dared use the flashlight. The backyard was just as dark as the side lawn. The outline of a stairway with a narrow railing of some sort—a kitchen window to the left, a smaller window to its left, probably the bathroom. She leaned against dewy shingles trying to hear through the wall, dizzy with excitement.

Sean Adams had cheated his last person, beaten up his last woman, purloined his last empty storefront. Claire swallowed her guilt and forged on. Holding the cake in gloved hands that seemed to glow in the dark, she stepped to the large black rectangle of the back door. The stoop was cement, three stairs. She tiptoed up and touched her fingertips to the handle of the screen door. A cheaper model, coarse aluminum with a single square of screen at the top. She pulled on the small lever handle. It unlatched easily. No rattle, no metallic squeak or even a click.

Claire opened the door inch by tedious inch, propped the door against her hip and touched the inside doorknob. It was cool metal and turned easily. Best of all, it wasn't locked. She twisted it so slowly that if anyone had been in the kitchen in broad daylight, they wouldn't have seen movement. The house was silent—deadly silent.

The door moved two inches before the first squeak. She stopped, waited, listened. Nothing. No barking or scratch of toenails on linoleum, if Sean had linoleum. Maybe it was tiles. Or wood. Or…

The door moved another millimeter. Another squeaky protest. An absolute screech in her ears. What was that smell? She sniffed again, assaulted by the vision of her father, slouched in his chair, head lolled to one side, beer can dangling from his fingers. She thrust the image into the recesses of her mind and stepped inside, easing forward till the screen door was closed but not latched.

The odor was stronger now and she knew it well. She'd never gotten to know her father as a person. Until her teens, she'd cursed his drinking and scorned his inattention to her and her brother. Gradually Claire realized the real trouble came from her mother, who waited till the kids were in bed, dressed in her best cotton dress, and went out, coming home smelling like someone else's aftershave just before dawn. Her mother was the biggest reason Claire decided to give Sean up for adoption. Genes had a tendency to replicate. She shut her eyes and counted to ten.

Sean's kitchen was backlit by the glow of the streetlight through the front picture window. She could see large objects: counters, cabinets, table, a large dark thing on the table. A box? No, it was roundish and lumpy looking. Laundry? Claire sometimes dumped her laundry on the table to fold it.

She took a step toward the long rectangle of countertop, still eyeing the mass on the table. The closer she got, the more certain she was that it was clothing. A coat maybe, tossed there as someone passed. She took another step, intent on putting down the cake and getting the hell out of there.

The pile moved!

Claire stiffened, the plate held ridiculously out in front, like a weapon. Or a shield.

The bundle moved again, growing before her eyes—her very wide eyes. Perspiration squirted out her pores, as though her body was a giant corn popper. Hysteria produced another vision, of the popcorn building, deepening, surrounding. Soon it would envelop her completely, and she'd be trapped in this beer-scented house.

Something rose up from the pile. A head. God, someone was here in the kitchen. Sitting in the dark. Drinking. Had to be Sean.

Claire made like a statue, praying her silhouette wasn't emblazoned against the wall like an actor on stage. If she remained perfectly still…

The head moved.

Her right leg began to tingle. She needed to flex it, hop up and down, do something to get her blood flowing.

The head wobbled. "So, you came back, you cunt." He sat up straighter in the chair but had to prop his palms on the table to steady himself. "You got balls, girl. Anybody ever tell you what big balls you have?" He staggered to his feet. The chair thumped off the half wall behind him. Sean tottered there for a moment, then moved toward her.

How had Claire's mother handled her father when he got like this? Her stomach shriveled at the thought. She took a step backward and whispered, "It's me, Sean. Claire. Claire Bastian."

Even in silhouette, his hesitation was evident. She tried again hoping familiarity would plow through his fog. "I-I came to. I-er, brought you a piece of cake." She held out the plate. "I made it… just for you." Would he remember how much he enjoyed her chocolate cake?

He took a step away from the table. His right arm fumbled for something to grab onto. "I told you to get out and not come back.

I said I'd kill you if you came back, and I meant it." He took a step.

When she spoke, her voice was scratchy but calm. "Sean, I'm not MaryAnn. I'm Claire Bastian, the librarian. Remember you got books the other day? Books on redecorating your restaurant."

"There is no restaurant."

What?

"Cake. Have a piece of cake, Sean."

He stepped closer. Sparks danced in his eyes. He planned to thrash her and enjoy every minute of it. But she wouldn't go down without a fight. She hadn't gone to all this trouble to have it end this way.

"I told you to get out and stay out."

She leaned toward the counter, the plate in her left hand. "I'm just going to put it here for you." In her nervousness she set the plate down an inch too early. It slipped. She groped for it, caught it, and slid the plate onto safe territory.

He took another step. His breath was cloying, hot on her face.

Claire made two fists, the feeling of the cotton gloves comforting. "What do you think you're going to do to me?" She leaned into him, making contact with his abdomen. "Let's see what a big guy you are. See if you can get the better of someone half your size." She poked her fists into him, feeling the heavy resistance of his sternum. "Well, what are you waiting for, you little pussy?"

"You..." He only had a chance to breathe the single word that smelled exactly like her father's breath. Her rush of anger was unexpected. Both fists flashed out. One struck him in the nose. The other hit him in the stomach. He doubled over and dropped to the floor.

"That's the thanks I get for being neighborly. For baking you a special cake."

He didn't speak or move, but she didn't wait. She slipped outside and into the deepest darkest shadows she could find. She stopped under a dripping lilac branch and listened. Nothing. No light turned on. No yelling for the bitch to come back and take what was coming to her.

Her greatest wish, second to the one that needed him off the planet, had been to watch him exclaim over the luscious piece of cake. Now, there was the likelihood of him not eating it at all. The chance he'd toss the whole damn thing in the trash.

Claire stumbled into her house, despondent and exhausted. The horizon was a puke-yellow strip just above the tree line, signaling the arrival of dawn. It was 4:30. All she needed was a cup of tea and a few rejuvenating hours of sleep. But there was one more thing left to take care of.

There was always one more thing.

She removed the plastic trash bag from under the sink. The aroma of the mashed chocolate cake rushed out. She held her breath and fed it down the garbage disposal with a large serving spoon. Several times, she had to put down the spoon and rush to the back door for a breath. Then a thought hit her—the fumes couldn't be toxic. Mamie had inhaled them while cleaning up the mess last night. Claire held her breath anyway and went back to shoveling cake down the garbage disposal. The little motor whirred away the last of the brown glop. She poured bleach, then boiling water, and then more bleach down the drain.

The teapot's insistent whistling broke through her reverie. Steam poured from the spout, wafted up and tangled in the hood over the stove. She made tea and carried it upstairs, and climbed into bed wondering how to dispose of the trash bag, and the gloves. Too bad she didn't have a fireplace.

In a few hours they'd all be down in the harbor waiting for the horn to signal the start of the season's first race. She'd arranged for Sarah to take her shift at the library. Once again, Claire thought about retirement. She'd made some wise investments and was fairly well off. But what would she do with her time, sit in that comfy chair in her front window and watch the world go by? She drank tea and lay on her side.

Would people be surprised when Sean didn't show up for the meet? No, probably not. They'd probably assume Frank Simpson had been stuck in another business meeting, and the men had decided not to participate.

The dreams weren't pleasant; she was seventeen, sitting at the Formica table in her parent's kitchen, amid the stench of beer and cigarettes, with the icebox and three-legged woodstove. Her mother jabbed her finger in Claire's chest. "What do you mean you're pregnant? How could this happen? You whore!"

"You *know* how it happens, Mother." Claire's words garnered a stinging slap on each cheek.

"Who's the father? Who've you been fucking?"

Claire stood firm as her mother named off every boy she could think of. Wouldn't his identity just blow her mind? Not a boy. A man. Passing through town. How could Claire explain why she'd succumbed to the man when she didn't even know herself—not until years later. For a few fleeting moments that man embodied everything her childhood lacked. Tenderness, love, protection.

"Well, I guess that's it then," her mother had said.

"What?" Claire hadn't needed to ask. She was on her own to raise her child. Didn't Claire's mother realize she'd never see her grandchild, never hold his hand to cross a street, never show him how to…what? Just what did her mother do that should be taught to a young child?

With a heavy heart, Claire had packed her belongings in a suitcase and large paper bag and walked. For miles and miles. Eventually, she'd gotten a ride. As they passed through Sackets Harbor, she'd made the driver stop and let her out. Thankful she looked older than her seventeen years, she'd been offered a job at the library. She and head librarian Edna Adams took to each other right away. Within weeks Edna was voicing some of her deepest, darkest troubles to Claire, one of which was her desire to have a child. That was when Claire burst into tears and told the whole story.

Claire woke in a cold sweat. She got up and shut the shades, then climbed under the comforter still in her cake-delivery clothing. The tea was cold but she drank the rest in two swallows. She fluffed the pillows and looked out at the gray sky, the dream still too vivid.

Edna and Rodney had paid for Claire to go away and have her baby. They took what they told everyone was a much needed vacation. When they returned, they brought with them their newborn son, Sean. He was a handsome child, with downy blond hair and a turned-up nose. And his bright blue eyes, so knowing, so intelligent. Claire remained true to their agreement: she wouldn't interfere with Sean's upbringing so long as she could be close and watch him grow.

At first Claire made excuses for the boy's school behavior, saying it was the change from a doting mom to the freedom of the school life. It was just a phase he was going through.

Then something happened when Sean was twelve that Claire thought would scare him straight. He woke one morning to find both his parents had been stabbed to death by burglars. Sean's behavior improved, for a while. He went to live with his godmother, Edna's sister, Elaine. Things had been good—for a few years. Then he'd returned.

FOURTEEN

Claire watched the news for an announcement about Sean's death. She went out and bought a newspaper. Nothing.

Probably MaryAnn never came home. The body wouldn't be discovered until Sean neglected to open the café. If he had eaten the cake. If the poison worked.

Claire ate a bowl of cereal then went downtown and visited Payton. They sat together on a long flower-patterned sofa.

The shop door opened and a dervish whirled in, pushed ahead of the early morning rain. The woman was encased from head to foot in yellow plastic. "Whew!" she cried, stomping water on the mat inside the doorway. The hood flung back to reveal a pretty face with high cheekbones and the pale skin of a person who spent too much time indoors. Mid-length brunette hair exploded from the confines of the hood like cotton from its boll. "Whew!" She finally stopped moving long enough for identification.

MaryAnn, in her mid-twenties, had gained quite a lot of weight over her eight years with Sean. Claire didn't think it was from sampling the decadent French food. The stress of living with him would turn anyone into a comfort eater. Her smiling face said she didn't know about Sean's death.

There was a definite discoloration under her left eye. She'd tried to cover it with makeup, but rain had become her enemy. Anger pushed into Claire's limbs. She gulped down the emotion. At least Sean wouldn't hit anyone again.

"MaryAnn! My goodness, Mamie and I were talking about

you just yesterday saying we hadn't seen you in ages. Have you and Payton met?"

MaryAnn shook more water from her raincoat. "Sure have. I'm her new employee."

"We walked up from the dress rehearsal together," Payton explained. "And it just happened."

"I didn't see you at rehearsal," Claire said.

"I was hiding. Sean would have made a scene."

"Claire, would you like some coffee?" Payton didn't wait for a reply; she headed for the back room and returned quickly. "The water's heating."

At that moment, a large box van rumbled into the side parking lot. Payton looked out the window. "Sorry for the interruption; my delivery is here. They're switching living room sets around." Payton picked up a pair of pink flowered African violets from the end tables and set them on the front counter.

"I'll do that for you." Claire moved pillows and knickknacks.

"Did Payton tell you she and I are racing *Zephyr* today?" MaryAnn asked.

"No." It seemed there was a lot she didn't mention. Claire's disappointment was palpable. She thought she and Payton were friends. Friends told each other things.

"It's only for this week though," MaryAnn continued, "so she can see how the boat goes. Since Sean and I are divorcing, he's got to give me back *MaryAnn*."

"He doesn't own *MaryAnn*?"

"He was really pissed last night when I reminded him." MaryAnn gestured at her eye.

Claire lowered her voice. "Excuse me for asking why you'd live with a man who strikes you."

"I'm a slow learner. Excuse me, I'll get the coffee." MaryAnn returned with three cups and a jar of powdered creamer on a small tray. "I could only find one spoon."

When the deliverymen left, Payton stood with her arms

crossed, surveying the room. "That's probably the ugliest upholstery I've ever seen."

"I don't think it's so bad," MaryAnn said. "If you do this." She squinted and tilted her head at an odd angle.

Payton laughed and shoved the sofa to the side.

"You throwing it out?"

"No, I just want a different arrangement. I think the couch would look better against the wall. Well, really I think it would be best hidden under a tarp, but…"

Giggling, MaryAnn took the opposite end and pushed. The sofa in place, Payton appraised the room again. "Doesn't help."

There was another rumbling in the street and a second truck turned into the lot. Payton stood. "That's my other delivery. While I supervise, would you go out back and see if you can find some throw pillows or an afghan to help deflect some of this pattern?"

MaryAnn followed Payton and returned carrying an armload of solid-color pillows. She dumped them on the sofa beside Claire. "I brought as many as I could find." MaryAnn spent a moment arranging them. "There aren't enough."

"There can't be enough."

Look how cool and innocent they were. How completely unaware their world was about to change. When the news about Sean came out, would MaryAnn cry? Payton wouldn't. In the privacy of her home, she might even do a little dance.

An hour till race time. An hour till they realized Sean was missing.

Something bounced in Claire's stomach, flipped over twice, and jumped into a rhythmic pitterpat. She put a hand against it, but it didn't ease. She jumped up. "I've got to go."

"So do we." MaryAnn picked up the tray. "Gosh, I hate the idea of meeting up with Sean."

"Don't let him get to you. Be the stronger person." Claire's heart thrummed against her ribs like it tried to escape. She ran to the door.

"Your purse." Payton handed it to her.

"Wouldn't be good to forget that, the stopwatch is inside."

"We'll walk down with you."

Claire didn't want to walk with anyone. She didn't want to see anyone's reaction to Sean's death. Didn't want to time a race. She only wanted to be home, safe in her four walls.

She envisioned Sean's body lying on his kitchen floor in a pool of vomit. Claire took a breath and rubbed a palm on her stomach.

Fifteen

The big white tent was visible from the top of the marina driveway. Claire could see the crowd and the buffet tables. Buffet! Everyone was supposed to bring a dish. Not only hadn't she brought one, she hadn't made anything.

"Are you all right?" MaryAnn asked.

"Yes, fine."

"You look pale."

"I just realized I left my dish at home."

"Looks like they've got plenty," Payton said.

"You can eat it for supper," MaryAnn said.

People were everywhere. No one crying, no one looked the slightest bit sad. Sean's body hadn't been discovered. Well, at least the race would go off as planned, though they'd be minus one racer. The only one who'd worry when he didn't show up was Frank, his partner. Claire couldn't see him in the crowd.

Helen disengaged herself from a small group and came toward them. She wore white slacks and a sailor top with a navy blue tie. "Good afternoon, ladies. Isn't it nice the weather broke for us?"

Claire hadn't noticed. The rain had indeed stopped. The dark clouds gone. A mix of sky and puffy whites looked down on them. Sun beat down in all its glory. The temperature must be ninety degrees.

"Are you excited about your first race, Payton?" Helen asked.

"A little." She held out the dish of tossed salad.

"Just find a spot on a table."

MaryAnn followed Payton. Helen bent toward Claire. "Is that a black eye I see on MaryAnn?"

Claire nodded. "She reminded him that *MaryAnn* belonged to her."

"Damn him." Helen shook her head. "I used to really like him. Dear, are you all right? You're all flushed." She laid the back of her hand on Claire's forehead. "You don't have a fever."

"I'm a little nervous. Timing the race is a big responsibility."

Helen smiled. The movement made the crinkles at the corners of her mouth turn into craters. "Me too."

Payton returned and stood beside Helen, who said, "Come, I'll introduce you to the Chaumont team."

People milled around the long food tables. Sylvie and her partner, holding almost-empty plates, wore serious expressions. Sylvie pointed at the harbor, then down the bay, obviously talking race strategy. Nearby stood Aden, Edward, Amanda and Seymour, all holding plates or cups. To their left was an industrial-size coffee urn, beside it, Frank Simpson. He forked something into his mouth and chewed. He gazed around, at ease, seemingly unconcerned about Sean's tardiness. Claire thought about going to him, seeing if he'd heard from Sean.

Someone stepped from behind the urn. Athletic, handsome, smiling. Claire's knees buckled. She groped for something solid, finding one of the oak poles that held up the tent. Fingers closed around the wood, expression tightened, brain churned. Sean Adams spotted her and smiled. Claire squeezed her eyes shut. When she opened them, the phantasm still looked at her. Frank touched his sleeve. Sean broke eye contact to heed his partner.

Sean still lived. The monkshood didn't work! She hadn't used enough leaves. The cup water was too warm, too cold. The cooking temperature killed the poison; too many variables to determine the culprit.

Strong hands grasped her waist. Guided her downward. Something enveloped her backside. "There, there, sit. Take it easy." Claire squinted into sunshine. Aden Green smiled down on her. "Someone get her a glass of water."

She tried to rise. "I'm all right. Really."

Aden's hand held her in the chair. "Just sit a minute. It's very hot out."

Someone handed her a bottle of water. She drank, feeling the liquid trickle down her esophagus and strike the boiling lava in her gut. She could almost hear the sizzle when the two made contact. She coughed down the explosion, leaned forward, arms wrapped around herself, afraid to open her mouth for fear steam would come out.

"Someone call an ambulance." She thought it was Aden's voice, but it could have been anyone.

Many concerned legs appeared. Her eyes followed one pair, clad in white gabardine, upward. Pale blue shirt. Clean shaven chin. Nicely shaped lips. Sean Adams' eyes. He knelt before her. "Are you all right? You look like you've seen a ghost."

He'd found out somehow. Claire blinked. He was still there. He grinned. A shark's grin. What would he do? Surely he'd get retaliation.

His face blurred, and spun. Worried voices grew louder, closer, then wafted away.

PART TWO

SIXTEEN

Payton watched the ambulance speed out of sight. She wished they'd allowed her to ride with Claire. "Heat exhaustion," they claimed, but Payton wasn't so sure. The past few days she'd seemed distracted.

"Gather round, folks!" Edward raised Sackets Harbor Yacht Club's brand new burgee on the pole, tying it off ten feet below the Stars & Stripes. The breeze lifted the sleek emerald flag and alternately displayed the gold crossed mainsails with the SH on the left and the YC on the right. Everyone cheered.

In a Billy Grahamesque gesture, Edward raised his arms in the air, palms facing the crowd. Silence fell. Even the terns stopped their incessant squawking. He lowered his hands and clasped them in front of himself. "Before we say our regular race prayer, let's have a moment of silence for Claire. The EMTs said it was probably heat prostration and she'll be fine in a day or so. For that we're thankful. We're also thankful Felicia has agreed to be her understudy and take over timing our race." There was a polite round of applause.

"Lord, please watch over our race today," Edward said. "Keep the waters smooth and the participants safe…"

"…And could you see your way clear to putting a prevailing tailwind on *Paves the Way*?" Helen added.

A chorus of groans went through the crowd.

Payton remained silent. Claire shouldn't be alone right now. Cameron had died alone. Stabbed through the heart on her kitchen floor. Not that Claire was in danger of dying, but still, she should have someone there. The psychiatrist's words spoke in her head: "Face your fears. Face your troubles. You'll find out how strong you really are."

Not strong. Not strong at all.

"Did you say something?"

Amanda stood beside her. Payton shook her head as Edward finished the prayer. "Thank you Lord. Amen." Murmured amens, and everyone shook hands, wishing each other good luck.

Payton took another step backwards. The air was cloying, heavy with something above and beyond the heat of the day. It wasn't something palpable, or even definable in words. Something was wrong. So why did everyone act so normal? Was she the only one who could feel it?

Feet thumped down the dock heading for individual sailboats. Aden appeared on Payton's left. "Nervous?"

"A bit."

"Try not to worry about Claire. She'll be fine."

Payton stopped at the tip of *Zephyr's* bow and ran her hand along the polished surface. "Thanks for the support," was all she could think of saying.

He kissed her cheek and patted her on the behind. "Happy sailing."

MaryAnn giggled from *Zephyr's* deck. Aden was undaunted. "Just sail 'er like you did the other day and you'll do great. Maybe you'll even beat us."

"You can bet on that," MaryAnn called.

"Bet, you say?"

Payton moaned. "We're not wagering on our first run in a strange boat."

"Come on, live dangerously."

MaryAnn stuck out a hand to help her aboard.

"Good luck!" Aden called and strode away, his footsteps silent in the boatshoes.

Payton checked the riggings. MaryAnn bent over the rail

and cast off the mooring lines, then turned the key and the motor chugged to life. Payton knelt on the deck as they headed to the starting line.

As they passed *Diplomat,* both Aden and Brighton tipped their caps. Aden hollered, "It's not too late to lay down a bet!"

Payton groaned, but it was erased by the sound of the waves swooshing against the fiberglass.

"Got the stopwatch and compass?" MaryAnn shouted.

Payton reached inside her shirt and pulled the silver chain from which hung the requested items. She dangled them so MaryAnn could see. Not only would Felicia time the race from shore, but each individual boat ran their own times, later comparing leg times, water and wind conditions against previous races.

Payton unfurled the sail in her charge, hauling hard on the lines, feeling the familiar bite of rope on her palms. Aden had been right, she felt better already. The wind caught in the white fabric, sounding like thunder. Memories roared through her brain: Cameron hauling on the mainsail ropes, his powerful muscles rippling from shoulder to spine. Uptilted face serious, brilliant green eyes squinting into the sun, jaw tense. Payton let the wind dry the pair of tears as *Zephyr's* bow cut through the water. Now wasn't the time for nostalgia or regrets. She inched the sail up a little more, trying to gauge the wind and currents and distance to the starting pin as the boats lined up. Timing had to be perfect; *Zephyr* could not reach the committee boat before the starter gun sounded. It echoed down the lake.

Their timing was off a bit. The gun cracked .073 seconds before they hit the pin. Valuable time lost already. A flood of adrenaline rumbled through her veins.

The race committee gave thumbs-up to the *Zephyr.* Payton raised the jib sail to its fullest point and tied off the line. The wind was strong and the craft fairly flew atop the choppy waves. To their port side, Aden and Brighton both worked to maintain course and increase speed, as did the crew of a Chaumont boat on the starboard side. Exhilaration throbbed against Payton's ribs. She held tight to her perch and let adrenaline overwhelm all thoughts.

"Wind change SSE!" MaryAnn shouted from her spot beneath the mainsail.

Payton adjusted the jib accordingly.

"Another boat starboard, be ready to luff off!" MaryAnn hollered.

Diplomat approached rapidly, its hull cutting through the water like a hot spoon through ice cream. The sound of it sent a rush of memories crashing inside Payton's head. MaryAnn's voice became Cameron's. *Zephyr* became *Ace.* The warm air blew with the chill of a Minnesota spring, the scent of fresh pine became factory smoke, Lake Ontario the Mississippi. "Racing is like sex," Cameron always said. "Reading winds, adjusting to currents, anticipating your boat's needs is just like making love to your woman." At this point he'd put his hand on her breast, flick a thumb across her nipple then roll the pert nub between his fingers. "Pilot her unerringly around the first pin," he'd add, and do it again.

MaryAnn bent forward, the boom rode over her back, and the boat headed crosswind toward the second pin to the northwest. The distance across the bay would be 2.3 miles. The sun was hot, the sky brilliant blue. They were in open water, the wind propelling *Zephyr* through the still-cold Lake Ontario water. The mainsail line thunked against the mast.

Two meters to port were Helen and Carter in *Paves the Way.* Just behind them Chaumont Team 3. To *Paves the Way's* starboard glided *MaryAnn.* Sean and Frank hollered back and forth, but the wind whipped away their words. Funny how distance always made voices sound angry. The heavy whoosh of water behind Payton made her turn. *Diplomat* was about halfway past them. Both Aden and Seymour waved. MaryAnn waved with her middle finger.

At the second pin, MaryAnn came to, letting *Diplomat* have the right of way. Just as they finished making the turn, a gust of wind whipped the mainsail line out of Aden's hands and the boom flew out to one side. The boat canted and *Zephyr* shot past. Payton gave Seymour a thumbs-up but knew she might have to take it back later on.

After rounding the pin, Payton felt intoxicated realizing they were in fourth place. The wind changed again, blowing down the Saint Lawrence against their port side. The Canadian shoreline whizzed past. In one short week, the scenery had changed immensely. The lanky oaks still carried many of their fluttering copper-colored leaves of last season, but the maples and willows were almost fully leafed. Their immature greenness contrasted against the darker greens of the surrounding evergreens. Cottages were open for the season, shutters thrown back, colorful awnings flapped in the breeze, toys littered shoreside lawns, boats waggled on moorings like bobbers at the end of fishing lines.

Payton watched Helen adjust the jib sail as Carter maneuvered *Paves the Way* into the final leg of the race right beside *Zephyr.* Just then, *Paves the Way* lost its wind. Carter maneuvered the sail, but not before they'd lost several lengths to both *Diplomat* and *Zephyr.* For several adrenaline-pumping seconds, the two boats coursed side by side. MaryAnn expertly matched her movements with Aden's. For more than a mile the tack worked, but all at once *Diplomat* surged ahead as though they'd acquired a hundred horsepower outboard. Seymour, at the jib, grinned widely. Payton gave them the Victory sign.

Chaumont Team 2 took the lead. Three meters behind was *SHARE,* and in third came Chaumont Team 1. *Diplomat* closed fast on all of them. Apparently Aden's new boat ran just as fast as *Zephyr.* If *Zephyr* sailed so well, why weren't she and MaryAnn in the lead? Or at least directly behind *Dipomat?*

Diplomat was ten meters from the finish line, passing all but Chaumont Team 2. Their crew scurried around the deck like children late for school. Whatever they did, it wasn't enough. *Diplomat* squeezed past. In Minnesota, the crowd would be roaring, cheering for one boat or the other to surge forward.

But this crowd was quiet. Dead quiet. Payton scanned the

shoreline. These spectators weren't even watching the race. En masse, they were looking at something behind her. Some held binoculars, most had arms across foreheads shading their eyes, but all were looking behind *Zephyr*—and still, no one was cheering. What was going on?

Payton swung under the boom and shielded her own eyes. Behind, on the starboard side, were the other two Chaumont yachts and *SHARE*. Five meters behind, and two to *Zephyr's* port, was *MaryAnn*. But it wasn't aiming for the finish line.

MaryAnn's mainsail was up as it should be but was void, flapping like laundry on a clothesline. Payton couldn't see anyone on the deck. A trick of the light. Had to be.

Something was wrong. Sean's boat veered off course. There was no one aboard *MaryAnn*. Payton hollered for MaryAnn to bring the boat around. MaryAnn shoved the boom over her shoulder and turned *Zephyr* for shore. Under full sail they closed rapidly on *MaryAnn*.

Now Payton could see Sean and Frank. Both lay on the deck, two dark, unmoving lumps on the stark white fiberglass. Without a pilot, Sean's boat made a course—directly for shore!

The crowd gaped at the events unfolding before their helpless eyes. Payton screamed Sean's and Frank's names. Over and over, till her throat hurt. Neither moved.

Sean lay on his stomach, arms and legs splayed like a skydiver. Frank was on his back, like a beachgoer soaking up rays.

"Can you jump across if I get us alongside?" MaryAnn shouted.

Payton nodded without thinking, then experienced a spontaneous flood of terror. She couldn't have heard right. Was MaryAnn actually proposing Payton jump from one moving boat to another?

Sean's boat was on a course for the narrow strip of beach and stone wall surrounding the battlefield. That black unyielding barrier approached at an alarming rate. On shore, the crowd finally realized the gravity of the situation and scurried away.

Payton lowered the jib and tied off the line, recalling movies where someone leaped from one moving vehicle to another, even from one plane to another. Although she walked and sometimes jogged, she wasn't a swimmer, or a jumper. Not to mention Sean didn't rank as one of her favorite people, and she didn't even know Frank Simpson. On top of that, could MaryAnn guide *Zephyr* without squishing Payton between the hulls?

She peered frantically for someone, anyone, near enough to remove this awesome responsibility from her shoulders. The other boats were completely out of range. None of their crews seemed to realize the problem. Even though the spectators watched with increasing horror, no one could possibly help—except to call for an ambulance when it was over.

MaryAnn pulled parallel to her namesake and matched the runaway sailboat's speed knot for knot. The two decks were a half-meter apart now. Payton knelt, gripping the rail with her left hand. She swung her right leg over and perched her knee on the outer parapet. One errant movement would catapult her into the icy water.

Mere inches separated the two decks. Payton's knuckles were white as she put a death grip on the rail.

"Jump as soon as it looks safe!" MaryAnn yelled.

What exactly did safe look like? Was it tangible? MaryAnn had to be freaking insane. So did she for even considering this.

Payton pasted her eyes on *MaryAnn's* deck, waiting for just the right moment. The crowd's screams grew to a roar inside her head. Neither man had moved. The boom swung back and forth over Sean's inert body. If he'd been hit by it wouldn't he have regained consciousness by now? Surely the boom couldn't have hit both of them.

She tensed. And leaped.

A wave hit. *Zephyr* pitched. The two decks crashed in a gut-wrenching fracture of fiberglass and wood. Payton felt herself heaved into the air.

Seventeen

Payton spun in the air like a kid's pinwheel. Whirling. Impotent.

A jarring belly flop. The tidal surge pushed up, offered her to the sun. Momentary relief propelled instinct into her limbs. The surge withdrew, sucking her back under.

White hull looming. Instinct battled terror. She swam, imitating the strokes she knew should save her. She plunged downward. *MaryAnn's* hull raced across her spine, the hydraulic force propelling her to depths unknown.

Wave-swell pushed her up again, lent more hope and a glimpse of shore. An ebb rescinded the dream with unabashed disregard. She moved her arms and kicked her feet in endless succession.

A breath. Just one. The simple wish went unanswered inside the relentless noise. Horrifying power. Muddy taste.

An endless circle. Lake Ontario enfolded Payton in its chilly embrace and sucked her into its womb. Darkness engulfed her senses, filled her up. Mother Lake's caress was persuasive, comforting. Cameron beckoned. Handsome. Smiling.

Reaching for her.

Go to him.

The lake swelled again. The tide rolled and shoved.

Cameron's love flowed over her with all the lake's power. *I'm coming!* She stopped flailing and waited for the water to take her. Waited for the immense pressure in her lungs to subside. She wouldn't need them any more.

The wave crested, vomiting her upward, spewing her into the bright sunshine. Payton blinked, coughed, breathed and felt overcome by overwhelming sadness. It wasn't time. She wouldn't see her beloved.

Her head broke the surface to the cries of the crowd. She was pushed higher, the lake's compulsion to rid itself of her. Payton inhaled. The breath brought with it the urge for another. And another. Blue sky. Sunshine and life.

Cameron pointed toward shore.

She coughed. Swam. Someone screamed her name. Memory returned. The race. Sean. Frank.

Ahead was a wall of white that was *MaryAnn*, her bow shattered against the rock barrier. The broken main mast lay atop the wall. The sail snapped angrily in the wind.

People clambered across her deck. Two men stood at the rail, pointing at Payton. She waved. Choked. They pointed again and yelled something that the wind tore away. Yes, she was okay.

"No!" They pointed left.

A flash of blue rose, and grew, like shaving cream—denim jeans, legs. Payton sucked in a ragged breath. The wave waned and didn't take her. For another instant she was sorry.

More blue, then yellow. Sean!

Payton summoned failing strength and plunged toward him. Fifteen feet was like miles. Her body ached to be done with this watery hellhole. Her lungs burned for air not mixed with lake water. There he was, blond hair arced around his face in an incongruous halo as he bobbed for a millisecond on the surface. The water ebbed, driving him toward her. Payton found his shoulder.

He was dead. He had the same look as Cameron that night. Angry, but resigned to his fate. Payton felt the tears as searing heat on her cheeks. She wrapped her arm under Sean's and around his chest as she'd seen Mitch do so many times on *Baywatch*. It had been one of Cameron's favorite shows. She sobbed, a child now.

Swim.

Don't want to, the child cried.

Do it!

If you insist.

Payton and Sean were cast up on the next swell—a quick glimpse of sun and sky and life. She kicked, her left leg striking Sean's body with every frontward motion. She drove with her left arm, muscles on fire, lungs saturated.

Something touched her arm, just a tickle at first, then firmer. And a voice. It spoke in her ear, but elation forced the words away and left simple relief. Strong arms took Sean. More arms gripped her, holding her face out of the water. She was set on the tiny stretch of sand and turned over. Intense pressure on her back. Up and down.

Water erupted from her lungs, burnt her throat. Just as the lake vomited her, she returned the favor. Anxious voices edged into her head. Sirens. The scent of seaweed. Grit in her teeth. She was alive.

Not yet, love, Cameron said. *You have a lot of living left.*

Payton rolled on her side, pushed herself up, sand biting her palm in a welcome chafe. The gentle hands guided her to sit. She coughed. Gagged. Hands pounded on her back.

A face loomed through the brain fog. Suntanned skin, salt and pepper mustache, green searching eyes. "Welcome back. My name's Dennis." He pulled her head onto his shoulder and wrapped his arms around her. "You're safe now."

Eighteen

Payton lay in a lounge chair under the big white tent, a paper cup in one hand. Every breath produced an inferno in her throat. A sip of water cooled it—until the next breath. Water ran down her forehead, dripped off her nose. Someone dabbed it away. Anxious voices were distilled by the ordeal. A blanket fluttered and was tucked around her from shoulders to feet. She shivered, a deep down trembling that swallowed her whole being.

"Thank goodness you're all right."

She rocked her head right, toward the familiar voice. Helen's face took shape through the blur. "We were so worried about you, dear."

Aden appeared on the other side, lines at the corners of his mouth loomed closer. He kissed Payton's cheek.

"Sean?" she asked, already knowing the answer.

"He's dead," Aden said. "Frank, too."

Sean's face, contorted in pain, bobbed before her. His body drove toward her. Her arms around a dead man. Saving someone she disliked. A roll of nausea blasted through her. A bucket pushed under her chin. A damp cloth wiped her mouth. She breathed deeply, swallowing the embarrassment.

"Will someone take me home?" Her voice was hoarse, unfamiliar.

"You should go to the hospital," Edward said. "Let them look you over."

"You almost drowned," Aden said.

"Home."

"I'll keep an eye on her," Aden promised.

Out of the crowd of concerned townspeople, a sea of tan materialized. Payton blinked the color into focus. A pair of stocky but very long legs. There was a tiny spot of something brown on the left thigh. A little higher, a shiny belt buckle with the initial E. Higher up Payton's sight was obscured by a paunch above the belt. The legs moved, folded, and brought the torso into her line of vision. A round, fatherly face peered at her, smooth cocoa colored skin, maybe South American descent, dark solemn eyes and a neatly trimmed beard. A shiny silver name tag proclaimed him to be Sergeant Espinoza of the Jefferson County Sheriff's Department.

"I'll be working this case. Do you feel up to talking to us?"

Case? What case?

Because of his name Payton expected him to have an accent, and he did, straight out of the Bronx. She didn't—couldn't—smile even though this struck her as humorous.

"Officer," Aden said. "Can't it wait? She's not in any shape for this."

Sergeant Espinoza nodded and stood erect. "I'll come see her later this evening." He slipped a sheet of paper from his notebook and handed it to Aden. "Would you have her make out a statement?"

Helen took the cup. Aden and Edward gripped her upper arms and helped her up. When Payton's feet touched pavement, her knees buckled, but the hands held her upright.

"I really think the hospital should check her out," Edward said.

"She doesn't want to go. I'll stay with her," Aden said.

MaryAnn raced toward Payton. Her face was flushed and she was out of breath. "Golly, are you all right? When you fell in the water—I'm sorry for suggesting—Oh, God, I could've been responsible..."

Payton nodded, a little bobbing dog in a car window.

"The boat's battened down. Seymour helped."

She nodded again.

"She's full of lake water," Aden said, chuckling. "I'm going to take her home and pump her out."

"I'll watch the store. Take care. I'll talk to you later." MaryAnn gave Payton a hug.

Payton lay against a mountain of pillows, a steaming cup of tea in one hand, Aden gripping her other. Outside the window, it was dark. Normally she'd have shut the shades by now. "I can't believe they're dead," she said, for the tenth time.

"We didn't know what was happening until the race was over. We thought it was strange no one cheered for us as we crossed the finish line." Aden gave a little laugh. "I didn't think people felt *that* angry about us winning so often." He took the cup and set it on the nightstand. "I can't tell you how I felt hearing you'd almost drowned while I was having fun."

"Does anyone know what happened?"

"Vaughn said it looked like a freak wave knocked them overboard and they drowned."

She closed her eyes. A mental tidal wave hit, cloaking her in its embrace. Her eyes flew open.

"You all right?"

"Yes."

"I have some phone calls to make. Will you be all right for about an hour?"

"Of course. I'm not a child."

He bent and kissed her cheek. "I know." His lips moved across her face, to her lips. The kiss was short but let her know he definitely didn't think of her as a child.

She was so tired. She closed her eyes.

Sean's face exploded out of the water, eyes bulging, mouth open in a silent scream that prickled the hair on her arms. Payton flung off the bedclothes and sat up. Pain rocketed from every corner of her being. She closed her eyes and the aches melded into a single entity.

After a moment, the clouds parted and she stood. She went to the sliders and stepped outside. Below, the harbor looked calm. Suddenly, the waves swelled. She ran back indoors.

Payton sat on the edge of the bed and waited for the dizziness to abate. She gave a longing look at the pillows and a wistful one at the deck, then got up and tiptoed downstairs. Payton dropped onto the loveseat in her sitting room. It was dark now. She could make out objects, but not details, outdoors. It wasn't too dark, though, to see a State Police cruiser in Aden's driveway and a light in his living room. Something tickled the back of her brain. They wanted to talk to her. About what? She hadn't seen the accident. She and MaryAnn had been busy keeping their boat on course. MaryAnn was the one who spotted her namesake veering off course. And Payton swallowed every ounce of common sense and half the lake attempting to save Sean and Frank.

Vaughn suggested a strange tidal surge knocked both men off the boat. They'd been the closest boat to *MaryAnn* if there'd been such a wave, wouldn't she and MaryAnn have felt it?

The police were coming. She should be dressed. Aden had helped her change into her worn but comfortable sweats when they returned from the lake. She didn't want anyone to see her in these old things. A tiny laugh squeezed from her throat. She hadn't wanted Aden to see her in them either. She hurried upstairs as fast as her aching body allowed.

Twenty minutes later, Payton sat on a stool in her kitchen. Sergeant Espinoza stood across the counter with his notebook open before him. She noted a thin silver band embedded in the flesh of his left hand. An enormous high school ring weighed down his right. He turned to a blank page and wrote. She looked up from the statement she filled out.

"Tell me what happened." His voice sounded like a father asking his daughter what had gone on in school that day.

"Isn't that what I wrote here?"

"Humor me. Where did your boat start in relation to *MaryAnn*?"

"It was our first time on *Zephyr* and we got a slow start. Most of the boats were out ahead of us." Payton stopped talking and tried to arrange the placement of the boats in her mind. "I don't remember seeing Sean and Frank till we rounded the first pin. Something about their conversation made me think they were arguing."

Sergeant Espinoza glanced up from his page. "You heard them yelling?"

"We all yell. It's the only way to communicate over the sound of the water and the air pushing out of the sails." Payton ran a hand through her hair. "I couldn't hear *what* they were saying. I was busy, but something about the *way* they were yelling struck me."

"You mean their body language?"

"Yes, I guess that's right. Sean was standing kind of stiff, and Frank was a little bent over, like he was carrying something. He staggered toward Sean."

"Staggered?"

"Again, it's the only way to walk on deck." Payton thought, then said, "All I saw was him taking one or two steps, sort of bent over. I got busy maneuvering the boat around the pin."

"Were Mr. Simpson's steps angry? Or just regular?"

"I think…he was walking fast but not stalking. Yeah, I'd say he was just in a hurry."

"When did you see the men again?"

"On the home stretch. I wondered why the crowd wasn't cheering. There were so many spectators. But they were looking behind us. I looked but didn't see anything unusual. *MaryAnn's* sails were loose, that's about all."

"Are loose sails normal?"

"If the wind changes suddenly."

"Where were the other boats at that time?"

"Helen and Carter were just in front of us. Or maybe it was Sylvie. I'm not sure."

The sergeant made a note.

"That's when MaryAnn spotted Sean's boat going out of

control. The sails were really flapping and the boat veered off course. MaryAnn yelled that she'd get *Zephyr* alongside if I wanted to try and leap across to—"

"Where were Mr. Adams and Mr. Simpson at that time?"

"I don't know."

"You couldn't see them?"

"No. I—"

"If you couldn't see anyone, then why were you going to jump across?"

Payton's brow wrinkled as she concentrated. She put her head in her hands. It couldn't hurt to let the afternoon's horror replay for just a moment, could it? She let the waves break, heard the crowd's screams, felt the wind in her face. She felt dizzy when she looked up. "They were lying on the deck. I remember thinking Sean must have been hit by the boom, but then I saw Frank lying near the helm. The boom couldn't have hit both of them. Not that distance apart."

"They were both lying down? Not stooping or bending?" The sergeant flipped to a new page.

"Sean was on his stomach, Frank on his back. Wait." Payton felt herself frowning. At first she didn't know why. Something was off kilter. She put her face in her hands to block out the policeman. Finally the image cleared and she looked up. "Sean and Frank were lying on the deck. Lying down."

The sergeant nodded. When he said, "The coroner said they were already dead," he watched her very closely.

"They didn't drown."

"They were already dead. We don't know how yet. Tell me what happened next? You saw them lying on the deck."

"MaryAnn brought us alongside. I jumped. The next thing I remember with any clarity is someone sitting on my back, squeezing water out of me."

The sergeant was busy writing. Payton thought of Aden. Where was he? Why wasn't he here buffering the space between her and authority?

"Who pulled me out?"

"A man from Massachusetts. His name is—" he thumbed through his pages. "Dennis Rogers of Chatham."

"Do you know how I can contact him? I'd like to thank him."

"He's gone home already, but I have his number." He scribbled then tore out the page and passed it to her.

Nineteen

Payton turned on the lights in the shop and puttered around, picking off dead leaves, dusting. She stood in the patio area for a long time, absorbing the aromas and melding them with the sounds of the wakening town. Did it sound different without Sean Adams? Was there a palpable difference in the atmosphere?

When Cameron died, she'd definitely thought so. But Cameron was well loved. His death impacted not only his immediate family but members of the business world. Echoes of his murder reverberated as far as Europe. Payton didn't think Sean's death would be that far-reaching, yet the air did hold a similar aura. Death lent a massive weight to those left behind, her analyst had told her. And she'd been right. Payton still carried the burden of her husband's death, just as MaryAnn would. Neither divorce nor death could take away what a couple once had.

Payton twisted the knob for the outdoor sprinkler system and set the timer. It was just a little egg timer on the counter, but one time she'd forgotten to turn it off and customers had to slosh on wet ground all morning.

Payton returned inside intent on making coffee. MaryAnn appeared in the doorway. Her cheeks were hollow and she fidgeted her fingers around the strap of her shoulder bag.

"Good heavens, what are you doing here? I wanted to call to tell you to take the day off, but I didn't know where you were staying. Here, sit down." Payton settled her in the middle of the ugly-patterned sofa and sat in the facing chair. She wished there was some brandy in the place.

MaryAnn's purse dropped off her shoulder as she fell back into the cushions. "I came to see how you were."

"I ache all over and have a bugger of a sore throat, but otherwise I'm good. What about you?"

"I slept in Sean's bed last night. I don't know why." Her face puckered. "Payton, shouldn't I be sorry he's dead? I'm not. I just feel dead myself." She shook her head as if to dislodge hair from her face. "He really did love me, you know."

"Of course. Did he have a will?"

The first giggle burst from MaryAnn's throat like a rocket. She laughed, doubled over until Payton laid a hand on the girl's thigh. When she looked up, Payton asked, "What's so funny?"

"Sean had the strongest will of anyone I ever met!" Then as if someone flipped a switch, she grew serious again. "A will. Yes, we did them when we first got married. Sean thought it was romantic. I thought it was morbid but went along with it. I went along with lots of things back then."

Scuffing shoes in the doorway made them look up. Helen stood there, her eyes adjusting to the lighting. She held something in her left hand. "Oh, there you are." She started across the room, but when she recognized Payton's guest, she tossed the item on the counter and went to sit beside MaryAnn. "What on earth possessed you to open the shop this morning? Look at the two of you; you look like hell. When was the last time either of you had anything to eat?"

"Aden fed me soup last night."

MaryAnn shrugged and leaned forward a little. She hadn't bothered to cover up her black eye. "Will you help me with the funeral arrangements?"

"Of course." It was the second time in two days Payton agreed to something without thinking. It was also the second time she regretted the words the instant they were out of her mouth. "We'll get busy with it this afternoon, after you've eaten and rested."

MaryAnn started to get up.

"Wait, dear," Helen said. "Why don't you just sit here a while. I'll go find you something to eat."

"I'm not hungry, really."

"Well, I am. My whole routine is off. Carter and I didn't get home until after two a.m. He's still sleeping, poor thing."

"They kept you there that long?" Payton asked.

"Asking questions. What did we see? Where was everyone?" Helen rubbed her eyes. "Who can remember all that when they're so busy? I just talked to Felicia. She said first thing this morning the police were hauling the Marches down to headquarters."

"Heavens, what for?"

"To go over the videotapes of the race."

"They're probably trying to figure out what knocked the men overboard," Payton said. "They kept asking me about a rogue wave. I didn't feel anything, did you?"

MaryAnn shook her head.

"I find it odd they'd both be washed over at the same time," Helen said. "Very odd indeed."

The door opened. Claire became silhouetted in the morning light. "Morning, ladies."

"Well, hello." Helen rose and went to her. "I was on my way to visit you in the hospital, but I bumped into Vaughn and he said they'd sent you home. After I checked on these two, I was heading over to see you."

"Are you all right?" Payton asked. "Perhaps you should be home resting."

"Look who's talking," Helen said to Payton, then turned to Claire. "What happened to you, dear? Was it heat stroke?"

"That's what they told me. I feel better this morning. I was looking for MaryAnn. I drove to Chaumont." She spotted MaryAnn on the couch. "Oh there you are. How are you?"

"I think she's in shock," Helen said

Claire settled on MaryAnn's other side. She patted MaryAnn's hands, folded in her lap. "Why don't you come with me? We'll get some food into you. I bet you haven't slept either. You're wearing the same clothes as yesterday."

The timer on the front counter pinged. The women started. Payton went to turn off the water. When she returned, Claire was leading MaryAnn to the door. "I loved him," MaryAnn said. "In spite of everything."

"I know," was all of Claire's reply Payton heard as the door closed.

Helen handed a copy of the *Watertown Daily Times* to Payton, thumping a forefinger on the large bold headline. "Take a look at this. I'll make coffee."

Sackets Harbor Drowning Deaths Suspicious

Payton sat on the nearest available chair to read. *Two deaths on Lake Ontario stunned the close-knit Sackets Harbor community yesterday. Sean Adams, owner of The Taste of Gay Paree Café, and Watertown businessman Frank Simpson, president of Watertown Computer Graphics, drowned when they were thrown into the water during the first Sackets Harbor Yacht Club race. The six boat Sackets Harbor team faced off against the three boat Chaumont team just hours before. What caused both men to be tossed into the relatively calm waters at the same time is still under investigation.* Payton laid down the paper.

"What a brave thing you did, dear," Helen said.

"It was insane! I don't know what got into me."

"A fellow human being was in danger."

Payton went to the back room to make coffee. Whe she returned carrying a tray and a bag of chocolate chip cookies, Mamie stood beside Helen. Her eyes were red-rimmed, her face white. She had a wad of pink tissues in one hand. "I didn't sleep all night." She looked at the floor.

"By the time I got home," Helen chuckled. "There was hardly any night left."

"God knows I don't feel like doing anything, but Miles is

on his way with a crew. We have to start moving things today."

"I forgot it was today," Payton said. "I assume you came for the key." Payton drew a key from her purse. It was attached to a red and white fishing bobber. "You may keep this one."

Mamie took the key and dabbed a tissue on her nose. "Have you seen Claire? I tried calling the house but there was no answer."

"She was just here. She took MaryAnn home with her."

"I'm worried about her."

"So am I." Payton told how wan Claire had looked yesterday morning. "Something's been bothering her. I didn't get a chance to ask what it was. There were people here, and then it was time for the race. Now I'm angry with myself for not making more of an effort."

"Claire's very close-mouthed," Mamie said.

"I'll check on her later." Helen took a sip of coffee and said to Mamie, "I know I'm sounding like I'm a cold fish, but since Sean won't be using the shop, you're welcome to it. I'm saying it now, before you go to all the trouble of moving into Payton's house. Heaven knows I feel bad enough about how this all happened in the first place."

"Thank you, Helen. I should accept and let Payton off the hook, but I just don't think I could go in that place after what's happened."

"I don't blame you a bit, dear. My offer still holds though."

"Thank you." As Mamie left, Payton thought she heard Mamie talking.

Helen nodded. "She's absolutely right."

"What did she say?"

"Something about how things would be easier for everyone now."

"I hate to say this, but she's right," Payton said, very softly.

As the morning wore on, tourists flocked into the shop by the dozens. Payton knew they only came to see the lady who'd almost drowned trying to save an already dead man. They inundated her with questions regarding her ordeal, pretending concern that was just morbid curiosity. There was an upside to it all. Sales tripled.

At lunchtime Payton went out to the sidewalk to water the pair of ficus plants. She stood for a long time looking across at the café. She saw movement inside. With the glare on the windows, she couldn't see who it was. Maybe Helen making sure things were turned off.

Payton flopped on the ugly couch, kicked her feet up on the coffee table, leaned back and closed her eyes. Was she strong enough to get through another police investigation? Sackets Harbor was a small town, but she didn't fool herself thinking they'd be any less thorough than the Minneapolis authorities. For some time, she'd been under intense scrutiny for Cameron's death. It was the authority's job to suspect her. But after a while they'd left her alone in that fabulous penthouse apartment with the spectacular views of the city, the empty rooms and the permanent stain on the kitchen floor. She'd moved into a hotel and put the place up for sale as soon as she'd been allowed. The police went away. Cameron's death went unsolved. Doctors and family recommended the change of scenery, but it hadn't been what she needed. The nightmares continued.

Payton's stomach growled. She called the *Galley* to place a lunch order, ran up the street and back in less than five minutes. Someone had arrived during her absence. The ugly chair held a familiar face.

Aden looked confused. He stood up and walked toward her, bending to kiss her cheek. "I thought you were in the bathroom. Come sit down." He took the Styrofoam container and led her to the sofa. "Why didn't you call me? I would've brought you something to eat."

"I thought you were on a plane to Prague. Why aren't you?"

"I called in sick."

"Who…to whom does an ambassador call in sick?"

"Bigger ambassadors. How are you?"

"Sore throat, but otherwise fine." She sat on the couch. He

inspected the contents of the container and handed her half the tuna fish sandwich.

"I'm sorry I didn't get back over last night. In order to postpone today's trip, I had to prepare my colleagues for a meeting today. I spent the night on the phone."

"I saw the police at your place."

"Eat."

"Helen said they asked a lot of questions. She and Carter were at the station till two a.m." She took a bite of the sandwich.

"What I don't get is how two men could be washed overboard at the same exact time in fairly calm water."

"They were good swimmers?"

"People who spend a lot of time on the water are most always good swimmers." Aden grasped her wrist and eased it up to her mouth. She took another bite of sandwich.

After swallowing, she said, "They didn't tell you—that Sean and Frank were dead before they went over the rail?"

His lips tightened. "No. They sidestepped my questions."

"The cop didn't come right out and say so but what else can it be but murder?" Payton coughed, trying to hide the last word from the pair of women who'd just come in the shop. "Sean wasn't very nice so it is no stretch to imagine someone wanting him gone," she whispered. "But who'd want to murder Frank? And how was it done? They were alone on the boat."

"There are dozens of ways to murder someone without being there. Did you see any blood?"

"I never got on the boat. All I saw was them lying on the deck."

"Were they near each other?"

"Frank was near the helm. Sean had been working the mainsail."

"You saw them in the water after that?"

"Just Sean. A wave pushed him into me." She shivered. "There wasn't any blood that I remember."

"Could have washed off. Tell me how he looked."

"Like he was in pain. Bad pain."

"Did you see anyone else in the water?"

"There were people all over the place."

"I mean before you did the dumbest thing of your life."

"Don't remind me." She gave the question careful thought, just as she had when the sergeant asked last night. "I don't remember seeing anyone else at all."

Aden was thoughtful, watching the customers browse nearby.

"What are you thinking?" Payton asked when they were out of earshot.

"In my line of work, we sometimes see things like this. Emirs and emissaries drop dead right in the middle of peace talks. It most always turns out to be poison."

"Poison?" Payton exclaimed. One of the customers turned around. Payton quickly took a bite of sandwich and averted her eyes.

"Some poisons are obscure. This had to be something fast acting, something that would at least incapacitate them over the course of the race."

"Like what?"

"There are hundreds of chemical compounds which would produce that result."

Twenty

After promising to have dinner with Aden, Payton found herself alone in the store. She wandered to the patio, now cast in shadows. Clouds had rolled in off the harbor and the sky was a deep charcoal black. She sat at the wicker patio set, of which she'd already sold two, and leaned her head back on the poufy cushion.

Who'd want to kill Frank? He was married with four kids, a football coach and a 4H leader. He didn't live in Sackets Harbor, nor did he have friends in common with Sean, that she knew of. The answer was simple. The murderer had inadvertently got him.

The bell over the door jangled. She rose and went inside, heaving a sigh seeing Sergeant Espinoza's bulk in the door. After Aden's comment about poison, she didn't feel at all comfortable seeing the officer standing there. "Good afternoon, Ms. Winters."

He sounded pleasant, like he'd come in looking for a birthday gift for his wife, but his motives weren't sociable. He'd question, cajole and badger everyone until the case was solved. She couldn't blame him, just like she hadn't blamed the Minneapolis authorities. They were doing their jobs. One good thing about this case, she wouldn't be on the suspect list.

"I thought we got the questions out of the way last night."

"Don't you watch Columbo?" He grinned. "There's always something we forget the first time."

The bell over the door tinkled behind him. He stepped out of the way. It was Felicia. Her eyes widened seeing him there. She spun on her heel and left before he could get all the way turned around to see who it was.

"Who was that?"

"Felicia Featherstone."

His brow puckered and he leaned to watch her hurrying up the sidewalk. When she'd disappeared, he turned back to Payton. "Do you have a minute?"

"Not here."

"What time do you close?"

"Five thirty."

"I'll come to your house."

"I, er…have an appointment later. Can't we do this tomorrow?"

Espinoza put his notebook back in his pocket and opened the door. "I will be at your home at five thirty-five."

At 5:37, Payton stepped out of *Payton's Place*. It was drizzling, the air heavy, a downpour imminent. She tilted the umbrella forward to keep the mist out of her face. Her thoughts were a jumble. The most recent was regret for offering her house for Mamie's exhibit. Now wasn't a good time to have strangers milling about. She wanted to be alone, to hide in her office working on her book. The psychoanalyst's words rang in Payton's ears. "Get out of your rut. Do something therapeutic." "What the hell might that be?" Payton had asked and she'd replied, "Write a book. Cameron's death made national headlines, but no one ever heard the personal, inside story. It'll be therapy for you and will let people know the man they read about for so many years. Like Aristotle Onassis, how much had you heard about him before he married Jackie Kennedy?"

So Payton bought a computer and started on her novel—*Winter Chronicles*. In Minneapolis, ghosts pervaded her every waking minute—and most of the sleeping ones. The analyst recommended moving away and she'd picked Sackets Harbor. The choice had been easy. She and Cameron had spent their honeymoon here away from paparazzi, cameras, news. It was a small town where no one recognized him.

Unfortunately, when Payton moved here, so had the ghosts. They gummed up her keyboard, cluttered her thoughts. She had to get out of the house, busy her mind with something other than Cameron. The result was the shop. So far it had been a wonderful distraction.

The wind changed, blowing the mist from behind. Payton tipped the umbrella back but it did little good. She turned left onto Broad Street, now the mist blew in from the left. Just a few blocks to go. Maybe having the gallery at the house wouldn't be so bad, it would only be open two nights a week, Friday and Saturday, and only until 6. She was at the shop until 5:30 every day anyway.

The rain blew down the neck of her raincoat. She shivered. Even so, she turned and walked the other way. The library would be open about twenty more minutes, and she suddenly needed to talk to Claire.

Payton stood in the library vestibule shaking off the water. She leaned the umbrella against the doorframe. Rhythmic squeaking came from the nonfiction area and Payton went that way.

Claire pushed the book cart out of the way. "I thought I heard someone come in."

"I didn't feel like going home. That sergeant is waiting for me."

"What more could they ask anybody? I think I even gave them my underwear size."

"I know what you mean."

Payton gave a shudder, which Claire must've mistook for a reaction to the weather. "Want a cup of tea or something?"

"No, thanks. You got a minute to talk?"

A flicker of surprise crossed Claire's face but quickly vanished. Payton followed her into a cluttered office behind the main desk. Claire apologized for the mess. "We're getting ready for the annual book sale. We get a lot of donations. It's a good fundraiser. I don't suppose you'd volunteer to help out?"

"Sure." Payton sat in a hard wooden chair. The one behind the desk squeaked when Claire dropped into it. Payton leaned forward and spoke low. “Sean and Frank didn’t drown, they were murdered.”

Claire’s hand went to her breast. Her eyes showed white all around. She got up and looked out into the library. Payton was pretty sure this was a delay tactic. Claire needed the time to gather herself. She returned, cheeks flushed. She didn’t sit. “That’s why I came to your shop this morning. I thought we could talk.”

“That was nice of you to take MaryAnn home. How is she?”

“I put a sleeping pill in her tea.” Claire sat again. “What else did Aden say?”

“He thinks they were poisoned.”

“P-poison?” Claire blinked several times then gave a thoughtful nod. “It makes sense. What else could kill two otherwise healthy men at the same time? I never believed Vaughn’s theory about a freak wave.”

“There was no wave. I was there.”

Claire frowned. “But, the timing—” The clock out front chimed 6:00. She went to lock the door.

“I don’t know what you mean,” Payton asked. “What about the timing?”

“What?”

“You mentioned something about timing.”

Claire shook her head. “Sorry, I lost my train of thought.” She removed her jacket from a hanger on the back of the door and took a string of keys from the pocket. Payton trailed her through the big doors and watched Claire lock the building.

“You walked? In this weather?”

“The weather report said sunny and seasonably warm. Thank goodness I keep a raincoat and umbrella at the shop.” Payton popped open the umbrella and set it over their heads. Claire unlocked her car. “Do you want a ride home?”

“All right, thanks.” Payton had hoped Claire would offer. Maybe she could jog the woman’s memory on the subject of timing. But the determined way Claire turned the hatchback onto Broad Street and the firm set to her jaw said she’d “remembered” all she could. She was silent all the way to Payton's house.

"Want to come in? There's a bottle of brandy that's been calling to me all afternoon."

Claire's manner softened. "Yes, I'd like that."

They headed up the newly laid brick walk. "Your house is a showplace."

"Thanks, I like it."

The house *had* turned out even better than she expected. It was now a full-fledged Spanish hacienda, complete with pastel stucco and a jade tree out front. Granted, the tree would come indoors in winter, but it fit the setting perfectly. It was especially nice right now because it *wasn't* decorated with a police car.

Aroma from the pair of *luculia gratissimas* on the small table in the sitting room wafted out when she opened the door. Payton inhaled and smiled, closed the umbrella and leaned it against the wall. The place had undergone a noticeable transformation since morning. The walls were collaged with paintings and murals. Sculptures and figurines decorated tabletops in place of her Mexican vases and statuary.

"Mamie and Miles have worked hard." Payton hung her raincoat in the hall closet and kicked off her shoes. A light went on upstairs.

Tap tap, came a sound from upstairs. Tap tap.

"Mamie?"

Mamie's head and shoulders popped into view over the railing. "Hi. Come see what I've done up here. Oh, hi, Claire."

When Payton and Claire reached the upstairs landing, Mamie pulled Payton into a bear hug. "I can't tell you what this means to me."

"You've thanked me enough. I'm glad I could help. We need to celebrate. Come have some brandy with us. Is Miles still here?"

"I'll just finish hanging this last painting. No, he left an hour ago."

Payton took the bottle from the hutch against the stairway wall. Instead of her heavy ceramic plates, the shelves now held tiny ivory statuettes. In the kitchen, she turned on a low-watt lamp that threw a delicate glow around the room. She took three snifters from the cabinet above the stove and set them on the counter.

"Claire, would you pour for me? I have to make a quick phone call."

Payton didn't bother turning on a light in her office. She pushed speed dial number one. There was a ring at the other end. Aden's voice said, "Hello."

"Hi."

"How's it going?"

"All right, I guess."

"Busy day?"

"The worst. All those people coming in just to ask questions."

Aden laughed. "All that matters is they spent big bucks."

Payton felt his enthusiasm and chuckled too. "My biggest day so far."

"Are we still on for tonight?"

"Can't wait. Can you pick me up a little earlier though? That police sergeant said he was coming. I want to be gone before he arrives."

The sound of a throat being cleared came from the doorway. There stood the big sergeant with a not so fatherly look on his face.

Twenty-One

Sergeant Espinoza rotated on a shiny booted heel and left the room. After a moment, both Claire and Mamie passed the doorway wearing deer-caught-in-headlights faces. They slid into their jackets in stunned silence. The sergeant stood behind them, arms crossed, legs splayed.

Claire poked her head around the office door. "I'll call you later."

"Payton!" came Aden's voice through the phone. "Are you all right? What's going on over there?"

"N-nothing's wrong, I have to go." She hung up the phone.

The front door closed. Espinoza stalked into the office and sat. With the slow precision of a Rolex, he opened his notebook, withdrew a pen and poised it over the page. Payton swallowed hard.

"Care to explain what I just heard?"

She wanted to say, "not really," but opened her mouth and told the truth. "Simple, I just don't feel like answering any more questions."

"In fifteen years with the department I've learned two things: there are no coincidences and…nothing's ever simple."

"Well, you'll have to change your theory because that's all it was. I have a date tonight and—" As if on cue, the front door opened and Aden stormed inside. If surprised, Espinoza didn't show it. He did get up from the chair and expand to his full height and breadth, which didn't intimidate Aden one iota.

"What's going on here?" Aden growled.

"Just some questions."

"I don't like your tactics. I heard her voice on the phone. You've got her scared to death. After what she went through yesterday…"

"Look at her, sir. She's no more frightened than you or I."

Payton tried to don what she thought was a troubled look, but Aden's expression said she'd failed. "He overheard me tell you to hurry and he took it to mean I have something to hide."

"Aaaah." Aden drew out the sound while he processed the information.

"I guess he thinks I poisoned Sean then dove overboard to try and rescue him."

The sergeant perked forward like a Doberman on guard. "Who said anything about poison?"

"Aden and I were talking, and we decided that's probably how Sean died."

"I'd like you to leave now," the sergeant said to Aden.

Aden backed out of the room, giving the officer an "I'll be keeping my eye on you" look.

Sergeant Espinoza sat, crossing right leg over left. There was a smudge on his boot. She figured a man so well pressed and polished would want to know about it, so she didn't say anything.

"Where were you Wednesday night, the night before the race? Start around supper time."

Why did he want to know her whereabouts? He couldn't possibly think she had anything to do with this. "I closed the shop and walked home. I cooked dinner and worked in here a while. Then I went to bed."

"Alone?"

"What sort of question is that?" The words were no sooner out of her mouth when she realized their significance. "You're checking my alibi. But, why me?"

"Did you leave the house at all? Go for a walk? To the supermarket? Gas station?"

Payton pretended to think, even though she was sure of where she'd been—right here. There was no way she could prove it except for when Aden had called around 10 p.m.

Where did Espinoza want her to have been? Probably somewhere around the marina. Whatever happened to Sean and Frank must have something to do with the *MaryAnn*. Thankfully, she'd never taken Sean up on any of his proposals. Her fingerprints, or whatever evidence they collected, was nowhere among any of his things, except maybe in the café dining room where she'd eaten once, weeks ago.

"I didn't leave the house."

"Did you use the phone?"

"I made a couple of calls."

"Mind telling me to whom?"

"Yes, as a matter of fact, I do."

"Tell me and I'll go away," he said in that infuriatingly calm, even tone of voice.

"I think you're going anyway." Payton pushed her chair back, hard.

Espinoza didn't get up, though he did uncross his right leg and cross the left one over it. Payton leaned wearily against the desk.

"What sort of relationship did you and Sean have?"

"Sean Adams and I didn't have any relationship, and I resent you insinuating that we did."

"I didn't mean *that* sort of relationship. Necessarily."

Of course he hadn't meant that right off the bat. He'd beat around the subject first. "I'm sure you've heard Sean and I didn't get along."

Espinoza waited.

Should she tell him? He already knew they disliked one another. It was possible he already knew why. "There are paintings for sale in his restaurant. I asked about one by Frederic Edwin Church. We couldn't agree on a price."

The sergeant's eyes took in the imported furnishings and antique books on the shelf behind him.

"Just because I can afford expensive things doesn't mean I buy them."

"Continue."

"That's all."

"What about the argument you had in the middle of the street?"

"It was about the painting. He asked for his money. I told him I'd never agreed on a price, and it went from there."

"Were there any threats made?"

She thought back. The exact content of the discussion escaped her, but she couldn't recall any specific threats. She shook her head.

"How did you feel about him besides that situation?"

"I didn't like him. He was too full of himself. He wears women as badges of honor."

"He ever ask you out?"

"Yes. And no, I didn't go."

"How did he react to that?"

"He said I'd change my mind." She picked up a pen and began twirling it in her fingers. "Besides, Sean is married. I don't date married men."

"I understand he's getting divorced."

"It's what I heard."

"Many women don't care whether a man's married or not."

She slapped the pen down. "I'm not one of them."

He was trying to make her angry and almost succeeded. She folded her arms and let her irritation pour out through fingertips clutching the fabric of her blouse. "Look, Sergeant, I'm new in town. I haven't known Sean long enough to want him dead."

"It doesn't take long to develop a hatred for someone. Take the man who rapes a woman. In one brief flash of time, she's been violated beyond anything she's ever experienced. She feels hatred, revulsion and horror. She could conceivably do something completely contrary to her calm nature and kill the perpetrator."

"If that's what you're trying to suggest happened here you can forget it."

"No, Ms. Winters. I was just making a point. Now tell me why you believe Mr. Adams was poisoned."

"Aden said that in his line of work—"

"What experience has Mr. Green got with poisons?"

"Well, none that I know of. He said he's seen it happen in his line of work, a prime minister or emir just keels over dead. He said it always turns out they were poisoned."

"What sort of poison do you think might have been used on Sean?"

"I don't know anything about poisons. It was just talk. I bet half the people in town are talking about it right now. We're all curious to know how Sean died. Simple as that." She stressed the word simple.

"So you expect me to believe you didn't kill Sean."

"Of course that's what I want you to believe. Sean was just a pain in the neck, like a mosquito."

"What do people do to mosquitoes?" The sergeant smacked the notebook shut, stood and shook out the creases of his slacks. Payton didn't follow him to the front door.

She wiped her palms on her slacks and marched to the kitchen. The three glasses of brandy Claire had poured were on the counter. She downed the contents of one, and then the second. The silky liquid spread a blanket of warmth down her throat, insides and then into her somewhat steadier legs. She took the third glass and went out to the patio.

The rain had stopped, but the feel of it was still heavy in the air. The newly planted garden scents: oregano, thyme and lavender were calming. She sipped the brandy, feeling more like the Payton of several years ago. The Payton she wanted to be.

Another sip gave her the energy to go inside to dress for her date with Aden. She'd been thinking of asking him if they could stay home tonight but suddenly she couldn't wait to get out of the house.

She shut the sliders and started when she saw him standing there, a mixture of emotions playing across his face. He took the glass, set it down and wrapped her in his arms.

"It'll be all right." His warm breath tickled a strand of hair against her ear. He patted her bottom. "Go get dressed. We'll get the hell out of here."

Twenty-Two

Even though sun poured into Mamie's gallery, the air was somber and sad. Their voices echoed in the near-empty room. Claire wrung her hands. "It's all my fault." Payton handed her a tissue, which she dabbed against her nose.

Mamie said, "It was just a sailing accident, Claire. It's a terrible thing, but it happens."

Mamie taped a large poster on the door proclaiming the opening of the new gallery at:

213 West Broad Street

11-5 Tues.-Thurs.

11-6 Fri. & Sat.

"It happens," Mamie repeated.

"No," Claire said softly.

"Yes."

Payton had tried to talk to Aden last night, but he refused to allow the topic of Sean's death in their conversation. After dinner and a nearly wordless drive up the coast, they'd returned to his house where he undressed her, ushered her to his bed and held her in a brotherly embrace all night. Payton couldn't sleep. The warmth of Aden's body, spooning her from behind, brought unwelcome thoughts into her head. She hadn't slept with anyone since Cameron, hadn't even considered it. Around 3 a.m., she'd nearly given in to the unbidden thoughts. There was a half hour stretch where she would have liked nothing more than a straightforward roll in the hay.

Here, Claire paced the squeaky floor. Payton stepped in her path and pulled her into an embrace. She wasn't a hugging type of person, but if she'd had a friend two years ago, maybe the nightmares wouldn't have been so bad. Maybe she could make it easier on Claire.

After a minute, Claire pulled away. "I'm all right now. It's been such a shock."

Outside Felicia was crossing toward them. She carried a plastic bag with the bookstore's logo. Mamie waved her inside. "Morning, ladies." Felicia peered around the big room. "Will you be keeping both places, Mamie? Now that the other is available again—"

"I'm not sure what's going to happen yet. Miles and I have been very busy."

Felicia frowned. "The man has galleries in big cities all over the world. I can't help wonder why would he want one in this godforsaken town."

Claire hissed in exasperation. "Felicia, not everyone thinks that way about Sackets Harbor."

"Not to be rude, but if you hate it here so much, why do you stay?" Payton asked, though Felicia's question bore consideration.

"Sometimes I wonder myself." Felicia gave a heavy sigh.

"You mean because of Sean?" Mamie asked.

"Indirectly."

"Did you see anything of what happened?" Payton asked.

"God, the cops have been all over me asking the same thing. I was timing the race. My eye was on Aden and Brighton in the lead." Felicia shifted her bag from one hand to the other. "If a freak wave didn't wash them overboard, what the hell happened?"

"I guess we'll have to let the authorities figure it out," Payton said.

Mamie moaned. "They're going to be crawling all over the place, poking their heads into everyone's affairs until they do."

"Is this a problem for you?"

All four women jumped at Sergeant Espinoza's voice.

"Your sneaking up on people is a problem, sir." Felicia's eyes narrowed. "What are you doing here?"

"I came to ask Ms. Coutermarsh a few questions."

Mamie leaned the broom against the wall. "Me?" she squeaked. Her cheeks paled, then reddened.

"Nothing to be alarmed about."

Payton wasn't falling for his manner, but Mamie did. She visibly relaxed and looked around the shop. "Will it take long? My gallery is opening later this morning, and I still have so much to do."

"This will only take a minute." Sergeant Espinoza's eyes flickered over each woman but he lingered longer on Claire, who wiped her eyes with a tissue. No disguising that she'd been crying, and he wasn't trying to hide his curiosity over it.

Felicia, Claire and Payton filed outside, like children being sent to the principal's office. The sergeant had taken out his notebook. Mamie slid onto her stool, fidgeting her fingers in her lap. Payton gave her a thumbs-up, said bye to Claire and ran to her shop, not realizing till she entered the building that Felicia had followed.

Felicia cupped her hands around her face and peered across the street. "I wonder what he's asking her."

The question didn't seem to require a reply. Payton went to sit on the new couch, replaced this morning by the furniture store. When a customer purchased the ugly set, she'd barely been able to contain her delight. This set was very pretty, white brocade with pastel pink hibiscus flowers among grassy green leaves. It had two matching chairs and a lovely carved-leg coffee table.

"They've questioned me twice," Felicia called over her shoulder.

"Last night was the third time for me. The sergeant wanted to know how Sean and I got along."

"What did you tell him?"

"The truth."

"Did he believe you?"

"I hope so."

"Did he ask about that painting Sean wanted you to buy?"

"I volunteered about our disagreement over price. Someone's bound to tell him anyway."

"I'm glad you didn't fall for Sean's rhetoric about the painting." Felicia crossed the room. She remained on her feet. "How could I let him talk me into paying so much for *Sunset*? When Brighton goes to pay Aden for his half of that new boat, he'll see I drained our account. And he'll kill me."

"Can I ask you a question? Tell me to mind my own business if you want, but there's a rumor circulating town."

"About me and Sean, right?" Felicia gave a wan smile. "When Sylvie saw us in Chaumont, I knew it was only a matter of time until talk got around. There's no relationship. I can't—couldn't—stand the man. We met by accident, believe me."

"Sylvie said you looked very serious."

"He wanted me to buy another painting. I said no way." She glanced toward the street. "I've got to be going."

Payton remained on the couch for a long time after the door closed. Much of Felicia's recent unease had been explained. Payton sat up straighter. Felicia said Brighton would kill her when he found out. What if he already knew and had killed Sean rather than her? Or, what if Brighton heard the rumors about her and Sean and killed him because of that?

Maybe, fearing Brighton's reaction, Felicia killed Sean. Possible, but why wait till now? The purchase was made weeks ago.

Once thing Payton learned from this conversation—Felicia wasn't all snob and arrogance as everyone said. She had a vulnerable side. Could vulnerability translate into murder?

Twenty-Three

Payton spent the afternoon shooing reporters away from the front of the store and dodging a hundred questions each time she poked her head outside. One photographer caught her wagging a threatening finger at them. Helen would get a kick out of seeing that on the six o'clock news. So would Aden, for that matter.

Reporters weren't the only people clogging the sidewalks. The police contingency questioned storeowners, townspeople and tourists. No one was left out. Contrary to what she expected, the authorities hadn't chased business away.

At the marina, authorities went over Sean's boat again before pulling it from the water and wrapping it like holiday leftovers. They loaded it on a big trailer towed by a truck with the Coast Guard logo on the side. They examined rental dinghies, sidewalks and the entire docking system at the marina, virtually shutting the place down. All this information came from Sylvie French.

At 5:30 Payton walked home. The weather had cleared, but intermittent clouds sill cast a gloom over her spirits. No sign of the sergeant. And she hadn't seen Vaughn since the day of the murder. Helen said his nose was out of joint at being usurped by the Coast Guard and State Police in the investigation. Vaughn was a nice guy, a good cop and determined to solve the case, but Payton saw their point. Vaughn was too close to the people of Sackets Harbor to be objective.

Aden's BMW was in his driveway. He'd mown his lawn today. The whole neighborhood smelled fresh and sweet. When she got to her property, she realized he'd mown hers also.

A rousing "Hello!" brought her alert. She went up Helen's walk.

"How was your day, dear?"

"Okay, considering."

"Are the police hovering like buzzards? I'm quite upset with that sergeant; he had Mamie in tears. That's uncalled-for."

"They're just doing their jobs."

"I have to admit, she's miles stronger than when Donald died."

Payton ran a hand through her hair, raking fingers through the tangles caused by the wind.

"She fell totally apart back then. Thank goodness she had Claire and me to hold her up." Helen stopped for a breath and a change of subject. "I've got a crockpot of chili, if you're hungry."

"Thanks, but I promised Mamie I'd help put finishing touches around the house." Payton gestured toward her house. "Was it busy over there today?"

"My word! Cars were parked along both sides of the street all day. I don't know how the neighbors will react if it keeps up."

"I never thought about parking when I offered the place to Mamie. I just wanted to help her out of her jam."

"The crowds will ease off once everyone's had their fill of seeing your house." Helen smiled. Payton frowned. "I told you how curious everyone has been ever since you began renovations, dear. Tell you what. I'll encourage her to get that empty shop in shape and move everything back over there. I'll say how much better the location is or something."

"No need. I've opened this can of worms. I'll live with it. Well, I'll be getting home."

"I'll bring over chili for two."

"Thanks."

She stepped through the back sliders and into her kitchen. Safe and sound. No police. No reporters. Mamie was seated at the dining room table sipping a cup of tea. She gave a guilty start and gestured at the cup. "I hope you don't mind."

"I told you to make yourself at home."

"Would you like a cup?"

"Yes, but don't get up." Payton dropped her jacket over the back of a chair and went into the kitchen calling over her shoulder, "Helen said it was busy today."

"It was. Miles called. He was very impressed when I told him I made three sales." Mamie said this not looking up from her cup.

Payton brewed tea and took the cup to the dining table. "You make out all right with the police?"

Mamie nodded. "Yes. That sergeant said it's all routine." She stood up and pushed in the chair. "I guess I'll be heading home. I'm exhausted."

"Why not stay a while? Helen's bringing over some chili."

"That's nice of her."

"She brings me food all the time. She thinks I don't eat enough."

"I agree." Mamie looked Payton in the nose. "By the way, since the Main Street gallery is empty, I thought it would be a good time to start the painting classes… If you still want to, that is. I thought I'd offer the first class next Monday night."

"Anyone else signed up yet?"

"Helen, Edward and Amanda so far. A while back, MaryAnn mentioned wanting to paint. Do you think it would be insensitive to ask her now?"

"No, it might be good therapy."

The chili was delicious, Mamie left at 7:30, expressing total exhaustion. Payton agreed. The past few days had sucked the life from the whole town.

She went to her office and, before turning on a light, peeked out the window. Aden's car wasn't in his driveway. She wondered briefly where he'd gone, came up with no answer, then turned on her computer. She opened a new file and typed *Winter Chronicles* at the top of the page. Working from the outline she'd hand-written over the past weeks, Payton began the first chapter and somehow managed to immerse herself enough to finish seven pages. She did a spell check and word count, shut everything down and looked out the window again. 11:30, and Aden still wasn't home.

She dropped the curtain and went to the living room where she looked out again. No movement on the street. No lurking police vehicles. No stray cats. No Aden. Why was she watching for him? She enjoyed his company, but that was it.

Right, that's why she'd wanted him to make love to her the other night.

That was nothing to do with him in particular.

The last time she and Cameron made love was the night before he died. Emotion brought tears. Tears brought an overwhelming need to be moving. Payton slipped into a jacket and went outside. She turned right and walked briskly, keeping her eyes averted from Aden's house. Where was he?

Helen's living room light glowed, but she saw no movement inside. With determined footsteps, Payton crossed the intersection at Main and Broadway. She slowed her pace near Claire's house. The bluish glow of a computer shone through sheer curtains on the second floor. Payton hadn't thought of Claire as a computer person. She wondered how MaryAnn fared and almost stopped to check.

Sylvie's house sat diagonally across from Claire's. No lights there at all. Sylvie's Chrysler was in her driveway. Payton turned and retraced her steps home. Instead of going in through the front, she walked around to the patio. The hard work had been worth it. The place looked wonderful, even in the meager light oozing out from the kitchen lamp. She sucked in cool air, deeper, deeper, until her lungs would hold no more. She blew it all out, till her insides deflated, empty of the feelings that had rooted there since Sean's death.

Payton went upstairs and undressed. For better than an hour, she watched shadows march across the ceiling, fighting the desire to close her eyes. Finally the compulsion to sleep became too strong. She got up and threw on a robe. Fighting the urge to see if Aden had returned home, she went out on the deck. The bay looked peaceful and calm. Few lights shone on the opposite shore. Wispy clouds, like 70's fishnet stockings, floated past, alternately obscuring then displaying the tiny wedge of moon. She lay on the lounge chair, pushing both hands through her hair before settling them inside the folds of her robe.

She would not sleep. Nightmares would be in full-assault mode.

She scrunched her mind shut. Appreciate the serenity. Don't think about Sean. But the more she told herself not to think, the more she did. How had he uncovered her secret? "Conduct unbecoming a teacher." Payton slammed her palms on the arms of the chair. Why had he investigated her in the first place? All she'd done was refuse to buy a very expensive painting from him. What was the big deal?

Payton suspected the "big deal" had very little to do with paintings and a lot to do with saving face. Multiple times, she'd turned down his date requests, in front of his townsfolk. She hadn't fallen all over him and he couldn't bear it. So he investigated and found the skeleton in her closet.

Cameron had been her strength during that terrible time with school authorities. He carted her off to Greenland where she moped while he conducted long distance business. In a month, she'd begun venturing out of the hotel. In three more weeks Cameron deemed her healed enough to return home, where the fervor had died down and Payton could go out without feeling as though all eyes stared. Well, almost. She still watched people's reactions, still waited for the signs of suspicion, fear, anger, but never said anything to Cameron.

Four months later, he was killed in her kitchen. Like a child's tower of blocks, Payton's world had tumbled. But this time she didn't have a shoulder to lean on, a sensible voice promising things would be okay.

She propped her bare feet on the railing. Sean said he had evidence. Where would he keep something like that? At home probably. Then she sighed. The police probably had it already.

That's why they'd been around. They were waiting for her to let something slip.

The doorbell sounded. Payton started violently as the plinky chimes echoed through the house. The image of two burly State Police officers, handcuffs at the ready, popped into her head. A throbbing began at the nape of her neck and thumped into her forehead. How bad would she be hurt if she leaped over the railing and made a run for it?

Twenty-Four

Payton leaned her head against the cool glass, fingers squeezing the bridge of her nose. Inside, on the bedside table, the clock said 2:34. The bell rang again. The LCD display flickered to 2:35. Couldn't they wait till daybreak? Not if they had a warrant. Not if they thought she'd run.

A third ring.

A fourth. More insistent. Payton stepped indoors, tightened the belt on her robe and tiptoed downstairs. Through the tall narrow window beside the door, hands were cupped around a face. A male face, flattened frighteningly against the pane.

She opened the door. Aden didn't wait for an invitation. He stepped inside and eased the door shut. "I saw your bedroom light on. I thought you might have had another nightmare."

"I haven't been to sleep yet. Aden, I don't think I'm up to having company."

He steered her toward the kitchen, sat her down and set a Pyrex bowl on the table. He fished a fork from the drawer. "Close your eyes."

She heard him unsnap the lid. The most wonderful smell wafted at her: garlic and oregano, seafood and olive oil.

"Keep your eyes closed and guess."

"Seafood fettucini."

"You peeked!"

"No, I didn't." She opened her eyes. "How did you know this

is one of my favorite dishes in the whole world? And where did you get it this time of night?"

"You told me it was one of your favorites."

"When did I say that?"

"The second day we met. I figured you wouldn't have eaten today and thought this might be just what the doctor ordered." He forked some of the food for himself.

"I did eat. Helen brought chili."

Aden smiled slyly, stabbed a piece of crab and raised it to her mouth. Her stomach growled again. Two against one. She chewed, savoring the sheer wonder of the flavors.

"I found this recipe in an old cookbook of my mother's."

"You made this?" Suspicion overwhelmed the wonderful scents. So, where had he been all evening?

"What's wrong?" he asked.

"Nothing. Come on, you're going to make a guy think he slaved all afternoon for nothing. A roll?"

"No thank you."

The fork clattered to the table. He grasped her hands. Her first instinct was to pull away. Her brain suddenly cluttered with thoughts that had no place being there. She kept reminding herself Aden meant nothing; he was just a considerate neighbor. He'd be out of her life soon, just like everyone else she'd ever loved.

"Are you sure you're all right?" he whispered in her ear.

"Yes."

"Lean on me. I'll be strong for you."

"Aden, I can't do that. I've got to learn to depend on myself. To face up to life."

He laughed. "That sounds like analyst talk."

She let a smile poke through the serious set to her lips. "It was, but she was right. How can I make it if I can't depend on me to be there when I need me?" She laughed now. "That didn't come out right."

"I know what you mean."

Aden held her for a long time. She listened to the steady thump-thump of his heart. She felt both energized and weakened at the same time. He put two fingers under her chin and tilted it up. His lips were soft and gentle at first. The tip of his tongue traced the outline of her mouth and she accepted his tongue inside. She returned the kisses.

His hand left her chin and traced a path down the front of her blouse. She felt each finger even though he put no pressure at all. She didn't react when the fingers fumbled with the buttons. Nor did she try to stop him when he swept her into his arms and carried her upstairs.

Payton woke to the sunlight streaming through her bedroom windows. She rolled on her right side to put her arm around Aden, but found his side of the bed empty. The bedclothes were turned back and thoroughly rumpled, so it hadn't been just an amazing dream. The shower wasn't running. There was no happy whistling in the bathroom.

"Aden?" No answer. She really hadn't expected one. He'd used her and gone home.

Payton rolled onto her stomach and cried into her pillow, feeling as empty as the container of seafood fettucini on the kitchen table. She sobbed for a very long time. A sound from downstairs made her squint at the clock, 9:30. Mamie.

She just about flung herself to the shower. Pausing only a moment to look at red-rimmed eyes in the mirror, Payton turned on the faucet and got hit with a blast of frigid water.

The aroma of brewing coffee trickled upstairs. She lifted her nose and sniffed, then smiled. Perhaps he hadn't deserted her after all. Payton usually lingered in her closet, trying to choose just exactly the right outfit, but today she picked the things closest to her hand.

Downstairs, on the counter, was one plate containing a cellophane-wrapped muffin. One spoon, one knife, one fork. He'd set the timer on the coffeemaker.

The sudden urge for tears was pushed aside as she noticed a sheet of her pink notepaper propped against the plate.

My Dearest,

I have to leave town. An emergency I must tend to. More sorry than I can say. Last night was wonderful. Please call my cell phone if you need anything. ***Anything.***

Regards, Aden

The second anything was bolded. He'd traced over the letters two or three times with the pen. She crumpled the paper and tossed it into the wastebasket, poured a cup of coffee, savoring the first sip and letting it slid down her throat. Hot, smooth, sweet. Just like his gentle yet mind-blowing lovemaking.

Payton gave an indignant huff and dumped the remaining coffee down the sink. She turned off the pot and gulped down the newest barrage of regrets. As she picked up her raincoat and umbrella, intending to take it back to work, the front door opened and Mamie came in.

"Good morning," she chirped. "What a beautiful day. Isn't life wonderful?"

"It is," Payton lied.

She went to her office and put yesterday's bookkeeping and an order printout for plants into her backpack. She slipped the straps over her shoulders and said good-bye to Mamie, who had already busied herself refilling the spaces of three items she'd sold yesterday.

"See you later," Mamie twittered, sounding like the robins on the front lawn.

They hopped and pecked and plucked worms without a care in the world. Payton, her legs feeling as heavy as lead, walked to work. She passed Aden's house, determined not to look for his car in the drive. But her brain had other ideas and turned her head in that direction anyway. No car.

She stood in the doorway of her shop, absorbing the aromas of herbs and flowers and soil, hoping they'd help improve her mood. They did, a little. She inhaled one last time before moving the ficus trees outside to the sidewalk. She picked off a few dead leaves and tried not to think about Sergeant Espinoza's official vehicle parked in front of the café. A second car bearing the Coast Guard logo parked behind his. She saw movement inside the restaurant and a number of people near the windows.

Payton put the money into the cash register drawer and set the timer for the water on the patio. She placed a phone order; a dozen African violets, three each of oregano, thyme and sage, a dozen mixed ivy and a half-dozen monkshood. The front door opened and two women entered. Payton gave them a brief glance and a good morning. She shut the patio water off. The women browsed for a half hour, bought the last of the miniature African violets and left without asking any questions or making the slightest reference to Sean.

Payton sat on the stool behind her counter and put her head in her hands. Would the authorities think she had a motive to want Sean dead? Was it enough motivation to want her past to remain hidden? Most definitely yes. What if she swore Sean never told her what he'd learned?

At 1:00, Sergeant Espinoza and another officer stood on the sidewalk. Espinoza held a sheaf of papers in his left hand and shook them in the air while he spoke. Once or twice they glanced toward Payton's shop but neither made a move to cross the street.

An excited female voice called from somewhere up the hill. "Officers! Officers, wait." Felicia, shopping bags flopping against her hip, ran across to them. Even though Payton's door yawned open and she wasn't standing more than two feet from it, the hum of traffic obliterated the rest of her words. Felicia seemed different today. Her face was animated. First she said something, then glanced from one officer to the other as though waiting for a reply. They remained calm and serious. Said nothing. Once, Sergeant Espinoza sneaked a glance at Payton's shop. Almost immediately, his eyes flickered away. In that briefest of glances, she knew they were talking about her.

A third vehicle pulled up in front of Espinoza's. A plain-clothed man hopped out, holding a sheet of white paper. Espinoza had obviously been expecting it because he nodded and set it atop the papers he carried. Why did the words search warrant come to mind? The newly arrived officer left without further conversation. Espinoza said something to Felicia, which Payton determined to be good-bye because they got into their cars and sped away, leaving Felicia standing there looking like a lost child.

Payton went out to water the ficus. A familiar "hello" made her look up. Her smile widened seeing MaryAnn, looking awake and alert, far different from a day ago. "How are you?"

"A little better every day."

"I'm glad you're recovering. Are you still staying with Claire?"

"She's been like a mother. Last night I went to the motel. I felt like I was imposing."

"I'm sure Claire didn't feel that way."

"No. Another reason was to escape the authorities. Just for a few minutes. You know what I mean?"

Payton and MaryAnn went inside.

"Do they have any suspects yet?"

"Not that I'm aware of," Payton said.

"Claire told me the spouse is always the first one they suspect. She said I should be strong and tell the truth." MaryAnn touched the corner of her left eye where the bruise had turned a yellowish-green. "I guess I had a good motive to want him dead." MaryAnn shrugged. "They were very nice. Never accusing or anything like that. I came because I thought you might want some time off. I know you've been putting in a lot of hours between the shop and helping Mamie open the gallery. How is it, by the way?"

"Mamie's like a dove soaring above the clouds. She arrived this morning just about tweeting."

"That's good. Why don't you go get something to eat? I'll watch the shop and close up later."

"I can't let you do that. You've been through hell lately. Besides, if you're trying to avoid the cops, here isn't the place to do it."

"I got some sleep. I'm ready to face them." MaryAnn gave her a little nudge. "I'll call if I start feeling sad." MaryAnn nudged her again. "Go. Relax."

Payton hugged her and retrieved her purse and backpack. She hadn't done any paperwork, but the idea of a few hours of freedom was as appealing as a bowl of Ben & Jerry's hidden under homemade whipped cream. That thought struck her as amusing and as she headed up Main Street, ducked into the *Galley*, took a table in the front window and ordered lunch. What she'd do when she got home, Payton wasn't sure. Maybe work on her book. Mamie had considerately taped a sign to the office door: "Staff Only Beyond this Point."

Payton dawdled, savoring every bite, licking the hand-whipped banana cream from the corner of her mouth with the tip of her tongue, instead of a napkin. She felt like a child and it showed in her steps as she started for home.

But what she saw in front of Aden's house changed everything.

Twenty-Five

Sergeant Espinoza's car sat in Aden's driveway, in the BMW's usual spot. Two other vehicles parked along the edge of the road. There were actually a lot of cars parked along the road. Lately, most were customers in the gallery, but these stood out like mold on cheese. Both wore New York State government plates.

Uniformed and plain clothed men hovered in Aden's front yard. One came out the front door carrying a plastic bag. Espinoza unlocked the rear door of his vehicle, waited while the man deposited the bag, then relocked the vehicle. Chain of evidence. The words slashed a path through Payton's good mood.

Aden's note said he had to leave on a business trip and she should call him if she needed anything. She took out her cell phone and dialed his number. It rang four times and Aden's voice came on the line. "Hello…" "Oh, Aden, I'm so glad—" "This is Aden Green. I'm not available…" The message finished and the beep sounded. Payton spoke again. "Aden, it's Payton. Call me. It's important."

Another officer came out carrying a bag about the size of a sandwich. There was something blue inside. Once again, Espinoza unlocked the car and the bag got swallowed. So far her approach had gone unnoticed. She took a breath to steady her nerves and went across the street. The sergeant didn't look surprised to see her. He took several steps to close the distance between them.

She kept her voice steady. "Where's Aden?"

"That's what I was just about to ask you."

"I don't know."

"When he left your house this morning he didn't tell you where he was going?"

They'd been watching. Of course they would be; she was their prime suspect. The lunch did a flip-flop in her gut. "It's not what you're thinking."

Espinoza's eyebrows rose an inch, then returned to their fatherly position over his dark eyes. "What am I thinking?"

"Aden came over because he knew I was upset."

"And what had you upset?"

"That should be obvious. I almost died the other day. Aden saw my lights and brought me something to eat."

"What did he bring?"

"Seafood fettucini." Why did she feel the need to defend Aden? He was a man, like all other men, out to get something from her and then leave. Wasn't his desertion proof of it? He'd left her to deal with the police.

"Something wrong?" Espinoza asked. "You suddenly looked as though a dog crapped on your shoe."

"Nothing's wrong."

"Prove it."

"What's the point? You've already formed your theory. Nothing I say can change that. What I don't understand is why you think either Aden or I had anything to do with Sean's death."

"The jury's still out on you, but Mr. Green had two motives, at least." The sergeant took Payton's arm and led her toward his vehicle. He opened the passenger door and helped her inside. He walked around and got in the drivers' side, sliding his right knee onto the seat. "How well do you know him?"

"Not that well."

"He didn't come to your defense when Mr. Adams harassed you?"

"Oh for heaven sakes. I already told you, the thing between Sean and me was nothing."

"His behavior didn't anger Mr. Green, make him jealous?"

"Jealous? There was no reason for either of them to be jealous." Payton opened the door and got out. "And I don't appreciate you insinuating otherwise."

She slammed the door and ran across the street. Mamie was waiting. "What's happening?" She kept her voice low. The house was full of gallery-goers.

Payton ducked into the pantry, dropping her backpack on the ceramic floor. "They think Aden killed Sean to keep him away from me."

Mamie's eyebrows lifted into an upside down vee.

"Do you know of any sort of relationship between Sean and Aden? Anything at all?"

Mamie looked Payton in the eye and shook her head. "They talked once in a while, at the yacht club meetings, that sort of thing."

Payton picked up her bag. "I'll be in my office a while."

"I'll bring you coffee in a few minutes."

"Thanks," Payton said, although right at that moment she really would have liked something a lot stronger than coffee. She smiled at a woman examining the painting of an Italian landscape and went in her office. She pushed the curtain aside. Espinoza and the others were still there.

She dialed Aden's cell again. After seven rings an automated voice said, "The number you've dialed is out of service at this time."

Payton squinted back tears. There was a gentle tap on the door and Mamie brought in a small tray that she set on the desk. "Are they still there?"

"Yes." Payton tucked the phone back in her purse.

"Were you able to reach him?"

"His phone's out of service." Payton dropped into her chair.

Mamie's look of polite regard almost caused Payton to blurt out all her troubles. It would be so easy. Mamie seemed like a good listener, more concerned for others than herself. Payton opened her mouth, then closed it again. Mamie had enough of her own worries right now.

"You can tell me, you know," Mamie said, as though reading her mind. "I'm stronger than I look. And I can keep a secret."

Payton laughed. It came out more as a chirp and both women laughed. Mamie dragged a chair close. "Tell me what's worrying you."

Payton laced her fingers before her on the desk. "I can't help thinking Aden left town because he knew they were onto him."

"What!"

"This morning there was a note on my kitchen table saying he'd been called away."

"He *is* an ambassador, you remember. He's often called away. He misses a lot of yacht club meetings."

"I know. Are you sure you don't know of a relationship between Sean and Aden? Maybe something that goes back a few years?"

"As far as I know, the only thing they have in common is sailing."

"What about Wanderlust or another group?"

Mamie gave the question serious thought. "Sean stopped coming to Wanderlust about seven years ago. It was just after Aden started coming. Oh my, Aden had some wonderful tales. Trips to the Far East, Europe, and a city with a silly name. Uz-something."

"You said Sean stopped coming soon after Aden started. Was there a confrontation, any kind of conflict between them that might've made him stop coming?"

"I don't think so. It seemed like coincidence." Mamie slid the coffee in front of Payton. She waited till Payton had taken a sip.

"How do you know how I like it?" Payton asked.

"I watched you at Wanderlust," Mamie said shyly, then gestured at the tray that also held a plate of cookies. "I thought you might be hungry, too."

"Thank you. You're a good friend."

All at once, Mamie began crying. Payton rose and put her arm around the wide shoulders. It was more than a minute before Mamie could speak. Her previous statement, "I'm a lot stronger than I look," seemed ludicrous. Mamie was just what Payton had always thought, a wonderful, considerate woman, but weak in both mind and spirit. It was exemplified in her oh-so-rarely being able to make eye contact with anyone.

Gradually Mamie got herself under control. "I'm sorry. I don't know what happened. This whole thing is such…"

"A mess."

"Yes." Mamie accepted a pat on the shoulder, gave Payton a weary smile and left.

"Mamie, wait. Why doesn't Aden come to Wanderlust any more?"

"He said it wasn't his cup of tea."

Payton nodded. "I wouldn't have thought so either."

"If anyone knows of a connection between Sean and Aden, it'll be Helen."

Payton spun the chair so she could look out the window again. One of the official vehicles had gone. Probably gone to get the warrant to search her house.

Twenty-Six

Payton escorted Mamie to the door. The street, especially out front of Aden's house, was empty of cars. Payton called him again, and again came the automated voice announcing the number was out of service.

"Aden, where are you?"

Payton slipped on her shoes and went out through the sliders, ducking between the trees into the Mortensons' back yard. A low-watt bulb burned on the wicker table in their new breakfast room. Two figures in deep shadow sat at the table. The larger shadow, Carter, held a glass in his left hand. Helen was talking, waving her hands as she always did. The low murmur of voices, but no words, penetrated the tempered glass.

Helen spotted Payton and welcomed her in with a hug. She said she'd get her something to drink and disappeared into the house before Payton could tell her not to bother. Carter waved her to a chair. She leaned back in the comfortable thickness of the padding and put her feet on the crossbar under the table.

"To what do we owe the honor of this visit?" Carter asked in his usual right to the point manner.

Payton laughed. "Do I visit so infrequently?"

"No, just never at night," Helen said, returning with a tall glass with ice tinkling against the sides. She also held a plate of something that she set on the table closest to Payton. "Have a walnut bar, dear."

Carter reached across and received a slap on the hand. He

didn't pull back, just continued reaching. "You didn't specify which 'dear' you meant."

Helen made a hissing sound and leaned back in her chair. Payton took a sip of the fresh lemonade, just the right amount of sugar. She leaned back thinking how very much Carter resembled Rhett Butler. "I've been thinking," she said.

"Uh-oh," Carter said.

"I imagine you saw the police at Aden's."

Carter roared with laughter. "You just made her night. She's called everyone in town, but nobody knew a thing—"

"Carter!"

"You didn't call me," Payton said.

"Yes she did, but Mamie said you were working in your office and she wouldn't disturb you."

"Go watch TV, Carter," Helen said.

"I think that would be prudent." He got up and went up the steps into the main house muttering something about "gossiping women."

"He's a hoot," Payton laughed.

"I guess other people would see him that way. I assume the cops think Aden killed Sean."

"I had the idea they were gathering evidence about me."

"You!" Helen's glance flickered toward the door. She lowered her voice. "Why would they be gathering evidence against you?"

"The way that sergeant talked, I thought they were focusing the investigation on me."

"For heaven's sakes, why—because of that silly thing between you and Sean?"

"That's what I was thinking."

Helen shook her head, the tight cap of curls not moving a bit. "No way. They removed way too much stuff for it to be you they're looking at. No doubt, they suspect Aden."

"And you think he ran?"

"It's the only thing that makes sense."

Payton leaned her elbows on the table and dropped her head

in her cupped hands. Helen remained quiet. After a while Payton looked up. "It can't be. Aden would no more kill Sean than I would." Then something dawned on her. "Helen, you know more than you've said. There's a relationship between Sean and Aden, isn't there?"

Carter appeared in the doorway. "What other relationship?"

"We think the police think he killed Sean," Helen said.

Carter returned to his chair. "I figured as much, what with the cops there all day."

"That sergeant thinks Aden wanted Sean out of the way so he could have me. I told him it couldn't possibly be true because Aden and I don't have a relationship."

"You lied to the police?" Carter put a palm to his chest and rolled his eyes.

"No!" She accented the next words, "We don't have a relationship."

"She doth protest too much." Carter threw his head back and roared. When he noticed them gaping, he put on a serious expression and folded his hands on the table. "Sorry. What was the other reason?"

"Espinoza didn't say. And I didn't want to appear too worried, so I didn't ask."

"Sean grew up here in town," Helen said. "He and MaryAnn married about five years ago. She paid his way through cooking school. I can't remember where. They both worked extra jobs while saving money to open his restaurant, which he did about a year and a half ago. As for Aden..." Helen ran her hands up both cheeks and rubbed her knuckles in her eyes. "He came to town I'd say, fifteen years ago. Built that beautiful little Cape."

"Was he always an ambassador?"

"Far as I know."

"Why did he move here?"

"He said he wanted to live somewhere quiet. He'd lived in the City his whole life and wanted a change."

"But why Sackets Harbor? It's not like it's convenient to New York City."

"His aunt Charlotte lived here. Charlotte Green. Aden came here summers from the time he was a small child."

"Were he and Sean friends?"

"He was too old to have been a playmate of Sean's," Carter added. "There's maybe fifteen years between them."

"Did Sean work for him? Did Aden sell him a boat? Did Sean steal something from him? There has to be a common denominator...besides me."

"Sean wasn't the soul of honesty. Don't you remember when he was arrested for taking that Boynton kid's bike?" Carter asked.

"He said he traded for it," Helen said.

"The Boynton kid said that wasn't true."

"But Sean had the Atari game to prove it," Helen said. "And Edna vouched for him."

"Helen, you know you've always had a soft spot where Sean was concerned."

Helen sighed. "I know. I just always felt sorry for him, Edna and Rodney being murdered the way they were."

"So you can't think of any time Sean and Aden had dealings?" Payton asked. "Is it possible he mowed Aden's lawn or watched his house while he was out of town?"

"Harry Brice, the one who owned your house, always watched it."

"Didn't mow his own lawn but took good care of Aden's when he was out of town. They were quite good friends. It was a terrible blow to Aden when he found the man dead. Brice had been dead more than a week." Helen made a face.

"How did he die?" Payton asked.

"It was about eight years ago. He tripped and fell down his cellar stairs."

"Right," added Carter. "It was November."

"The day our niece Ann was born. We were getting the news of the birth on the phone while they were moving Harry's body out the back door."

Seemed like Payton was always surrounded by death. Now she'd be awash in the vision of Harry Brice lying at the bottom of her cellar stairs. Death probably occurred in lots of houses, but the owner didn't usually hear about it. She rose, suddenly aching to be out of doors.

Outside, Payton did just as she'd promised herself. She breathed. In and out. God, it felt so good. She didn't go home. She walked toward town, past Aden's dark house.

Aden. Had he run away? Would the man she'd had wild and wonderful sex with just hours ago run like a frightened child? No, he wouldn't leave her dangling like that.

At the intersection she continued on Broad Street, past Claire's house, a large, well-kept Victorian with the small Ford in the driveway. The place had a homey look to it. As two nights ago, behind a trio of tall, narrow windows, the bluish computer light glowed. A dark figure sat with his back to the windows. The person turned suddenly, as though sensing someone watching. Payton ducked into the shadow of a huge oak then continued walking. She went as far as the bend in the road near the big cornfield, turned and headed back.

A figure appeared on her left; she jumped in fright.

"I didn't mean to scare you," Claire said and fell into step beside Payton. "I saw you walking and thought you might want company."

"How are you?"

"Good as can be expected. This whole thing has been a drain on the town. I heard the police were at Aden's today."

"Yes."

"So it's true. Did they arrest him?"

"Not that I know of. I think he's out of town."

"I heard they were taking evidence from the house."

"They were, but I have no idea what it was."

Claire's grip on Payton's upper arm tightened. "Well, at least they didn't arrest him."

Twenty-Seven

At 7:30 Payton took her morning coffee to the sitting room loveseat, one leg tucked underneath her and turned sideways so she could see Aden's house. The street was quiet. His porch light remained off. No police vehicles in sight. She'd slept well in spite of Claire's final words orbiting inside her head like a rocket ship. "At least they didn't arrest him." What a strange way to say it.

Outside, an orange striped tiger cat crossed the street. A jogger ran into Payton's line of vision and her first thought was that Sean would never jog past her house again. He'd passed there almost every morning since four days after she moved in. This runner was a woman, jogging hard and struggling. She wore a grey sweat suit—matching pants and zip-up hooded shirt. Something about her was familiar. She stopped in front of Helen's house and leaned against a small maple to catch her breath.

Payton set down the coffee, got on her knees and pressed her face against the window. "Claire!"

Claire doubled over and seemed to have breathing difficulties. Was she all right? Payton slipped into her sneakers, then opened the front door enough to peek out. Claire had leaned away from the tree trunk and stood without aid. She looked across at Aden's house, breath heaving.

Payton hurried to the phone and dialed. A sleepy voice answered. "Helen, look out your front window, quick." Payton heard the phone being laid down and rapidly shuffling footsteps on a wood floor. She heard Helen say, "What the..." and steps returning. "What's she doing?"

"I don't know. She was jogging and stopped. It looked like she was about to have a heart attack, and I was just about to go help when she started watching Aden's house. She looks all right now."

Carter's voice in the background called, "What's wrong, Helen?"

"Nothing, dear. I'll tell you in a minute."

When Carter spoke again his voice was much closer. "Why are you hanging out the window?"

Helen told him what was happening, then she said to Payton, "He's looking out the window."

"Now ask him what he thinks about gossiping females," Payton said.

"Not on your life!" Helen shouted the same time Carter called, "She's gone."

Helen spoke two words, "Jogging? Claire?"

"She's been talking about getting in shape."

"But jogging?"

"Sure, why not? Stranger things have happened."

"Sorry I woke you."

"I had to get up anyway…for Sean's service."

Payton hung up the phone. Things were really getting strange. Steadfast, somber men were running from the law, and down-to-earth, middle-aged women were taking up new hobbies. She wondered briefly if something was wrong with Sackets Harbor's water.

Sean's memorial service was scheduled for eleven at the United Presbyterian Church on Main Street. There wouldn't be a wake or a regular funeral until authorities released his body. Nobody seemed to know when that would be. Sergeant Espinoza had told someone—rumor lost its original owner—they were waiting for toxicology reports. Didn't that pretty much cement Aden's theory about poison?

Which raised another question. If Aden killed Sean, why force attention on himself by talking about it? Why not lie back and let nature, or the authorities, take its course? Or get the heck out of town right away? Surely someone with Aden's connections could lose himself anywhere in the world.

A paralyzing thought hit. What if she was responsible for him being a suspect? If she hadn't mentioned poison…

Payton stood on the stone steps in front of the church, submerged in the same dizzy sensation as when she dove overboard to save Sean. Thankfully, people were both behind and in front of her and the momentum of their movement kept her from sagging to the floor. She slipped into the first pew and sat. Her thoughts swam in muddled confusion. If she hadn't told the sergeant Aden's concerns, suspicion wouldn't have been generated in his direction, and he wouldn't be on the run right now. Despair clouded her vision. Desperation forced her to her feet. She pushed through the people still making their way inside. Barely touching the steps, she flew to the sidewalk and sprinted for home.

Church bells chimed behind her, but she ran on.

Payton needed to be alone. Her world was crumbling again, an avalanche of wood, mortar and brick that flowed like lava. She felt only the air pressure on her back at first, and then the tickle of the dust shoved her ahead of the deluge. And now the force of the shards themselves propelled her indoors. Payton fell to her knees in her hallway, gasping, trembling, sobbing.

Twenty-Eight

The noise broke through her stupor. Insistent hammering.

With immense effort, Payton lifted her head and peered through a tangle of hair. Helen and Claire stood at the sliders, Helen's fist making the most god-awful noise on the glass. When she saw Payton moving, she stopped pounding and signaled for her to unlock the door.

Payton moved slowly, every muscle, nerve and even her brain screaming. She let the women in. Helen put her arm around Payton while Claire pulled out a chair and helped her sit. Payton buried her head in her hands.

"Are you all right, dear?"

Payton thought how often people had been asking that question lately. Finally she nodded.

"What happened?"

"Aden," was all she said.

"Has something happened to him?" Claire asked.

"He's gone. It's my fault."

"Your fault?" Claire's voice carried a hoarseness that made Payton look up.

Helen handed Payton a tissue. Claire cleared her throat and repeated the question.

"I told the sergeant that Aden thought Sean had been poisoned. Now he's gone."

Helen frowned and left Payton's line of sight. The front door opened and shut. Helen returned carrying a thick copy of the

"Watertown Daily Times." She slapped it on the table and swiveled it so Payton could read the headline.

Sackets Harbor Man Poisoned

Payton held her breath and read the short article. *Last Wednesday, two prominent businessmen died during the Sackets Harbor Yacht Club race. On Thursday, this paper reported that both Sean Adams and Frank Simpson had been murdered. A subsequent report determined they had been poisoned. "Although Mr. Adams ultimately drowned after rolling over the gunwale into Lake Ontario, the amount of poison in his system would most definitely have already killed him," stated Daniel Grayson, New York State Coroner, yesterday. "Manner and variety of poison have not yet been determined. Though it's often difficult to pinpoint a type of poison, we are following several leads. We should have toxicology reports in a few days."*

Payton looked at Helen. "So Aden was right."

"What does it say?" asked Claire.

Payton slid the paper across the table. As Claire's eyes neared the bottom of the article, a strangled sound came from her throat. Helen put a hand on her arm. "I'll get you a drink of water." But before she could move, Claire sprang from the chair and dashed outside.

"What on earth is going on this morning?" Helen asked.

"I think there's something in the water," Payton said, completely serious.

Head throbbing, she dashed outside. Rounding the front of the house, she felt herself being wrenched backwards. Her captor was a tall man wearing the tan uniform of the New York State Police. "Where do you think you're going?"

Her reply was cut short when Helen pounded the officer on the arm. "Let her go, you bully."

Sergeant Espinoza stepped up, took hold of Helen's arms and yanked her away from the officer. "We want to talk to you."

"Not now," Payton said, jerking from the officer's grasp.

"Now!"

Payton didn't stop, didn't even turn.

"Follow her," the sergeant shouted.

Somehow Helen already had the car running and the door open. Payton leaped inside. The Buick's tires squealed on the pavement. She raced directly to Claire's house. Her car wasn't there. It wasn't at Mamie's. And it wasn't at the library.

Payton was suddenly sweating and trembling all over. She clenched her hands in her lap and ordered herself to concentrate on finding poor Claire. Sorrow could make a perfectly stable person do the most abnormal things. She leaned forward, pressing the seat belt strap tight, looking down driveways on the right side of the road while Helen did likewise on the left.

"Where could she have gone?" Helen asked.

Helen inched past the shops, even though they could both see Claire's car wasn't there. Helen turned into the marina driveway and stopped. Behind them, the police car jerked to a halt as if surprised by their actions.

Claire wasn't at the marina either. "Where did she go?" Helen repeated. She backed as far as she could, avoiding the officer's car, turned and went back up the hill. The shadow-car did likewise.

As they passed Payton's shop, Payton hollered, "Stop!"

Helen slammed her foot to the floor, pitching Payton forward against the restraints. "Sorry."

"She went behind the cafe."

Helen drew up to the curb. Payton and Helen flew out of the car and cupped their hands to peek in the café windows. "There's no one in there," Helen announced.

"Let's go around back."

They ran down the alley to the left of the building and stopped at the corner. Claire's empty car was there. It was running and the door stood open.

A tiny metallic squeak brought Payton's eyes up to the top of a flight of wooden steps. A white, raised panel door waffled back and forth in the breeze.

"That's the door to the kitchen," Helen explained.

Payton went first, up the stairs. Her stomach was in a twist, not from fear but worry for Claire. The officer was nowhere to be seen. Payton almost told Helen to go back and get him.

She poked her head in the kitchen. The place was cold as a tomb. A large cast iron stove filled most of the right-hand wall, vents and blowers above it. Directly ahead, all the cupboard doors stood open. On the left, the refrigerator was ajar and empty. A long counter, with shelves both above and below, was clean and bare except for an enormous knife rack. One wooden handled knife was missing.

A scratching noise came from the dining room.

Payton made no sound crossing the gleaming white-tiled floor. She inched her face up to the round goldfish bowl type window. Claire stood in the middle of the dining room, amid the round metal tables. Each table had a pair of chairs tipped upside down on top.

Claire clutched a white apron to her chest. Her hands wrung it in a long rope shape, twisting it tighter and tighter, the string ties dangling to the floor. She turned in a complete circle, looking at everything, and nothing. Her back was to Payton right now, but they knew she was crying. Her body heaved and jerked as she struggled to catch a breath between sobs. Helen's arm touched hers as she peered through the second round window.

"What do we do?" Helen whispered.

"I'm not sure. Maybe it's best to let her get it out of her system, whatever it is." Then Payton remembered the knife missing from the rack on the counter. "Uh-oh."

Helen squinted for a moment. She shook her head. "What's wrong?"

Had Claire carried the large French knife into the dining room? Nothing on the tables. Nothing tucked in her waistband. Perhaps the knife was in the dishwasher or something. There was nothing to indicate Claire had it. Payton fortified herself with a breath and pushed the door open.

Claire turned.

Payton stopped. She couldn't see the knife. That didn't mean that if Payton rushed to Claire, it wouldn't be jammed between her ribs. For what reason Payton couldn't imagine, but Claire wasn't acting like a woman in possession of all her senses.

Whatever Payton expected, it certainly wasn't for Claire to crumple to the floor in a heap. Payton and Helen did the best they could to lift her and wrap her in a protective embrace. Claire sobbed even harder now. Intense gasps and snorts racked her thin frame.

Payton put her left arm around Claire's back, her right arm on top of Claire's hands, still clutching Sean's apron. Helen's right arm clutched Claire's waist. Her left hand lay on Claire's knee. They leaned their heads on each other. There they sat, an ungainly statue, mourning the loss of someone nobody had liked.

Payton felt more than saw the officer arrive. A change in air pressure. A fuller feeling in the air space, perhaps. Didn't matter. If they needed help, he was there.

Helen looked up from where she'd been leaning her head against Claire's. "Get out." And he obeyed.

Behind them, the door to the vacant shop opened. "Oh my," came Mamie's voice. Then rushing feet. She stopped in front of the women and dropped to her knees. "Is someone hurt? Should I get help?"

"No," Payton said softly.

With Mamie's help, they eased Claire to her feet and out into the passenger seat of her car. "I'll take her home and get her to bed," Mamie offered.

"She's in shock," Helen said.

"Do you think she should be treated?" Payton asked.

Mamie started the car. "I'll stay with her."

"I hope she's all right," Payton said as they drove away.

"Claire just needs rest. I'll go back up to lock the door."

The officer, standing near the corner, approached Payton. "You will come with me now."

"I'm going back. But I'll ride with Helen."

Helen slammed the upstairs door, making Payton jump. “I’ll have to get a new lock. Claire broke the other one.”

“Now,” the officer said.

Payton eyed the young man, too small, in Payton’s mind, to be a policeman, a defender of the wronged, fighter for the right. She wondered what he’d do if she suddenly popped him in the balls and bolted across the parking lot and into the line of trees behind it.

“Now.” He made his voice deeper, putting her in mind of the wrestlers Cameron used to watch on television, men who never talked in their own voices.

It was a short drive to her house, but today the trip passed as though in some sort of science-fiction time warp.

Twenty-Nine

At Payton's, the sergeant waited at the patio table in the herb garden. He gestured for her to sit across from him. Sun beat down, heating the metal past bearability. He laid the ever-present notebook on the table. Payton waited for the questions to begin.

He looked at her, pen ready, brown eyes somber. Those eyes didn't fool her. She'd been taken in by the "I'm-your-Daddy" routine once already. "Ms. Winters," he began, and Payton felt suddenly quite lonely. "Can you tell me any reason why Mr. Green might have wanted Sean Adams dead?"

"I didn't have an answer the first time you asked, and I don't have one now."

"All right. Tell me what you did last Tuesday during the day."

"I went to the shop early to put in an order, dust and do some bookwork. On the way I picked up a cup of coffee at the Galley. I moved the ficus plants outside, turned on the patio sprinklers and watered the plants inside the shop. Just before putting the Open sign in the window, I went to the bathroom."

Espinoza frowned at her overly detailed description but didn't say anything. "A lot of people come in during the day?"

"Only everyone who'd read a newspaper or listened to the news."

"Any local people?"

This was where she was supposed to throw her townspeople to the wolves. Yes, so-and-so was here. Yes, she talked about the murder. No, she didn't mention wanting Sean dead, but she was carrying a hundred pound bag of arsenic and an Internet printout of how to murder Sean.

"Felicia stopped in. She wanted to know what I was bringing to the potluck before the race. I told her I'd bring a salad. After lunch there was a dress rehearsal for the race and we all went there."

"Dress rehearsal?"

"Yes. It's when we take the boats along the course to familiarize ourselves with the route. I sailed with Helen and Carter."

"Not in your own boat?"

"I don't own one. I've been thinking of buying *Zephyr*."

He gave a slow nod and took notes. "What about Sean Adams?"

"Sean's partner was unavailable and he sailed alone."

"This can be done?"

"Not easily. But remember, it was only to familiarize ourselves with the route."

"Who else was at this dress rehearsal?"

Payton counted on her fingers. "Helen and Carter. Sylvie and her partner—I don't know her name. Amanda and Edward. Brighton and Aden. That's it, I think. After rehearsal we all went back to work."

"Who took care of the shop while you were gone?"

"I left a note on the door telling everyone to come watch. Most shop owners do that."

"And next?"

She thought a moment. "Mamie came for the keys to the house. She was meeting Mr. Arenheim here. Then MaryAnn came looking for a job."

"That right."

Payton didn't say the words that wanted to come from her mouth: "Yeah, that's what I said." She didn't want to piss off this man. There were too many skeletons in her closet.

"Did you hire her?"

"Yes."

"Was she qualified to work in a flower shop?"

"You don't exactly have to be a rocket scientist to sell plants. She's hard working and came with good references. That's enough for me."

"What happened next?"

"I gave her a plant book so she could familiarize herself with some of the most common plants. Then Claire and I remembered the *Wanderlust* meeting."

"So you went to the meeting. Did you close the shop?"

"I left MaryAnn in charge. It was slow. I was only going to be a couple of minutes away. It seemed like a good time to break her in."

"Where was the meeting?"

"Helen's. She wanted to show off her new breakfast room."

"Who else was there?"

"The usual members. Amanda and Edward. Sylvie French. Claire and Mamie."

"Do Mr. Green and Mr. Adams attend?"

She shook her head. "Aden calls them 'a group established for the betterment of Sackets Harbor's gossip.'"

"Was there any talk about Mr. Adams?"

She tried but couldn't remember. And told him so.

"Where is Mr. Green right now?"

"Uzbekistan, I think he said. I've tried reaching him but keep getting a message that his number is out of service. That's all I can tell you." She started to rise, expecting him to flip shut his precious notebook and get the hell out off her property.

But he didn't. He turned to a fresh page and wrote *Payton Winters—continued* at the top in letters so big she could read them upside down across the table. "All right, will you get me the telephone numbers of the people you said you spoke to the night before the murders?"

"What possible reason would I have for—"

"If...if Aden didn't kill Sean, who do you think might have reason to?"

"Like I said before, I've only been in Sackets Harbor a few months. Since I've been here, I've heard rumors about things

Sean's done to people."

"Tell me some of them."

She put her hands on the sides of her head, her hair drifting between her fingers and falling down to cover her face. This little movement gave her some needed privacy. Time to think. Just what had she heard? Helen had been forthcoming with a lot of stuff about the town and its goingson through the years. How much of her chitchat was anything more than idle gossip? Should Payton tell this man and let him sort through it? Was it her problem? Helen had an admitted soft spot for Sean and would probably have glossed over a lot of his behaviors. That meant he'd most likely done worse things than she reported.

What did Payton know firsthand? That he beat up MaryAnn.

Was it her business to repeat any of it?

"Ms. Winters, would you be willing to give us a sample of your DNA?"

Payton pushed her hair behind her ears and lifted her head to stare at him. This was unbelievable. She shrugged.

"Okay. Now, think back to *two* days before the murder, to Monday, and tell me what you did."

She'd taken inventory. Had lunch with Helen and Amanda. Did bookwork. Brought Aden's gargantuan pile of newspapers in and put them on his counter. Oh God! She'd been in his house. No wonder Espinoza was acting so suspicious.

"Ms. Winters?"

"Oh, sorry. I was thinking." She told him about the newspapers.

"You have a key to his house?"

"Not really." The sergeant stopped writing and looked up. "Helen and Carter watch his house while he's away. Helen loaned me the key to bring in the papers. Simple." Again she stressed the word he disliked so much.

"Will you give me the names of the people you spoke to on the phone last Tuesday night?"

She shot him a wan smile. "You're not going to like one of them."

"Mr. Green?"

She nodded. “The other was my friend Marcy from back in Minneapolis.” She slid his notebook from under his arm and wrote Marcy’s phone number in the top margin. “I talked to her from around eight thirty to nine thirty.”

“What time did you talk to Mr. Green?”

“Around ten.”

Espinoza’s eyebrows did an up and down thing.

“I know what you’re thinking. I told you the other day he was concerned about me—as a friend. He called to check on me.”

“What made him think you might be up?”

“He probably saw my lights on. You’ll have to ask him.”

“Would you do me a favor?” asked Mr. Friendly again. “Would you watch the tapes of the race and see if anything strikes you as odd?”

“Do you want me to do that now?”

“What if I leave the tapes and you can do it tonight instead of watching television.”

“I never watch television.”

“What do you do for entertainment?”

“I’m writing a memoir.”

He got up and slapped the cover of the notebook shut. He peered at her over the top edge.

Why did she suddenly have the feeling he still hadn’t asked the one question he’d come about?

He called for shadow-officer to retrieve the tapes from the car, whispered something and came back to sit. They were silent until he returned with two DVDs and a small black plastic bag. He laid them on the table before the sergeant.

Espinoza opened the black bag and took out a white envelope with a black logo of some sort in the left hand corner. From this envelope, he removed a second envelope. It was also white, but with no logo. From this he took out a long handled swab, like a giant Q-tip. He brandished it toward her. “Open your mouth, please.”

She obeyed while he swabbed the vile object around inside her left cheek while she stifled her gag reflex. He placed the swab in the white envelope, wrote her name and vital statistics on it, then sealed and slipped it into the larger envelope. She folded her hands in her lap so he wouldn't see they were trembling. He placed the envelope back in the black bag and laid it on the table.

When he sucked in a breath that filled both lungs—she could tell because his shirt strained at the buttons—she pictured them popping off like little bottle rockets and shooting all over her floor.

"What do you know about Mr. Adams' financial status?"

"Nothing. The café appeared to be prosperous. I did hear him ask Helen to have pity on him and offer a really good deal on the rental of the empty store. I have no way of knowing that meant he was hard up for cash, concerned about costs, or a cheapskate."

"Why did you move to Sackets Harbor?"

She'd known this question was coming but hadn't prepared an answer. She also knew it was leading up to his most important query of the afternoon. Her silence must have gone on too long. He'd let out the breath, his shirtfront returned to its pristinely pressed status.

"To write. I wanted a small town. A quiet place." She laughed. "A quiet place."

"That didn't really answer my question, did it?"

Now it was Payton's turn to sigh. "I'm sure you're aware that two years ago my husband was murdered. I came to…recover."

"Ms. Winters, how many poisonous plants do you carry in your shop?"

Thirty

Payton's telephone rang. She considered not answering, but the image of Aden appeared before her. Maybe he was calling to ask her to harbor him in her home. How would she respond? Did she feel sufficiently thankful for what he'd done for her? Did she want to have him around the rest of her life? That's what it would be, two souls who knew too much about each other, clinging out of need rather than the love and devotion a relationship should embrace.

The next ring seemed more insistent. "Hello."

"Hello, dear. I just called to see how you were."

Helen had called for gossip, but right now Payton didn't care. "I'm fine. Thanks."

"What are you doing?"

"Watching videos of the race." Though she hadn't been able to concentrate, visions of every poison plant from the shop kept floating onto the screen.

"Did the police badger you badly?"

"Nothing worse than before. Just more questions, like, what I did the two days leading up to the murder. Who did I talk to? Did I have any poisonous plants in the store."

"What?"

"They didn't say which one. And no, I didn't ask."

"So Sean was killed with a poisonous plant."

"Helen, what if someone bought the murder weapon in my shop?"

"You're not responsible for what people do with plants once they get them home."

Payton couldn't respond.

"Payton, if you owned a hardware store and someone bought a hammer to use as a murder weapon, you wouldn't feel responsible, would you?"

Payton gave a nervous laugh. "Probably."

Now Helen laughed too. "Well don't." Her voice turned pensive. "Who do you think did this?"

"I have no idea. It's all I've been able to think of."

"Do you want me to come over?"

"No thank you. I'm going to replay these videos and go to bed."

Payton laid the cordless receiver on the desk. What if she had sold the plant that had killed Sean? Could plants really be used in that way? They could be used to make drugs that people smoked or injected into their veins, so probably it could be done. She'd known about poisonous plants, of course, to warn her customers as the law required. But she definitely hadn't known any of them were *that* poisonous. She hadn't thought "poisonous" in that context meant anything other than a tummy ache and diarrhea if your kitty chewed a leaf.

The sergeant's voice boomed in her mind. "To whom have you sold poisonous plants?"

Payton had a sudden urge for a tall, strong drink with a ton of ice cubes. She crossed the living room to the cabinet where Mamie's little statuary dotted the shelves now instead of her hand-painted Mexican dinnerware. Payton's favorite of the figurines was the little brass whale: tail flexed, poised for his next dive, she could feel the awesome power of the animal. She brushed two fingers down its satiny spine and along the outstretched fluke.

The liquor was locked in the bottom of the cabinet, away from prying fingers. She sorted through the mostly full bottles and selected the small one at the back. Frangelico. It had been Cameron's favorite bedtime drink. Not something that was usually to her taste. For a long time, she cradled the bottle against her chest. She took a crystal glass and went to the kitchen, ignoring the tears blurring her vision.

As she passed the cellar door, she opened it and peered into the darkness of the stairwell. Harry Brice had fallen to his death here. Aden must have suffered a serious guilt trip on discovering the body, wishing he'd been home days earlier to have perhaps saved him.

She put the bottle and glass on the counter and dialed Aden's cell phone. Several clicks and weird noises were followed by ringing, and more ringing. She listened until the automated operator began her spiel about Aden's number being out of service. Maybe it was just as simple as him leaving his phone charger at home.

If that were the case, why hadn't he called on a regular phone?

By moonlight, she poured a couple of ounces of the smooth brown liquid and took it to the patio. The breeze chilled the tears on her cheeks. Golden stars sparkled in an ebony sky. A few lights shone in the harbor below. Conversational voices wafted between the trees. Fireflies flickered inches above her lawn that needed mowing. Aden wouldn't be doing it for her. Not any more. He'd spend his time stamping out license plates in the penitentiary. Would she go visit him? She shivered at the thought but decided she probably would. But wait! Aden hadn't bought a poisonous plant. He hadn't bought *any* plants.

Why use a plant as a murder weapon? Why not a knife or gun? Why take a chance the poison wouldn't work, or might kill someone else? Which it had.

Was a similar sergeant questioning Frank's friends and relatives as diligently as Espinoza was working the Sackets Harbor residents?

What was the killer plant? Payton wished her plant book were here instead of at the shop. She thought about going down to get it; she'd even taken her jacket from the closet when an awful thought hit with the physicality of a club. What if the killer purposely used a plant from her shop in order to incriminate her?

She hung up the jacket, went to the kitchen for a larger glass, filled it to the brim and went to boot up her computer. But Payton didn't open the book file. She clicked on the Internet and, after some searching, found botanical.com, a site featuring poisonous plants. It had a frightening list that in the end didn't help Payton determine what plant it might have been. There were so many that could kill. The site also said that most plant poisons were indefinable after death. That was probably why Espinoza wanted her to pinpoint the plants she'd sold—to narrow down the possibilities.

7 a.m. The doorbell rang. Payton was already up but still wearing beat-up velour sweats. Sergeant Espinoza stood on the stoop.

"Don't you ever sleep?" She backed to let him in, shut the door, returned to the kitchen, slid on the stool and went back to eating breakfast. She could feel him standing in the doorway behind her. "Pour yourself some coffee. Mugs are just above the machine."

He obeyed and then sat across the table, pushing the cup forward and laying that irritating notebook before him.

"I assume this isn't a social call. Did you find Aden?"

After a couple of long beats, Espinoza said, "I have a warrant to search your shop. I wanted to get to it early so you can still open on time."

"That was very considerate of you." His expression said she hadn't been able to keep the sarcasm from her voice. "Are you looking for poisonous plants?"

"Mostly."

"What makes you think the plant came from my shop?"

"We're checking nurseries too, if that makes you feel any better."

"Not really." She stood up. "I'll be dressed in a minute."

Payton watched out the window of the sergeant's car. She was pretty sure a curtain moved in Helen's upstairs window and stifled a wave. Two carloads of officers in unmarked cars sat in the parking lot beside the building. She let the men in and went to sit behind the counter, surprised not to be the least bit nervous. She took out the sales book while the men pawed through her store.

Espinoza approached. "You mentioned a book on poisonous plants. Could I see it?"

"I don't have a book on poisonous plants. I have several on 'regular' plants and it tells which ones are poisonous in the blurb describing each one." She reached under the counter.

"You could save time if you told me which ones to look for."

She grinned and reached into her backpack on the floor behind her stool. "I made a list last night." Seeing his raised eyebrows she explained, "After you asked about poison plants I was curious." She handed him the list. "I got these off a site called botanical.com."

He read out loud, "Larkspur, poinsettia, lily of the valley, hydrangea, monkshood, buttercup, oleander, Star of Bethlehem, and several varieties of lily. Do you sell any of these here?"

"In stock I have lily of the valley, the monkshood and hydrangea. I had the Star of Bethlehem until the other day. I just ordered more. If I were you, I'd check the monkshood first. Apparently the entire plant is poisonous, even the root. Lily of the valley is too, but to a far lesser degree. The active chemical ingredient in monkshood is aconite and it's highly toxic. One fiftieth of a grain will kill a sparrow in a few seconds. A tenth of a grain can kill a rabbit in five minutes."

A slow hiss of air escaped between the sergeant's teeth as he scribbled.

"One problem," she continued. "Over the past ten years, scientists have discovered the medicinal properties of aconite. Cold pills, ointments and tinctures now contain some. Last night I wondered whether it was possible to make a poisonous mixture from one of the medicines."

Espinoza made notes. "You said you do have monkshood here in the store?" He shadowed her out to the patio.

She pointed at the plant sitting innocently in the center of the wicker table. "This is *aconitum napellus*. Apparently this variety is the most toxic."

Sergeant Espinoza hesitated only a second before picking it up with his fingertips. "I'll need to take this to headquarters."

"I'll box it so it won't bite you."

When Payton returned carrying the plant, most of Espinoza's team had gone. "I'll need a list of people who bought these, and your supplier's name."

"I'll get it, but there's something you might be overlooking. One: someone could conceivably come in and have stolen parts of the plant. Two: this plant grows wild in the woods. It enjoys shady spots with lots of water. Like on the edge of a marsh. There must be dozens of areas like that around here."

"How many leaves would someone need? What would they do with them?"

"I don't know."

"Tell me about MaryAnn Adams. How did she come to ask for a job?"

"She's been trying to save money so she can afford to move out of the house she and Sean shared. She wanted a job that paid more than the Galley," Payton lied. Let the sergeant find out the real reason for himself: that she'd left because of someone Sean had been dating at the restaurant.

"She hasn't been back to the house in Chaumont since he died."

"Do you blame her? Sergeant, you can't be thinking she killed Sean."

"Don't you feel it's a little suspicious that the day before her husband dies, she comes to work in a shop that contains poisonous plants?"

"I suppose someone in your position might look at it that way." Damn, had MaryAnn come there for that purpose? No way. The woman suffered Sean's abuse for years. She was just about to move out of his life. Why would she suddenly decide to kill?

Maybe, faced with the reality of her departure, Sean wouldn't let her go. MaryAnn represented his failure in their marriage. Failure was one thing he didn't handle easily. Payton glanced at the sergeant and saw in his eyes he knew what she'd just been thinking.

"I understood she moved out of their house Wednesday night," Payton said.

"Telling, don't you think?"

"You'll have to ask her."

"Where is she?"

"She told me she got a motel room but didn't say where."

"We've checked all the surrounding motels and she's not in any of them. When is she scheduled to work next?"

"Today, but she's been in shock. I'm not sure she'll be in."

"Tell me about your husband's murder."

Payton's breath went out of her as though she'd been struck from behind. Her head spun and she grabbed for something solid, which ended up being the sergeant's arm. He lowered her to the stool. When her vision cleared, she said, "No. I will not talk about that."

Thirty-One

"If everyone will sit down, we'll get started."

Five metal folding chairs were arranged in a semi-circle in front of Mamie's stool. Her easel, holding a tall pad of paper, faced the empty chairs. Payton, Helen, Felicia and Amanda chatted near the refreshment table while waiting for the class to start. Helen stood uncharacteristically to one side. Her face was pale. She held her keys in her left hand and rattled them in an unconscious gesture. Payton took them from her fingers and dropped them into her oversized handbag, receiving an appreciative look from Felicia who slid the bag under the middle chair.

"We'll get started as soon as Sylvie arrives."

"Claire's not coming?"

"I don't think so. She hates painting. Besides, she just not—lately she's just not right."

"I don't think Sylvie is either," Helen said.

"Coming…or quite right?" asked Felicia. No one responded.

"Yesterday Sylvie told me she would be here." Mamie said.

"We had a…a confrontation," Helen said. She sat heavily in the end chair. Her knuckles were white against her black flowered dress. "I didn't have time to bake anything for our get-together so I stopped at the supermarket on the way here. I was trying to decide between the pastry and the cookies when Sylvie came up beside me. I said hello. She looked at me, her face turned red and she started shouting at me. Shouting. She said I was the l-lowest form of scum on this earth and I should be ashamed of myself.

She said I should c-crawl in a hole and die."

A chorus of "nos" and "whats!" came from the women.

"Did she say what was wrong?" Felicia asked.

"I haven't spoken to her since the day of the race." Helen's round body trembled. Amanda poured her a paper cup of water. "Everyone in the place was listening. It was terrible. The manager came over and told us to take it outside like we were some sort of street brawlers or something."

Suddenly Amanda laughed, and then so did Felicia. Payton almost did too. The vision of Helen and Sylvie rolling on the supermarket floor, pulling hair and screaming obscenities among spilled oranges and yams, was very vivid.

"I'm sure it didn't help that I threw a tomato at her," Helen admitted softly.

"What!"

"I couldn't help it. I was so mortified she'd spoken to me that way. You all know me. I've always said that if any of you have a problem, just come to me so we can talk about it."

"Helen," said Mamie, the only one of the five able to maintain a totally serious air. "I can't picture you throwing things."

"Are you all forgetting that time at the Wanderlust meeting when Sean told everyone he was going to become a life insurance salesman?" Felicia said with a laugh. "She threw a blueberry scone at him saying what a terrible agent he'd make because he'd chase all the wives and he'd be the one to need the policies."

The corners of Helen's lips twitched.

"You really did that?" Payton asked.

"'Fraid so," Helen said.

"I always felt sorry for his poor mother," Mamie said. "Having him late in life the way she did, and then having him turn out to be such a bad boy."

"In what way was he bad?" Payton asked.

"He was always into something," Mamie said. "Conning kids out of their lunch money and toys. He was arrested at least once for breaking and entering when he was about twelve."

"Didn't he also get arrested once for rape?" Felicia asked.

"Attempted," said Helen. "It was that young Brice girl, Zoe."

"Isn't that the family who lived in my house?" Payton asked. "I thought Harry Brice only had one son."

"No, there was a daughter too. She left town just after the trial. She's never been back, that I know of. The judge practically laughed the case out of court. She was a bit of a…"

"Tramp," finished Amanda. "Where did she go? I mean, she couldn't have been more than fifteen."

"Sixteen, I think," Helen said. "She went to live with relatives in Oregon. The family had been about to send her away anyhow. She'd been in a lot of trouble."

"So Sean didn't really rape her?"

"No. At least nobody thought so at the time." Helen shifted in her chair and sighed. "I'm sure my escapade in the supermarket will make the front page of this week's *Gazette*." Some of Helen's color had returned and she was seeing a little humor in the situation.

"I can see the headlines now," Felicia said. "Helen Mortenson's first pitch of the season is a strike."

"What was she angry about?" Payton asked.

"That's the thing. I have no idea."

They finally got down to the lesson, but the air was heavy.

It wasn't fifteen minutes before Payton wondered how Mamie could possibly be such a bad teacher. She was impatient almost to the point of being rude. At one point Helen looked at both she and Felicia and raised her eyebrows.

Mamie seemed nervous, glancing often at the clock. Several times Payton almost asked what was wrong. But Mamie was a naturally anxious person; this could be perfectly normal behavior.

Payton's mind wandered as she worked on her painting of an herb garden. What had upset Sylvie to the point of making a scene? Could it have something to do with Sean's death?

An hour later, Felicia and Amanda left carrying the new portfolios Mamie had provided. Payton snapped the art case shut and picked it up by the two narrow handles. "Is everything all right between you and Claire? You seem a bit out of sorts."

"No. Yes. Oh, I don't know. Claire's been...strange since Sean's death. So serious. And so—I don't know—weird. Did you know she's been out jogging?"

"What's strange about that?"

"She always said it was a waste of time and wrecked your joints. I don't know what's wrong with her. And I don't know what to do."

Helen patted Mamie's shoulder. "This whole thing's hit her hard. I'll go see her on my way home. I'll tell her about my run-in with Sylvie. That should get her laughing again."

"I'm glad to see you're over it," Payton said.

Helen shrugged. "Eventually I'll find out what ticked her off. Till then, I'm not going to worry about it. There're enough immediate things to keep my mind occupied."

Mamie locked the door. Payton refused rides home and walked, downtown instead of home. Dusk had descended. A pale gray-yellow light outlined the opposite shore of the lake, near Long Point. Payton crossed the street and let herself into her shop. An uncomfortable feeling lurked at the back of her mind. As she sat behind the counter, the feeling took shape in the form of a headache, carving a relentless path through her brain. She dug through her purse for a bottle of pain pills. As the ache marched from the nape of her neck up between her ears, her thoughts grew jumbled. There was something she should be remembering.

Almost in a trance, she locked the door, leaving the ficus plants on the sidewalk. She gave them "you'd better be there in the morning" glances and started up Main Street. Statistics said that traditionally women used poison as a murder weapon, but could she picture any of her friends actually doing so? There was obviously some animosity between Felicia and Sean. Was it enough to compel her to murder?

And Helen. She admitted being one of Sean's advocates, chalking his exploits up to youthful exuberance. Was his last deed with the empty store enough to finally make her realize what a low-down snake he was? What about Helen's husband, Carter? On the surface, he seemed easygoing and agreeable. He'd stayed out of Sean and Helen's business dealings, but could he be sick of Helen sticking up for Sean all the time?

Using the empty shop as a motive, wasn't it possible Mamie killed him? She wanted the contract with Miles Arenheim more than anything in the world. Even though Payton offered her home, had Mamie been unable to let go of the emotion?

Amanda said if Edward found out what she'd paid for Commodore, he'd kill her. Would he be more likely to take his anger out on Sean? If Claire had a motive it totally escaped Payton. Claire was far too levelheaded to let Sean talk her into buying paintings she didn't want. She was too logical to let what he did to Mamie rule her emotions. She was the type to go out and find Mamie another venue. It's said anyone can murder given the right set of circumstances but Payton just couldn't picture Claire as a murderess.

Who else? Sylvie? Payton didn't know anything much about her except what she'd been told: she was in her early sixties, had been divorced for quite some time and owned Sackets Harbor Real Estate. And that lately Sylvie was acting out of character. Payton had seen signs of the opinionated behavior for herself. Suddenly she had the urge to talk to the woman. Thankfully, seven thirty wasn't too late to make a social visit. She made tracks to Sylvie's house.

Sylvie's house was the same Victorian style as Claire's but not in as good condition. Sylvie was either not a very successful real estate agent, or else she chose to do other things with her money. Maybe Payton could use real estate as an excuse for her visit. Another house? Sylvie wouldn't believe that. And it was far too soon to be thinking about enlarging the shop. So, what to use as a reason for the visit? Simple, she'd come to patch things up between she and Helen. She pushed the ancient brass doorbell.

Sylvie opened the door only enough to peek outside. Seeing

Payton, she pulled the door open about a foot. She was wearing a striped blouse and polyester slacks from the sixties. Swollen ankles stuck out between the hem and purple veined feet. "I suppose Helen sent you."

"She has no idea I'm here," Payton said.

"You should look for a new friend."

Payton sucked in a breath and said, "Maybe I am."

Perhaps it was just idle curiosity that made Sylvie step back and allow Payton to enter.

She had just enough time to determine she was in a hallway before the door slammed shut, throwing them into sudden and near-complete darkness that emoted the hallway into a long soundless cave. The still air enveloped Payton in a most distasteful scent; bitter and acerbic. The only light was a skinny rectangle around a door at the end of the hall. It did nothing more than mark the location of the next room.

Without speaking, Sylvie walked toward that elongated rectangle, her bare feet scuffing on what sounded like linoleum. Payton followed with her own shuffling steps, trying to recall, in her brief moment of sight, whether she'd seen any furniture that would trip her up. Holding her breath against the odor, Payton took a few halting steps and came up short when a sharp object jabbed into her left hip. Feathering her fingers over the flat surface, she decided she'd bumped into a table. She moved around it, one hand rubbing the sore hip, the other probing for more obstructions.

Sylvie threw open a door. At that moment, two things hit Payton: the first was the stark fluorescence of a ceiling light. Her pupils contracted, throwing her once again into total blindness. The second was an accretion of the aroma against which she'd been holding her breath. A wall of stink moved at her like an invisible enemy. Ammonia burned the inside of her nose. The tiny hairs in her nostrils shriveled. Payton's instinctive inhalation only succeeded in drawing the burning into her lungs.

"I don't suppose it's anything like your house."

"I don't choose my friends because of where they live."

Between rapid blinks of traumatized eyes and restricted intakes of air, Payton saw she was in Sylvie's kitchen. To her right was a Formica table with molded chrome legs and four matching chairs. Sylvie dropped into the chair at the far end. She didn't invite Payton to sit. Payton, dizzied by the smell of ammonia, pulled out the nearest chair and sat anyway.

Payton felt like she'd somehow stepped inside a time machine—back to 1969 to her grandmother's house. Her kitchen had been exactly like this, long and narrow, running the width of the old house. Linoleum floor, white metal cabinets and double porcelain sink. The only redeeming thing about this room was that it didn't have avocado-color fixtures.

"This is wonderful period decor," Payton lied. "Have you maintained it throughout the house?"

"Y-yes." Sylvie's voice betrayed her confusion. She recovered quickly. "I have. Shag carpets, vinyl living room set, the works."

"A virtual trip into the past. Wonderful." Payton glanced around for something else to praise. "Those cabinets are in wonderful condition. I haven't seen metal ones since..." She was about to say "my grandmother's house" but didn't think that would be construed as a compliment. So she let the sentence hang.

"Originals," was all Sylvie volunteered.

By then Payton's eyes had adjusted to the unbounded reality of the fluorescent lights and she realized, with a flicker of horror, just what was causing the horrific odor.

Cats.

Everywhere. Like hairy doilies, they decorated every available surface: counter, stove, windowsills, the top of the refrigerator. Payton's right elbow suddenly bumped something solid. A black cat with a white patch on its head eyed her with disdain from the corner of the table.

Payton reached out to pat the Holstein-colored creature. It tilted its head and half-closed yellow eyes. The animal appeared to be purring. She ran a palm down its back a couple of times hoping to gain a bit more of Sylvie's trust. "How many cats do you have?"

"I'm not really sure. They're always bringing home friends."

By the aroma coming from what must be an overflowing litter box, Payton had trouble believing any of these pets ever went outdoors.

"Phoebe had five upstairs in the guest closet," Sylvie said with pride. "They're almost eight weeks old."

Payton withdrew her fingers from the short, coarse fur.

"So, tell me again why you came. I'm sure it wasn't to meet my kitties."

She gave Sylvie her most direct gaze. "I thought maybe you could help me. Help the people of Sackets Harbor."

Sylvie's eyes narrowed.

"I assume you know Aden is under suspicion for Sean's murder." Sylvie nodded, her expression beginning to make Payton feel a bit uneasy. "Do you have any idea why he might want Sean dead?"

"To have you for himself."

Was that what everyone believed? "Did Sean and Aden have anything in common besides me?"

Sylvie thought seriously for several moments. Her left fingers drummed on the table, the others held the side of her face as though her head suddenly grew too heavy for her neck. "No." She sounded so certain Payton didn't try to draw her out any further.

"It just doesn't set right with me. Especially now that Aden's missing."

"Missing? Well…that just about solves it, hey?"

"He works in the Mideast, Sylvie. There could be a dozen reasons why he's out of touch. What I was trying to say is that the authorities are looking at other people."

"Like who?"

"I don't know specifically, but this morning they searched my shop." She lowered her voice. "I got it out of that sergeant that the poison used to kill Sean was from some kind of poisonous plant."

Sylvie's eyes widened. She put down the tabby she was holding and leaned both elbows on the table. "I knew something was going to happen with those things all over the place. I just knew it."

"Sylvie, we tried to tell you at the time, they're not—"

"Obviously you were wrong." She picked up the cat again, watched it turn in a circle and lie down on her lap. "What types of plants are poisonous?"

"Lots really. Poinsettia and lily of the valley to name two."

"Lily of the valley," Sylvie said thoughtfully. "How does somebody use a plant to kill somebody?"

"I have no idea. The authorities are waiting for test results that show how the poison got in Sean's system."

"Do they suspect you?"

"I hardly knew Sean."

"That's not how the rumors went."

Payton shrugged. "I have no control over what people say. Sean was merely a thorn in my side, a mosquito." She recalled Espinoza's comment about the demise of the pesky insects. She shivered, banging her elbow against the innocent cat. It got up, stretched in a way that would send most humans screaming for a chiropractor and hopped to the floor. "From their questions, I got the idea they think the killer is a woman. Poison is usually a woman's weapon. And Sean came in contact with a lot of women. The ones he worked with, spoke with at meetings or in shops, sold paintings to." Payton knew she was rambling but was spurred by the curious expression that had crept onto Sylvie's face. Guilt? Suspicion?

What if Sylvie was the murderer? Payton didn't know of a possible motive, but she didn't know Aden's either, at least not the one the police kept under wraps. Sylvie had lived in town a long time. It was conceivable she'd have been affected by one of Sean's escapades.

Sylvie still didn't speak.

The black and white cat returned and stood between Payton's shoes, looking at her with big yellow eyes. It crouched, leaped and landed in her lap. Payton stroked the shiny fur. Whatever could be said for Sylvie's litter box cleaning habits, at least this cat appeared to be well fed.

"So, will you help me find out who did this?" Payton asked.

Finally the iceberg melted. Sylvie's features softened, smoothed out. "Yes. I think I'd like to do that."

Payton set the cat on the floor. "Were you born here in town?"

"Uh, yes."

"Married?"

"I was...once. C'mere kitty kitty." Sylvie bent over and put her hand out to a cat that had hopped off the windowsill. She spent an inordinate amount of time scratching between the animal's ears and cooing little nothings.

"Where were you last Tuesday night?"

The tone of Payton's voice hadn't been accusatory, just conversational yet the iceberg returned. Sylvie's eyes transformed into black slits, her mouth to a skinny pink line.

"Sylvie, I'm just trying to piece things together in my mind. Whatever was used to kill Sean obviously had to have been put on his boat the night before. I know where I was—home—alone. Helen and Carter went to the movies."

"How convenient they can alibi each other. I was here. Alone. I came back from the office around five. Cooked supper for me and my children." She arm waved to include her furry companions. "We watched television until about ten and then went to bed. Not very exciting. Not like what you probably did."

Payton smiled. "I did about the same things, except I only fed myself. I don't have any pets."

"Don't you like animals?"

"I do. I just don't happen to have any. Who do you think had reason enough to want Sean dead?"

The reply was simple and to the point. "MaryAnn. On *NYPD Blue*, the spouse is always the one who did it. She took a lot from him. She worked her ass off to put him through cooking school. Then there was the abuse."

"You knew about that?"

"Everyone knew. You'll ask why people put up with it." Sylvie made an exasperated sound with her tongue. "We all tried to get her to leave him, or press charges. Even Officer Vaughn did. But she wouldn't. I always wondered if Sean had something on her. I mean, why else would a woman take what he did?"

"Weak women do that sometimes."

"She doesn't seem weak to me."

Sylvie had a good theory. If Sean was indeed holding something over MaryAnn, that would explain a lot of things.

"I understand you saw Sean and Felicia in Chaumont."

"Another of his conquests."

"An unlikely pair. What was their demeanor? Did you hear any conversation between them? See any gestures? Did they hug or kiss, or anything like that?"

"They were standing in front of a restaurant, a foot or so apart. If that's not the posture of people who know each other very well, I don't know what is."

"Could it have been simpler than that; two people having a conversation over the sound of traffic?"

Again Sylvie thought. Then she nodded. "I suppose it could have been."

"Did you see anything else?"

"I wanted to watch them but couldn't find a spot to park. I went to turn around, but when I got back Felicia was gone. Sean was still standing there."

"Do you know of any relationship between Amanda March and Sean? Besides sailboats, I mean."

"I don't think it's possible. Edward rarely lets her out of his sight. He's a tough bastard, if you'll excuse my French."

"Is he that strict?"

"Last October, I overheard them arguing. He was using the worst vocabulary you can imagine, saying she'd better phone next time she was going to be late, or else."

"He really said 'or else'?"

"He did."

"Where had she been?" Payton asked.

"It was Helen's birthday. We were all at Mamie's. He knew exactly where she was."

"How did you come to overhear the argument?"

"I took a walk to the battlefield during my lunch break. They were in the marina parking lot."

Payton put down the cat and crossed her legs. "Helen was really upset about your meeting at the supermarket."

"That's the real reason for this visit, isn't it?"

"I'll admit it's a part of it. Helen and I are friends and I'm understandably concerned. She doesn't know I'm here, nor did she suggest it. I really do want to get better acquainted with you. Of all the people I know in town, I think you're the most logical one to help me find the real killer."

Sylvie thawed a little more. "Sometimes Helen makes me so mad. I can't believe she *believed* Sean's tale about Mamie's gallery troubles. Everybody knows *never* to believe anything Sean says. The thing that got me was when Helen said 'she got what was coming to her for being such a pantywaist.'"

"Helen said that?"

"She sure did."

"Are you certain she was talking about Mamie? To whom was she talking?"

"Carter. At Sean's memorial service. I was sitting behind them."

Sylvie talked a while longer, obviously happy to have someone besides her cats. She wasn't forthcoming with any more helpful gossip, and Payton soon made an excuse to leave. Though not before she'd been given a complete tour of the smelly, rundown Victorian. And been introduced to the adorable "kids" in the bedroom closet.

At the front door, Payton was surprised to hear herself inviting Sylvie for coffee "one of these days." From the way this offer was received, Payton had no doubt Sylvie would come knocking very soon.

Outdoors, she breathed deeply of the clean air. Could she picture Sylvie as a killer? Possibly. Hadn't she said that Sean cheated her out of a commission on the house he'd bought through her? That was years ago though.

Sylvie's seeing Sean and Felicia in Chaumont might be important. It was remotely possible they were having an affair. But more likely they'd been, as Felicia admitted, discussing *Sunset.*

Then there was Sylvie's assessment of Edward and Amanda's relationship. From what Payton had seen they were always polite and considerate to each other. On the other hand, if Sylvie was right, that would explain Amanda's fear of Edward finding out what she'd paid for the painting of the old commodore.

She passed Claire's house. No lights on. Not only had she supported Mamie through her troubles, but she'd also taken MaryAnn under her care. She had to be worn out. It was no wonder her behavior had become erratic.

At home, Payton checked her answering machine. There was nothing from Aden. Why should she be worried about him? He was a low-down rat for leaving her alone to face the cops. She undressed in the dark, looking out over the harbor. Stars glinted off the mirror-like water. Where could he be?

A laugh squirted between her lips. All this time she'd been worried about Aden and her friends, but more than likely she herself was at the top of the suspect list. She'd had means—the probable plant right in her store. She had no alibi. Flimsy as it was, she had a motive. And on top of it all, she had something none of the other suspects had: another unsolved murder in her past.

She'd been a suspect before and survived.

Before, she didn't have a motive to kill Cameron. And she'd been out shopping when he was killed.

So, how to keep the cops off the doorstep?

Find the real killer.

Easier said.

As she climbed into bed, the painting class replayed in her mind, from the moment she put her packaged chocolate chip cookies on the table to the click of the door when Mamie locked it for the night. They had talked about Sean, his personality, his deeds and misdeeds. They'd talked about Sylvie and Helen's confrontation. They'd made jokes. Commiserated.

The Brice girl had taken Sean to court, not surprising really. She'd been young; parents would be understandably upset learning their daughter had relations with anyone. They'd talked about Claire's erratic behavior. There was a clue somewhere in all that talk. Darned if she could see it.

Payton curled into the security of a fetal position, watching the clock. As the numbers flicked from 4:11 to 4:12 and a twinge of dawn's light lit the room, Payton flung herself upright. She clutched the eyelet lace coverlet to her bare breasts, her nipples erect as though they'd been alerted to the same realization their owner had just made.

Thirty-Two

By 8 a.m. Payton sat in Helen's glassed breakfast room. Carter voiced his intention of "letting you girls talk" but he remained there. Payton sipped Helen's fresh-ground hazelnut coffee and leaned back in the white wicker chair, purchased at Payton's shop at a 10 percent friendship discount. She dropped the bomb. "I've decided to investigate Sean's death."

This was obviously not what they'd expected her to say. "Why?" they both asked at the same time.

"Because…" Payton hesitated. "I—"

"Because you're scared they're looking at you?" Carter asked, his usual teasing manner serious.

"Right," Payton admitted.

"That's absurd. Why would they suspect you before people who've known and despised Sean?" This also came from Carter. In response to the scathing look from Helen, he said to his wife, "I thought we decided you were done sticking up for Sean. Your attentions, although misguided, were well intentioned but will stop here."

A light flush colored Helen's cheeks.

"Did you ever buy insurance from Harry Brice?" Payton asked.

"Er, yes," Carter replied.

"Did anyone else in the neighborhood?"

Carter laughed. "It was hard *not* to buy from him."

"What could this have to do with Sean's death?" Helen asked.

"I don't know yet. Do you know if Aden bought a policy?"

"I wouldn't be surprised. They were friends," Carter said.

"Aden was Harry's only friend."

"That's not true," argued Carter. "I was his friend."

"Hrmph. That's why you didn't even know the man was dead." This was clearly the first time Helen voiced the thought aloud. Carter's expression registered both shock and disappointment. Helen was quick to apologize.

"Harry was diabetic," Helen said, "plus he was suffering some sort of post traumatic stress from an injury in Korea."

"What sort of injury?" Payton asked.

"He was shot in the leg," Carter said. "Walked with a cane."

"So he was unsteady on his feet?"

"He was careful."

"Do you remember when Aden first started coming to the Wanderlust meetings?" Payton asked.

Carter chuckled. "That was back when men were allowed to come."

"Men are still allowed," Helen said. "Sometimes Edward shows up."

"That's because he won't let Amanda out of his sight."

There it was again, another contradiction to the March's relationship. "If Edward thought there was something between Amanda and Sean, what might he do?"

"Simple. He'd kill Sean," Carter said. Suddenly the air in the room changed.

"Oh God," Helen said.

They sat silently with their thoughts for several moments. Finally Payton spoke, "I can't see him buying a plant and mixing up a poison concoction though. That takes planning."

Carter pointed at Payton. "Wait. Explain."

"The police were at Payton's store, searching for poisonous plants," Helen said. "They insinuated Sean had been poisoned with a plant."

"No way Ed would use a *plant*," said Carter. "If he killed Sean, it would be in a fit of anger."

Payton nodded. “I think a woman killed Sean.”

“Anyone in particular?” Carter asked.

“No. I’ve been talking and listening a lot, that’s all so far. What do you think about Amanda?”

“No!” Helen said but then leaned back, blinked twice and said, “Maybe.”

“She’s as gentle as a lamb. I’d more likely picture Helen—Ouch! Stop kicking me.” Carter bent down and rubbed his shin.

“What kind of thing is that to accuse me of, Carter Mortenson?”

“Oh stop it. I just meant that personality-wise, you’re more the type because you’re more logical, more likely to plan. Amanda’s sort of a scatterbrain.”

“I never thought of her that way,” Payton said. “So when did Aden start coming to the meetings?”

“Almost right from when he moved to town,” Helen said. “We dragged him everywhere at first.”

“Ha!” Carter threw back his head and roared. “You dragged him everywhere, little Miss Matchmaker. He really disappointed her, though. He never went out with one of Helen’s setups more than once.”

“When did he stop coming to the meetings?”

“He didn’t come very often because of his job. I think he just sort of petered out.”

“What about Sean? Did he ever come?”

“In the beginning, yes.” Helen took a sip of coffee.

“When did he stop?” Seeing Helen’s mounting confusion she said, “I’m trying to piece together a timeline. Was Sean still coming when Harry died? Did he and Aden ever come at the same time?”

“When Aden found Harry dead, Sean was still attending the meetings. I remember because Sean made a rude comment about Harry. He said ‘the old gimp shouldn’t be trying to act like a kid.’”

“No, that’s not exactly right,” Carter added. “He said ‘Old gimps shouldn’t try and do kids’ jobs.’”

“You’re right,” Helen said. “That made Aden angry. He picked

Sean up by the front of the shirt and shook him. Sean's feet were right off the floor! Then Aden gave him one hell of a lecture about being respectful to his elders." There was silence a moment, during which Payton tried to picture Aden angry. She failed.

"You know," Helen said, "it doesn't seem as though Sean came to many meetings after that."

"Tell me about Sylvie."

Helen wrinkled her nose but leaned back in her chair. "She grew up here. Married Garson French. He was a captain in the Air Force, and for a few years they lived on bases around the country. Moved back here when he got out, but things weren't good between them. They got divorced a short time afterward. He moved away. She stayed. Never married again. I don't think she dated anyone either."

"Has she always been in real estate?"

"No. She was a high school English teacher back then. I can't remember exactly when she opened the agency. I went to work for her—"

"She talked you into working for her," Carter interrupted.

"Yes," Helen admitted. "I stayed as long as I could take it, then went out on my own."

"She was hard to work for?"

Carter chuckled. "In case you haven't noticed, Sylvie's not a people person."

"But she knew it," Helen said. "That's why she asked me to come in with her. Paid for real estate classes and everything."

"When you left, was it amicable?"

"Yes and no. We had a falling out but patched most of it up afterward."

"What do you know about her life now?"

"You mean besides the cats?" Helen asked.

Helen didn't mention the smell so neither did Payton. "Did Sean and Sylvie have any real estate dealings? Any relationship at all?"

"There was something, while I worked there." Helen put a

finger to her lips, thinking. “Sean put a deposit on a piece of land. A few days later, I saw Sylvie tear up his check and accept someone else’s. When I asked about it, she said only that he’d backed out of the deal. But later, Sean was livid, so I knew she was lying.”

“Interesting. Do you recall who bought the land?”

“No. Sorry. It’s probably in the town tax records.” Helen’s phone rang.

Payton looked at her watch. “I have to get to the shop.” She took her cup to the kitchen, rinsed it and put it in the sink. She practically danced across the lawn to her house. Things were really taking shape. Get people talking and there was no end to what you could find out. She retrieved the shop keys and her backpack. Claire hadn’t arrived yet, so she locked up and headed for town.

Just as she’d thought, Aden and Sean had a previous relationship that ended on a bad note. And so did the relationship between Sean and Sylvie. Payton couldn’t wait to visit town hall and find out more about that land deal.

Thirty-Three

MaryAnn wasn't scheduled to work, yet she arrived at noon bearing a large white bag. "I thought you might be hungry." She drew out a pair of Styrofoam containers. "Eat. I'll go out back and get drinks."

"I'll take these to the patio. It's too nice to eat inside."

MaryAnn brought two Cokes, moisture already beading on the sides of the cans. Payton took a long sip and sighed.

"Hard day?" MaryAnn asked.

"Not really. I'm tired." A few flowers had fallen from the monkshood plant onto the table. Payton picked them up and piled them on her napkin. "How are you holding up?"

"I started cleaning out the house yesterday. I thought about putting it on the market but changed my mind."

"Can you handle living there?"

"I think so. Once I get things cleaned out, repainted. You know what I mean."

"Can I help with anything?"

"No. Thanks. Uh, you know what? I really would like—not help really—just someone to be there with me."

"There must be a lot of memories."

MaryAnn bit into a ham sandwich and chewed, looking out at the passing cars.

"Did Sean have any friends?"

MaryAnn swallowed. "Not since we got married. I can't believe it's been five years."

When Payton asked, "Did he ever tell you about being accused of rape?" MaryAnn's eyebrows shot up into her bangs. "The guy who owned my house had a daughter. The girl was loose, as Helen calls it, and charges got dropped, but I wondered if you knew anything more."

"This is the first I've heard of it. Was this recent?"

"No, back when they were teens."

"He raped me once." Payton didn't say anything. MaryAnn added only "he was drunk" and seemed inclined to say nothing more.

They sat in silence for a while. Payton watched sparrows flit through the lattice, pecking at bugs on the plants, chirping as though they hadn't a care in the world. She thought about how she'd misjudged Aden. He appeared carefree and easy-going on the surface. Yet, he'd physically manhandled Sean.

Across the table MaryAnn had finished her lunch. She pushed the Styrofoam package away. Though pensive, she didn't seem affected by the talk about Sean being a rapist.

Payton stood and pushed the chair close to the table. "I'll be off. Thank you for bringing lunch." She dropped the containers, dead flowers, and her can into the shopping bag.

"Anything special you need done?"

"Nothing I can think of." A tour bus rumbled to a stop in the parking lot. "Maybe I should stick around a while."

"No need. Tourists are rarely in a hurry. I'll manage. Where's the Wanderlust meeting today?"

"At the battlefield. Are you sure you'll be all right?"

"I'm fine. Really."

Payton squeezed MaryAnn's arm. "Call if you need anything." She turned left out of the store and waved through the lattice.

At the battlefield, several blankets, looking like a giant patchwork quilt, were spread on the freshly cut grass. Shade from the elderly maples deflected the heat of the afternoon sun. A warm breeze riffled Payton's hair against her cheek. She brushed it away, savoring the day. Helen, Felicia and Amanda were already there.

The wind turned over the corner of a rectangular green blanket. Helen straightened it and sat down with a grunt of satisfaction. "Let's see it pop up now!"

Felicia and Amanda manned other corners. "We're human anchors," Amanda laughed.

"Okay, I'll take one." Payton sat cross-legged on the fourth corner.

Sylvie came down the hill. Payton eyed Helen watching her.

"You okay with this?" Felicia asked.

"Yes, it's in the past." Helen's voice was calm, but her hands fidgeted in her lap.

Sylvie nodded hello to Payton and set a foil-wrapped plate on one of the blankets. "I brought brownies."

"Potato salad for me," said Helen.

"Fried chicken," chimed in Claire.

"I didn't expect we'd be sitting on the ground though," added Sylvie. "Amanda, could I have some of that tossed salad, please?"

"Well," Amanda said, handing across the bowl, "nobody offered to bring chairs."

Sylvie lowered herself heavily onto a nearby blanket, facing the water, Payton noticed, so she didn't have to make eye contact with Helen. "I'm down, but someone might have to help me up."

"No problem," Amanda said. "But what I wonder is who's going to help the first person up."

Payton laughed. "Maybe we can flag down a tourist."

"Where's everyone else?" Sylvie asked.

"Claire and Mamie are coming down the hill now," Amanda said.

"Mamie's packed on a few pounds," Sylvie offered.

"That's not a subject most of us are comfortable talking about, Sylvie." Helen laughed, her weight was often a humorous topic of conversation. But Sylvie scowled and Helen shut up.

Claire and Mamie soon settled, but both seemed out of sorts.

Claire's eyes darted back and forth, like roving Christmas

lights. Mamie seemed nervous, too, but demonstrated it by looking only at the food in her lap. Payton was used to her not making eye contact, but today she never once looked up from her plate.

Finally, topic of the meeting turned to Sean's murder. There was an unspoken moment of silence for the two men, after which Sylvie said, "Never much liked Sean. Don't know how he ever got hooked up with that nice Frank Simpson."

Amanda nodded slightly, but even Sylvie was content to let the subject drop.

Payton wondered at the logic of mentioning her intention of finding the killer. If either of the three were guilty, they'd be on her thick as honey. Would any of them resort to a second murder if she got too close? What was she saying—Helen and Carter were no more murderers than her. Sylvie on the other hand…

Sylvie's voice brought her senses alert. "Bullshit. You could kill as easily as anyone else, given the right set of circumstances."

"No," Felicia said. "I believe my inborn desire not to hurt anyone would overrule the part of me that's angry enough to do something like that. Heaven knows, I've been in that position often enough with Brighton."

They all laughed, but there was no humor in it.

"Haven't you all been so angry you wanted to hurt someone? You manage to stop yourself, don't you? Well, I believe that, even given those considerable circumstances, I could hold back."

"This wasn't a crime of passion," Helen said. "This was cold and well calculated in advance."

"You ought to know about cold and calculating," Sylvie said.

Helen bent forward, hand knit sweater almost in her potato salad. "Sylvie, what is your problem? What did I do to make you so angry?"

"It's your big mouth, that's what. You telling your husband Sean got what was coming to him."

"What!"

"I heard you, don't try and deny it."

"I never said such a thing."

"No!" Sylvie got to her feet without any of the difficulty she'd proclaimed she'd have.

"You must have misinterpreted something I said," Helen protested.

"Ladies," Payton said.

"You're the one who should learn a little decorum," Helen said.

The word obviously stymied Sylvie for a moment, but she finally realized that whatever it meant, it wasn't a compliment. "How dare you?"

"If any of us could do such a thing as murder, it's you."

"Ladies!"

"What reason would I have for killing somebody, assuming I could do such a thing?"

Lightning bolts from Sylvie's eyes hit Helen squarely in the barricade that had, so far, controlled her temper. It broke with an almost audible snap. "You have as good a reason as anyone, Sylvie French. when you sold that parcel of land out from under Sean, he vowed he'd pay you back. And he did, didn't he? He made sure you couldn't get the variance on that strip-mall deal."

Sylvie spluttered, like a fire with ice water thrown on it. But she wasn't ready to be extinguished yet. She balled her hands and shook them at Helen. "You're saying I cheated Sean out of that land?"

"Give a trophy to the lady. Yes, that's exactly what you did. Sean gave you a ten thousand dollar deposit. I saw the check myself. You tore it up and went with a higher bidder."

"I—"

"I was there, remember? Sean's check was dated four days before the Carlson Corporation's."

Sylvie shot another volley of lightning at Helen then stormed off up the hill.

Amanda was first to break the awkward silence. "Well."

Helen pushed onto her knees and then to her feet. "I'm going home."

"We might as well all go," Felicia said. "I feel the urge to apologize to Brighton."

"For what?" Amanda asked.

"All the times I wanted to pound him into mush."

Together they folded the blankets, wrapped the uneaten food and went their separate ways. Mamie and Claire—who hadn't spoken a word throughout the meeting—and Payton walked up the hill together.

"Claire, tell Payton your plan," Mamie said suddenly.

"I wanted to tell everyone at once, but…I'm going to ask Helen about reopening Sean's café."

The words "you're kidding!" squeezed between Payton's lips before she could get her surprise-reflex under control.

"Someone should be carrying on his legacy. MaryAnn doesn't want to. She's even selling his house."

"She's decided to keep it."

"Good. Well, I'll try and corner Helen at home. I want to get things rolling as quickly as possible." Claire waved good-bye and strode away, not limping at all on her bad ankle.

Mamie's eyes focused on Payton's top button. "Crazier and crazier."

Thirty-Four

Payton sat at her kitchen counter, perched on a stool. She gave a bored glance at the folded copy of the *Watertown News* and pulled it toward her. For the past two days, the story about Sean and Franks' deaths had been relegated to the fourth page, but today it was once again splashed across the front—"Poisonous Plant Used in Sackets Harbor Deaths." The article was short and didn't state the specific plant that had been used. Either the police weren't releasing the information or they didn't know. Yet. She recalled the research saying many plants couldn't be detected after death.

The phone rang and Payton went to retrieve the cordless handset from the dining table. "Hello."

"Hello, dear."

"Hi, Helen."

"Did you hear the news about Claire? She was just here asking for a lease to reopen Sean's café."

"I heard. What's wrong with that?"

"She doesn't have any restaurant experience. She admitted it to me just now. What's going on with her? With her job at the library she wouldn't have time to run a restaurant anyway."

"Something's definitely going on."

"Would you try and talk to Claire tomorrow? You know, talk her out of this ridiculousness."

Payton wasn't sure ridiculousness was a word. "What have the cops been up to? I haven't seen them around lately."

"I heard they're back questioning Amanda and her husband."

"Really?" Amanda had bought a few plants. Payton couldn't recall exactly which—except one had been monkshood.

"Dear, are you still there?"

"Yes. Sorry. What did you say?"

"I asked if you had any idea why authorities would want to talk to them again."

"No. Unless they found something on those videos."

"Did you see anything when you watched them?"

"No. And it was awful watching myself almost drown."

"All right, dear. Take care. Let me know if you find out anything."

Payton pushed the OFF button and ran a hand through her hair. The burnished strands filtered between her fingers like water over a dam, glimmering in the overhead kitchen light. So the police were questioning the Marches. She tapped the ON button and dialed MaryAnn's number.

"Hi, it's Payton. I wondered if you wanted some company."

"You must have ESP. I was just thinking of calling you."

Payton found a pencil and scribbled directions to MaryAnn's house. "See you in a bit."

The house was a respectable ranch in a middle-class neighborhood. The houses were close together, even more so than in Payton's neighborhood but all were well kept, with newish cars in the yards. The porch light was on and before Payton reached the top step, MaryAnn opened the door. She wore jeans, a baggy pink t-shirt and a welcoming smile.

"I'm really glad you called. I was feeling a little down."

"I brought refreshments." She brandished a bottle of merlot and followed MaryAnn into a well-furnished home. It was clean and smelled of furniture polish.

MaryAnn handed her a corkscrew and opened cabinet doors. "I know there are wine glasses here somewhere."

"It doesn't matter," Payton said, twisting the opener into the cork.

MaryAnn finally gave up and took two tumblers from the dish drainer.

"Did you make the cake?" Payton pointed to a plastic wrapped plate on the counter.

"No. And I have no idea where it came from. Someone at the restaurant must've made it for Sean."

"Why didn't you eat it?"

"I'm deathly allergic to chocolate. You can have it if you want."

Payton picked up the plate and peered at it closely. Two layers, moist, creamy looking frosting. Suddenly she wished she could bake, to turn out something this luscious looking. She pulled back the plastic wrap, dipped her finger in the frosting and put it in her mouth. "Oooh, this is fabulous."

"Eat it. I'm just going to end up throwing it away. Hold on, I'll get you a fork."

Payton pulled the plastic down and put the plate on the counter. "Maybe later. I want some of that wine first. I want it so badly I'm not even letting the bottle breathe first." She poured both glasses full. Fruity and smooth, it flowed like mercury from a thermometer.

Claire's words about the world's best chocolate cake echoed inside her. Maybe this had been what she'd been referring to. Payton dearly wanted to eat that cake but felt a little awkward with MaryAnn not having something herself.

They carried the glasses down the hall. MaryAnn stopped at the master bedroom. "This was Sean's room."

The room was definitely a man's domain. The bedding, crumpled in the middle of the king-sized bed was red and green plaid. The walls were painted white; a sportsman's border had been applied near the ceiling. Two dressers, one with a mirror and one tallboy were good quality. A photo of Sean and MaryAnn on their wedding day sat atop the tall dresser. She'd worn a simple blue pantsuit and held a bunch of miniature white roses. Her face was innocent and unmarked. Payton picked it up. "When were you married?"

"April fifth. It was seven years ago. I was sixteen."

A million questions swirled inside Payton's head, but she didn't ask them. The time wasn't right. A framed photograph over the bed caught her eye. It was of a seaside cottage, its weather-beaten shingles gray, the roof spotted with white bird droppings. Water pounded the marsh grass strewn shore where a small boy, obviously Sean, in a red bathing suit splashed in the gray/green surf.

MaryAnn climbed on the bed and took down the photo. "Sean's parents used to rent a cottage on Cape Cod." She gazed at it tenderly for a moment and then hung it back on the wall.

MaryAnn had been cleaning out Sean's things. In one corner squatted a large box. It was half full of folded clothing, probably destined for the thrift shop. Payton pictured MaryAnn running her hands over each item, recalling when they'd bought it, or what memories each evoked. She'd have tears coursing down her cheeks. Payton knew exactly how it felt.

"If this is too much for you, I can do it. You can work in another room."

"I'm okay. If you could do the dresser and his personal things, that would help the most." MaryAnn hauled a cardboard box out of the closet. "I'll go through this one. I'm thinking we put the stuff in three cartons; that one for the thrift shop, this one is for Sean's aunt in Amarillo and the one near the doorway for the trash man."

"Does Sean have any other relatives?"

"Only Elaine. She's his mother's older sister."

"Why didn't she come to the memorial service?"

"She's an invalid."

Payton opened the bottom drawer. "I assume you want the jewelry and knickknacks in her box?"

"Right." MaryAnn's voice sounded muffled. Payton turned to see her nearly upside down in a large cardboard container.

Payton set to work pulling the contents out of the drawer. It was mostly sweatpants and shirts, all in good condition and smelling like Polo cologne. She dropped them into the thrift shop box. "He sure had a lot of sweat clothes."

"He jogged most every day and I'm not very good at doing laundry."

They worked in silence for a long time, Payton slogging her way through Sean's summer clothes and dress shirts and MaryAnn starting on one she dragged from the depths of the walk-in closet.

It gave Payton a creepy feeling to be sorting through Sean's things, a man she not only disliked, but one whose bloated face kept appearing before her. The next drawer held his underwear. Without noticing anything other than they were mostly all new, she picked them up in two handfuls and flung them in the trash.

She hadn't had to do this with Cameron's things. In a heavy funk, she'd moved from the penthouse to a hotel. Months later, when she finally emerged from her walking coma, the penthouse had been cleared, furniture placed in storage and the apartment put on the market.

MaryAnn held a worn leather jacket. Her eyes brimmed with tears. "He wore this on our first date."

When MaryAnn dissolved into great heaving sobs, Payton wrested the garment from her fingers and heaved it in the trash. As it left her fingers, something solid in the pocket made her retrieve it and dig deep. She came out with a beautiful silver money clip. MaryAnn was still sobbing, so rather than ask about it, she laid it on the dresser in front of their wedding picture.

She sat beside MaryAnn on the floor and wrapped her in a hug. Payton rocked her gently. The digital clock beside the bed clicked around to 9:10. Payton had to blink to bring the numbers into focus and realized she too was crying. Not for the death of an inconsiderate man. Not for the loss of a human being, but for the town who'd felt its reverberations to its very soul.

After a while, MaryAnn sniffled, disentangled herself and plucked two tissues from the box on the bedside table. Payton went to refill their glasses. She put the almost empty bottle on the counter and picked up the plate of chocolate cake. Payton pulled up the edge of the plastic and scooped two fingers-full of the delicious frosting. She opened a drawer and fumbled out a fork.

"Payton," MaryAnn called, "come see what I found."

MaryAnn still sat in the middle of the room, but instead of crumpled tissues, she now held a gray metal box. "Any idea what this is? It was in with the things the cops returned."

Payton swished her tongue around her teeth, savoring the chocolate taste and really wanting to run back to the kitchen. She pushed aside a pair of brass bookends and put the glasses on the dresser. "It looks like one of those fireproof boxes. You said the police already saw this? Where's the key?"

"I think I remember them asking for one, but I didn't know anything about it."

"Did they find one?"

"I guess so. Or else they would have broken into it, right?"

"Possibly."

MaryAnn retrieved her glass and took a long drink, then smacked her lips. "Good." She giggled. "When I was a kid, we had wine with every meal."

Payton set the box atop the mess on the dresser. She picked up her drink and sat on the bed. "Where are you from?"

"San Luis Potosi, a small city near Mexico City."

"You don't look Mexican."

"My mother was Mexican. My father was a salesman for a chemical company."

Payton giggled. "What nationality is that?"

MaryAnn held her laugh in with her free hand. "I think he was French. My mother met him when he was there on one of his trips. For twelve years, he came twice a year. I was born in the sixth year." She grinned. "I have three brothers. One older, two younger. And who knows, by now there might be six or seven more."

"Why did you leave Mexico?"

MaryAnn took a long fortifying drink. Her eyes had begun to look a bit glassy. "Papa was like a god to me. I wanted to go live with him. To be able to live in *América*! It was a dream. So when I turned sixteen, I sneaked across the border and hitchhiked north. In New York I got a bus to Watertown where he lived. I walked from the bus station to his house in the rain. I must have looked like a drowned rat when I knocked on his door. *La señora* opened it. She was *muy hermosa*, very pretty, with blonde hair and blue eyes. I'd never seen *los ojos* like hers." MaryAnn kept lapsing into her native tongue. She leaned back against the closet door and closed her eyes. "I asked her for mi padre and she stared at me like I was crazy."

"Was he there?" Payton asked.

"Ha! No, the woman was his *Américana* wife. There were toys and bikes all over the yard." MaryAnn gave a snort. "We didn't have any bikes."

"I'm sorry."

"It was a long time ago."

"You don't have an accent."

"Sean helped me get rid of it."

"How did you end up in Sackets Harbor?"

"I ran from that woman, and into the street. Sean almost hit me with his car." She shrugged and said, "The rest is *l'historia*," with a finality that told Payton it really wasn't. MaryAnn wiped her eyes and got up. "I need some more of this stuff."

Payton followed her to the kitchen where she splashed the rest of the wine into Payton's glass. Then she fished under a cabinet and came out with a large bottle of Seagram's. MaryAnn smiled and giggled. "It's not like what you brought, but it'll work."

She poured her glass three quarters full of the amber liquid. They went back to the bedroom and sat on the bed. Payton leaned against the headboard sipping her wine. She giggled, spotting an ugly painting of a man in uniform on the far wall. "Where have I seen him before?"

MaryAnn looked up and snickered too. "Amanda has one in the marina."

Payton got up to look more closely at it. She trailed her

fingertips across the rough-napped paint. The signature in the lower right hand corner said *Henry Woodward*. Payton didn't know much about art, but it looked genuine. "Do you know anything about this?"

"Sean had it hanging over the fireplace until last year. Then he moved it in here. I was really glad. It's awful."

"Do you mind if I ask why you stayed with him so long?"

MaryAnn sighed and looked into her glass. "*Sería largo de contar.*" She sighed again and closed her eyes. After a minute, she said, "He was really a sad little boy inside. He did a lot for me. I owed him." MaryAnn opened her. "Sean married me so I wouldn't be deported. I am illegal."

For a fleeting moment, Sean Adams climbed in Payton's esteem. He'd done something nice by offering to marry MaryAnn. There didn't seem to have been anything in it for him. Nothing except the companionship of a hardworking woman. Theirs hadn't been a conventional marriage. The relationship hadn't turned into one of love and respect as some did under these circumstances. Sean had to have been disappointed in their union. MaryAnn admitted to being a poor housekeeper and cook, both things a perfectionist like Sean would demand. This must have frustrated him, and in response he'd abused her both physically and mentally. Suddenly Payton understood why MaryAnn was so accepting of his affairs, and that spark of respect she'd felt for him took a nosedive. He'd probably told her "that's what Americans do." Her biological father was a perfect example.

Was it possible she'd had enough and decided to kill him? What were the deportation laws in these situations?

Payton put down her glass and went back to work. There was only one drawer left, and it slid open without a sound: ties, hankies, watchcases, coins and a confusion of other things. Payton dropped the ties into the thrift shop box. She plucked up the pile of both white and colored handkerchiefs and was about to toss it too, but felt something solid. Buried between the layers was Sean's wallet. She rolled it over a few times: average-quality leather in a deep brown color, tri-fold style, worn at the edges.

Payton turned intending to show it to MaryAnn. The girl's head lolled to one side and she snored lightly. The glass tipped in her hand and some of the liquid sloshed on her jeans. Payton took the glass and set it on the bedside table. Then she opened the wallet. License, credit cards…all current. What man leaves his home without his identification?

She picked up the metal box and Sean's wallet and turned off the bedroom light.

Thirty-Five

In the living room, Payton turned on a table lamp and sat in a deep leather recliner in a beautiful shade of mahogany. A man's chair, she knew because a matching one in cranberry corduroy sat nearby. Knowing it had been Sean's chair disturbed Payton. She picked up the items and went to sit in the other chair. She opened the wallet first. Sean's license with a pretty good picture of him. He would turn twenty-eight on September 12th. He had three credit cards, a photo of MaryAnn, $72, and a dog-eared social security card. She put the things back in the wallet and laid it aside.

Payton slid the metal box onto her lap. Where would Sean keep a key? She went to the kitchen. Lots of people kept keys on a rack near the door. Not so with Sean. Where would he keep a key he rarely used? In his dresser, most likely, but she'd cleaned out every drawer and the only key had been to an automobile Sean had sold back in '97. MaryAnn had suffered a fit of giggles relating stories of the car's undependability.

Payton sipped and thought, but nothing occurred to her. She tiptoed down the narrow hallway. MaryAnn had turned onto her side. Payton pulled the comforter around her shoulders and as she turned to leave, her eyes fastened on the bedside table, one on each side of the bed, each with a drawer at the top.

She opened the nearest one, but besides three packages of condoms and another box of tissues, it was empty. The other table yielded a jackpot, the tiny gold key on a length of household string. Payton managed to stifle a whoop of elation.

Back in the living room, in the corduroy chair, with the box in her lap, Payton slid the key into the tiny lock. She twisted it.

"Man, I guess I fell asleep," said a voice in front of her.

Payton flew out of the chair, the box tumbling to the floor. "Oh jeez, you scared me." She laughed. The box lay on its side, the tiny key glinting in the light of the 60-watt bulb. Payton picked up the box.

"What're you doing?" MaryAnn asked.

"Trying to figure out what's inside." As Payton handed MaryAnn the box, she palmed the key. She wasn't sure why, but it was too late to turn back now.

"There should be another key, wouldn't you think?" She teetered in place for a moment. "I suppose it could be on his regular key chain." She shook the box beside her head. "What do you suppose is in here?"

"It sounded like paper to me. If I had one I'd put my will, the deed to my house, birth certificate, insurance forms, anything I didn't want lost or burned. If my house caught on fire I could just grab the box and run. Are you all right?"

"Yeah." She rolled vague eyes in Payton's direction. She flopped into the leather recliner. "For more than two years I've imagined some angry husband running Sean off the road. Or somebody shooting him, trying to rob the restaurant. And I wasn't sad. You know?"

Payton got up. "Come on. It's time for bed."

MaryAnn allowed Payton to lead her to the second bedroom, still clutching the metal box. So this was MaryAnn's room, all pink. The bed was neatly made; a collection of colorful stuffed animals obscured the surface. The only furniture was a dresser and a wood rocking chair. No pictures or paintings. No knickknacks. Just a few cheap cosmetics and a hairbrush on the dresser.

"The police stuck a Q-tip in my mouth," MaryAnn mumbled.

Payton brushed the animals to the floor and pulled down the chenille spread.

"I've been sleeping in Sean's room," she said, which explained the mussed bed in the other room.

"Sit."

MaryAnn obeyed, and Payton removed her shoes and socks. MaryAnn lay down, still gripping the box. Payton attempted to slip it away, but MaryAnn held tight. Payton tucked the covers around her friend and shut off the light.

"Leave the door open, please."

Payton dropped the small key and Sean's wallet in her jacket pocket and headed for home. What was in that box? Maybe she was being overly suspicious, but something told Payton the contents of that box were very important to someone in Sackets Harbor. Maybe important enough to kill for.

Sergeant Espinoza was sitting on Payton's stoop when she arrived home at 2:10 a.m. She spotted him immediately even though she'd forgotten to leave the porch light on. She almost decided to go in through the garage entrance and leave him sitting there but took her time getting out of the car instead. He rose as she approached.

"Gee, if I'd known you'd wait up, Mom, I'd have called."

Espinoza followed, wordless, into the house. She dropped her purse on the floor beside her desk, took off her jacket, and started to toss it across the back of the loveseat. Suddenly she remembered Sean's wallet and key and hung the jacket in the closet.

"You know, Sergeant, you're here so often my neighbors are going to think we're having an affair. What do you want this time?"

"We discovered the identity of the poison that killed Mr. Adams and Mr. Simpson. Thanks to your research and kind plant donations, the toxicologist was able to match up the plant DNA with the residue found in the men's systems."

"Glad I could be of help. Couldn't you have called to tell me this—in the morning?"

"Could have. But then I wouldn't have seen the surprise on your face when you came home at the crack of dawn."

"You didn't tell me not to leave town. And it's not the crack of dawn."

"How is Ms. Adams by the way?"

Silent, she poured two cups of leftover coffee and popped them into the microwave. She pushed the creamer and sugar bowl to him when she was finished preparing her own. "MaryAnn is fine."

He took a sip, and then another without putting the cup down. "The poison was from the monkshood plant. It didn't come from medicine. And the chemists are fairly sure the serum didn't come from a wild plant."

"Wild?"

"Yes, the plant is in-indigenous to the area."

"Gotta watch those big words, Sergeant," she said, not able to let his verbal hesitation pass. "How can they tell it wasn't a wild plant?"

He shrugged. "Different plant genetics or something."

"So, you've convinced yourself the murder-plant came from my shop."

"There's only one other nursery in a thirty mile radius that sells them. Chances are it came from here. Now I need a more detailed list as to who bought them from you."

"Couldn't this have waited till morning?" she asked wearily.

"It is morning." He wiped his mouth with the back of his hand. "The trail grows colder by the minute."

"And this should worry me why?"

"The thought of a murderer in your midst should worry you, Miss Winters. Once a person has killed, they often do it again."

"So, have you finally eliminated me from the suspect list?"

"No."

"Then you'd better watch how you phrase your comments, you said 'he.' And as far as a murderer in my midst, you know what? It bothered me at first but then I realized that, even though Sean Adams wasn't a Jeffrey Dahmer, he was a thoroughly rotten human being, and—don't look at me that way—I happen to think whoever killed him, did the town a favor. "

"Can we get to it? I'd like to catch a few hours sleep before daybreak."

It was obvious the sergeant wasn't used to going without sleep. She suddenly felt a bit superior, happy that she was keeping him from the pursuit of physical comfort. She couldn't help asking, "Does your wife wait up for you?"

"She used to, and be so anxious by the time I straggled in, she started taking sleeping pills whenever I'm on a case." He withdrew the ubiquitous notebook from his breast pocket and then looked up, his dark eyes edged in the red of exhaustion. "Ms. Featherstone has a monkshood. Did she purchase it from you?"

Payton nodded.

"And Ms. March?"

Another nod.

"Miss Bastian?"

"Yes."

"Anyone else?"

"Helen Mortenson." Payton ran a hand through her hair. "I think that's all. The records are at the shop."

"Which of the women would you think the most likely to—"

"Oh no! I'm not going to rat out one of my friends."

"I'm just asking your opinion. I assume since you're investigating things yourself—which, in a moment I'm going to warn you against—that you've formed an opinion."

She held up her hand. "Stop now. One, I'm not going to share my thoughts. They're my friends and my opinions are just that, opinions. Two, as for investigating on my own, I'm only asking the questions you probably already asked. And three—"

"What questions did you ask Ms. Adams?"

Payton's slow smile seemed to disturb the sergeant, his lips tightened, but for only a second. "It's none of your business, and you won't believe me, but I went to her house to help her clean out Sean's things. She's my friend."

"What did you talk about?"

"Childhoods, marriages, school. Girl talk."

"Did she give any indication that she wanted her husband dead?"

"No. Sergeant, I'm sure she and most other people in town have already told you about MaryAnn and Sean's relationship. I have nothing new to add. Now, I'd really appreciate it if you go so I can get to bed."

"No insomnia tonight?"

"I don't know yet." Payton took her still full cup to the sink.

The sergeant got up too and pushed his chair under the table. "Heard from Mr. Green?"

"No." She didn't say she was really beginning to worry. "Was Frank Simpson's death an accident?"

He gave a small nod.

"How was the poison administered?"

"Can't you guess?"

"Well, the newspaper said there was nothing toxic in their stomachs so they obviously didn't eat it. I can only guess since they were the only two on the boat, it wasn't injected, and since they were in open air, it wasn't gas." She stopped as an idea flickered inside her head. "Maybe it could have been gas. Maybe it was in the cabin below." Then she shook her head. "No, can't be. They were racing, there wouldn't be any time, or need, for them to go below. So the poison had to be absorbed through the skin."

A look of admiration appeared on Espinoza's once-again fatherly countenance. "Someone made a paste and painted it on the ropes. The idea was obviously for it to come off on Sean's hands when he raised the sails."

"Was it on all the ropes?"

"Yes." He'd begun walking to the front door but stopped and came back. "What are you thinking?"

"The person who did this wasn't a sailor. The members of the yacht club would know exactly which lines Sean manned during a race. We never changed positions. You get proficient at one job and stay there. See what I mean?" Payton could almost hear him rubbing his mental hands together in anticipation as he flipped the notebook shut, locked it securely behind that small round button, and left her house. This was a man who wouldn't get any sleep at all tonight. The thought made her grin.

Across the street, Aden's house was black. Payton went to

the closet and switched Sean's wallet and key to the pocket of her winter coat hanging at the far left. She pulled the dry cleaners' plastic down and smoothed the creases. She put on the jacket and went outdoors, walking confidently, in case any other insomniacs lived in her neighborhood, across the street and onto Aden's front porch. Most people kept spare keys somewhere near the door. Aden didn't seem like the type to do this, but he also hadn't seemed like the sort to run away from a murder investigation.

Payton searched above the door and under the mat, anywhere she could think where someone might hide a key. She even checked the rocks in the garden, having seen artificial stones with crevices for such things. Nothing. She stood in the shadow of the maple at the street and eyed the house.

Where might he hide a key? She traipsed through the dewy grass around the house. Not over the door. Not under the mat. Not under either of the enormous geranium planters. Not under the stone to the right of the steps. But tucked into the slot in the fake left hand rock was Aden's house key.

The door made the tiniest click as Payton slipped inside. The place smelled faintly of vanilla. The officers had left a mess. Not the sort of mess that occurred during a home invasion, but just a disruption of neatness. For example, the books on the shelves of the entertainment center were off kilter, the sofa pillows were lopsided. What she expected to find here that the cops hadn't, she had no idea.

Standing in Aden's bedroom, she suddenly felt very stupid. She had no reason to suspect Aden of anything, least of all murdering Sean Adams. Sean's pestering her was her problem alone. Aden hadn't cared enough to defend her honor. He didn't care enough to stay around and make sure none of his friends were accused of murders they didn't commit. Payton stomped a sneakered foot and stormed from the house. It wasn't until she got back inside her front door that she realized she still had his house key in her hand. She peered at it lying innocently in the palm of her hand and then flung it against the wall.

Thirty-Six

The key hit with a tiny ping and bounced off the hardwood floor. Payton dropped on the sofa and cried until she felt staggered by exhaustion. All energy drained, she couldn't even raise her head from the cushion. As the hall clock struck 9 a.m., even the realization she would be late opening her shop didn't produce enough adrenaline to do more than wipe hair from her face. Strands of it clung to wet cheeks and eyelashes. One strand had even found its way into her mouth. She felt the tickle of it in her throat and plucked it away. Still she couldn't move from the sofa. She didn't care about the shop. She didn't even care which friend was a murderer.

She also didn't care that someone was banging on the sliders. But as the sound grew louder, Payton realized whoever was outside could see her lying there, arms outstretched, legs crunched up to fit her height into the small space. If she didn't move, whoever relentlessly pounded on the double-glazed glass would eventually feel the need to break in. So Payton moved, first her right arm, to push the hair from her face, then the left, pins and needles striking like barbs as she raised it from its dangling position off the edge. The tingling burst into her brain, shocking her awake.

Helen stood with her nose pressed to the glass, hands cupped around her face giving it a ghoulish look that in the dark might have startled Payton. But right now, she was incapable of feeling anything more than simple annoyance at being disturbed. She inched off the couch, muscles and nerves screaming in indignation. Helen lowered her arms as Payton staggered to the door and unlocked it. She didn't open the door, just went back to the couch, sitting instead of lying down.

"Dear, do you know what time it is?"

Payton's brain told her to say it was nine o'clock. So she did.

"Are you going to open your store?"

"No."

Helen joggled Payton's shoulder. She rubbed the spot and stood up. "No," she said more succinctly than before. "I didn't forget. I just..." Payton started for the stairs, and a shower. Late or not, she needed the bracing hot needles to bring her senses to life. She turned. "Did you come for something in particular?"

"No dear. I didn't see you leave and wondered if you'd overslept. Give me your keys. I'll go down and man the ship so you don't have to hurry."

Payton's brain wasn't functioning well enough to tell her where she'd left the keys. Helen found Payton's handbag and brought it to her. Payton fumbled around inside.

"Are you sure you're all right, dear?"

"I had a rough night." Payton came up with something jingly and handed it to Helen. "Thank you, you're a lifesaver."

"What kind?"

"Peppermint," Payton muttered and shuffled upstairs, still wearing her wet sneakers.

An hour and a half later, Payton sat on the stool behind the counter in the shop. She'd absorbed two cups of coffee—which Helen had been thoughtful enough to make—and sent Helen on her way, thanking her several times for her kindness, and somehow managing not to give a plausible explanation for her behavior. Helen knew of Payton's insomnia and probably assumed it finally caught up with her. That was partly it, but at Aden's, she'd had a re-realization of where she stood in the grand scheme of the world. It was a sobering thought to know that if you disappeared from the earth, few people would notice.

Payton thumbed through the phone book and dialed Claire's number. "Hi, it's Payton. I wondered if you'd like to get together for lunch today. MaryAnn's due here at one, want to meet me here? We can go to the Galley." Payton set down the phone and laughed. If MaryAnn was in any condition to show up. Well, if she didn't, she and Claire would just order in.

The sky threatened rain. The streets were quiet. Even the tourists seemed to be sleeping late. Payton wondered if the sergeant finally got to sleep, or if visions of Sackets Harbor's women carrying buckets loaded with monkshood paste down to the dock kept him awake.

Why hadn't the investigation resulted in MaryAnn's past coming to light? Being illegal, she couldn't have a birth certificate, social security card or even a driver's license. That explained her not owning a car. It wasn't because she couldn't afford one, as she'd said.

MaryAnn did arrive, and on time. She looked bright and ready to face the day.

"How come you look so good?" Payton asked.

"Don't know."

"Question: why didn't the cops arrest you for being illegal?"

MaryAnn looked at Payton for several seconds, her dark eyes vacant, as though she'd forgotten she'd divulged her deepest secret. She sighed. "About six months after we got married, Sean paid a guy to make me all the official papers. As far as the government is concerned, I am legal."

So MaryAnn really did owe him. Payton understood the gratitude of such a situation, but couldn't believe MaryAnn would swallow every last ounce of her pride to pay back a man who cheated, lied and stole.

"When I got home that sergeant was waiting. They figured out how the poison was given to Sean. It was made into a paste and painted it on the rigging lines. When the ropes went through Sean and Frank's hands, the poison got onto their skin."

MaryAnn paled.

"It's awful isn't it?" Payton said.

"They must have suffered." She rose and shook herself like a dog coming out of the lake. "You should go home and rest."

"Can't. Claire and I are going for lunch. I will fix my face though."

When Payton returned, Claire and MaryAnn were seated in the patio area. Claire stood up, looking as disheveled as Payton felt.

"We'll be back soon."

"Have fun."

They stepped out onto the sidewalk. Sergeant Espinoza's car was parked in front of Sean's cafe. No one was in sight. Payton picked up her pace.

"You still want to go to the Galley?"

"Sure. Did you remember there's a race today?" Claire asked.

"God, I don't feel like sailing today."

"Don't then."

They found a table near the window where they could see the street.

"Tell me about your plan to reopen Sean's café."

"I've been doing a lot of research, looking for French recipes and all that."

"Maybe he left some cookbooks in the restaurant."

"Helen said she didn't find any when she cleaned out the place."

"I didn't see any at his house either. Ask MaryAnn when we get back to the shop. Maybe she knows where they are. Did you try a search on the Internet?"

"I don't have a computer. Well, I do, but it's broken. I'm so excited about this."

Broken? It was working a couple of nights ago.

"I'm hoping to open the first of August. I, er, gave the library director my notice."

"Claire, are you sure this is what you want to do?"

"You aren't going to try and talk me out of it too, are you?"

"No, of course not. I'm just worried you're getting in over your head."

"And at my age…"

"I didn't say that."

"Mamie did. She said I should be thinking about retiring and not bogging myself down with a career that's known for its pressures and—oh, Payton, it is the right thing to do, isn't it?"

"Only you would know that. I'm just worried about your health. Since Sean's death, you've been different."

Claire said softly, "We've all been different. I think someone should carry on for Sean. We owe him that."

Payton didn't think any of them—most of all MaryAnn—owed him anything. But Claire was right about one thing, Sean's death had changed them all. Payton ordered a chef's salad, realizing she hadn't eaten since stealing the frosting off MaryAnn's cake last night.

"What are you laughing about?" Claire asked.

"I was just remembering the last thing I ate. I was at MaryAnn's helping clear out Sean's things. There was this slice of chocolate cake on the counter. I stole some of the frosting. Claire, I swear it was the best frosting I've ever had."

Claire rocketed to her feet and raced from the restaurant. Payton stood up and groped in her purse. She tossed some bills on the table but Claire was already running up the sidewalk. By the time Payton made it to the curb, she'd climbed into her car and sped away, squealing the tires. Payton went back inside and asked the waitress for the meals to go.

"Well, that's about the wildest thing I've ever heard," MaryAnn said between bites of Claire's chicken salad.

The sergeant came out of Mamie's gallery then drove two hundred feet down Main Street and turned into Sylvie's parking lot. Payton let out the breath she'd been holding because she'd just figured out what Espinoza was doing—following up on the leads she'd given him in the wee hours of the morning. The thought gave her a heavy feeling, and Payton pushed the half eaten lunch away. "Will you be all right for a while? I think I'll go for a walk."

"Sure. While you were gone earlier, I thought I'd learn a little more about plants, but I couldn't find the book. Did you take it home?"

"The cops have it. Anything you can't find around here, they probably have." Payton donned her raincoat, turned left out of the store and walked down the hill. Sergeant Espinoza was still at Sylvie's. Rain had begun, first as a gentle mist as she passed Sylvie's real estate office. It became heavier as she passed the Information office. Payton pulled up her hood and ducked her face to the wind that had picked up off the harbor. As she crossed the battlefield, rain pummeled the treetops above, rattling the new leaves and sending some to earth, fluttering and dipping like monarch butterflies in July.

She stood on the stonewall, at the spot where *MaryAnn* ran aground. Directly below, etched into the man-made rock barrier, was a permanent reminder of the incident. Maybe someday the white paint would fade, but the disruption to the evenly stacked stones would remain. The water washed over Payton's memory—Sean's face, paralyzed from the effects of the poison, rose up, pushed on the waves. The vision was so real she couldn't stop herself from flinching away. This time Payton didn't try to stop the images. Maybe if they played themselves out, she'd be able to rid herself of the nightmares. That's what her analyst had told her. "Face the trouble head on. Let the memory come, over and over so that your mind gets used to it. Become familiar with the images, like a coroner steels himself against death. That's what you've got to do with Cameron. Let him come to you."

Unable to face the pain and horrific waste of a wonderful human being, Payton had been unable to do this. But she wasn't emotionally involved with Sean. The images didn't propel her into the same emotional state as Cameron's. So she stood atop the wall with her eyes closed. And let it come: *MaryAnn* off course. Sean and Frank toppling into the water. Her stiff form poised on *Zephyr's* starboard rail. As she leaped a swell pushed *MaryAnn* up. She missed the deck and went under. And didn't come up. Not for a long time. When she did, the sight of her own bloated face made Payton gasp.

Finally she turned and headed back up the hill, feeling

rejuvenated and determined to find Sean and Franks' murderer.

Payton walked home, grateful not to see a police car waiting. It had stopped raining, but the clouds remained. She hung her raincoat in the closet, giving a pat of reassurance to Sean's wallet inside the tan cashmere winter coat. Checking that neither Mamie nor any customer was in sight, she pulled up the crinkly cleaners' bag, slipped out the wallet and took it to her office.

The leather creaked as it unfolded. She took out his license and social security card and set them on the desk. The photo of MaryAnn was the square Polaroid type with wide white border and age-crackled face. It must have been taken soon after their wedding, maybe on their honeymoon; the background was some sort of carnival. In the picture MaryAnn was youthful, at ease, without the tense lines around her mouth or the extra pounds she wore today.

The credit cards, Visa, Mastercard and Exxon gasoline, were in Sean's name. None appeared too well used, no scratches on the laminated surfaces, not even a signature on the gas card. There were two twenties, three tens and two ones. Payton poked into the wallet's nooks and crannies but found nothing besides a 1905 dime tucked under a flap.

The social security card must have been the original; the heavy-weight paper was dirty and worn. He hadn't bothered to laminate it. His assigned number was 210-72-2891. She leaned back in her chair. Something she'd read recently nagged at her. Something about social security numbers being issued in a particular order. Each state had a specific code. On the computer, she located a Website telling her that the first three of Sean's social security numbers, 210, originated in the state of Pennsylvania, which brought a frown. She'd assumed he was born right here in Sackets Harbor, which would make the first numbers somewhere between 050 and 134.

Things were certainly getting interesting.

Thirty-Seven

Most of the gang already gathered under the white tent in the marina parking lot. But something was wrong; the voices were too loud, too forced. Payton nearly turned in her tracks and ran back up the hill. Conflict she didn't need today, especially when it was delivered by none other than Felicia Featherstone. She stood out from them a bit. Wearing a red top and creased white capris, she pointed a red-lacquered fingernail at the group. "Don't tell me you're not all wondering what she's doing here in Sackets Harbor—"

"Felicia, we expect this sort of behavior from Sylvie," Helen interrupted, "certainly not from you."

Felicia was undaunted. "She doesn't fit in with this small-town atmosphere—"

"Any more than you."

Felicia sputtered a little but kept on. "Didn't you see the way they acted around each other? You can bet there was something going on." Still, no one did more than stand open-mouthed. "Don't any of you think it's at all strange that she no sooner moves to town and Sean dies?"

"Sean was a worm," Amanda said. "He was bound to be killed sooner or later."

They all spotted Payton about the same time. Most had the grace to blush or look away. She didn't wait for their embarrassed explanations. She couldn't *grin and bear it* as Granny used to recommend when her brothers taunted her. She turned and ran up the hill, past her store. *This little piggy went to market. This little piggy ran all the way home.*

Payton startled Mamie and a customer as she burst in the front door. "I'm not here," was all she said. She raced upstairs and shut herself in the bedroom. She didn't fling herself on the bed as she used to back in childhood Virginia. She opened the sliders and went out on the deck, shutting the door to close out sounds of life from below. Face still hot with betrayal, she leaned her elbows on the railing and lowered her head. The cool breeze did nothing to alleviate the pain. She'd thought Felicia had accepted her as one of them. They hadn't become friends as such. There was that wall they'd each built around themselves.

Mamie wasn't a big enough bouncer to keep the determined Helen away. She came out on the deck as if she owned it, sidled next to Payton and put arm around her waist.

"How can she think I killed Sean?"

"She doesn't…not really," Helen replied. "The police were at her house for a long time yesterday. Brighton walked in while they were discussing *Sunset* and there was a huge row. She's feeling a mite overwrought. You should have stayed around to see how Edward blasted her. Brought waves of delight to these old bones, I can tell you that."

Payton spun around, realized her knees were wobbly and leaned against the rail. Helen's face looked flushed. "Felicia was in tears when I left."

Payton went back to looking at the harbor, now alight with afternoon sunshine. Where had the storm clouds gone? Then she laughed. "I was wondering where the storm clouds went. Then I realized I swallowed them."

Helen laughed too, and all at once they were giggling, unable to catch their breaths. Tears rolled down Payton's cheeks, her breath came in staccato bursts. "How come no one's racing?" she finally managed to ask.

Helen managed a semblance of seriousness. "I don't know."

There wasn't much else to say. They leaned elbows on the

railing, watching for activity in the harbor. It wasn't hard to convince Helen to go home; the woman was itchy for more gossip.

Payton tiptoed down to her office. Mamie tapped timidly on the door to say that Amanda had arrived. One by one, the rest of the Sackets Harbor Yacht Club members came—all but Felicia—voicing regret for what happened. Payton half-heartedly accepted all apologies.

Once the gallery closed, Payton sat in her love seat with a glass of chardonnay and suddenly couldn't stop thinking about Sean's social security number. What difference did it make where he was born?

She dialed Helen's number.

"Can I bring you something to eat, dear?"

"No thanks, Helen. I've eaten," Payton lied. "What do you remember about Sean's birth?"

"Not much, really. In those days, Carter and I were struggling financially. He worked for a Watertown construction company, and I worked for an attorney in Watertown. Most nights I brought work home and there wasn't time for socializing. The point is, it seemed as though all of a sudden Edna had herself a baby. Payton, I honestly don't remember the woman being pregnant."

"Uh-huh," was all Payton could think to say. Her mind was going a million miles an hour.

"Is this important?"

"I don't know. It might be. Thanks." Payton hung up.

She was finishing bookwork when the doorbell rang. She dragged herself to the hallway, hoping it wasn't Felicia. A confrontation with her just wouldn't work right now. But Sylvie stood on the stoop, cuddling a longhaired white kitten. As soon as Payton's eyes spotted the little feline, Sylvie stuffed it into her arms. "I thought you might need a friend."

Payton stifled a groan of dismay. What was she going to do with a kitten? Its untroubled blue eyes gazed out beneath long silky whiskers. The kitten's tiny body trembled with its purrs and Payton couldn't help clutching it to her chest. "What's his name?"

"*She* doesn't have one yet." Payton stepped back to invite Sylvie in but she waggled a finger. "I'll be right back, I have to get something in the car."

"I hope it's not another cat." Payton laughed, meaning it.

Sylvie returned, dropping a box on the hall floor. "It's a litter box and food."

"Gee, Sylvie, I really can't keep a kitten."

"Why not?"

How could she say, I just don't want the responsibility, and make it sound like she wasn't completely heartless? "Would you like a glass of sherry?"

"Love one."

They went to the kitchen. She handed the kitten to Sylvie and got glasses from the cabinet. Settled in chairs on the patio, the two women and the kitten sat in companionable silence watching the lights twinkling on the bay.

"Sylvie, do you remember when Sean was born?"

"Not really, why?"

"Helen said she never knew Edna was pregnant. I would think someone—especially someone like Edna, who'd tried so hard to have a baby—would be so excited they couldn't keep it quiet."

"You would think so." Sylvie sipped the sherry.

"I keep having this unsettled feeling, like there's something I've missed."

"Can I help?" When Payton didn't respond, she added, "You did ask for my help."

"Two things keep sticking in my head, Sean's birth and the three paintings."

"Three paintings?"

"Felicia's *Sunset.* Amanda's *Commodore.* And yesterday I found an identical Commodore in Sean's house."

Sylvie put a finger to her pursed lips. "What's wrong with that?"

"That's the problem. I haven't the slightest idea."

Sylvie's sharp laugh startled the kitten who stood up in

Payton's lap. After a minute, it kneaded her thigh a few times, then lay back down.

"Here's the question," Payton said. "Why are there are two Commodores?"

Sylvie's lips puckered a little more. "He was a historical figure in town. Why couldn't there be two?"

"I looked at them closely. They're just about identical."

"You're saying it's not likely an artist would paint the exact same painting twice."

Payton gave a slow noncommittal nod.

"Want me to do some research?"

"Sure. That would be helpful."

After Sylvie left, Payton prepared the kitten's litter box and put it in the laundry room off the kitchen. She set bowls of food and water on the kitchen floor, put the kitten down so it could explore and went to her office. Had inviting Sylvie's help been the right thing to do? Time would tell.

Payton dialed Aden's cell phone and received the same "the number is out of service" message. She dialed another number. This was answered on the second ring. She said, "Hi, it's Payton." The kitten padded into the room. "I was wondering if you'd like to take me out to dinner tomorrow night... Good, I'll see you then. Good night."

Thirty-Eight

As Payton's office clock finished striking 9 a.m., she dialed Pennsylvania's Hall of Records. Five phone calls and 40 minutes later, she hung up satisfied but thoroughly confused. Sean Stephen Adams was born at 4:12 a.m. on September 12, 1978, in Scranton, Pennsylvania to Edna and Rodney Adams.

Why would anyone travel over 200 miles to have a baby when there was a perfectly good hospital less than 10 miles away? Payton leaned back in the chair and tapped the pencil on her blotter. It didn't make sense. A woman who's due date is upon her doesn't travel unless it's an emergency. Her prenatal doctor, hospital room, everything at home is planned and ready for the new arrival. The security of being around family and familiar surroundings would keep a woman close to home, wouldn't it?

Payton hugged the still-nameless kitten good-bye, rolled up her raincoat and stuffed it in the briefcase beside the umbrella then walked to Claire's house.

Claire answered the door wearing a welcoming smile. "Good morning, come in."

It was Payton's first visit here and she wasn't quite sure what to expect. Since her impromptu call on Sylvie, she viewed many things in a different light. "I'm sorry for not calling. I wondered if I could ask you a couple of questions."

If Claire was surprised, she gave no indication. She opened the door and waited for Payton to enter. Claire's home was the complete antithesis of Sylvie's. The place smelled like Pledge and Lestoil.

"Do you want a cup of coffee, or tea?"

"No thank you. I won't keep you," Payton said as Claire shuffled along the buffed hallway floor on the plastic soles of blue slip-on bedroom slippers. Payton and Claire sat at the kitchen table. Claire pushed aside a basket of artificial fruit and waited for Payton to speak.

"Do you remember the name of Edna's pediatrician?"

Claire frowned, not from intense concentration. It was more a look of confusion. "Why would you want to know something like that?"

"Humor me, please."

Claire looked as though she was trying to recall, but in the end, shook her head. "I really can't remember. What's this all about?"

"Sean's social security number says he was born in Scranton, Pennsylvania. I think it's odd that Rodney and Edna would travel two hundred miles to have a baby when there's a perfectly good hospital in Watertown."

"What possible difference could it make?"

Payton gave a one-shoulder shrug. "You know how song lyrics can get in your head and no matter what you do, you can't get rid of them? Well, I can't stop thinking about this."

Claire appeared to give the matter a bit more thought, then seemed to come to a decision. "I wouldn't like for you to spread this around. Even though all the parties are dead now, I just wouldn't feel right."

Payton nodded.

"Edna and Rod were having marital troubles. I think mostly it was because she was so determined to have a baby. She talked about it to me every day, so I'm sure she bombarded Rod with it. Years went by and it just didn't happen for them. She finally begged him to adopt."

"He didn't want to?"

"He was adamantly against it. Anyway, when Edna found out she was pregnant, she was just about soaring through the clouds, you know what I mean? But, there was still a lot of tension between them. So, they decided to go away to have the baby."

"You were close to them?"

"Edna was head librarian at the time. She gave me my first job when I came to town. I was just a kid then. When she died, I took over her job."

"Do you know where they went?"

"I suppose it could have been Scranton. I still don't understand why you're asking."

"It's a puzzle with a piece missing."

Claire smiled. "One piece?"

"There are a lot of missing pieces."

"When I have a puzzle with lots of pieces missing, I usually throw it away."

"Do you know if either Edna or Rodney had relatives there?"

"I don't know about Rod. He wasn't a real social man, and the only relative I know Edna had was a sister, Elaine. She lived here in town until maybe ten years ago. I don't know where she went. But it wasn't Scranton. She went someplace warm."

Payton rose to leave. "Do you know if Mamie had the painting of the Commodore authenticated before Amanda bought it?"

Another vexed frown from Claire, and then a nod. "She did. Sean asked her to do the documentation, but she said she wasn't qualified. She got someone from the City."

"Was Amanda there during the documentation?"

"Not that I heard."

Payton spent the rest of the morning in a thoughtful muddle. MaryAnn arrived a little before one, looking more like her normal self. The color had returned to her cheeks and her eyes sparkled. She carried a brown paper bag, which she deposited on the counter. "I brought lunch." She placed a ham and Swiss grinder before each of them while Payton went out back to get cold drinks and cups. They sat on the patio to eat.

MaryAnn wadded a mouthful in her cheek. "Oh! I have to ask you something. Did you eat that slice of chocolate cake on my counter?"

"Huh?"

"The cake. Remember I said you should eat it?"

Payton grinned. "I tasted the frosting. It was to die for, but I held back from eating the whole thing. Why?"

"When I got home last night it was gone."

"You mean like a mouse came in and ate it?"

"If he did, he ate the plate and the plastic wrap too. It was there that morning, because I was going to bring it to you. But I forgot. And when I got home, it was gone."

Payton laughed. "You can't guess how many times I've thought about that darned slice of cake. The taste of that frosting has been on the back of my tongue ever since."

"It's very strange. Nothing else is missing."

"No idea." Payton took a bite of sandwich, shaking her head in disbelief. "Hey, guess what? Sylvie brought me a beautiful blue-eyed kitten yesterday."

"You should bring it to the shop."

Payton giggled. "I can see that. Walking to work everyday with a cat on a leash. Or worse yet, in one of those backpack things!"

"Or one of those strollers!" MaryAnn's grin died. "I was thinking about getting a dog, or a cat. It's so quiet."

"Sylvie has lots of kittens. I'm sure she'd give you one. Question: do you remember Sean's Aunt Elaine's last name? Or do you possibly have a phone number?"

"Her last name is…Johnson. She lives in Amarillo. Sean sent her a Christmas card every year so her address must be around somewhere. What's up?"

"I'm working on an idea. I'll tell you if it pans out."

"Want me to go home and see if I can find it?"

"If you wouldn't mind," Payton said. "Finish your lunch first."

MaryAnn was back in just over an hour. She thrust a piece of yellow lined paper at Payton. "I only had her mailing address in Texas. I tried to get the phone number through information, but it's unlisted. Then I went through Sean's personal phone book, but it wasn't there."

"Thanks. This will work."

MaryAnn's eyes narrowed. "Just what have you got up your sleeve?"

"Could you watch the store for a couple of days?"

"Sure, but tell me what's going on, the suspense is killing me."

"I'm going to Amarillo."

"Okay, but what do you think she will be able to tell you? As far as I know, the only contact Sean had with her was through Christmas cards. That's what I told the police when they asked about her."

"I need this trip to be a complete secret."

"I don't get it, but I won't tell." MaryAnn made both a cross over the heart and a Girl Scout salute. "Did the cops tell you not to leave town?"

"Nope. You?"

"Yes."

"Another question: do you know of any artists Sean might have been acquainted with—ones who paint with oils?"

"Mamie?"

"She works in water color."

"Oh yes. Then I don't know."

"Maybe you can go through his address book?"

"What are you thinking?"

"I'll tell you later. Thanks for lunch."

Payton walked home, pushed along by the energy of her suspicions. If what she suspected had been going on, at least two people in Sackets Harbor had really good motives for wanting Sean Adams out of the way.

Mamie greeted Payton from the top of the stairs. She had a fluffy blue duster in one hand. "I just sold that big painting of the harbor," she said, descending the stairs. "For three thousand dollars."

"Awesome," Payton replied, then made a squeaking sound to call the kitten. After a few seconds, it poked its head out from under the couch. Payton picked her up and cuddled her.

"Where did you get that?" Mamie asked.

"Sylvie brought her yesterday."

"I had no idea there was a cat in the house."

"I apologize. I forgot to leave you a note. You aren't allergic or anything, are you?"

"No. I like cats." Mamie scratched the kitten between the ears. "What's her name?"

"I was thinking about calling her Magnolia. We had a tree outside our back door where I grew up, and the flowers were just the color of her fur. We could call her Maggie for short."

"Nice."

"Can we talk a minute?"

They sat on the love seat bathed in the passive solar heat of the afternoon sun. The kitten curled into the fetal position in Payton's lap, purring.

"What can you tell me about Amanda's painting of the Commodore?"

A cloud rolled past the window as Mamie looked at Payton's top button. She took a breath. "Last year, Sean came to me. He said Amanda wanted to buy the awful thing but wanted documentation before she'd spend that kind of money. I didn't know anything about documentation so I called galleries in the City. One of them sent me to Miles. He came and did what needed to be done. That's the last I knew of it until a few weeks ago. Amanda came to me crying that she'd shown the painting to someone from the City—who said it was a forgery."

"Forgery?"

Mamie shrugged. Her eyes moved up, but only as far as Payton's chin. "I told her all I knew was I got it authenticated."

"Is it possible a forgery was substituted after the documentation?"

"I wondered about that, but why would anybody bother? It's not like it was worth a lot of money."

"Amanda said she paid a lot."

"Fifteen hundred dollars. I guess she might consider that a lot."

"Have you seen the painting lately?"

"I went…after Amanda came and yelled at me."

"When was that?"

"A few weeks ago. She accused me of being in c-cahoots with Sean. I was so humiliated." Mamie sniffled and looked out into the street. "After that I got to thinking of something Claire and I saw: Sean and Amanda were in the café kitchen. They were arguing. One of the waitresses went through and while the door was open we heard Amanda tell him his little scam wouldn't work and that she was going to tell Edward."

"What happened then?"

"Sean laughed. And Amanda ran out."

Payton stroked the kitten's back.

"What did you say?" Mamie asked.

"I didn't realize I said anything." She smiled. "I think that after Miles authenticated the painting, Sean swapped the original for a forgery. I'm pretty sure the original is in the master bedroom of his house." Mamie's eyes narrowed. It was then Payton understood. "All this time you've been thinking Miles faked the papers."

"How did you manage to work with Miles the past couple of months if you thought he was unethical?"

Suddenly tears were streaming down Mamie's face. "I wanted the gallery so badly. I'm ashamed to say I was willing to do anything to get it."

"What did you do after Amanda yelled at you?"

"I went to Sean, of course. He swore up and down the painting was the same one Miles documented." Mamie's hands were a blur of motion. "I didn't know what to do. Amanda begged me not to say anything."

"Because of Edward?"

"Yes, he's got quite a violent temper. But also, she was afraid for the business. Things like this can affect how people view you as a businessperson."

"So, what happened with Sean?"

"He seemed so upset I believed him. I-I convinced myself Miles had made a mistake. That's happened before, right?

Somebody got fooled by a forgery."

Payton understood Mamie's emotional turmoil. Sean had a way about him that inspired confidence. Whatever "it" was hadn't worked on Payton, though, and he'd known it right from the moment they met.

She held the kitten in the air and gazed into its big blue eyes. "What do you think about the name Maggie? Do you think that'll suit you?" The kitten continued purring. "I'm not sure if that's an 'I hate it' or a 'that's all right with me' purr, are you?" Payton asked Mamie, trying to ease the tension. "By the way, would you mind watching Maggie a couple of days? I've got to go out of town."

"Be happy to keep an eye on her."

In her office, Payton looked up the number for Southwest Airlines and made reservations for a flight to Amarillo Regional Airport the next morning. Then she called Amanda and made an appointment to see her at three thirty, which left Payton a half hour to kill before walking back downtown. She went upstairs and chose some clothes for her date; a white tank dress with a handkerchief hem. She set out antique jewelry trying not to think about Cameron's grandmother, who'd given the turquoise necklace and earrings to her on her first "anniversary" in the family. High-heeled sandals and a lacy teal shawl completed the ensemble. Satisfied, Payton went downstairs, draping the shawl across the newel post at the bottom. She wondered where he'd take her.

Of course, since she'd called him, he might expect her to have selected the site. In that case, Payton chose a small restaurant in Watertown, one she and Helen had eaten at a couple of times.

Payton and Amanda walked out of the marina parking lot and along the narrow beach fronting the tall stone wall. Both had removed their shoes and left them on the wall. Waves lapped on Payton's bare feet. The water was cool but not uncomfortable.

"I wanted to talk about your painting of the Commodore," Payton said.

Amanda's manner turned wary. "What about it?"

"About it being a fake."

Her expression registered *who told you?* but her words said, "That's old news."

"Was Edward really angry?"

Amanda sniffed. "That's not even the word to describe his reaction. He stormed out of the apartment. I saw him go down the dock. I figured he was getting things ready for the race and went back to my housework. I found out the next morning that he'd given Sean two black eyes."

Payton remembered those eyes, bursting up out of the surf. She'd thought the bruises related to his situation. "What happened after that?"

"Payton!" Amanda's words came like a blast of dynamite. "You aren't thinking my husband killed Sean!"

"Someone killed him, Amanda. And I think the reason you're so volatile lately is because you think so too."

Payton crossed her arms and tried to look at the water as something other than an enemy. Lake Ontario had tried to swallow her. "Where was Edward the night before the race?"

"Just where I told the police he was, down at the marina working on our boat. He came upstairs about nine o'clock."

"Do they know about his fight with Sean?"

"He told them the whole story."

Then why hadn't authorities confiscated either of the paintings?

Who painted the forgery? She almost laughed thinking of the fiasco of a painting class the other night. Surely it couldn't be any of them!

Payton thanked Amanda and put her shoes on.

"I think I'll stay here a while," Amanda said.

Thirty-Nine

Officer Vaughn Spencer's pickup stopped in front of Payton's house at exactly three minutes to seven. He got out and sprinted up the front walk. She'd never seen him in street clothes before, khaki slacks with a pastel striped shirt. He was younger than she, maybe ten years, and two inches shorter. His head was freshly shaved and gleamed like the proverbial bowling ball. Payton didn't like bald men, particularly self-imposed baldness. Those were probably the same men who, when nature caught up with them for real, would rush off to the store for their first bottle of Rogaine.

Vaughn stabbed a bouquet of carnations at her. "I didn't know what kind you liked. I mean…I didn't know your favorite."

"These are beautiful. Make yourself at home while I get a vase."

She opened the plate cabinet, moved aside the knickknacks waiting for Mamie's exhibit to be over so they could regain their proper place on the shelves, and took out a hand painted Columbian vase. It was made of clay and fired to a hard glossy surface. Someone had painted a desert scene in bold simple strokes. Payton filled it with water, arranged the flowers and brought it to the dining area. "Do you want a drink before we go?"

"No thanks, I don't drink."

"Not even wine or brandy?"

"Not really. Well," he said, a blush creeping across his pale skin, "I've never had wine."

"In that case, I have something you might like." Payton retrieved a bottle of merlot from the cabinet and poured an inch in the bottom of two long stemmed glasses. She watched while he took a tentative sip.

His eyes widened in surprise. "This is good."

Satisfied, Payton took a drink of her own.

"I gotta tell you, I was surp—er, glad to hear from you. I thought maybe we could go to this place called Debonairs in Watertown." He downed the rest of the wine, waited for her to do the same and took both their glasses to the kitchen. "You ever been to Debonairs?"

"I don't get out of town very often," she said.

"I-I thought you and Aden…"

"We went out a couple of times. But not there."

Vaughn reached out to help with the shawl but obviously didn't know anything about them and stood helplessly as she draped it around her own shoulders. He laced his arm through hers as they walked to his truck. He must have spent the whole day polishing it. There wasn't a speck of dust or a fingerprint anywhere. He opened the passenger door and waited till she'd buckled herself in before shutting it.

Vaughn drove slowly, too slowly, along the narrow stretch of Route 3. He might have been trying to impress her with his cautiousness, or maybe trying to prolong their date. He certainly didn't impress the drivers behind them. Payton mostly looked out the window, commenting on this or that about the scenery. About halfway to Watertown, she pointed out a pair of whitetail deer in a field and he pulled off the road to watch them nibble the tall grass. The animals didn't even look up as vehicles whizzed past. After a while the animals wandered into the tall brush at the edge of the field.

The restaurant was quiet and plush, lighting subdued. Flickering wall sconces, resembling candles, cast just enough light so a person wouldn't trip on the maroon paisley carpet. They were ushered to a quiet corner table and Vaughn helped her off with the shawl. He folded it carefully and set it on the back of a vacant chair.

"What kind of wine was it you served me? Maybe we could order it," Vaughn suggested.

"When the waiter comes, ask him for Yellow Tail Merlot. It's Australian."

They each ordered rare prime rib with steamed broccoli and baked potato. Vaughn asked for extra sour cream. The meal was excellent, the meat tender and juicy, but Payton wasn't there for romance. She wanted answers.

He chattered like a magpie about sports, weather, tourists and movies, both ones he'd seen and ones he wanted to see. He spoke as though this would be the first of many dates, talking about things they could do together "next time." Till tonight, Payton had thought Vaughn would be one of those who couldn't leave his job at work, that he'd be aching to talk about the murder and the excessive amount of time it was taking State Police to solve the case. But he didn't say one word.

Afterward they went dancing. Payton tried not to think about the last time she'd been dancing—more than three years ago. Payton had to hold her questions; the music was so loud it made discussion impossible without yelling. And she could hardly holler, "Who do you think murdered Sean?" at the top of her lungs.

Around midnight, they left the club and stopped at a quiet diner for coffee and dessert. Not only didn't Vaughn talk about the case, he didn't even leave an opening in their conversation to interject a question about it. Of all the television shows this man watched, apparently none of them had anything to do with murder, poisons or police.

He was a fun date, otherwise, his topics of conversation were varied and interesting, and he never said a bad word about anyone. If she'd been searching for someone to fill her lonely moments, Vaughn might have been the perfect partner. She felt relaxed in his presence, drawn to his calm manner and almost told him about her planned trip to Texas in the morning.

In front of her house, he shut off the engine and leaned back in the seat.

"I had a good time," Payton said.

"So did I. What are you doing tomorrow night? There's a musical I thought you might like to see." This he said shyly, not showing the confidence he'd exhibited all evening. Payton almost smiled.

"Not tomorrow," she said, "There's something I have to do."

"Oh," was all Vaughn said, leaving the impression of a little boy whose mommy told him he couldn't have a candy bar. "What about Saturday?"

"Okay. I'll see what's going on and call you."

"Sounds good."

She pulled on the handle, and by the time she was out of the truck, Vaughn was around the other side, waiting. They walked up to the house together; she put the key in the lock. "Would you like to come in for a nightcap?"

"No thanks, it's late." He gave a slow shake of his head. "I just never thought something like this would happen in my town." He clapped a palm to the side of his head. "I'm sorry. I told myself I wouldn't talk about this tonight. I know how hard the whole thing has been for you."

"Murder happens everywhere." *Talk!*

"I know, but nobody expects it to happen around them."

"Thank you for being concerned." She sat on the stoop and patted the spot beside her. After Vaughn sat, she asked, "Am I a suspect?"

Silence for a moment. "I guess they haven't eliminated you. But I want you to know, I don't think you—"

She patted his hand. "I know." She lowered her voice, "Who's at the top of the list? Never mind, that wasn't fair to ask."

"I *can* say it's a woman."

She counted on her fingers. "Helen, Sylvie, Claire, Mamie, Felicia and Amanda? And me."

"Pretty much."

"I'm sorry. You're not supposed to talk about these things."

"It's not that. It's just that the local force really hasn't been involved in the case. The Attorney General thought we were too close to things, you know what I mean?"

"Sure. But I think they're wrong. Local cops can give important insight into things—and people."

"We do. We've given profiles on everyone in town, just about." He shrugged. "Sorry if I made you think I was more important than I was. I get carried away sometimes."

"I've always loved mysteries. Even as a little girl. I read all the Nancy Drew stories, then graduated to Erle Stanley Gardner."

"That's the Perry Mason stuff, right?"

"Yes. Then I moved to Agatha Christie. I bet I read *all* eighty-something of her books. My favorite character was Hercule Poirot."

"I've seen him on TV."

"The man who plays Hercule, David Suchet, is absolutely perfect. Exactly like the Hercule in the book." She giggled. "Except he doesn't walk the way the 'real' one did. Sort of like a penguin, I always imagined. I also like Lawrence Block. He's got a great series where the main character is a burglar. You find yourself rooting for this lovable guy the whole time."

"I never was a reader, but you're making me think I missed something."

Payton asked the question she'd been holding inside all evening, but the reply to that too was a disappointed, "I really don't know."

Forty

Payton was shown into the recreation room at the nursing home where about a dozen elderly people sat, played cards or chatted. Light rock music played through invisible speakers. She followed an orderly to a table in the corner where he introduced Payton to a white-haired woman in the wheelchair. She looked up. Though her hair was white and her skin wrinkled, the eyes behind gold wires rims glittered with light that belied her age. They shook hands. Elaine Johnson's hand wasn't fragile and gnarled the way Payton remembered her grandmother's. This woman was strong and alert and pumped Payton's hand with enthusiasm.

Payton introduced herself. "I won't keep you long."

"Nonsense," said Sean's aunt. "It's rare enough I get visitors. They told me you were coming. Sit down, please."

Payton pulled up the closest seat, a softly padded card table chair. "Mrs. Johnson, I—"

"Call me Elaine."

"All right. Elaine. I assume they told you your nephew Sean died?"

"Yes. The New York police called. Terrible thing to do over the phone. They asked me a lot of questions. I'm afraid I wasn't much help." The hand-knit blanket on her lap had started to slip and she pulled it back up. "Have they caught who did it?"

"Not yet. I'm afraid that's why I'm here. I'm a friend of Sean's wife."

"MaryAnn?"

"Do you know her?"

"We haven't met, but Sean spoke highly of her."

"She's a sweet girl. But I'm afraid she's a suspect."

Instead of being surprised, Elaine said, "Of course she is. Isn't the wife always the first suspect?"

"Is there anything you can tell me that might help prove her innocence?"

Elaine gave the notion serious thought. "Are you a police officer?"

"MaryAnn works for me in my flower shop. She's my friend and sailing partner."

"I've never been sailing."

"It's wonderful. Exhilarating."

Elaine laughed. "I don't think I could stand anything exhilarating any more."

Payton laughed too. "I feel that way sometimes lately."

Elaine patted Payton's arm. "Keep active. That's the key to a long life."

"I'll remember that." She took off her glasses and blinked as though the light was too strong. She leaned forward, putting a hand on Payton's arm. "I told the police I only heard from my nephew at Christmas, but that wasn't quite the truth."

Payton allowed her brows to lift slightly. Elaine grinned, showing her original teeth, still white and straight. "You look like an honest girl." She hesitated only a second before saying, "If I tell you—you need to keep what I say to yourself."

"I'd like to promise, but if you tell me something that helps find the murderer, I would have to report it."

Elaine nodded. "Fair enough. My nephew was adopted. I see you didn't know. My sister Edna couldn't have children. She so wanted them." She shook her head sadly. "I lived in Sackets Harbor, just a few blocks from she and Rod. A girl, hardly more than a teen showed up in town one day and Edna hired her to work at the library. Even with the age difference they became fast friends. It wasn't long before Edna suspected the girl was pregnant."

"Do you know the girl's name?"

Edna raised a finger. "Give me a moment, it'll come to me."

Payton's elation soared. She didn't need to hear a name. Claire Bastian had been pregnant when she arrived in Sackets Harbor. Giving up her baby to her best friend probably seemed like the perfect solution. Thinking she'd get to watch him grow up must have eased that measure of guilt she had to feel. But, watch him grow into a naughty child, an immoral man, a philanderer, a thief—all things that offended Claire's sense of morality had to be one of the hardest things she'd ever had to endure.

This was more than interesting. But how did it relate to Sean's murder?

"The girls' parents threw her out when they learned she was pregnant. I can't understand parents. When their child needs them the most they throw them out like week old hamburger. Edna asked my opinion about adopting the baby. I thought it was a great idea. The three of them went away together. When the baby was born, the young lady returned to Sackets Harbor. A month later, Edna and Rod went home with their little boy, Sean Stephen." Elaine pursed pink Cupie-doll lips. "Ooh, the girls' name was right on the tip of my tongue. No fear, I'll remember it."

"Is she still in Sackets Harbor?"

"She was in '95. That's when I moved here. I thought I wanted a warmer climate. Since I've trusted you so far, and you haven't said anything to disappoint me, I think I'll show you my other secret."

Elaine accepted Payton's offer to push the wheelchair. "Turn right here."

Elaine's room was clean but absolutely clogged with memorabilia, from family photos to framed newspaper clippings, magazines and knickknacks. She laughed. "I just can't seem to part with anything."

"No need to apologize."

Elaine wheeled herself to the closet and slid open the door. "Would you mind getting that cardboard box in the back?"

Payton ducked inside the closet that smelled of a combination of mothballs and herb potpourri. She lifted the breadbox size carton over a half-dozen pairs of shoes and set it on the bed. She stood back while Elaine opened the flaps.

"A long time ago—probably ten years or so—Sean sent me an envelope and asked me to hold it in case something happened to him. Every once in a while since then, he's sent similar envelopes. I've stored them all in this box. I think it's time I passed them along. Maybe something here can help find his killer." She wheeled backward then gestured at the box.

"You're sure you want me to have this?"

"Yes. You're MaryAnn's friend, and you were Sean's, so I think you're the best person to take charge of it."

Payton asked one last question before heading back to the airport. "Did Sean know he was adopted?"

"Edna never told him. She was waiting until he was old enough to handle it emotionally. But something he said a couple of years ago led me to believe he did know. He said, 'My real mother would never have done that,' and hung up before I could ask what he meant."

Could Sean's parentage have anything to do with his death? Had he somehow found out the truth of his birth? From what she knew about him, he wouldn't take the news lying down. He'd insist on knowing his mother's real name.

On the plane, Payton sat with several of the envelopes in her lap. Each was sealed and bore a date—all written by the same hand—somewhere on the front. The first was dated April 16, 1990, when Sean was almost twelve years old. It was difficult picturing him as a child. The hard lines at the corners of his mouth must have been softer, the blue eyes more innocent.

She slid a fingernail under the flap. Inside was a newspaper clipping, the creases sharp, the ink still clear—"Prominent Sackets Harbor Couple Killed in Burglary." *Last night, in a daring home invasion, Edna and Rodney Adams were brutally murdered while their twelve-year-old son slept in an upstairs bedroom. Investigating Detective David Currier stated that he received a call from the hysterical boy at three minutes past seven in the morning. The child was nearly incoherent as he tried to explain how he'd awakened to find his parents dead.*

Currier arrived on the scene and immediately determined that Rodney must have heard sounds coming from the living room as the burglars went through their belongings. It looked as though he'd gone to the room carrying Sean's baseball bat but had been stabbed several times before he could use it. There was no hair or blood on the bat. Currier then found Mrs. Adams in her bed, stabbed also, once in the heart.

Sean was able to point out a number of items that were missing: a television, a pair of silver candlesticks, a set of dinnerware, a silver money clip, and a painting of Commodore Melancthon Brooks Woolsey.

"Holy shit," Payton whispered, receiving an indulgent smile from her seatmate.

Though Sean had only been 12 years old, she was now absolutely certain he had killed Edna and Rodney. The fact that he was in possession of two of the stolen items—the horrific painting and the money clip—was proof incontrovertible.

Payton ran a possible scenario through her mind. He'd learned of the circumstances surrounding his adoption and savagely stabbed them when they refused to divulge his birth mother's name. To make it look like a random burglary gone bad, he'd taken some of the Adams's most valuable belongings. Trouble was, he hadn't been able to part with them.

The next envelope was dated November 1994. Inside was a newspaper clipping. The headline screamed "Insurance Salesman, Longtime Resident of Sackets Harbor Found Dead." A dreadful feeling pelted her like sleet off the bay. The sensation didn't improve as she read how Aden discovered Harry Brice's body at the bottom of the cellar stairs. Brice's death was listed as accidental, his physical problems blamed for his tumble down the old stairs. Another small clipping documented the case Brice had filed against Sean on behalf of his sixteen-year-old daughter. The case had been dropped.

Payton wished she had a very strong drink, because the whole thing suddenly made sense. Aunt Elaine's box of goodies wasn't a collection of papers and tidbits about Sean's life; it was a documented list of his exploits. Not only had Sean murdered his parents, he'd also murdered old man Brice, probably as retaliation for socking him with the lawsuit. But the charges were dropped.

Maybe the charges were dropped because Sean threatened the family. A migraine formed at the nape of her neck. Payton rubbed her forehead, then tucked the article and the envelope into her bag and leaned back on the seat with her eyes closed.

What to do with the information? If she told authorities about Sean's adoption, they'd ultimately find out about Claire. That would ruin her reputation, and she'd done nothing but desire a better life for her son. It was obvious Sean hadn't been able to beat the information about his parentage from Rodney and Edna—if that was the real reason they'd been killed. If he had, he'd have been all over Claire, possibly murdered her too. Payton shivered, garnering another tolerant look from the man in the seat beside her. So how had he found out?

What could any of this have to do with Sean's murder?

It was well after midnight when Payton pulled into her driveway, with a migraine to rival all migraines. She pushed the garage door button and drove inside. She'd turned off the key, removed her things from the trunk and gotten all the way into the kitchen before realizing there had been a car in Aden's driveway. Elation pulsed through her at the same rhythm as her headache. Aden was back!

She ran to the living room and pulled the curtain aside. Aden's bright silver BMW was in its usual spot. The porch light wasn't on. That was unusual. There were no lights inside. That was unusual too. When home, he always kept a light burning in the hallway.

Payton considered rushing across and banging on his door until he opened it, bleary-eyed and wearing that gray pinstriped dressing gown that made him look so handsome. Okay, it made him look sexy. Either way, he'd put out his strong arms and she'd rush into them, and cry until she was depleted.

Instead, she let the curtain drop, turned and started for her office but tripped on something. She smiled and picked Maggie up. The kitten's obvious happiness to see her made Payton feel better than a pound of chocolate. Cuddling the cat, she returned to the office and checked the answering machine. While the tape went through the preliminary motions, she fondled Maggie's soft fur and laid her cheek against the tiny rib cage, listening to the ragged purring.

A click and Helen's voice said she needed to talk to her. A beep, then Claire's voice saying pretty much the same thing. Something had happened, but right now Payton wasn't curious. Tired. She was so tired. The third message was from Aden. "I'm home. Missed you very much. Can't wait to see you. Am wondering where you are so late though. I hope everything is all right." The machine clicked off.

She downed a pair of pain killers, picked up the meowing Maggie and leaned her forehead against the cool glass of the sliding doors. What a horrible burden Sean had bestowed upon his aunt. All the way home, Payton's adrenaline had pumped, anxiety propelling her to dig further into that box, but now that she was here, the urge had waned. She didn't want to know what else Sean had done.

Part of her wished she'd never gone to Texas.

Payton and Maggie lay in bed. Maggie didn't have any trouble sleeping, but once again Payton lay with her eyes open and her mind working overtime. Sean Adams. Handsome, suave, exuding class and sophistication—until he opened his mouth. His words, his smile, and his attitudes contradicted it all.

What else was in the box Elaine had entrusted to her? Was there was an envelope dated somewhere during the past month—an envelope telling about Payton's dismissal from the St. Angelina's School? How Sean had gotten hold of the information she had no idea. The news never hit the outside world. Even though Principal Barrett let Payton go, he'd said he hadn't believed a word of the boys' allegations. For that she was grateful, because she hadn't done anything wrong. The boy, a Richard somebody—Payton tried, but couldn't recall his surname. God, what was wrong with her that she couldn't recall the name of the person who'd ruined her career? This Richard kid had come to school to pick up his sister Stephanie. He came every day to get her. Carlson, that was the name. That afternoon Stephanie had gone to the school library to get something, and was gone when Richard came to retrieve her. Payton had told him where she was yet he elected to wait around.

She vividly recalled how he laid his backpack on the desk nearest the door. She saw Richard's creased blue jeans, striped t-shirt and cotton jacket as clearly as if he stood before her now. He'd run a hand through his too-long hair and walked toward her desk. Closer. Too close for comfort, but she didn't want to embarrass him by moving, or asking him to back away. He said a couple of pleasantries about the weather and she had looked out the window. Yes, the weather *was* nice, she agreed, admitting she'd been so engrossed in grading the tests that she hadn't even noticed. He'd suddenly bent down and kissed her, on the mouth. Instinctively she reached up and shoved him away, hard. He stumbled over his own sneakers, hadn't fallen, but had leaped up, furious.

Stephanie backed her brothers' story even though she'd been nowhere around. The school board tried to remain on Payton's side. She had an impeccable record, and the Carlson kid had been trouble more than once, but the Carlson parents were unflappable. Either Payton left or they smeared the school's reputation all over the newspapers. So she'd gone home to Cameron, who did his best to soothe her wounds by taking her to Greenland.

Payton's fist pounded the sheet, making Maggie glance up. Teaching was all she'd ever wanted to do. How much further would Sean have gone if he'd lived? The cops must be wondering the same thing.

Forty-One

The bright sun woke Payton at 8:05. She unfolded herself from around Maggie and stretched. Her first thought was of Aden. She flung off the sheet, padded into the guest room and peered out the window. His car was still in the driveway. The morning paper, wrapped in bright red plastic, lay on the front stoop. He wasn't up yet.

Payton went back to her room. Maggie sat perched on the edge of the bed, still too small to jump down. Payton carried the kitten downstairs to use her litter box, started the coffee and went upstairs to shower. Payton was dressed and halfway down the stairs when the phone rang. She rushed to pick up the cordless handset. "Hello," she said a little breathlessly. "Hi, Helen."

"What time did you get in? Did everything go all right?"

"A little after midnight. Everything's fine. What did I miss?"

"Aden's been arrested. The minute he turned into his driveway, they slapped cuffs on him." Payton groped for the nearest chair and fell into it. Why would they arrest Aden? For leaving the country when told to stay in town? It had to be something like that; it couldn't be something more radical, like murder. Aden wouldn't kill Sean. Would he?

Payton fed Maggie and collected her briefcase. Should she take an envelope or two from the box to read at the shop? She rubbed her temples, the site of yesterday's headache and decided against it. She hugged the ball of white fur waiting by the front door, somehow knowing that her owner was going out again. Payton considered MaryAnn's idea about taking the kitten to the shop. Instead, she told Maggie, "I'm really glad Sylvie brought you to me. I'll be back later. You'll have someone to play with anyway, Mamie should be here soon."

The humidity hung in the air like wet cotton batting. Aden's house looked forlorn, as sad as the heavy June morning air. Would they let Aden out on bail? Probably not. He'd be considered a flight risk. But did the authorities really have anything to hold him on? Even if they didn't, she believed they could hold him up to 48 hours. Payton thought about calling Vaughn to find out what he knew, then remembered their tentative date for tonight. She'd said she'd call him.

Payton spotted Sergeant Espinoza clomping toward the shop just before noon. She greeted him with as much spirit as she could muster. What could he want—again? He got to it soon enough, asking first if Aden Green had purchased one of the monkshood plants.

"I heard you arrested him."

The slight lift to his fuzzy brows denoted his surprise.

"I assume since you're asking about the plants again that you've arrested him for murder. You're making a big mistake."

"Would you mind just answering the question?"

Payton counted on her fingers "He didn't buy a plant. He doesn't keep plants because they would die while he's away. He's been in the store once, and I didn't have *any* plants here yet, so he couldn't even have stolen the necessary leaves." She dropped her hands to the countertop. "Why are you here? We both know you aren't stupid. You didn't forget I gave you all this information before."

"Why do you think I'm here?"

"You want to know if I found out anything in Texas."

"You went to Texas?"

She stood up and walked around the counter. "The man you had tailing me wasn't very discrete."

He was undaunted. "So, what did Mrs. Johnson say?"

"You really shouldn't let private citizens do your job for you."

Espinoza recovered quickly. "I talked to her. I'm sure you know that."

"She wasn't impressed you delivered news of her nephew's death via phone."

"I would like to know what she told you. You were in that nursing home far too long for her to have said 'sorry, I can't help you.'"

"Would you believe we became fast friends? We realized we had a lot in common. What's wrong with that?"

"Name one thing you had in common."

"MaryAnn. Sean. Sackets Harbor." She added, "Sailing," just for something else to say.

"We can do this the hard way…at headquarters."

"Don't threaten me, Sergeant."

How much, if anything should she divulge? She didn't want to withhold anything that might help, but she also didn't want their fingers digging into things with the potential to destroy reputations of innocent people. She decided to wade through the rest of the envelopes before saying anything at all—if they didn't already know about the box. Surely, if someone were watching her…

"I'm sorry. She didn't tell me anything that would help the case."

He moved so quickly, she didn't have time to brace herself. He stepped close. She tried to back away, tripped and went down hard on her rear. The sergeant knelt beside her, true concern on his face. "Are you hurt? I didn't mean to frighten you."

"Yes you did. You thought you could scare me into telling you something I don't know." She allowed him to help her up.

After Espinoza left, Payton tried to do some bookwork. The trail of numbers was interrupted by a single thought. She hadn't been tailed *from* Texas or they would know about the box.

At home, Payton greeted Maggie and Mamie in that order. She went to the pantry, removed two more envelopes from the box and took them to her office. There were several people browsing downstairs, so Payton waited for Maggie to scamper inside and shut the door. With the kitten settled in her lap, Payton examined the envelopes, dated 1/1/95 and 3/17/95. The one dated in January contained a handwritten invoice in the same penmanship as the date on the envelope. It described a sale Sean had made to a man named Rich Saunders, no contact information given. The price was $15,000. The invoice said "for painting titled *Lake George* by Church" and stated official documents had been provided. There was no copy of such papers in the envelope, nor was there information as to who'd made out the validation papers. Why did the name Church ring a bell? He must be pretty good if his stuff sold for that much. If the painting was so valuable, why would Sean sell it? He loved having beautiful things around him. Maybe he needed money—possibly to open his café. She made a note to see if the dates coincided.

The second envelope provided the answer to her previous question. It, too, was a sales invoice in the amount of $15,000. This one to a woman, Glenda O'Connor, for the sale of *Lake George* by Church.

So, Sean was in the business of selling forged paintings. Was it possible the same person had painted the one of Amanda's *Commodore*? Who'd provided documentation on the Church paintings? Could it also be Miles Arenheim? A sinking feeling told her it was. Payton put Maggie on the floor. She went to the door and called Mamie, who waddled in.

"Two things: Are you familiar with an artist named Church?"

Mamie assumed a puzzled expression. "You must mean Frederic Edwin Church. Why do you ask?"

Payton shrugged. "I saw a painting of his that I liked. Is it possible he painted two of the exact same painting?"

Mamie's confusion increased. "I suppose it happens on occasion, but there are always differences."

"Is Miles returning soon?"

"I have no idea, why?"

"My husband owned a number of buildings in Minneapolis. Well, I own them now. I was wondering if Miles would be interested in setting up another gallery there." Payton finished the long-winded commentary and took a breath.

"He hasn't been around to see the gallery since we opened. Maybe I can get him here and you could tell him your idea. Can I use your phone?"

Mamie went to the kitchen to make her call. Payton used her cell phone and dialed the number on Espinoza's business card and left a voice mail for him to call her. Mamie returned wearing a wide smile, Miles would be able to come as soon as tomorrow, around noon.

Forty-Two

This time Vaughn bore no flowers. And this time he didn't hesitate to talk about the case. The only thing was, now Payton didn't want to talk about it. She had way more information than she wanted. She sat quietly looking out the window, the same as the last time, but now the atmosphere was different. Payton felt it, and she saw Vaughn did too.

He pulled into the parking lot at Briton's Mini Golf and smiled over at her, the smile intended as a question. She nodded. "I haven't played in years."

"They have a snack bar too. I thought we could grab a little something."

"Sounds good."

"Maybe it'll get this case off your mind."

"It's not off yours," she said.

"No, but police work is my life."

"And the suspects are my friends."

"I know."

"I thought you told me all the suspects were women."

"I did," he admitted.

"Then why did they arrest Aden?"

"Because he left town without letting anyone know and he didn't contact anyone while he was gone."

"So, he's really not a suspect?"

"That I'm not sure about." His tone said he wasn't happy about this. He undid his seat belt and watched it slide back into the slot.

"Sergeant Espinoza says you've been investigating."

Payton shrugged.

"You could have asked me what you wanted to know."

"You said you didn't want to talk about it. Besides, you told me you weren't privy to the case."

"I've had some of my own questions," he said. "Like what was Amanda doing out walking after midnight the night before the murder?"

What? "Did you ask her?"

"She said she couldn't sleep."

"With all her problems trying to keep Edward from finding out about the painting, I'm not surprised," Payton said.

"But Edward already knew by then."

"I heard he and Sean fought. Where did it happen?"

Vaughn ran a hand across his sweaty forehead then opened the pickup door. "You mean like, did Edward meet up with him on the street?"

"Right, or seek him out at the café? Find him on his boat? Where they met could be very important."

"The night they fought, Sean was at the marina preparing his boat for the race."

"So it probably happened down on the dock," Payton said.

Vaughn nodded.

"The poisoning had to be planned in advance. Which means Edward would've had the container of monkshood paste with him."

"Right. Not sure you know it or not, he passed a polygraph."

"Did they find any DNA evidence on *MaryAnn*?"

"The waves pretty much washed the deck clean."

Payton opened her door. Cool air pushed in, raising goosebumps on her arms. "The waves didn't wash the poison residue off the ropes though, right?"

"No. They retrieved good samples."

"Would someone have to be well versed in plant knowledge to have done this?"

"You kidding?" Vaughn laughed. "These days anyone with a computer can get information to do anything. Or anyone who watches CSI."

She laughed and got out of the car. Several couples were golfing. They laughed and joked as though without a care in the world.

Vaughn beat her two games to one. They stopped for a break and had steamed hotdogs with chili on top. The chili was a five-alarm batch Payton wasn't prepared for. The first bite sent her into spasms of coughing. Vaughn handed her a cold drink. It took several minutes, but she finally recovered.

Later, he beat her another two games. Then he took her to the A&W for root beer floats. Vaughn walked her to the door and once again didn't go in when she invited him. He planted a kiss on her cheek, a little closer to her lips than the previous time. Payton wondered how many dates before he actually kissed her full on the lips.

Aden's car was still in his driveway; his lights were still off. As far as she knew, the 48-hour period during which authorities could hold a suspect was just about up. Maybe they were planning to charge him with Sean's murder. Would Vaughn have told her?

Vaughn was serious about his job. He was down to earth, friendly to everyone and accessible, showing up inside shops instead of passing them by during his rounds.

As Payton picked up and greeted the meowing Maggie, a thought struck. Vaughn had access to the shops. Meaning he had access to the monkshood plant. Vaughn knew what sort of person Sean was; they'd grown up together. Maybe Vaughn was one of the kids Sean tormented. He was on duty the night the poison had been applied to the ropes.

She tried to swallow the lump in her throat, but it lodged like a car in a Minneapolis traffic jam. She poured a generous glass of Chablis and took it out on the patio, settling Maggie in her lap. But this was Maggie's first time outdoors and soon she wasn't content just sitting. After receiving a warning not to get lost, she was set on the ground to explore.

Could Vaughn be a murderer? Payton shook her head. It couldn't be.

Possibly the box held an incriminating envelope with Vaughn's "date" on it. She retrieved the kitten, who obviously didn't want her explorations curtailed, and went inside. "You can go out again tomorrow," she told the cat, shut the door and set Maggie on the floor. The kitten went back to the door and meowed. Payton ignored her and went to the pantry.

The next envelope was dated August 22, 1996. This held no invoices or newspaper clippings. It contained three handwritten pages documenting the real estate deal gone bad between Sean and Sylvie. Payton settled on the kitchen stool, sipping wine and stumbling over Sean's scribbled penmanship, trying to figure what it meant. The other envelopes contained sales Sean made, or news articles about events in which he'd been involved. But this seemed to be a record, more like a note to himself. Then Payton realized—this was information for future reference, possible evidence for blackmail.

Had Sean presented the evidence to Sylvie? It would be a perfect motive for murder.

The next envelope was dated April 4, 1997. This Payton recognized immediately. It was the day he and MaryAnn married. Inside were copies of her driver's license, birth certificate and social security card and a scribbled note saying he'd paid $5,000 for them. From whom, the note didn't say. She sipped wine and thought about MaryAnn, having to live with the fear of being deported. Having to accept his philandering with stoic silence. Taking his abuse with grace. Had she finally grown sick of it all? It just didn't fit. MaryAnn had been so happy to finally be moving out on her own.

Maybe, seeing her bags packed turned the divorce into a reality for Sean. Up till then it had been just talk. She was saving money and *someday* would leave him. Now it was real. Would he accept this with just a shrug of his shoulders? Payton didn't think so. The little boy in him needed her. MaryAnn accepted him for what he was.

Payton poured more wine and went for another envelope, not at all liking what she was thinking. This was dated December 24, 1999. Christmas Eve. The only thing inside was a sales invoice to a woman named Ann in the amount of $17,500. There was no address or notation as to what she'd bought. More blackmail evidence? Payton slipped the paper back in the envelope and returned the envelopes to the box.

Payton called Maggie, still sitting at the sliding door. Payton scooped her up. "You can go out again tomorrow. It's after midnight and we're going to bed now."

Forty-Three

Payton greeted Miles with a warm handshake and close scrutiny—mid to late forties with high cheekbones and a narrow nose that gave his face a pinched look, like something didn't smell quite right. Not bad looking in the grand sense of it though. Expensive haircut, longish sideburns, otherwise clean-shaven. No wedding band, just an onyx and gold ring on his right pinky finger. No other jewelry in evidence except a Rolex watch. The whole package presented a picture of financial well-being.

Was Miles Arenheim the sort who'd provide false documentation papers on forged paintings? Or had Sean duped him as he duped so many others?

A search on the Internet provided some information. David Miles Arenheim owned two homes, one in New York City and one in Aspen. He had no criminal record except an arrest for going 47 miles over the speed limit at the age of 17. He had a .45 caliber pistol registered to him in the State of New York. He had not been in the military. Last year he paid taxes on $2.7 million. Miles Arenheim was a noted authority on paintings, one of few in the United States licensed to provide documentation. His handshake was supposed to be his bond.

Payton needed a few uninterrupted moments to talk with Miles. Like a lost puppy, she followed him and Mamie around the downstairs, listening to Mamie's commentaries about pieces he'd sent up from the City, and how she would display them.

"I sold this just yesterday," Mamie said, touching a carved

teakwood statue of an elk. "I'll hate to see it go. Oh, where are my manners? Would you like some coffee or tea?"

"What I'd really like is a glass of brandy, or sherry if you have it." This he said looking at Payton.

"I'll get it," Mamie offered.

This gave Payton the opening she'd been hoping for. "Do you remember the documentation papers you provided on a painting of Commodore Melancthon Brooks Woolsey for Sean Adams?"

A clink of glass against glass made them both turn. Mamie gave an embarrassed smile and said, "I didn't know you were going to bring that up. I thought Amanda and Sean got it all settled."

Miles' brow knit in thought. "Ugly cuss? Uniform?"

"That's him."

"Long time ago, but yes, I remember. Why do you ask?"

"There's a forgery of it floating around town. A forgery with your papers attached."

"Shit." Miles accepted the glass from Mamie with a nod.

"Did Sean hire you to document other paintings?"

"Several."

"Was there ever a Frederic Edwin Church?"

"There was." Miles set the glass on the dining room table. He took off his glasses and laid them beside it. "What are you trying to say?"

"I think Sean was selling forged paintings. I found some papers in his things."

"His things?" Mamie asked.

"I was helping MaryAnn sort through them and found some old invoices and things. Anyway, he sold Church's *Lake George* at least twice."

Miles ran a hand through his hair, leaving a bunch on the left side standing straight out. Mamie put a hand up as though she wanted to brush it down but decided against it and jammed the hand in the pocket of her dress.

"Sean sold the painting twice for fifteen thousand." Payton turned to Mamie. "Do you know anyone named Ann? There was another invoice for seventeen five made out to a woman named Ann, but there was no note as to what it was for."

"I can't think of anyone by that name."

"I know a lot of Anns," Miles said, "but none who strike me as being related in any way to Sean."

"How well did you know him?" Payton asked.

"We met those few times I did the authentications. We never socialized. The day he burst in on Mamie and I at the gallery, I didn't recognize him. It wasn't till I was on my way home I realized who he was."

Miles helped Mamie wrap the elk carving for shipment to London, and Payton went into her office and shut the door. For the first time in ages she felt like working on her memoir. While the writing program opened, she listened to Miles and Mamie bantering in the living room. Apparently he'd picked up the kitten and was cooing over her. How bad could Miles be if he cooed to a kitten? Mamie tapped on the door and announced she was taking Miles back to the airport. Payton went to say good-bye.

"I'll check my records when I get back and call you," Miles said. "It was nice seeing you."

"You also. See you in the morning, Mamie," Payton shut the door on them and went back to her book. She worked for a couple of hours, but her brain kept sidetracking to Sean and his birth mother. Payton wondered how Claire would react if she knew Payton found out her secret.

She shut down the computer, gave the kitten a good-bye hug and walked to Claire's once again, without calling first. Definitely not apropos. Claire was in the side garden on her knees weeding. She grunted as she stood, dropping a handful of weeds atop a pile at the edge of the driveway. "Keep trying to get in better shape, but there always seems to be muscles I don't reach."

"It's looking beautiful," Payton agreed. "I'm surprised your monkshood is doing so well in this spot. Traditionally they like it shady and wet."

"Well, it's definitely not shady, but I have an underground

watering system that keeps it pretty moist. Would you care for a glass of lemonade?"

"No thank you."

"How's your kitten?"

"A hellion," Payton answered. "She's decided she wants to be outdoors. She's too little to let out on her own, so I have to drop what I'm doing to go out with her."

"I'll have to come see her sometime. I haven't seen Sylvie's cats in years."

Payton lowered her voice. "I'm in no hurry to see them again either. How do they handle it when she hosts the *Wanderlust* meetings?"

"Felicia ordered Sylvie to clean the cat boxes or we wouldn't come."

"I'd have a hard time telling someone something like that. It's sort of like telling someone they have bad breath."

"You trying to tell me something?" Claire asked, mischievously wrinkling her nose.

Payton laughed and pointed at one of the other plants Claire had purchased at her shop. "You really have a green thumb."

"What have you been up to? I haven't seen you in a few days."

"I worked on my memoir for a while this morning. Miles Arenheim came to see how the gallery was shaping up. Then I thought I'd come see how you were."

"That explains why Mamie didn't show up this morning. Sundays we most always spend the day together."

"She picked him up at the airport early. About an hour ago she took him back."

"What did you think of him?"

"Suave, sophisticated. Way out of my league," Payton said.

"Boloney! He's exactly your type."

Eeuw. "Is that how I come off?"

Claire plucked out a single weed and dropped it on the pile. "There's nothing wrong with sophistication and class."

"I guess not, but in my mind that usually means snob too."

Seeing Claire's averted eyes, Payton exclaimed, "No, not that!"

Claire gave a nervous laugh.

"People think I'm a snob?"

"In the beginning they did." Claire went to the back steps and sat on the top one. "When you didn't try to make friends…I think it was natural for them to think that."

"I hope they don't any more."

"They have other things to gossip about lately."

Payton brought up the reason for her visit. "Tell me about Edna and Rodney."

"He was short and squat, stoop-shouldered and bowlegged. Very sweet. He doted on Edna, and then Sean when he came along. They did all those father-son things together, fishing, boating, baseball." Claire gave a reminiscent laugh. "He bought Sean a little tiny baseball glove as a coming-home-from-the-hospital gift." Then she added, "Rod and Mamie's husband, Donald, were in the same graduating class."

"Were they friends?"

"Yes. Well, during high school anyway. After Donald married Mamie and Rod married Edna, they sort of drifted apart. You know how it is, people get involved in their lives. Besides, Don changed. He got hired by that laboratory and turned really weird, talking about experiments and discoveries all the time. I don't know how Mamie stood it."

"So Rod and Sean got along well," Payton said.

"Yes. Best friends, I guess you'd say."

"How did Edna get along with him?"

Claire laughed, a deep rolling one that began in the pit of her stomach. "She was so jealous of the relationship between her boys!"

"Must have been hard on them both when he started getting in trouble."

"God, yes, Edna was a wreck, Rod blamed himself. It wasn't their fault. They were so good to him." Her hands fluttered in her lap. "Maybe they were too good."

Payton took a breath. "It must have been hard on you."

Without hesitation, Claire asked, "How long have you known?"

An uneasy laugh squeezed between Payton's lips. "A few days."

"How did you find out?"

"It's a long story. It all began with Sean's social security card but ended with a visit to his aunt Elaine."

"So, she's still alive."

"And well, and living in Amarillo."

"Did he know, do you think?"

"I suspect he only knew he was adopted. They didn't tell him, though."

"They planned to. That was part of our agreement. When they—we—thought he was old enough. You've heard about his behavior. He wasn't ready."

"Was there anyone else who might have known?"

"No." She thought a moment, then repeated, "No."

"What about Mamie?"

"No. I've been so careful. It's awful to say this, but Sean's death has been a relief in some ways. To not have to watch everything I say. Not to have to worry what he's going to do next." Tears flowed down Claire's cheeks.

"It must have been awful for you, to watch him lie, cheat and steal from your friends."

Claire's shoulders heaved with her sobs. Payton put an arm around her. The move brought on a new round of tears. It was time Claire got it all out. After a long while, she looked up at her, squinting into the sun and between racking sobs, said very softly, "I pl-planned to d-do something about it."

Payton gulped and dropped her hand from around Claire when Mamie's car turned into the driveway. Mamie got out, all smiles. While she opened the hatchback and took out a basket, Claire sniffled and swiped her sleeve across her face.

"Well, I got Miles onto his plane. What it must be like to own your own plane I can't—" Mamie put the basket on the ground and went to her friend. "What's wrong, Claire?"

"Nothing. We were just talking about Sean," Payton answered for Claire. Payton stood. "I'll be on my way."

"We're going on a picnic," Mamie said. "Would you like to come? There's plenty of food."

"I'd love to, but I think I'll take a rain check. I'm behind in my bookkeeping. Take care, Claire, I'll see you soon."

Claire sniffled again and waved.

Payton walked to the battlefield. It was late afternoon. Few tourists were around. She walked to the spot where *MaryAnn* had run aground. Unlike the last time she'd been here, visions of the accident didn't storm her mind. So, Claire was going to do something about Sean. What did that mean? Tell folks the truth? Commit murder?

Could a mother actually bring herself to murder her son to stop the evil things he perpetrated on his townspeople? Could Claire feel *that* guilty for letting the Adamses adopt him, for subjecting them to those years of torment at his hands?

Claire said she *was planning* to do something about Sean. That meant she hadn't actually done anything. But two things Claire said recently came resoundingly back. Both that, at the time, seemed like nothing more than the ramblings of a person suffering severe sorrow. The first was when Payton mentioned about Aden being a suspect and that the police couldn't arrest him because he couldn't be located. Claire had said, "That's good then, isn't it?" The second time had been in Mamie's shop when Claire broke down, mumbling that it was all her fault. If Claire hadn't killed him, then what did the comments mean?

Claire's behavior had been odd, to say the least. First was the jogging. Then, the announcement that she was quitting the job she'd loved more than life itself to reopen The Taste of Gay Paree. Payton sat, pulling her knees up close and hugging her arms around them. She lowered her forehead on her knees. The news about the murders Sean committed had to come out. Payton couldn't delay telling authorities. What would this do to Claire? Probably send her completely over the edge.

During the walk home, Payton decided to drive to the detention center and see if they'd let her visit Aden. Right this moment she didn't care whether he'd killed Sean or not. She just needed to see his face. She ran upstairs to change into something more appropriate for visiting a jail but realized she didn't have a clue what that should be, so she left on the same blouse and shorts.

At state police headquarters, they wouldn't let her see him. Payton asked to see Sergeant Espinoza, but he wasn't there. She stopped at the same A&W she and Vaughn had gone to and ordered a hamburger. Dripping grease, just like she remembered from her childhood. That very moment, she desperately wanted to be in Virginia, in her family home, surrounded by family. For one fleeting moment, she pictured herself squealing the tires out of the A&W parking lot and onto the Interstate ramp headed south.

At home, she shut off the car and laid her head on the steering wheel as the garage door slid shut behind her. She didn't know how long she sat there, still considering packing a bag and heading back to the hills of Virginia. Family. People who loved her. She hadn't been back in a very long time. Hadn't even gone home after Cameron died.

The kitten met her at the kitchen door. Payton cuddled her, tears flowing. Maggie didn't seem to notice, just purred and cuddled and loved. Exactly what Payton needed. They sat on the love seat in the dark. It wasn't two minutes before she pulled herself erect and turned on the light.

She suddenly knew without a doubt who had killed Sean. Someone who'd been there from the start, known Sean since he was a baby, knew Edna and Rodney. Chances were good—very good—this person also knew Sean's other secrets.

Payton picked off a cat hair that tickled her nose and looked out the window. Aden's car was in his driveway, same as before, but now his porch light was on. This time she wouldn't wait for him to visit. She put the kitten on the floor and raced upstairs to wash her face and repair her makeup.

The blow came without warning.

Forty-Four

Payton landed on hands and knees beside the bed, pain ricocheting from ear to ear. The second blow glanced off the nape of her neck. She rolled. The third blow jammed her right wrist; her shoulder exploded out of the socket and she collapsed. Stay down, part of her said. The other part that controlled the lust for self-preservation said, get up and fight.

The air was heavy with his presence. In the shadows near the closet.

Her mind scanned the surroundings and fabricated only one possible weapon, the adored imported crystal lamp on the table, four feet to the right. She lunged, toes digging for traction, fingers groping. She missed the lamp, lost her footing and fell, fingers hooking the lace doily and jerking it from the table. She landed on her dislocated arm. Payton never knew a human could feel such pain and still live.

He came at her again. She saw him, not as a shape, but a darker spot in the dense shadows. Where was the lamp? She'd heard it fall when the doily pulled away. Her fingers groped along the floor.

He took another step and became outlined in the meager moonlight from the French door; he was shorter than Payton, but beefy and thick, probably outweighing her by seventy-five pounds. When he bypassed the opportunity to escape out the door, Payton knew with unqualified certainty that his objective wasn't burglary. It was murder.

"Who are you?" She backed two steps, her right arm dangling uselessly at her side, pain screeching into her fingers.

"What do you want?"

No reply.

Another step back.

"If you go away now, I promise I won't call Vaughn."

Still nothing.

The hallway was an endless five feet away. As if reading her thoughts, he lunged, one arm high overhead. Something glinted in his hand.

Payton spun and ran. She tripped and fell against the wall. She didn't lose consciousness but wished she had. Through the wall of agony a silhouette loomed above. The panther statuette—given to her by Cameron—was about to smash down on her head.

How dare he use her own possession as a murder weapon? Payton drove her left shoulder into his midsection, embracing his thick hips with her good arm. She dug her toes in the carpet and thrust all her weight forward. His muscles clenched as he fought to maintain balance. She pushed again, toes digging in. He staggered; should fall.

The cat statue—a precious third anniversary gift—drove into the middle of Payton's spine. Rather than debilitate, the pain spawned rage. Adrenaline bred strength. She squeezed her arm around him, used the rug as a launching pad and thrust forward. The heavy body tumbled against the dresser amid a torrent of obscenities. Payton fell atop him but quickly regained her feet.

So did he. Fury etched his silhouette.

Something cold lay against her right foot. Mercury couldn't have flowed smoother than Payton as she bent, picked up the lamp and wrenched the cord from the wall.

And aimed for his head.

He ducked. The lamp struck his right arm. Bones broke. The sound was like nothing she'd ever heard. He gave a low, agonized howl.

This time the statue caught Payton on the side of the head. Her vision swam. Became four assailants. Then ten.

She slashed the lamp in a wide, sweeping arc. He came at her anyway, statue held like a gun. A spark of moonlight illuminated its ruby eyes. This must be how it had been for Cameron, at the mercy of those wretched men who'd pummeled him with her kitchen utensils.

Payton stabbed the lamp at a spot that should be groin. The ensuing wail said she struck home. She crashed the lamp down. Once, twice. The bulb burst and they were showered with glass. She swung again. Each time she made contact with flesh and bone, yet still he remained upright.

He lunged. She swung. Lamp and cat collided. The lamp shattered in her hand. He took a step forward. She took two backward. Each bore an arm dangling at their side. Each breathed hard, though his was raspy and liquid. In an absurd dance they edged toward the door.

He prepared to strike again. Payton prepared to defend. There was a sudden, ragged intake of breath, and he collapsed at her feet. Not dead, she knew, because he was breathing in thick, mucousy gurgles.

She leaped over him. And started to run.

Fingers clutched her ankle and yanked. She kicked out, making contact with something rough. Her attacker grunted. The hand let go and she darted for the door.

He'd gotten upright again.

What did it take to bring this monster down?

This time he didn't charge. Didn't swing the statue. He raced from the room, taking the stairs two at a time. Payton sprinted after him, doing likewise. At the bottom, he suffered a moment's hesitation then raced to the back of the house dodging furniture and statuary.

He wrenched open the sliding door and slithered outside. Moments ago, she'd been willing to let him leave without impediment. Now, feeling all-encompassing outrage borne of invasion, betrayal and attempted murder, she dove at him. This time he dropped like a stone. The scent of rosemary surged around them as they tumbled into the herb bed, Payton on top. She thrashed him in the face, nose and ears. Over and over she pounded, feeling a rush as his blood gushed over her.

He planted his good hand on her left breast and shoved. She went airborne; her head thumped back onto the brick patio. Now he was atop her chest, his weight forcing her shoulders into the bricks, expelling a new battery of pain. Five fingers went around Payton's throat.

This time she would not heed Death's call.

She folded her legs, arched her back and hammered her knees into his spine. Unable to brace himself, he fell forward. Their faces touched. Breaths mingled. A scent. No, not a scent, because she couldn't breathe; it was more a perception, a familiarity. She arched her back and kicked again, but added a twist to the side that dislodged the hands and broke the bond of recognition.

Payton flew to her knees, gasping, sucking in lungfuls of precious air, helpless and impotent. She put out a hand in a gesture of supplication: like a child's time out. It wouldn't stop him, but it was all she had left. Breathe. In. Out.

Movement behind her attacker—a shadow, an apparition, or maybe an angel—Payton didn't know, or care. It moved with the speed of electricity, wrapping an arm around the attacker's neck and slamming him to the ground. There was a sound of intense thrashing and grunting. Payton lifted her head; maybe Aden needed help. But it was over, Aden was on his feet, brushing dirt off his hands.

She inhaled. That cool fresh air was the best thing she'd ever felt. Better even than any sex. Payton fell back on her haunches, breathing, just breathing.

"Are you all right?"

That's when she realized she was crying; if her squeaks and rasps could be called crying. Gentle fingers touched her elbow, helped her up. Strong arms wrapped her safely in their embrace and lifted. Her shoulder jostled against his and she screamed. It was a croak but there was no mistaking its meaning.

Aden guided her down into the lounge chair. He knelt, peering anxiously into her face. "I'm going to get the phone and some towels. Will you be okay for a minute?"

She stretched to peer over his shoulder.

"Don't worry about him right now."

Aden was only gone a moment. He returned with a phone against one ear and a bundle of kitchen towels in his free hand. "…lot of blood," he was saying. "Hurry." He gave Payton's address then flipped the phone shut and dropped it in his shirt pocket. He knelt again, shaking the folds from a yellow plaid towel. "There's blood all over you. Where are you hurt?"

"Everywhere."

He gave a grim smile, lifted her right hand and turned it. Her palm was covered in blood. A fresh flow ran from the middle of her lifeline. He swabbed it, but a fresh bubble burst up. He grunted and wound the towel tight around her hand. Behind him a black hulk grew out of the shadows.

"Aden! Look out!"

Seemingly in the same motion Aden leaped up and spun around. The hulk approached, entered the circle of light from the sliding doors. Vaughn's face appeared, came closer.

"Aden! Watch out!" She flinched back in the chair. It went off balance and tipped over. The scream that ensued probably woke the rest of the neighborhood.

When she came to, both Aden and Vaughn hovered over her, Aden's mouth in a straight line, Vaughn smiling. "So, you thought I was the bad guy, huh?" He tilted his head and pursed his lips. "If I wasn't so worried, I might be insulted."

"I'm sorry."

He patted her thigh. She peered over his shoulder. "Aden, something's wrong. Tell me what it is."

Aden finished fastening another towel around the back of her neck, then said, "Sorry honey. He got away."

"What!" She tried to sit up but fell back in pain. "How?"

"He probably skirted the shadows behind the properties," Vaughn said.

"It's not a he, it's a she," Payton said.

"What?" both men exclaimed at the same time.

The wail of an ambulance stopped further questions.

Forty-Five

Aden brought Payton home from the hospital just after 4 a.m. She'd insisted on returning home even though doctors wanted to keep her overnight. She lay on the love seat in the living room, pillows bundled under her head, a patchwork quilt someone had brought from the guest bedroom tucked tight. She could barely keep her eyes open. Whatever they gave her made her dopey as hell, but at least it eased the pain.

Three tired looking people sat in a semi-circle around her: Vaughn, Aden and Sergeant Espinoza. The sergeant was the only one who looked alert. He held the customary notebook in his lap, and a pen in his right hand.

"Why aren't you out looking for her?" Aden asked, aiming a glare at both Espinoza and Vaughn.

The sergeant scowled over a pair of half glasses Payton hadn't seen before. "I have a dozen men on it. She won't get away."

"She already got away. I want to know—"

"Calm down, Mr. Green. Overreacting won't get us anywhere."

"Overreacting? You people hounded me when—"

"Aden." Even though Payton could speak in little more than a whisper, the men stopped arguing. "Let them do their jobs."

"She's right," Vaughn stood. "I'll get out there and help."

"Is there anywhere else you can think of that she might go?" Espinoza asked.

"Outside of the places I told you, no," Payton said.

"So, you agree that this attack is related to Sean's murder?" Aden asked.

Espinoza nodded. "Since Ms. Winters took it upon herself to become, shall we say, a target, yes, I'd say the two situations are related." Espinoza stood and flipped the notebook shut. When he didn't slip it into the usual pocket, Payton realized it was because he didn't have a pocket. He was wearing pajamas, white with wide brown stripes that made him look like a clown. "I hate to think what might have happened here. Maybe this will teach you a lesson."

"Sergeant…" This from Aden.

Espinoza sighed. "I'm through here for now. I'll be back in the," he gave an exhausted glance out the window where the first signs of dawn were creeping over the houses, "morning. Take care."

Aden walked him and Vaughn to the door. Vaughn threw a wave over his shoulder. Did he also glare at Aden? Payton didn't want to think about male rivalry right now.

She caught the end of something Espinoza said, "…two men watching the house."

"Four," Aden and Vaughn said in unison.

The scent of rosemary washed over her along with the heat of her attacker's breath. The golden cat slashed downward. Familiar eyes gazed into hers for one second before the pain hit. Payton came awake with a start. She was still on the couch; cold because the quilt had fallen on the floor. Thank goodness she hadn't knocked Maggie off also. The little white kitten, curled in the fetal position, purred noisily near her waist. Payton was thirsty and tried to sit up but the shoulder brace hindered any movement.

She almost called for Aden. Where was he anyway? She blinked away the nightmare. The sun shone between the blinds. The length of the shadows said it was late. She should get up and open the shop.

The pain meds had worn off. Every inch of her screamed for relief. And coffee. Even so, Payton lay back down, picked up the quilt and pulled it over her. During the assault, she thought she'd been defending herself against a man who wanted to rob, and most likely rape her; a man who wanted to laud his power and strength over a weaker being. The fact that the assailant was a woman changed the complexion of the situation. Or maybe the situation changed when Payton's suspicions about the woman's identity became reality.

How foolish she'd been not to keep her suspicions to herself. She'd practically begged for this beating, from a person with the most amazing stamina Payton had ever seen. Adrenaline was an awesome thing. Hospital personnel had reinserted her arm in its socket and X-rayed her throat. No permanent damage—except to her psyche. Just another thing to make her stronger. Every time Payton had cried to her grandmother over something that had happened, Grandma had said, "All things happen to make us stronger, little one." And so, Payton had gone through life, stronger after each confrontation. More powerful than a locomotive. Able to leap tall…

Until Cameron's death. Then her whole building of bricks tumbled down on top of her. She sighed.

It didn't matter right now that Lake Ontario and her attacker had different motives. In less than two weeks, Payton had faced her own mortality twice. Both times she'd won. She couldn't help wondering if her luck was wearing a bit thin.

"Find her yet?" Aden asked.

The sound of his voice made her turn from where she sat at the dining room table. The meds were working. She'd gotten some sleep. Aden put a Gallery Closed sign on the door, but the house hadn't been the slightest bit quiet. All day, an army of forensic people tromped up and down the stairs.

Vaughn entered the front door and sat across the table. To his, "You okay," she nodded. Then he said, "I found bloody footprints on the sidewalk. Followed them until they petered out at the intersection of Main and Broad. From the amount of blood in your room, I don't imagine she could get too far. Don't worry, we'll find her."

Payton shivered at the thought of what her precious bedroom must look like. Aden set a glass of ice water beside the one he'd brought moments ago. Her hero. Make sure Vaughn knows who's in charge.

She snapped her fingers near the floor and made squeaking noises.

"Shh," Aden said and handed her a notepad and pen. "You know they told you not to talk. Write what you want and I'll get it for you."

Cat, Payton wrote.

"Cat?" His brow wrinkled.

"They're fuzzy, say meow and use a litter box," said Vaughn.

The sarcasm didn't make Aden smile, but it did Payton.

"She's got a kitten now," said Vaughn, inserting his bit toward male domination. "It's white with blue eyes. And its name is Maggie."

Aden scowled but went in search of the small feline. That's when Payton realized the sliders were open. She wrote *outdoors?* on the notepad. Vaughn too, set out in search of the white ball of fluff. She rose and shuffled back to the sofa. When she awoke the quilt was bunched against her chin. And a small white kitten purred under her chin.

Payton sat up and stretched anything that didn't ache; which wasn't much. Maggie meowed. Payton ruffled the soft fur. The house was quiet and dark. How long had she slept? A sound, soft like paper against paper, came from the kitchen. Maggie stopped purring, her ears went back and her fur stood on end. Knowing she couldn't jump down and be in the way, Payton set the kitten on the cushion and picked up a piece of bric-a-brac—one of Mamie's favorite pieces—but it was heavy and comforting in her good hand. She hefted it overhead and tiptoed to the kitchen.

She rounded the corner from the dining area, heart thumping like a bass drum. There he was, wearing that striped dressing gown and a wide smile. Aden put down the newspaper, stood up, took the statue and set it on the counter. He took her gingerly in his arms and held her. In this safe womb, she cried. And cried.

Aden was the first to break the embrace. He eased Payton onto a stool and set about dipping something into a bowl from a pot on the stove. He put the bowl in the microwave and punched buttons. Moments later he placed a delectable smelling dish of potato and herb soup before her. "I used herbs from your garden."

She could get used to this.

"A bunch of people stopped by to see you. News sure travels fast around here."

She wrote on the notepad. *Gossip committee in action.*

Aden laughed. "So, where'd you get the cat?"

Sylvie thought I needed a friend.

There was a knock on the glass doors. First Aden helped Maggie off the couch and then he flicked on the outside light and opened the door to admit Carter. Aden launched himself in Carter's face. "Where's your wife?"

Carter frowned but didn't back up. "At her mother's. She fell last night and broke her hip. Why?"

"Where have you been?"

"Dropping her off. She can't see to drive at night. I repeat, why?"

"What's your mother-in-law's phone number?"

Carter's frown deepened. Then he spun on a heel, slamming the sliding door.

Aden chased after Carter.

Forty-Six

Payton woke on the sofa. She counted eight chimes of the grandmother clock against the hallway wall. The house was otherwise silent. Aden must've gone home. Payton set Maggie on the floor and went upstairs feeling stiff but not too bad.

She didn't want to go in her bedroom. Memories would gush like floodwaters, but that's where the clothes were. She pushed open the door. The blood had been completely cleaned up. The bed was now covered in the colorful spread from the top shelf in the closet. The carpet had been scrubbed and everything shone with cleanliness. A pervading odor of copper permeated the air. Payton went to shower where she leaned against the tiles letting the hot jets beat her skin to a bright red.

An hour later, dressed and ready—mostly—to face the world, Payton pulled open her front door. And nearly lost her coffee when both Aden and Vaughn stepped inside. "Where are you going?" they asked, conjoined twins today, instead of rivals.

"I have a shop to open."

Aden took her elbow. "Come on."

They piled into Vaughn's pickup, Payton in the middle. Vaughn jammed his foot to the floor. She almost smiled as the old-lady-driver turned into Mr. Cop. They took the turn at Main and Broad on what felt like two wheels. Where were they going?

Her unspoken question got answered when they screeched to a stop near *Tin Pan Galley.* Across the street, flames flickered inside Sean's café. Two fire trucks and a gaggle of onlookers were already there. Vaughn sprang from the vehicle. Aden laid his arm across the back of the seat. Payton settled back in the comfort of his embrace and as though they were at a drive-in movie, watched the firemen work. Once she started to ask something, but Aden shushed her.

An hour later, the fire was out and cleanup began. Smoke billowed out and hung overhead, scenting the air and making eyes burn.

"I wonder how it started," she whispered.

"I don't know."

"I wonder if anyone's inside."

"They won't be able to check till things cool down. Now, stop talking or I'll take you home." A moment later he said, "I'd say it won't be worth opening the shop today."

She nodded.

"Want to take a walk?"

She nodded again, feeling like the little bobbing dog in the back window of her grandfather's T-bird. Aden helped her to the sidewalk.

They walked up the hill, arm in arm, like two people out for a Sunday stroll. Two people without the worries of an arrest warrant, burning buildings and maniacal murderesses. They walked a long time, along the farthest end of Broad Street, past the school and wide-open field where the air smelled less like lake and more like green, and clean. After a while, they turned and went to Payton's. She'd been worried they'd find it too in flames. But it stood strong with its fresh coat of pastel yellow atop brand new stucco. Every previous time she approached her house, she felt pride in what she'd accomplished. A woman alone can get things done, just like Grandma declared.

Aden touched her arm. "Come on," he said, tugging her off the sidewalk and across to his house.

Payton held back. "Maggie."

The kitten waited at the door. Payton couldn't help sniffing the air for fire. Nothing, not even the ubiquitous scent of blood.

But something was not quite right.

Aden picked up the kitten and headed out the door.

"Wait."

She could see him mentally tapping an impatient foot as Payton tiptoed upstairs and pushed open the door of the guest room. There, on one of the twin beds, was the object of last night's All Points Bulletin. Mamie was beyond being a danger. Blood, drying to the color of raw nutmeg, caked the side of her face where Payton stove it in with the bedroom lamp. Her stomach roiled at the sight of what she'd done. She stepped fearlessly into the room and dropped to her knees beside the bed. She put her hand on Mamie's arm, tears rolling down her cheeks.

Mamie's eyes fluttered open. Payton saw recognition. Mamie opened her mouth. A trickle of blood oozed from the corner, ran down her jaw and onto one of the red squares on the blanket. She whispered something Payton couldn't understand.

"What?"

Mamie opened her mouth again. Payton put her ear near Mamie's lips. "Sorry," came the soft words. "So sorry."

"Why?" Payton asked, but it was too late to list motives, to deliver explanations. Mamie gasped, shuddered and went limp. Whatever trials, troubles or worries had driven the woman to murder, were over.

Payton laid her head on Mamie's blood-encrusted sleeve and wept tears of sorrow and forgiveness.

Forty-Seven

Payton leaned deep in the crook of Aden's arm, the length of their naked bodies pressed together on his couch. Comfortable and secure. She laid her hand on his chest, palm flat, soaking up his strength. Last night, after the removal of Mamie's body, the investigation was deemed complete. The motive had been listed as a "disagreement over a vacant store."

Just after the clock chimed midnight, she got the courage to ask him where he'd been for more than a week. He gave a small chuckle. "Scared out of my mind, that's where. Payton, I'm forty-nine years old. Till now, I've managed, whether by choice or fate, to remain unencumbered by a serious relationship. Then you came along and changed it all. In a heartbeat, I found myself planning our future. I thought for sure I'd gone insane. I took some time off from my job and went to London. I thought you'd be able to reach me if you had an emergency. Believe me, I had no idea the phone didn't work." He stopped and took a breath. "To think of what you went through all alone. I'll never forgive myself."

He'd carried her to the bedroom, then, and laid her on the cool, soft sheets. Then he crawled in beside her. They spent the rest of the night that way.

When Aden's clock proclaimed 7 a.m. she flew into a sitting position, bringing Aden wide awake. He sat up, running a hand through his hair. "What's wrong?"

"I just remembered something."

"Don't talk," he said.

But she continued, this time in a whisper, "Sean's aunt gave me a box."

Hearing her mistress' voice, Maggie popped her head from under the blankets on Aden's other side. He helped her to the floor and got out of bed.

"I'll get it. I need Maggie's litter box too," Payton whispered and began dressing. "Maybe there's something that'll help us figure out why Mamie murdered Sean. It wasn't because he cheated her out of the store; I'm sure of it." She sat on the bed to put on her shoes.

Aden slipped into his robe. "What first put you on to Mamie?"

"Something people said kept rattling around in my brain. First, Amanda left my open house because Edward had work to do on the dock and they couldn't leave the store unattended. Later Mamie said someone could've substituted the forged Commodore painting because Amanda and Edward 'are always leaving the place unattended.' Another time she told me she never goes to the marina, had never even been inside their shop. None of the statements are telling in themselves."

"But combined…"

"That night I think she waited around for the docks to be empty, but everyone was there until quite late preparing their boats for the race."

"She must've overheard the argument between Sean and Edward."

Payton finished tying her shoes. "I'll be right back."

"You're not going alone. We'll take Maggie so she can use her box."

Moments later, at her kitchen table, Payton dug into the box. Only four envelopes remained. The dates read September 1, 1996, April 10, 2003, June 4, 2004, and June 8, 2004. The two June dates had to be related to Payton, and she left them for the time being.

Recalling that Donald had died ten years previously, Payton selected one dated 1996 and opened it, saying a short prayer that it would contain a motive, a sort of closure for the whole dreadful event. Aden read over her shoulder, digging his chin in the spot at the corner of her neck. It hurt, but she didn't ask him to stop. The envelope was thicker than the others. It contained several sheets of handwritten notes and two invoices. The invoices were copies of ones she'd found in other envelopes. With a sinking heart, she unfolded the pages of notes. Suddenly Payton knew what had happened. And she knew why Mamie had felt it so necessary to murder Sean Adams.

Payton pieced things together for Aden. "Sean always looked for ways to make an easy buck. Donald had been dead about a year. Mamie was just coming out of her grief. Claire talked her into following her dream of opening an art gallery, but Donald had left her broke and she had no way to come up with the money. Sean probably heard them talking. Whatever. That part doesn't matter. He got the bright idea to give her the money in exchange for one copy of a painting he had."

"The Commodore?" Aden asked.

"No, a Church."

"But."

"She desperately wanted the shop and did as he asked."

"But."

"But he didn't stop at one."

"Payton."

"What?"

"Are you forgetting? Mamie couldn't paint."

She continued, undaunted, "How hard it must have been for Mamie to hide her talent all those years. All the horrible water colors she produced just so no one would catch on if anything came to light about the forgeries."

Aden kissed Payton's cheek. "You are a genius."

"I wonder what pushed her to kill him though. This has been going on for years."

"When he screwed that empty shop out from under her she snapped."

"I wouldn't be surprised. I don't know what turned her onto

the monkshood. Maybe I have to take some of the blame. One day we girls were talking about poisonous plants and maybe it gave her the idea.

"I was at Claire's last Sunday when Mamie arrived. Claire and I had been talking about Sean and she was crying. Mamie asked what was wrong and Claire lied. Claire's not a good liar. I bet Mamie's guilt got the better of her and she assumed I'd just told Claire her whole secret."

"And she decided to kill you."

"Then burn the café so Claire couldn't open Sean's restaurant." Payton folded the documents and put them in the box.

"I'd better call the police."

While Aden dialed, Payton said, her voice very scratchy, "She was so strong. To be able to hide all those years. To not say anything when people so obviously disliked her work. To not protest when I bypassed one of her paintings for *Ocaso*. To not show her guilt for killing Frank along with Sean."

Aden hung up the phone. "How do you know she regretted that?"

"Because of something she said the day after the murder. We were in my shop. Of course Sean was the topic of everyone's conversation. Helen offered to let Mamie have the shop. Since Sean was dead, their contract became void. Mamie said, 'I don't think I'd be able to go in there, knowing what I do about this.' At the time we put it down to stress and sorrow, but..."

Aden nodded and moved the box onto the counter.

"I remembered something else. Amanda once referred to Felicia as Felicia Ann Marie Dawson Featherstone. I bet she's the Ann on that invoice. I bet her painting is also a forgery."

"Easy enough to check." He pulled a chair close and sat with his knees touching her leg. "Now, to happier topics." He adjusted his chair a little to the right. The heat of his thighs seared into hers.

"Will you marry me?" he asked.

For several moments, the only sound in the place was the crunch of Maggie chewing cat food.

Payton took a breath and let it out very slowly. "I can't."

Aden didn't speak.

So she continued. "Since I met you my head's been in a turmoil. I recognize there's something special between us. I don't know how much of my past you know. I'm sure it's well documented in that box." She gestured toward the counter. "I came to Sackets Harbor to escape memories of my husband's murder—that's what causes the nightmares. I realized recently that escaping wasn't what I needed to do." She fumbled her hands on the table. "I have to come to grips with Cameron's death before I can commit to another relationship."

"I understand."

"No, I don't think you do. Aden, I'm leaving town. I'm moving home to Virginia, to be with my family. It's where I need to be right now."

Sergeant Espinoza's car turned in Aden's driveway. Aden rose. "I'll go let him in."

She got up and stared out at the water. What if she just dumped the money Cameron left? Gave it all to charity. The old proverb that money didn't buy happiness was so true. Actually money was the reason for all her problems.

She recalled the first time she'd seen Aden, coming out of the bookstore carrying a bag she later learned held John Grisham and Robert Ludlum's latest releases. He wore a brushed twill coat and hat. Few people wore hats any more, but he managed it beautifully, setting it at a jaunty angle atop his salt-and-pepper hair. Payton let her mind watch him, distinguished and very sexy, stride down the sidewalk and get into his car. Her insides twitched at the memory.

Author Cindy Davis

Besides taking impromptu trips to far-off places like Sackets Harbor, New York, Cindy and her husband enjoy the sights, sounds and tastes in their home state of New Hampshire. From camping in upstate moose country to attending Monarchs hockey and Fisher Cats baseball games, and promoting books at summer fairs, they love it all. Cindy's computer goes most everywhere, but so far she hasn't made Bob squeal the motorhome's tires again.

Visit her books at www.cdavisnh.com and www.desert-magictrilogy.com. And also, the site of her daytime job www.fiction-doctor.com.

Praise for Cindy's other books

A Page from the Past, nominated for Book of the Year at Champagne Books.

Reviewed by Long and Short of It Reviews: In six words Cindy Davis grabs her reader's attention in a death-defying situation. "Our van sailed over the embankment…" For anyone who enjoys murder, mystery and suspense this is a book for you. Once you pick it up, you'll find it hard to put down again, so make sure you give yourself plenty of 'me' time and enjoy the way Cindy Davis unfolds her plots and her characters capture your imagination.

Final Masquerade

Reviewed by The Road to Romance Reviews: Cindy Davis creates a fantastic story of betrayal, suspense and intrigue in *Final Masquerade.* The tension in this novel makes this book hard to put down. The reader suffers along with Paige as she tries to make a new life for herself and feels her pain when she leaves friends behind each time she is found again. Cindy Davis has certainly created a winner with this novel.

A Little Murder—first in the Angie Deacon mystery series.

Reviewed by Midwest Book Review: Davis takes what looks to be a simple murder mystery and adds enough twists and turns to produce a real whodunit readers will be challenged to figure out. Characters are solidly developed and dimensional, the plot fast-paced and peppered with suspense.

Play with Fire—second in the Angie Deacons mystery series.

Reviewed by Long and Short Reviews: Play with Fire is one of those stories that is so beautifully written you forget you are reading it; you must know what happens. It's engaging and intriguing, the characters seem real, and the backdrop, Alton Bay New Hampshire, is simply perfect. I'd like to sit at the real Shibley's and read this again, and listen for the MV Mt. Washington's horns sound in the distance. Kudos to Cindy Davis - can't wait for the next one.

Hair of the Dog—the third in the Angie Deacon mystery series.

Reviewed by Midwest Book Review: This well-written mystery offers plenty of suspects as Davis takes the reader into two diverse worlds: the dog show venue and the cosmetics industry. Angie and Jarvis are unique in that they are portrayed so realistically, each with their own strengths and weaknesses; a couple trying to work out the kinks of their relationship. The mystery will challenge readers as they follow the clues and filter through suspicious characters and circumstances. Dog lovers will appreciate the presence of Guinness, an Irish Setter, along with a nice dose of information concerning dog shows and breeding.

Watch for the fourth in the Angie Deacon series, **Dying to Teach**, coming April, 2011.

Breinigsville, PA USA
04 March 2011
256937BV00004B/1/P